IN FEA[R]

'Ylia.' A soft murm[ur] unwholesome feelin[g] cannot precisely say why.'

'It is here. With us.'

Ylia's thought was a wild babble; somehow, half-ill with terror, she caught it and forced it still.

The Fear nudged at them, stealthily, then struck again, hard, just in front of them.

"Draw sword! Something unclean walks this ledge with us!"

Nisana sprang to the ground. The screel of several swords drawn at once was drowned by a terrified scream . . .

"We are living in a flood of generic fantasy and we can only be grateful for the better practitioners of it . . . Emerson is a welcome addition!"

—*Locus*

"Ru Emerson has a talent for tight plotting and strong characterization."

—Charles de Lint, author of *Moonheart*

Ace Fantasy books by Ru Emerson

THE PRINCESS OF FLAMES
THE FIRST TALE OF NEDAO: TO THE HAUNTED MOUNTAINS

THE FIRST TALE OF NEDAO

TO THE HAUNTED MOUNTAINS

RU EMERSON

ACE FANTASY BOOKS
NEW YORK

This book is an Ace Fantasy
original edition, and has never
been previously published.

THE FIRST TALE OF NEDAO:
TO THE HAUNTED MOUNTAINS

An Ace Fantasy Book/published by arrangement with
the author

PRINTING HISTORY
Ace Fantasy edition / February 1987

All rights reserved.
Copyright © 1987 by Ru Emerson.
Cover art by Martin Springett.
Map by Vicci L. Mathis.
This book may not be reproduced in whole or in part,
by mimeograph or any other means, without permission.
For information address: The Berkley Publishing Group,
200 Madison Avenue, New York, New York 10016.

ISBN: 0-441-79558-7

Ace Fantasy Books are published by The Berkley Publishing Group,
200 Madison Avenue, New York, New York 10016.
PRINTED IN THE UNITED STATES OF AMERICA

To Doug, sweet baboo and fellow masochist, with my love, and in fond memory of the East Fork, Devil's Punchbowl, the Old Green Tent, the thin Orange Bags and thinner boots, Turner Meadow, the Great Loop, 32-pound packs, the first dose of freeze-dried food and Kendall's Mint Cake, 20 pounds of Gorp (each). . . . Ready again when you are.

To Mom and Dad, for my first fix of mountains.

To my sister Vicci, for the aid and abettance, for the map, and in memory—not necessarily fond —of the East Fork and skinny logs. . . .

To Alec: Everybody knows this is Nowhere. Down to the Colorado & back in one day, but we lived to tell about it.

To Ginjer, with deep appreciation, for helping me refind the book I knew was in there.

To Mike Von Ree for the loan of the typewriter, July 1975, without, as they say, which. . . .

And to Arwen Elanor, 1974-1982, calico lady of exceedingly tart demeanor and a magic all her own.

Prologue

The heights had blown clear of snow, the past two nights; the warm winds, the AEdrith, were early, all the more welcome for it. Snow still lay in waist-deep greyed drifts in the vales and canyons, but even this was beginning to melt at the edges, forming little dripping caves. Water plopped in huge drops from winter-bent fir. The sound carried loud across the deep, bowl-shaped valley.

The tower stood as it had for hundreds of years, a blackened, torn hulk. Openings gaped where thick, opaque glass had shattered and still lay in multicolored shards beneath the snow, or where stone had been torn down, bronze and iron sills and doorframes twisted by the fury of long-burned-out fires.

Stood as it had, save for one thing: it was occupied.

Had any of the few hunters within the Foessa chosen to approach from the east, and had he survived long enough to reach the tower this particular night, he would have seen a clearing, a huddle of small, low barracks along the edge of the trees; across from them, the grand stair, the great balcony as large as many a lord's banquet hall—and, beyond the bank of windows letting onto that balcony, light.

Not the honest light of torch and lantern, no. A red, murky light, the color of a half-healed wound, the color of dried blood.

A hall ran the length of the balcony. The vaulted ceiling vanished in gloom; a polished, tiled floor caught light from the smoldering firepit and reflected a sudden red on pale walls. A dais, two grand canopied chairs were barely to be seen against the windows.

Shadows scurried across the room, not-reflections of things fluttering high above, things creeping about the edge of the firepit. A horror moved with them. Fear crawled across the floor, slid from the embers and shivered into the corners.

1

Two other shadows flickered against the far wall but did not move beyond the motion of the low-burning fire. Man and woman: human-shaped, at least, among the horrors that surrounded them. To these, the two paid no heed. He of the two turned to face the windows and spoke.

"It is done; Chezad has spoken. Even now the old shaman passes the war god's message to Kanatan. The Tehlatt will retake the Plain within days. Nedao will fall; after that, by our hand, Yls. *And* Nar."

"But my Lord—if the Lammior's power still does not rise to your bidding—"

"Oh, that." He laid an arm across the woman's shoulders, drew her to him. "He will answer me, eventually." Calm certainty. "In the meantime, I have drawn sufficient knowledge from this place to start down the path I have chosen—"

"*We* have chosen, my Lord," she reminded him. He nodded.

"We. They will see, all of them. Fools, all."

"All of them." Her voice was no less eager than his. "My father—she who would have been yours—"

"Ah." He laughed, a chill sound that sent the shadows quivering against the far walls and damped the embers to an even duller red. "Does it bother you so much, my sweet? That Scythia was the one I chose first?"

"Why should it?" The profile, seen against the half-moon, was delicate: Pale hair, near silver in the light, was piled in jewel-touched curls. "She matters to no one, she is already dead, though she does not know it yet. And *I* have what she was stupid enough to spurn."

"Dead." He laughed again. "She, the barbarian who stole her from me, their half-breed brat. All. An excellent beginning point, and a good test." He drew the woman with him to the great double doors set in the far wall. One hand on the latch, he turned, spoke a single word. The firepit flared, sullen red flame swirled and towered toward the ceiling, disturbing a number of huge batlike creatures and sending them flapping for the darkness.

The story is mine to lay before you, by right and by knowledge: alone of those who know the tale, I, Nisana, was present from its Nedaoan beginnings to their end. More: I was party before Nedao's involvement, and the whole of the histories are known only to me of all those who walk this great valley. Though we of AEldra blood who wear cat's form are brief of speech, still I take the telling willingly upon myself, that you may know the truth of it.

1

The sky was a spring-blue bowl arched over gently rolling plains. It caught to the west at enormous white-capped, harshly jagged mountains, faded pale eastward to even flatter ground. South, the River Torth faded into distance, edged by the yellow-green grasses of the great marshes.

North: There was, on such a clear day, normally the faintest hint of purple across the horizon to mark the distant bluffs across the River Planthe. Today, there was nothing save a smoke haze.

Tehlatt. The Northern barbarians rode from their strongholds in Anasela, burning and slaying as they came.

The King's City was a broken beehive, people running wildly through the streets, flying in a disordered mass down the close-paved road that led to the harbor. The double gates were flung wide to accomodate that hysterical traffic and the King's own household men stood at the gates, arbitrating sudden disputes, helping parents locate children—aiding the old and ill to conveyance.

The lone horseman lay across his mount's neck, hands wrapped around her, caught at each other by the wrists. His eyes were pain-narrowed, exhausted slits. The horse limped.

They went unnoted at first in the crush and panic. But then, his ancient charge and her meager bundle of possessions safely loaded onto a cart bound for the harbor, Narsid, a swordsman of one of the minor barons, turned to search out others in need of his aid. The horse staggered; Narsid called for aid and sprinted across the crowded gateway.

"There man, we've got you, you're safe." *What, in Koderra?* his thought mocked. A hasty glance back out the gates and northward assured him the line of burnings had come no closer.

A swollen hand, the nails black with half-dried blood, waved feebly. The rider coughed. "I am Gors—Corlinson. I —message for—the King."

"Gors," the swordsman whispered to himself. Hard to tell, under all that dirt, the blood-stiffened hair, but he spoke truly. It *was* Lord Corry's son, but by all the Mothers at once, *here*? He glanced up as shadow crossed them. His baron and his captain stood there. "M'Lord Grawn, it's Lord Corwin's son, he's hurt."

"Can see that, boy. Get him a healer!"

"He has messages for the King, sir."

"Messages." The wounded boy was reviving, a little. The captain knelt with water, then caught at his waist to help him up. Narsid ran ahead with word as Grawn came to the other side.

Brandt's Grand Reception was light but cold. No fires had been lit. The hall was filled nearly to capacity, crowded with nearby Lords Holder and their armsmen, a few of the household women and servants who had not yet been put aboard ships and sent downriver, and half the King's Council. The elders were already gone.

Tehlatt. The name was in every thought, if not upon every tongue. The Tehlatt rode south, vanquishing Nedao a horse-length at a time. This was no simple spring raid, such as had plagued the farmers and herders near the Planthe, such as that which had netted the barbarians the whole province of Anasela.

But there was another name on the tongues of those in the

Reception at the moment: Ylia. Brandt had just, again, pub-
licly named his daughter and only child his heir and extracted
Heir's Oath from them all. The girl—she was scarce of age
and still wore her bright coppery hair plaited—had taken her
vows to the King gravely; taken the oath of the Lords Holder
and the Council with the same aloof gravity that was clearly as
much fright as training.

Nervous whispers echoed across the chamber. It was bad,
serious, if he'd swear them to his chosen heir again. As though
he didn't expect to survive.

His choice; in Nedao it had always been King's choice, who
might be his heir. But Ylia—not all those present swore to her
with good grace. Her father was Nedao's King, one had only
to look at her face to see the young Brandt there. But her
mother was an AEldran noblewoman, a member of their Second House. Sorceress. And while not all Nedao felt as the
Chosen's new religion prated, that witches were a black evil,
few of the Plainsfolk were comfortable with Scythia's Powers.
Though, most admitted, she never flaunted them, and indeed
used little in public save her healing.

In her favor, the girl had little of the look of her mother's
kind, beyond the lighter coloring, the red-gold hair and the
hazel eyes in place of the Nedaoan olive skin and brown hair.
She was tall, but not as tall as the AEldra. And as to the
Power, well, she had *some* of it, she was after all half AEldra.
Fortunately, she seemed to have little skill and to take no interest in the witchery, though most of the Cityfolk were not
certain her interest in weaponry was much improvement.

But if she ruled after Brandt, the first woman to do so since
Leffna, 500 or more years before, she would need weaponry
and battle knowledge. That was law, and had been inflexibly
held to even during the Long Peace, 200 years before.

The swearing completed, most of those standing around the
chill room went back to their own nervous conversations. The
girl on the dais rubbed slender, capable hands down her dark
robes, laid them across the King's shoulders. He then laid his
own over them, smiled at her.

"Father—"

"Necessary, the swearing. You don't doubt that?"

"No." She didn't; Brandt knew his people well, and even
though she'd spent long hours at his side, she still had much to
learn before she could understand and act as well as her father

did. "But that wasn't what I was going to say."

Brandt laughed briefly. "That again? We will not argue, Ylia. You are safest away from Koderra, and the only way to manage that is to put you on the Narran ship, *Merman*."

"But I can be of use—"

"None to Nedao *or* to me if you die here." That silenced her, briefly, though her eyes were still rebellious. "You are my only child, Ylia." A shadow darkened his eyes momentarily: Beredan. *A man's sons were meant to survive him. I cannot let this child die as foolishly as Beredan did.*

"But I—"

"If I were to command you—I seldom do that, daughter. But in this matter—" He paused. "It is that important to me, Ylia. Believe me. What we do here, I will do better if I know you are safe." His grip tightened on her hands. "Promise me." Silence. "Promise?" She closed her eyes, sighed in resignation.

"All right, Father. I swear," she said evenly, "to take great care, that no harm come to me, that I may have the ruling after you. A great," she added with a smile of her own, "many years hence."

The King wrapped an arm around her and caught her close. "I don't like the sound of that, my girl. You're too much like your mother, you trap me with words." He sighed. "But so long as you board the *Merman* this afternoon—*swear* you will, daughter."

"I swear," she whispered. *And debark before she leaves harbor*, she added firmly to herself. Brandt, she knew, had no inner skill to hear her; the only Power of any kind he had was a sense of when her mother was near, and that was love, not AEldra. She tamped carefully at the inner voice—Scythia *could* hear her, and she had been as determined as Brandt that their daughter flee with the Cityfolk. And then there was Nisana. But the cat was on her own errands at the moment and unlikely to have an inner ear to *her* thoughts.

But it was as though a command were laid upon her, as though the Mothers had set a new pattern in her weaving, that she must stay. She must!

Conversation ceased; a pathway opened as Grawn and his captain brought the Lord of Teshmor's son slowly toward the dais. "Oh, gods," Ylia whispered. "Father, it's Corry's son." She caught at cushions and a thick fur robe; Brandt was at his side as they lowered the boy gently onto the soft pile. Gors opened his eyes briefly, winced and cried out faintly as someone raised him sufficiently to help him swallow a little wine.

"Sire. Father—sends word. The Tehlatt have—our walls—have them surrounded." He frowned; hard to remember anything. He hurt, but that took no memory, that just was.

"If he asks aid—" Brandt began unhappily. Gors shook his head once, stopped abruptly as pain knifed through him, swallowed hard.

"No. No aid. Too late—and—not enough. He knows you've—no one—to spare. He said—" The boy swallowed again and was silent for so long they thought he had fainted.

"Get my Lady, find her," Brandt hissed to those behind him. *My Scythia, the boy can't be beyond your skill.* It seemed moments, it seemed hours, and the only sound, torn, pained breathing, too shallow to hold for long. And then a warmth ran across his inner being: *Beloved.* He knew, always, when she was near.

"—he said," Gors whispered, sharply catching at the King's attention again, "to tell you that. And—that he was sorry—" he gasped for air; Brandt brought him a little more upright, Scythia came across to the boy's other side. "—he couldn't be of—more aid."

"Sorry," Brandt whispered. Tears blurred his vision; he blinked them away. *Boyhood friend. Corlin, how like you. But Gors—*the boy sagged, closed his eyes. Scythia's pale, slender fingers stroked the hair back from his brow, baring an ugly cut that ran above his left ear, a blackened and swollen bruise over his left temple. "Rest, boy." Concerned, near-black eyes caught at and held his wife's. Scythia shook her head faintly, shrugged. Uncertain.

"I will try. But Nisana—I've sent for her. She's—We'll try." She glanced around the full chamber. "My Lords! I need quiet, either keep it or leave, I beg you. Lord Corlin's son is gravely injured." A strangled outcry from near the center of the dais. Scythia caught at it, pinned down the source with her wide-set dark-blue eyes. Her mental voice stabbed into her daughter's thought. 'Oh, no. Ylia, it's Lisabetha. By all the Nasath, why did no one think to remove her?'

'I—I didn't see her, Mother.' But as she stood, started toward the shaking girl, Ylia's youngest honor maiden, Gors' sister, fell senseless to the floor. The Queen's old nurse, Mala-

eth, dropped heavily to the girl's side. Scythia turned her full
attention back to Gors.

Bad. A Nedaoan healer wouldn't waste his herbs and poul-
tices on one so far gone; most AEldran healers wouldn't even
attempt the task. The Nasath alone knew how he'd reached
the City with such a blow to the head. And he'd lost blood
—there were slashes through both sleeves, a deep cut in his
right calf. She cast a swift, sidelong glance at her husband. His
best friend's son, she couldn't let him die.

'Ylia.' The girl stirred as the inner speech once again
touched her.

'Mother?'

'He'll die if I wait for Nisana, you're the best I have. Join.'

Color burned in the girl's face; she knelt reluctantly. 'But—
Mother, I can't! Before all these people? And, you know how
little aid I can be, he'll die anyway, if you—'

Scythia's mouth set in a hard line. 'He won't die, if we can
help it! This is no time for argument, there's enough in you to
back me, and there's no time to move him. *Join!*'

Her face a hot red, Ylia caught at her mother's free hand,
closed her eyes, joined. Silence. She tried to concentrate on the
healing itself, on Gors—on anything but the anxious, curious,
staring people behind her, her own sense of inadequacy. *That*
never helped, her mother told her so, often enough.

Warmth—she could sense the warmth surrounding her
mother's hand, the chill of her own fingers as Scythia drew
from her. And Gors—she could sense him, too. Odd. Most
times she could not feel beyond the physical contact with her
mother. *Oh, Mothers, pain*: It knifed at her; frantically, she
tried to pull her thought away. But it was fading, already fading. The room blurred around her as Scythia dragged ruthlessly at her remaining strength. The boy sagged between
them. Ylia felt herself toppling over the edge of a black pit and
cried out. Hands caught at her shoulders, bit into muscle,
dragged her back to the moment.

'M—mother?' Her vision was blurred. *Mothers, I nearly
followed him into death*! Her mother's face swam before her;
tears ran, unheeded, down both faces.

'Gone. I—there was nothing we could have done. We tried.'
She shook herself, willed her daughter a burst of strength.
'No, I follow your thought—even if Nisana and my own
father had been to my aid, he would have died.' ''I am sorry,

beloved," she added aloud as Brandt wrapped her fingers around a warmed wine cup. "He was beyond my reach."

"I—it's all right." He blinked tears away. "Ylia."

"Father?" *Up.* She was exhausted beyond bearing, but she had trained her body hard; it knew how to go on when the mind denied she could. One of the King's housemen steadied her, gave her wine. She sipped gratefully, dispelling the chill that still shrouded her thought.

"Go, finish your packing. The Narrans wait only for you and your ladies."

"I—yes. All right." She cast an unhappy glance at the still form on the fur, his face mercifully covered over, strode from the Reception, oblivious to the still-staring nobility who parted to let her through.

Scythia ran a tired hand across her brow. "She is still displeased, isn't she?"

"Yes." Brandt's arm tightened around her shoulders as she stood. "But she swore she would leave."

"Well, then." Scythia shook her head. "Something's wrong. But then, everything is, just now."

"If you would leave with her?"

"No, Brandt. We agreed not to speak of that further. I do not leave you, not in this life. Nor in any that may follow."

Brandt sighed, but let it rest. Impossible to argue with his AEldra wife when the matter was so important to her as this. And, in truth, he knew he felt exactly the same.

The child is a good child, for one human: Brave like her father and as skilled, I swear by the One, as her mother, though she chooses as stubbornly as one of my kind to disbelieve. Half-blood! I, Nisana, am among the great wielders of the AEldra power, though my own blood has been cut more times than I can count. The Power is, *that is all. And so she will learn.*

The last boat sailed at dusk, oars splashing softly to guide it into the current. A triangular orange sail was hoisted awkwardly and the long pleasure craft, floating low in the water with its unaccustomed cargo, gathered speed and was gone. The *Merman* had left a long time since.

Ylia watched the River from a deserted upper chamber, a small black and orange cat against her arm. Nisana: Queen

Scythia's cat. But also AEldra, and so more than simply cat.

"I will keep my promise." Ylia spoke softly, though the rooms had been deserted for nearly a hundred years; not even servants came to this particular tower, and most of them were hours since fled down-River, anyway.

'Hah. You promised to board the Narran ship and seek safety in Yls,' the cat's tart reply filled her mind, continued an argument started over an hour before when Nisana, alerted to the girl's presence, had come in search of her.

"I did not, most carefully," Ylia retorted. "Father named me heir, I accepted that as I must. Because Beredan gainsaid it by his death, five years ago." She swallowed; her brother's death had been so *stupid*! Useless, foolish and stupid! And it still hurt, even after so long a time. "I promised to use full safeguards. But I made no promise to remain on that ship!" She stared out the window. "*You* did not go, cat," she added pointedly.

'Because your mother did not,' Nisana replied. 'I do not leave Scythia ever, unless I must. I have not, since her mother commended her to me at her birth. I intend at the last to lead her from the City by the tunnel.' Her head moved against pliant fingers. 'Two would be better at that. If your father dies,' she added, with a cat's blunt lack of tact, 'she will not wish to leave.' Ylia closed her eyes, swallowed dread. 'I must go to learn what I can of the defenses,' Nisana added, 'and to see what aid I can give. Stay here.' She dropped lightly to the floor. 'Unlikely, with all that passes at present, Scythia will be aware of your presence.'

"No. I remained to aid also. And I will not hide behind what I have done; I am not ashamed of it."

'So be it.' Despite the fact that she was irritated with the girl, Nisana was moved to a grudging admiration: unlike most humans, to take responsibility for their often foolish, emotionally bound actions. 'But stay a while. Lest they still find a way to send you hence. Wait, I will return.'

"All right, cat." Ylia turned back to stare into the night. *My less than worthless Power. Nisana could have saved Gors, she and Mother together. And I*—she suppressed the thought. Faintly, she sensed the cat's presence fading down-hall. One such as Scythia would have been able to follow her all the way to the Reception.

Nisana returned some time later and accompanied her to the

kitchen for a cold evening meal, and for biscuit, dried meat and fruit to fill a travel bag. As the girl ate, Nisana told her what she had learned. 'Plans are not yet complete and depend largely upon the barbarians. Scythia and I will create a *seeming* upon the walls, so that it appears we have more armed there than exist. Other than that—'

"Then I can be of some aid, perhaps. A little." Ylia swung the bag to her shoulder. "The Council Room, cat."

'No! If you—'

"Yes. I remained to aid. I cannot aid, unless they know I am here."

Nisana glowered at her, finally turned away and padded back toward the main halls.

A silence greeted the heir to the throne's entrance: She stood in the doorway, braced for the recriminations, the anger which must follow. Silence. Her mother laughed then.

"I told you, husband, I sensed *something*."

Brandt shook his head, bent to hide a smile under his moustaches. "Mmmm. Had there been less to worry this afternoon, I might have caught you out in your choice of words, girl! You boarded, eh? And then left at once, no doubt?"

Ylia flushed, shrugged. "Well—not quite at once." She grinned as she caught the smile that passed between her father and mother. "I had to wait a little, until the Narrans were away from the plank."

Scythia laughed again, drew her into the room and to the empty chair at her side. She and Brandt both ignored the unhappy looks from the others around the table; Ylia was too nervous to see them. "All right, child. You've made your point and cut your escape. And I can use you tomorrow."

"Nisana told me. You plan a *seeming* of bowmen."

"We'll keep most of our bowmen within the City, upon the outer parapets," Brandt said. "Most of the City's strength, swordsmen, landers, horsemen, go with me, to set upon the Tehlatt in full force. Since they know that we by habit send only a portion of our armed out at a time, they may think us a greater army, and turn away."

"But, of bowmen—" Ylia considered briefly. "We haven't enough to man a third of the outer wall, even with the Southern and Eastern holders to aid." She was more aware of the remainder of the men in the Council Chamber, now; flushed as she caught suddenly approving looks. The girl wasn't merely a spoiled creature; she was Brandt's child and had learned from him.

"No," said Scythia. "Most will be *seeming*. Between us, you and I can create and hold such a vision, daughter, and Nisana will reinforce the vision with her own strengths as need requires." *Can we, indeed*, Ylia thought sourly, thrust the thought hastily aside as her mother caught it and frowned at her.

"If they can fight—" one of the captains began hesitantly, but Scythia shook her head. "No. That we cannot do: The Powers granted the AEldra by the Guardians are for healing and peace, for personal protection only. If phantoms could fight, one with evil intent might use such forces to gain hold over a folk. A host of *seeming* bowmen there can be—one to take arms and defend Koderra, that there cannot."

"It may, as the King says, be sufficient." The captain didn't look wholly convinced, though.

"Levren leads the bowmen, and with him Marhan will stand, since he no longer sits horse with comfort," Brandt finished. "They will bring what men they can through the northern tunnel to the River if it becomes clear they can do nothing on the walls save die."

Ylia laughed. Death, at the moment, was a distant and unreal thing. "Marhan will not like being surrounded with phantom soldiery."

Her father laughed with her. "No, poor Marhan, he does not."

"Nor do any sensible folk." Familiar, hated voice. Ylia rose to her feet, all laughter gone, shook off her mother's restraining hand. She turned away, too, the warning thought that sought to touch her: 'Do not anger him, we need his strengths, daughter!'

"Vess." Hated, horrible cousin! '*Need* Vess, Mother? Why not bring also some of the green marsh-snakes and have done?'

Brandt's sister Nala's mystery son, the King's bastard nephew—there! Half a room away from her, he lounged at the foot of the table. Still too near. "Perhaps you have a better suggestion, sweet cousin. I'm certain we cannot *wait* to hear it."

He flushed at that. Almost immediately, though, he was once again the smooth, languid darling of Teshmor's ladies, but the light brown eyes that met hers were pale furies.

For years, since she'd been old enough to realize how Vess treated women, particularly those of rank greater than his, Ylia had loathed him. *Seducer.* That was the polite word for it. For his part, Vess disliked her openly and intensely. That a female be handed Nedao's throne! And a female half-witch, to boot! He had, after Brandt named her heir, attempted her death on several occasions, hoping thereafter to press Brandt into granting him a higher position in the succession. One could always, he reasoned, try.

Deep down, he found her attractive, sword, plaits and all. The certainty that she'd have rebuffed any of his skilled overtures had only intensified his already strong hatred.

"I was not aware *you* had skill in battle strategy, sweet cousin." It was Ylia's turn to flush. Her mother's hand became even more insistent.

"The equal of yours," she replied sharply, "and if that is little, at least it is not buried under many years worth of lechery and wine."

Vess leapt to his feet. "I've had enough of you, girl."

"Not as much as I've had of you, womanizer!"

"Perhaps you'd care to settle matters—right now!"

"Try me!" Her sword was halfway from its sheath; Vess' dagger gleamed in the ruddy light. Those around the table eyed the two nervously.

"Vess! Ylia!" Brandt shouted. Instant silence. "There is enemy enough to fight, without you killing each other. Lord Vess, you have learned all we have to say here. You are welcome to remain in Koderra, though I fear I cannot offer you safety."

"If I had wished safety, Sire, I would have sailed for Yls." Vess inclined his head respectfully. The dagger vanished back into its hidden arm sheath.

"There are still one or two small boats remaining in the harbors, nothing truly safe in open sea, but a chance against a certainty. There are the mountain passes. Or, if neither of those options appeal to you, sister's son, return to Teshmor." Another, colder silence. Ylia ventured a thought in her mother's direction as she sheathed her sword and dropped back into her chair. 'Father's furious with him! What went on before I came?'

'Vess suggested a venture to attract the attention of the Sea-

Raiders to aid us against the Tehlatt—hold your seat, girl! Your father has forbidden you to fight him, and I will not have him further upset!'

She subsided, unwillingly, but her hands itched. To smash that pale, smug, self-satisfied face—just once! *Sea-Raiders!* They'd swallow Koderra whole, given the chance! Nedao's ancient enemy at Nedao's side? How many kinds of fool was he? Or was it yet another of his endless plans for gaining Brandt's throne?

Vess bowed even lower. "My King." His voice was low, expressionless. "Teshmor is my sworn City, true. But Gors' tale, as the Lady told it," his tone of voice could not, really, have carried any suggestion that the Queen had lied, "leads me to believe a return journey to Corlin's walls would be my death. I need time to decide. If I do not go to Teshmor, if I could be permitted to join the bowmen?"

"Marhan will like that," Ylia muttered; Vess shot her a telling glance but risked no further comment.

"Your choice, sister's son," Brandt replied. Vess cast the King's heir one last, black look and strode from the chamber.

There was little else to discuss. The Southern Lords left moments later; Ylia, at her father's insistence, went back to her chambers to find what sleep she could against the next day's need.

But few slept that night, and many stood as she did, peering northward through the overcast, where the reflections of the burnings could be seen as a ruddy glow against thick clouds, and later still as small flame points scattered across the Plain. By dawn they were less than a league from the City.

I have lived long years, even as humans count them. But in all of them, there was never a worse day than that one, and it is still hard for me to tell of it. I had lost before—no one lives for 70 or more years and does not. Mother, brother—many others. I have never before or since lost as I did that day. It is seldom I envy humans anything that is theirs. When I think of my Scythia, I envy them tears.

2

Sunrise. Ylia stood at the outer gates as equerry to the King. Queen Scythia was already upon the inner parapet, staring across grey crenulated stone, the AEldra cloaking of Power playing rainbows across her white robes and pale hair.

Brandt gripped his daughter's shoulders, his eyes warm and proud, but fear rode high in his thought, so strong even she could sense its direction. She spoke impulsively: "If—if there is need, I will lead mother to safety. I know the tunnel, the lands about the River for many leagues. I will keep her safe, Father, I swear it."

"I know you will." And some of the fear went from his face as they clasped hands. "Take care, daughter and heir."

"And you, my father." He pulled her close; she was hard put not to cling to him and weep, but then he was gone, mounted and riding from the gates with the war banner of Nedao at his right hand, his housemen about him and several hundred foot and mounted armsmen following.

For the space of several pained breaths, she stood where he left her. Only when she regained control of tears did she dare

climb to join her mother. She was embarrassed, half-sick, and
her purpose in remaining seemed, suddenly, childish. But
Scythia's smile was warm as she turned, and she held out her
hands.

"Nisana will aid us from within the Tower. Join, daughter." Ylia smiled back, at least partly reassured, reached with
her weak inner strengths, her strong sword hand.

Her eye was caught by movement on the near hills, and
she stared in horror as a force of Tehlatta horsemen rode
toward the gates, outnumbering the Nedao army by at least
five to one. There would be no victory here, there could
not be. Only the purchase of time for those who had fled, and
hope of a swift death for those who remained. Her fingers dug
into the stone sill as the first of the barbarian horsemen spilled
into the City foreguard, and battle was joined.

Her mother's mind-touch dragged her sharply back to the
moment. 'Join!' A rain of arrows flew from the walls, driving
back those who had pressed toward the gates. A hundred or
more bowmen stood there, some on the inner walls, some on
the outer. Even with effort, she could not tell which were real,
which illusion, though she knew full well how few trained
bowmen Koderra had.

The sun rose ever higher, and still the City forces, embattled
as they were, held, though little of the fighting could be seen
from the walls for the dust churned up by men and horses. But
now and again the wind would clear a space, or another would
open as the Tehlatt force moved on, leaving dead and dying
behind.

Midday: hot for early spring and dry. The *seeming* held.
The King's forces held, though there were fewer than had ridden forth.

Ylia cried out and tore from her mother's grasp, as a sudden
wind from the Torth blew the battlefield clear, and with
nightmare clarity she saw the ground before the gates. The war
banner flopped wildly, sagged to the ground, its pole cut in
half, the bearer limp across his terrified horse. Brandt shouted
once, stood in his stirrups with his sword raised high; he went
down immediately under the attack of a dozen Tehlatta axemen.

She could not move, could not remember how to breath.
Could only stare, dry-eyed, as the wind faltered and dust ob-

scured the battlefield once again. Could not answer the mental demand that was Nisana: 'Scythia? Ylia! What chances without? *Scythia*?!?' But the Queen was gone.

Gone? Great Mothers, *no*! Ylia gazed frantically about, leaned precariously across harsh stone, her breath coming in anguished little gasps. Light flared across her vision—oh, Mothers, gods and Mothers, no—

Scythia stood directly above the outer gates, the Power flaring blindingly with the rage and pain of her loss. The bowmen, only seven in number as the *seeming* faded and was forever gone, drew back in sudden fear, shielding their eyes. A hollow boom shook the City: they were bringing rams to attack the gates. The few who defended before the walls were ringed on all sides, though someone had rescued the King's torn and broken standard and set it in their midst.

A voice rose high and terrible above the sound of battle and silence fell as defender and foe alike turned toward the gates. For Scythia had cried a blood-curse in the AEldra tongue, and the sun was briefly darkened as the Baelfyr blazed from her hands to strike down those below. She cried out once more then, and a horror of blue-white flame bloomed around her as she toppled slowly from the walls. A third of those who sought to breach the gates died when she fell, the rest fled.

'Ylia? *Ylia*! There is nothing you can do, come now!' Nisana's sharp command dragged the stunned girl from the wall. 'Your oath, remember it!' It was the right choice: Dagger-oath to her father and her people held her now; horror-sick and weeping, she tore herself away and pelted back into the Tower.

'The tunnel, girl! No, not as you are, you'll die the first night! Your pack, my bag—your cloak! Must I think for you?' Silence, save for Ylia's choked weeping. The cat rubbed against her leg. 'Weep later; save yourself and me first!'

'I—' with a terrible effort, Ylia caught at her breath, caught at the wall, hard. Pain—blood flowed from scraped fingertips, but it gave her back a little control. She scrubbed a sleeve across her eyes. 'All right, I'm all right. The food pack—my rooms. Go.' Her face was white, eyes huge and dark, and her teeth had left blood on her lower lip, but she was, momentarily at least, in command of herself again. Nisana cast her a worried glance, padded off downhall.

Food. The cat's travel pouch in which she rode on long

journeys—don't think of who always carried it before, it's yours now!—a heavy cloak, the warmest she owned. One last look at the airy, familiar rooms then, before she turned to leave. A faint, furtive sound brought her sharply back around, dagger at the ready. 'Where—and what?' No answer; Nisana was already scouting down the hall.

She moved quietly across the room, stopped at the entrance to her dressing room. Stared, blankly. Whatever she had expected, it was not this. "Malaeth?" Her nurse, her mother's nurse before that, knelt within the cupboard, tugging vainly at another—Lisabetha; Mothers, no. "Why is she here? And why are you, old woman?" Fear, surprise made her voice rough, overloud in the hushed Tower.

Malaeth recoiled in terror, gasped, then swung about in a pale-faced fury. "Did you think me so weak as to desert your mother?" she snapped. "And yourself, Lady Ylia? You were to be gone as well, I think, Lady Princess!" Nisana, her whole furry body a taut demand for haste, padded back up-hall. "As for this child," Malaeth continued, "I thought her gone. She *was* to have gone. She is in shock."

Lisabetha huddled in her corner, nearly hidden by hanging robes, eyes open but unseeing. Young for her 16 years, fragile for all her outward show of self-reliance, she was sheltered, a true Nedaoan noble's daughter, with no real inner strength to face such a situation as this.

Though she had reason enough for her present state. Father and mother—dead by now. Her brother, Gors—dead, and before her eyes. And her own death howling at the outer walls. . . .

Beyond the Tower came the sounds of battle; fierce cries tore at the air. Time was short. Ylia's face remained impassive; inwardly she quailed. *I, who cannot care properly for myself, must now help two even more helpless than I? Inniva aid me!* She steadied her thought with effort. The tunnel, the escape tunnel first. Then—whatever came next.

"We cannot leave her here, Malaeth."

"No." Malaeth crouched at the girl's side; sudden hope filled her. Scythia's daughter was strong; she'd not let them die. "But—"

"Nisana—cat, your aid, I cannot do this alone."

No censure for a change in the cat's thought, there was not time for her usual tart jabs at the girl's stubborn denial of her potential. Ylia's mind steadied as Nisana joined, lending her considerable strength of will, her Power.

She knelt beside Lisabetha, took hold of her chin and brought her face around so that their eyes met. Difficult, but not without precedent; Scythia had told her sufficient tales from the old days in which this thing was done: Find the place in the girl's mind, set there a command of following. "Bring her, Malaeth." Ylia dragged the girl to her feet, set her hand in Malaeth's. The old woman pulled a cloak across her shoulders, pinned it with shaking fingers, threw another round Lisabetha and drew the girl across the chamber. Brandt's heir drew sword as they ran toward the stairs. Nisana leaped rapidly ahead of them.

There was a sudden, tense silence: Silence both without and within the City, save for the pounding of Ylia's boots, the shuffle of Malaeth's soft slippers, and Lisabetha's occasional stumble, for though she followed where led, she went blindly.

The tapestry in the Reception had already been dragged aside, revealing the entrance to the dark tunnel beyond. They had scarcely reached it when a jarring crash filled the air, and echoed across the high ceiling. A triumphant shout drowned it.

"The gates!" Malaeth shrieked.

"I know." Now that the moment had actually come, Ylia was astonishingly calm. She turned, gave the two women a push. "Go. We dare not leave this entrance for the Tehlatt to find, they would take us immediately. And I do not know where the triggering device is placed." The old nurse made a convulsive movement, started back toward the entrance. "Await us in the grove, but if we are not immediately behind you, leave and that quickly! Cross the Torth by the old fords and stay low until dark." She pressed her heavy food pouch into the old woman's reluctant hands. "Go!" she snapped as Malaeth hesitated again. "Marhan may well be there, he was pledged to save what men he could and withdraw—go!" Malaeth cast one last terrified glance toward the outer gates, turned and hurried into the blackness, dragging Lisabetha after.

Ylia drew a deep breath, let it out slowly. Still that unnatural calm filled her. Mother, is this your aid in my time of need? Nisana leaped to her shoulder, balancing awkwardly on the mesh of the mail shirt. 'What need have you?'

'Help me find the trigger, so we can close the wall.' She recoiled, cried out involuntarily as loud cries echoed down the long hall. There was a sharp, terrible drain on her inner strength and a darkness swirled before her eyes even as dim shapes spilled into the Reception. The darkness solidified, became a wall that left cat and human in the silence and cavern-night of the tunnel.

'Work quickly!' Nisana snapped. 'I cannot hold such an illusion as this for long. No, use the Power!' she hissed, as her companion hesitated. 'A thing within the wall which is different. Use the Power and *look* for it, girl!'

Easy to say, for one who can build and hold so real a wall, Ylia thought sourly. If Nisana heard the thought, she gave no sign. So weak, that sense which faltered out to touch the damp stones. So far from true AEldra. But she dared not ask Nisana's aid, she could hear those in the great hall, knew how long they would live should that wall fade. She shuddered. Sweat started forth on her brow, burned her eyes; she pressed harder.

There. It *was* different, and easy to sense, once you realized how to find it. But she was too exhausted by the search to feel triumph. She fell to her knees, groped blindly, pressed hard against the odd brick. It swung out, stiffly, and a real wall slid to fill the opening, closing with a barely audible click. Sand spilled out. Nisana leaped to the floor, rubbed against her hand.

'I—rest here.' Barely audible thought.

'No, girl. Not safe.'

'I can't walk. Sorry, cat.'

'Not safe, come!'

Ylia shook her head. "No. I—I used all I had. I must rest," she whispered.

'Not yet.' Nisana was adamant. She sent a burst of strength; Ylia's vision cleared, a little. 'The wall will hold. But we must go; Malaeth will worry.'

Malaeth. She *would* worry, she'd be terrified, and she'd come back up the passageway, if they didn't appear shortly. It helped some. It allowed her to push away from the floor and, with the use of the wall, to gain her feet. They walked down the long and silent passage to the light beyond.

Malaeth, pale and wild-eyed with terror, stood just within the tunnel's end, another behind her, a bearded man in the plain brown of the Tower Guard. Ylia blinked, could no longer bring her eyes to focus. Her head ached; a horror and pain of loss was overwhelming her. But they must know, must be told—

"The wall is closed," she whispered. "They cannot follow that way, the Tehlatt." She swayed, felt concerned hands on her arms. "Malaeth, I must rest." Someone aided her to the ground and let the darkness cover her.

Since the long kin of the Nedao first took the Plain from them, the Tehlatt ever sought to reclaim it. And they, being men and short-lived, and fearing the truth, took no cautions against such an enemy, but gave praise to their gods, their Mothers, that the barbarians were never able to bind all their tribes together, knowing if they did it would be the end of Nedao. Yet, can they be looked down upon for such behavior? For did not the Nasath and the Folk themselves, in an hour even darker and in the face of the horror that was the Lammior, not act precisely so? They knew, the humans, the day Kanatan led his warriors down the final slope to Koderra's gates—though it was then too late.

3

Silence within the smoky ravine, save for the faint victory cries of the Tehlatt. Ylia coughed, sat up to gaze about. Not far away lay Malaeth and Lisabetha; the three of them seemed to be alone, though it was impossible to see far in either direction, and the upper ledges were shrouded in gloom. Scarcely four hours from midday, as near as she could tell, but the sky was black with smoke, the sun a blood-orange halfway to the mountains.

If the Tehlatt found them now—But that was unlikely. The exit from the escape tunnel had been well chosen, and from the City it could not be seen at all. The barbarians had enough to occupy them for the moment, without searching the Plain for such hiding places.

She narrowed her eyes against smoke, coughed again as she drew an injudiciously deep breath: Someone there—a man under the trees on the northern lip, keeping watch toward the City. Mothers, it was! Marhan, King's Swordmaster, her own tutor in arms. Someone else with him—but she could not see well enough in the increasing, unnatural gloom to place him.

The old man—Marhan was indeed well past Nedaoan prime —had only one eye for the Plain, the other directed downward, for with a word to his companion he pushed to his feet, and slid down the steep bank. A soft leather bottle of water gurgled agreeably in his left hand. He scowled, thrust it forward and she drank, keenly conscious of the wrath he was keeping, barely, in check. It broke free as she corked the flask and returned it.

"So! This is how Nedao's heir keeps dagger-oath to her King! You were to be aboard a Narran ship last evening!" Black eyes bored furiously into hers. "I should box your ears!"

"What would you?" Ylia demanded stiffly. Unwise to show weakness when arguing with Marhan, but unlikely *she* would anyway. "Would *you* have left, not knowing what chanced? Well?" Silence. "And, had I left, what of them?" She nodded toward the two sleeping women. "Do you wish to think of their fate? I would rather not!"

"Don't twist words with me, damn it!" Marhan turned aside and spat. "Of course it was good that you found them. But that you remained, that you took such fool chances—!"

"You would not have called them 'fool' had you taken them," she snapped. Always, with Marhan, it came back to this—that he might take any chance, being older, wiser—a man, though he ever furiously denied that as a reason—but should she do the same, it was stupid and pointless. "And I can take care of myself," she finished shortly.

"All right. So you can," he muttered. "But not against an entire hoard of Tehlatt!" Ylia sighed, shook her head. Apparently he accepted the gesture as some sort of apology, for his next words were less harsh. "They're occupied with sacking the City, haven't come so far south. They hold the fords and the harbor. We'll go once it's dark, the moon's a late one."

He hesitated, laid a hand across her forearm. "Your—your father." His face was bleak. Ylia closed her eyes, swallowed hard, shook her head so fiercely the plaits slapped against her mail. No, do not think, do *not*. Marhan patted her arm awkwardly.

He reached then into the age-darkened leather over-jerkin to bring forth a flat, oiled packet: a map, much folded, of the Peopled Lands east of the seas. "When we leave here, we had better have direction." His voice was husky and even more clipped than usual.

"So we must." She pushed pain away, forced her mind to the moment. "How many are we?"

"There were five of us bowmen left when the gates fell. The others keep sentry there." He gestured toward the rim.

Her heart sank. Four men at arms against a nation of Tehlatt? They were dead already. But—no. If they hid, avoided the enemy, skulked from the City. And they were six, for Marhan, though old, still had a strong arm. And she had learned well from him. "Six warriors, two helpless women and a cat." Nine alive from over two thousand armed Koderra. "Most of the folk dead, the rest scattered between the Sea and the eastern deserts." She swallowed again, leaned forward to study the map. "Which way do we go? You know the lands, your choice will be better than any I might make, Marhan."

"Hmmph." The Swordmaster snapped a dead branch in half, pushed dust and leaves to and fro with it. "Only two that I can see. Yls—" The stick traced the southern edge of the Lands, down the west bank of the Torth to the Sea, thence around the coast to Yslar. He met her eyes questioningly.

"No," she said finally. "Not sensible. There are no boats, and though I have never seen it, I know full well how the land against the Sea looks. If the Sea-Raiders did not pick us off, we would be half a year walking that route. And the land passes will be thick with snow a month from now. Malaeth and Lisabetha would die, and it would be too cold for the best-clad of us. Either way, a long and doubtful journey." And what welcome at the end, for the half-breed daughter of Scythia, coming as she would with news of her death? She buried the thought angrily. *No*. "Tell me the other choice, Marhan. It can be no worse, surely."

"Perhaps." He did not seem particularly certain of that. "But I see no others, none at all. Not without horses or boats.

And even then—Aresada." The stick pressed against a dark blotch north and west of Teshmor, ten leagues within the Foessa and sixty leagues or more north of Koderra. She rested her chin on drawn-up knees, thought hard.

"Then it must be Aresada. The Caves have been used before in time of need; folk would go there, if they escaped in the north or escaped Teshmor. And Lord Corry cached stores of grain, and dried food after Anasela."

"If the boats reach Yslar—"

"They will." She dared think nothing else for now. "The folk will be cared for." She sighed, suddenly desperately tired, weak with the thought of what lay before them. Before her. "I have never felt less like Brandt's heir, but I see where I am needed most, Marhan. And that is where we must go." Dark brown eyes met hazel ones. He nodded.

"So be it. But you are not alone, remember that." He went back to the map. "So. We are here. Caves, here. A long and hard journey, however taken, but the Foessa are our only road."

"I fear so. No matter where we go from here. It is said there are ways within the mountains, trails and paths. Though I have never seen them, save what remains of the old Hunter's Trail from Koderra."

"I know no more than you," the old man nodded unhappily. "I did take the pass to Yslar once, but it was a long time since. Hunters make and use the trails, but we of Nedao never used them. Why should we?" he added bitterly. "We had the Plain, *we* never needed the mountains." Ylia needed none of the Power to sense the direction of his thought: men lost, friends and arms-companions dead. No hope of revenge.

"No. But we need them now. And we will use what paths we can find, and make others. Stay well within the mountains. The Tehlatt fear them."

"So they do. There is that, at least. Where their gods live, they won't pursue us. And a few stragglers—"

"I—stragglers. Noteyen guard us." She sought, gripped his arm. "It's true, isn't it? We have seen the end of all we knew, Marhan. Nedao. All of it. We were soft, complacent, unwilling to face what we saw among the Tehlatt. And Kanatan brought all the tribes together."

"And made massacre. Not war, genocide," Marhan said gloomily. "You are right, I said it in Council often enough.

We were unwilling to face a fearful likelihood only because it frightened us." He stared at the map without seeing it. "Though I took the Tehlatt messages the past year no more seriously than the others, and that after Anasela."

"Even after Anasela," she agreed. "They took that ten years ago, killing everyone who did not flee. And we actually believed they would be satisfied with so much and would leave us in peace." They were silent for a time. Ylia traced her mother's calming charm across her inner being, fighting the encroaching fear that they might be the sole survivors anywhere across the Plain.

"Marhan," she said finally, steadily. "There is one other thing you and I must discuss before we leave this place. I am Brandt's heir, now Nedao's Lady. But I am also arms-woman." She paused to choose her next words with great care; the subject was a touchy one with the old armsmaster. "We face terrible odds. We may not even live, all of us, to cross the Torth tonight. And the road we have chosen, you and I—it may be all that the old tales make of it, it may be worse than anything we can imagine. I will not command any, man or woman, where we go. Nor is this the time to hold to Nedao's traditional protection of noble blooded and female. I will neither lead nor follow. I will give no order, and I will not allow you to care for me as we must Malaeth and the girl. We who can fight must be equals and arms-mates in this." Silence. "Do you agree?"

Marhan frowned. "Your oath to your father—"

Ylia stiffened, swallowed anger. "Safeguards, he said. I count my sword among them."

"Perhaps. You are not bad. But your sword is unblooded."

She laughed, mirthlessly. "Hardly that! Do you forget Vess' messenger this past winter?"

Marhan shook his head firmly. "You did not slay him."

"No," she replied flatly. The anger she'd felt then was still alive. "Not for lack of desire on my part. The guard came to my aid too soon."

The old man laughed grimly. "It does not matter. If we travel the Foessa, you'll blood your blades properly within a five-day, I'll wager you."

"No take," she replied soberly. "But if the need is there, by the Black Well I will." Another silence. The cries from the City were fainter, or so it seemed. "It is my fight as well as

yours, Marhan. You trained me for this.'' Keen eyes met hers.
He opened his mouth, shut it again, refolded the map with
great care and placed it in his jerkin. He was withdrawn for
some moments. His hand moved then, freed the dagger from
its arm sheath, and he laid it hilts down against his breast.

"That is how you mean it—arms-mate?"

She drew her own short blade, matched his gesture. "That is
indeed how I mean it." It was as though a weight had slipped
from her shoulders, and she could have laughed for the relief
of it: She'd won him over, however grudgingly. "What say
you, arms-mate?" she added challengingly, one hand gripping
his shoulder. "Shall we win through the Foessa to the Caves of
Aresada?"

His face was battle tight, his eyes glittered. "Aye, arms-
mate. Though an army stand between!" With one swift motion that belied his three-score years, he sheathed the blade,
rose and returned swiftly to the lip of the ravine.

Ylia lay back, suddenly weary. Arguing with Marhan took
much from her at the best of times. Nisana slid quietly from
under a nearby bush, stretched her sleek, dark body and
purred against the girl's shoulder. *Teacher, friend—constant
companion.* Ylia smiled, rubbed thick fur, and the cat leaned
hard against her cheek, moved down to curl against her body
and went to sleep.

Malaeth slowly closed the few paces separating them,
spread her cloak and lowered herself cautiously to the ground.
"Where do we go, Ylia, and when?" She cast one nervous
glance toward the unseen City. "And—and where is—where
are the others?"

"I—no one else is coming." Ylia swallowed, reached to
take the tiny soft hand in both her own small hands. "We are
all that remain, we here." Silence. "I am sorry, Malaeth."

The old nurse shook her head violently and tears flew. "I
knew it. I *felt* it—what she did. No." She fumbled at her gir-
dle for one of her bits of fine-broidered linen, dabbed at her
face. "No, do not be sorry; not for me."

Ylia patted her hands helplessly. She who had been nurse to
the Queen since her birth, forty or more years ago in distant
Yls, what could anyone say to her? But there was more she
must know. Ylia took a deep breath, plunged on. "We seek
Aresada, Malaeth, those of us left. With luck we will find

other survivors, perhaps from Teshmor but certainly from the
Western farms and herding villages. We must travel within the
mountains, though, for safety from the barbarians." The old
woman's eyes went wide. "We cannot attempt Yls; it is nearly
180 leagues to Yslar, across the highest of the mountains; and
we are afoot and poorly clad. It is perhaps a third as far to the
Caves." Silence. The old nurse continued to stare at her horrified. "I wish we had another choice, and I cannot command
you, Malaeth. But—"

"No. I served your mother, and I now serve you." Malaeth's voice trembled, but her hand was steady as she touched
her forehead in the Ylsan sign of service. "Even if our path lay
through the Tehlatt themselves. And someday," she added, a
more normal tartness edging her words as she eyed her charge
critically, "someday you will cease trying to ape the Swordmaster and realize you are a woman." She shook her head
grimly, the moment's fears forgotten in old argument. "You
need me, child. You cannot travel with men unprotected; I will
not have it!"

Ylia smothered a sigh. "Malaeth, I do not forget what I am.
Lady of Nedao, Scythia's daughter, she of the Second House
of the AEldra. Wielder of the AEldra Power, however poorly
I inherited from her. But also Brandt's daughter. *And*
swordswoman!

"The Power is no real protection for me, Malaeth, you
know that. And Father put little faith in such things, you
know that, too; he trusted to those strengths he could *see*.
Think if I had not had my sword, and the arm to wield it,
when Vess' man set upon me last winter! Had I not been what
I am, had I been instead the jewel on a lace cushion you would
have me be—"

"I wish no such thing," Malaeth replied reprovingly, and
untruthfully. "But it's no proper thing for a maid. Look at
you," she went on, "a form such as yours cries for soft
gowns, a wide belt to set off such a tiny waist. Such small,
dainty hands should wear jewels, not wrap themselves around
sword hilts! No. Your mother never cared for it, and I like it
even less."

Was one fated ever to hear the same words, year in and year
out, Ylia wondered tiredly. And as for her clothing, gods and
Mothers, she was wearing that silly mid-calf length tabard
over her sensible breeches and boots, wasn't that modest

enough? "Mother never liked it, but at least she saw the need." Scythia *had* understood—at least understood that Brandt's heir must be capable of leading Nedao's armed to battle. *That* Nedao insisted upon from its rulers, and those few women who had ever ruled had been warrior trained, warrior skilled.

Scythia had understood also, she was certain, the love her daughter shared with her father for the weapons themselves: the grace of a well-fought crossing, the joy of a difficult pass mastered. Though she probably would have approved less, had Beredan lived.

Ylia sighed again, deeply. *Beredan*: It still hurt, even with all that had passed in recent days. Beloved older brother. He'd given her first lessons, given her his own boy's wooden training blade when her hands were still too tiny to wrap around a real hilts. She'd worshipped him; all Nedao had. He'd died five years past, he and his entire company, protecting peasantry who'd finally been persuaded to leave the Eastern marches hard against Anasela and on the northern edge of the Planthe.

Brandt, after an interval of mourning, had named Ylia his heir, ignoring the advice of his council for once, reminding them of Queen Leffna, ignoring again their outcry that she had been "different" and in any case had ruled 500 years before. Male cousins, a royal uncle or two had been thoroughly enraged, none moreso than Vess. It was at about this time "accidents" occurred near the Princess Royal: two distant attempts at assassination—an arrow from across the River during a foot race that missed her by inches, the bowman never found; a knife thrown from the shadows when she returned to the Tower late one evening after a late practice session with the Swordmaster. And then the swordsman who'd engaged her just outside the walls. Vess' man, she *knew* beyond doubt. He'd swallowed poison when they took him, and not even her mother would believe her suspicions.

She forced her mind firmly back to the moment again. Malaeth, huddled at her side, looked old and frail indeed, as though twice her three-score and fifteen years weighed upon her. The old nurse's next words took her by surprise. "They owe us blood-price, the Tehlatt," she whispered fiercely. "And may the day of payment come soon!"

"It may," Ylia replied, but doubt showed in her voice. "In

a way unlooked for, perhaps. We are few, scattered. We must rebuild, for the present, and not think of vengeance." *And where shall we rebuild, my sadly lessened people and I*? "If the day comes, we will grasp it with both hands." She caught Malaeth's hands between her own again, a faint smile bringing one as faint and poor a thing in reply. "I will need you in the days to come, Malaeth, remember that. You are strong, I need your strength. And I will need you at Aresada."

A long, comfortable silence, broken only by the distant sound of the river and an occasional, faint, cry. Malaeth cleared her throat. "Ylia—I—what of the Foessa? They—if we go there—they are haunted, the mountains."

Ylia stared at her. Unsuccessfully fought a giggle. "Haunted? Malaeth, I have heard those tales since I was a child! Tales, that was what I thought even then. Be serious, that is all they are, stories to frighten small children!"

"Perhaps." The nurse eyed her darkly, clearly unconvinced. "Men hunting in the mountains seldom return. Those who do, speak of the fear that followed them in the dark, that they fled witless from it. Or of things that cried aloud and rolled stones upon them. Shadows that moved overhead swiftly on clear nights, strange prints, animals for which there are no names. I cannot believe this is all wild telling!"

Ylia rolled over to gaze through the trees to the west. Across the unseen Torth, the Foessa rose: Glorious mountains torn from the Plain, above a single line of tree-capped hills. Sharp-edged; jagged; snow-clad well into summer. "I cannot say," she replied finally. "Since I have seen none of these things myself, and have spoken to no man who has. And there is no point to gainsaying anything before it is known true or false. But, what need you to look for in mountains other than weather and wind to loosen stones, wind to cry strangely in the heights? And fear of a strange place can put terror into a man in the night, so that all he sees is distorted. And who of us is to say which prints are strange when in the Foessa they may all be? I," she added with an assurance she hoped she felt, knew she must force upon the old woman, "will put trust in the swords among us, and in our need to reach the Caves. And I will fear nothing to which I can set steel!" Malaeth gazed at her unhappily, but finally nodded.

"I said I would follow you, and I will! But I feel, in the core of my inner being where the Power still stirs, that trouble will come of this!"

"And I will hope that you are wrong, Malaeth. But we cannot use the Plain; we have no choice in our path." Time to change the subject. "How is Lisabetha?"

"She still sleeps." Malaeth glanced over her shoulder to the huddled form on the ground. "What will you do with her?"

"Let her stay as she is, we can take in turns to lead her. I used more strength than I thought I possessed merely to close the passage behind us, and that was not all I used this day. I dare nothing else just now if we are to leave quickly at full dark. Rest while you can, Malaeth," she added. "The way will not be easy, and we will need as much speed as we can muster." Malaeth sighed, but touched her forehead again and rose heavily to her feet.

It wasn't the kind of company that would have been named in one of the old tales, and quite frankly not the one I'd have chosen myself, given our destination and the way we must travel: The presumption of humans! Consider: mountains that have killed or defeated strong men fully prepared, and they intended to breach them half-clad, ill-armed, and with such strength. An untried girl, whose blades still bore the shine the smith put on them; an aged and half-blind old man and an even older woman—a stunned and terrified girl, who had to be led by the hand. Two men who openly loathed a third and another so young he'd scarcely finished his height. Well, fortunately for them, they also had me, even though most of them didn't realize yet how grateful they'd be of that.

4

The day crawled by. Impossible to guess the time, for smoke obscured the sun totally.

Again and again she murmured the AEldra words which slow pulse, relax muscles; as often she rubbed damp palms against coarse brown breeches. Their luck had held so far, but how much longer? Inaction ate at her; finally she could no longer wait below. Even if there was nothing to be seen, she could look, could take her share of the watches. She roused Nisana and they climbed the steep, crumbling ledge.

Marhan sat alone, back against a tree, gazing across the darkened landscape. To the right, fires, fewer than the sky would have led one to believe, burned at the City walls. Westward, the red sun cut briefly through cloud and smoke, began to edge behind the mountains: within the hour they could leave. But as she opened her mouth to speak, the old Swordmaster gripped her arm, dragged her down to his side. He gestured with his chin.

Tehlatt. A band of warriors rode from the gates down the wide road to the harbor. Though they were half a league and more distant, the refugees dropped even lower, peered cautiously through tall grasses. The barbarians vanished from sight over the low bluff that edged the water. Marhan shook his head unhappily.

"Won't do. We can't risk the crossing if they don't return."

"You said others had—"

"Others came this way earlier. Two. And they came back. These might be searching."

An idea came from a third source. Nisana rubbed against the girl's arm. 'Tell him.'

'Cat, if I tell him *that*—'

'Tell him!'

Ylia scowled at her, turned back to the old man. 'All right, and I'll catch the blame—seven hells.' "If we wait until full dark, if we stay close together, Nisana can screen us. We could cross under their very noses and not be seen."

One dark eye regarded the cat warily. "Magic." The word fell like an epithet. "No." he said flatly. "Unless there is no other—" He broke off. The barbarians were returning from the harbor; even more swiftly than they had come forth, they rode back to the City. Marhan sighed with obvious relief. "No need."

Nisana's amusement pressed against her. Ylia scowled at the old man. For one so undeniably brave to fear the Power as he did! "Marhan, it cannot *hurt* you!"

"Huh. You speak like your mother. And I believe it just as much as your father did. Give me defenses I can see!"

Nisana's amused snort reverberated through Ylia's mind, did nothing to sooth her irritation. 'You did that on purpose, cat!'

'Nonsense.'

Marhan rolled aside, sat up and waved an imperative, if prudently low, hand. Moments later four men, clad in the dusty brown garb of the Tower Guard, slipped into the grasses beside him.

"Brel. Did you keep count?"

The boy nodded. "As many out as back, Swordmaster."

"Good. We leave shortly."

Nisana clambered onto Ylia's lap, studied the armsmen gravely. One of them, the bearded man who had helped Mala-eth when Ylia staggered spent from the escape tunnel, gazed back in stunned disbelief, and with patent disdain. "A cat. By all the gods together, what next?" Softly spoken, but Ylia caught the muttered words and flushed angrily.

"A cat. I am glad you came through battle with your eyes intact." It was the armsman's turn to redden. "Nisana," Ylia went on, fury clipping her words, "is indeed a cat, but my mother's. She is of AEldra blood, as I am; she has my mother's skills, more of them, and better, than I have. She is no fragile lady's pet, but a wielder of the Power. We need every weapon we can muster among us. Or perhaps," she demanded, "you doubt Queen Scythia's Power?"

The bearded armsman leaned angrily forward but the lad Marhan had first addressed laid a hand on his shoulder, pressed him aside. "Bren; let me. We do not doubt, Lady Princess," he added. His own color was high, but it was a flush of embarrassment. "Bren knows. The Queen healed my knee last winter after my horse fell with me. I'd have been a year or more recovering had I been left to the healers. The Lady's ways are not common in Nedao but real enough, I'd vouch for that. If ye say the cat is like to her, I do not doubt ye." Northern by the accent. So much like his companion they must be brothers, and now she remembered them: Brelian and his elder brother Brendan, sons of Broln, who had been Captain of the Gate Guard in Teshmor until his death two winters since.

She knew neither well. She met them, was at her father's side, when they first came to Koderra and the King's service. She seldom spoke to the armsmen, of course, as she was keenly aware of how most of them regarded her. She had likely never spoken to these. But she recalled something Marhan had said about Brendan's astonishing weapons-skill. He was handsome, yes, undeniably that. *Just ask him*, she thought sourly. Brelian, a pleasant looking boy, seemed considerably more human.

Brendan, she noticed with dry amusement, had managed

somehow to clean his jerkin, and his long breeches were neatly laced and tucked into boots that were scuffed but clean. His cloak lay in tidy folds across the field pack which held his arrow-pouch and food. His bow, strung, lay loosely in his left hand, which was considerably cleaner than her own hands. Only his short-sleeved mail did not shine.

His brother, by contrast, was as rumpled as Marhan, as rumpled as she herself must be. His mail was greened from hiding in the trees, his belt-pouch skewed to one side, and black ash smudged one high cheekbone.

She smiled as she turned to the next of them. "Lev." She had known him all her life as she had Marhan, for Levren was right-hand man to the Swordmaster, Bowmaster in his own right. He had taught her, though she had less skill than either of them wished. Less than Beredan, who had first pushed her into the training. Levren, near the King's age, hair and moustache beginning to grey, easy-going, unlike the sour and brusque Marhan, and yet, like Marhan, a man to depend upon when there was need. It always came as a surprise to her, that he was not that tall; but then, he was so often surrounded by children—his own young ones and, it often seemed, half those in Koderra as well—as he went about his duties.

His only serious flaw that she had ever seen was that unreasoning xenophobia that would have set him at the throat of anyone not Nedaoan, and when he could not control it, he quietly absented himself from offending company. Here, fortunately, there would be no problem. At least—she gazed blankly from Levren to the last of the company. *Oh no. Gods of the Black Well.*

Golsat. Alone of Brandt's armsmen, she knew this man well, had crossed blades with him once or twice, defended him against certain of his comrades. He had come to Koderra three years before from Lord Corry's Teshmoran Guard, and before that from Anasela when it fell to the Tehlatt. Had they captured him, then or today, the barbarians would have burned him alive, a fate they reserved for traitors. For Golsat's mother was Tehlatta, and he resembled her more than his Nedaoan father. Though not much older than Ylia, his somber mien and non-Nedaoan features gave him the appearance of a ten of years more. He was pragmatic, taciturn, aloof. Not through pride, but because he felt the cast many put upon his mixed blood and did not wish to foist himself upon anyone. A man, altogether, of rare composure and strength.

A good man. A good friend, though, really, she knew very little of him. Would Levren be able to deal with Golsat at all? The tension in the clearing was palpable, the air around the Bowmaster crackled with his effort to keep his balled fists to himself. He moved, finally, a little beyond Marhan, turned to gaze out across the Plain. Golsat, keenly aware of the Bowmaster's problem, backed a few paces away and eased himself down against a tree.

"Thank you, Brelian," Ylia met his eyes, with a faint smile. "But, no ceremony between us, we are all cut of the same cloth in our need to escape the Plain. For now, I am no more Lady Princess than you are dagger-sworn. Besides," she added, a genuine smile touching her eyes, "I wager my face is fully as sooted as yours." Brelian smiled shyly in return, scrubbed his nose on his sleeve. Ylia forced aside a shyness nearly as overwhelming, suddenly, as his, gazed from one of the men before her to the next, then to Marhan, who nodded. "For now I am Ylia—sword-mate to all of you, if you will have it." A deft motion freed her dagger from its leg sheath. Brendan cast a dark, sidelong glance at the Swordmaster, hesitated briefly, finally drew his own blade. *Does he dare humor me?* she wondered hotly. *If he does, he will regret it!*

The other three appeared to have no such doubts, for they had drawn their blades at once and with visible good will. Levren, she noticed with relief, was choosing to ignore his half-caste companion. Better than any alternative she could, at the moment, conjure. Brendan—it figured, given his unbending appearance and Northern heritage—cast his dark ally a dubious glance, but he spoke the oath without other outward misgiving.

At Marhan's order, they broke up, slipped back into the trees to watch and wait for darkness. Ylia moved back into shadow, stood to survey the Plain until the harbor road could no longer be seen in the encroaching gloom.

Silence. With concentration, she and the old Swordmaster could hear celebration within Koderra's high walls as night drew in, bringing with it ragged clouds and a few stars.

"The luck's with us," Marhan whispered. "Moon's no more than a splinter, and it won't rise until near dawn." He gazed out across the Plain himself, though his own eyes were weak and it was unlikely he'd see anything unless it were on top of him. "Time, girl. Go waken Malaeth, get ready. We'll leave as soon as we're all together."

"Good." Ylia scrabbled down the dark ravine wall. The burden of waiting, at least *that* was over.

Darkness was near total as they started toward the River, keeping in file behind Levren, who knew the path well enough even though he could not see. Marhan and Golsat brought up the rear.

The Torth was deep, fast with runoff. Marhan held up a hand and went forward alone at the water's edge, vanished into thick reeds. Nisana, curled into the travel pouch at Ylia's back, nudged her. 'Join.' Dubiously, considering her faint reserves of strength, Ylia added her own thought to Nisana's. The cat began an intense, rapid mind-search of the area around them.

In the space of forty cautious breaths, the Swordmaster was back. The others crowded close so he could speak. "Not guarded. Water's high and treacherous though."

"The fords?" Levren asked. Marhan shook his head.

"No. They're held. Dangerous. Can't risk it."

"Well, then, how do we cross?" Brendan demanded in a low voice. Impatience in his stance, in the turn of his mouth —so much Ylia could see with the second level of Sight. 'Trouble, cat; he'll be trouble every step of the way.' 'Perhaps, girl. He's upset; give him a chance to sort himself out.' "We are not much burdened, but the women cannot manage that river alone."

Marhan rubbed his moustache with a thick forefinger, frowned at his boots. He glanced back at the water, nodded to himself, turned back and began to speak. But the mind-search Nisana had loosed closed at that moment about strangers— near! She clawed free of her pouch, pulled onto Ylia's shoulder and flung herself growling to the ground. Dark shapes —they would not have been visible with straight vision—loped down the ravine toward the River.

"Golsat!" Ylia hissed; her right hand gripped her sword, tore it from its sheath; the dagger was already in her left. Brelian leaped to push Malaeth and Lisabetha flat into the brush as Golsat whirled. The first of the Tehlatt fell with a gasping little cry. Golsat ran back up the trail as another threw himself forward; his sword crashed against Ylia's and she found herself fighting in truth.

But the sudden ferocity of the attack drove fear from her mind; instinct long honed took over. One clash of blades that numbed her arm, a second. He was all strength, no skill, and her blade slipped easily under his guard. She turned away as he fell, but there was no further need for her aid. Brendan, who had held two at bay, slew the first with a clean thrust, dropped the other with a blow from his dagger hilts and pushed the barbarian into the Torth. Marhan knelt over a dark huddle near the water's edge, and Brelian was already aiding Malaeth to her feet. Levren, arrow fitted loosely to the string, was moving silently back up the trail. Golsat materialized at her side.

"My thanks, friend," he began with his usual grave formality. "He would have killed me before I was even aware." He wiped his dagger against his breeches, peered into the dark at her feet. "Well. The Swordmaster cannot fault your sword now, can he?" He laughed rather grimly, and knelt. His dark face was void of expression as he looked up. "He is not dead." Spoken so matter of factly Ylia stared down at him blankly until she saw the gleam of starlight on his blade.

"No." She dropped to one knee. "Equally I said, and so I meant." *If I think what I mean to do.* She forced aside thought of any kind, brought her gaze to the fallen Tehlatt, swiftly dragged his head back by the hair and buried the dagger in his throat. He jerked once, lay still. Golsat took the knife from her limp fingers, wiped it on the brush and restored it to its sheath, then pulled her to her feet. A few paces from the others, he stopped. His grip stayed hard and reassuring around her shoulders until she could stop shaking.

"That was bravely done." He spoke quietly. "To slay in battle, to slay before another kills you, that is far different from what you have just had to do. Remember, lest it seem easy to take lives. But never forget you have killed an enemy this night, one who would have killed you had your places been exchanged!" Ylia could not speak, could only nod. He patted her arm.

When they moved back to join the others, Marhan and Levren were again discussing the crossing. "We had better leave now, as quickly as we can." The Bowmaster might have been discussing a summer picnic.

"I cannot fault that," Marhan growled. "What we must do is—spread out, all the way across. Pass cloaks, weapons, whatever else need stay dry. Pass Malaeth and the girl."

Brelian and Brendan had dragged the bodies down into the water, and they now returned, Brelian's young face unnaturally pale. The older brother listened impassively. "I see no better way myself. Let us go, now." He turned, waded out into the River.

The rest followed. The water was bone-chillingly icy as it slid past knees, nearly to the waist. Though it fortunately went no deeper than that, it was difficult to keep balance against the current. Ylia, on whom the water came nearly breast high, had been given the place nearest the west bank. Even so, she would have been hard put to hold had it not been for the boulders down-River.

Once in position, they were little more than arms width apart, and reached nearly shore to shore. Packs, weapons, bundles of cloaks and food, Brendan's mail, all came across in such a fashion. Then Malaeth grasped Lisabetha's hand and led her into the shallows. Three steps allowed her to put the girl into Brelian's arms and slowly, cautiously, she was passed across. Ylia waded ashore long enough to lay her among the packs and unwillingly waded back out to help bring Malaeth over.

Malaeth caused considerable difficulty: Though shorter and much lighter than Lord Corry's daughter, she was awake and terrified, while Lisabetha had been limp as a child's doll. Malaeth fought to keep her body above water, and nearly caused Marhan a complete dunking. For a wonder, though, she held a tight-lipped silence throughout, and was finally across. The rest followed, pausing only long enough to wring out wet clothing, and empty boots. The steep Hunter's Trail loomed before them, a faint pale line against dark brush and rock.

For as long as Nedao had dwelt on the Plain, the Trail had been there, cutting through the foothills, across the eastern edge of the Yls Pass and then to an end a league or so beyond the Pass. It was Marhan's hope to reach the trail's end by dawn.

He fought impatience and anger as they paused for breath, more frequently than he'd hoped, but the way was steeper than he'd recalled. At least there were no sounds of pursuit, no sound but nightbirds and the Torth far below. Fire burned high as night came on, turning the City walls and the Tower ruddy. Their mood lightened when they topped a ridge and began the descent, for then Koderra was hidden from view.

But the going was still slow, even after the ascent lessened, for clouds filled the sky and darkness became absolute. Marhan and Levren took turns at first to lead, much to Ylia's and Nisana's impatience, for the cat could see quite clearly, and Ylia, with the second level of Sight, could see much better than any of the rest of them.

Finally the Swordmaster relented and Ylia took the lead, Nisana on her shoulder, aiding her even in this simplest of all uses of the AEldra power, using her own cat-vision to assist. They traveled faster for some time after that, for even though those behind could see no more of the trail than before, Ylia called out changes in direction to those who followed, warned of rocks and holes.

The only mishap occurred when Golsat missed one of the sudden turnings and tumbled off the trail. Although the drop was steep, the area was thick with the previous year's grasses, so he took no real hurt. But he was in a foul mood for the rest of the night. The others could hear him mumbling to himself as he combed prickly seeds from his hair and beard with his fingers, and he was still pulling long-tailed barbs from his mail shirt the next afternoon.

By middle night, a longer rest had become absolute necessity. It was well over a league, mostly uphill, from the Torth. Just over a low rise, Ylia found a dell near the path with a deep-cut brook running down one side. It was sheltered from the chill little wind that had risen. They lit no fire, for not even Marhan could guess how near the Pass they were, and it was possible, if not very likely, that the Tehlatt had sent a party up the ancient road. They huddled close together, shared a little of what food there was, mostly biscuit and dried meat. Poor fare, but at least filling.

"Beyond the Pass road, we'll be able to hunt, to properly cook what we catch, without fear of the Tehlatt," Levren assured them.

"Not the Tehlatt, anyway," Brendan said. Ylia glared at him, indicating the old nurse with a swift motion of her head; Brelian whispered something against his brother's ear. Brendan rolled his eyes but made no further remark.

Ylia spared him one black look, then went back to her study of her companions. Malaeth and Lisabetha, of course, had brought nothing at all with them; Malaeth had barely retained sufficient wit in her terror to get both of them winter cloaks. But they had already been dressed for the journey to Yls and so wore travel skirts, thick but divided for ease in walking, shorter than the traditional robes. Lisabetha even wore sturdy boots. For so much she could give silent thanks, though Malaeth's beaded slippers could not possibly last an entire five-day.

The armsmen were clad for warmth and against rough usage, as she was. And armed. Levren was a good hunter, perhaps the brothers were. Or Golsat. If there was meat in the Foessa, they'd not starve. Those dressed for battle were also unlikely to freeze.

She spared no concern for Nisana: of all the company, she was the most self-sufficient.

Well. She sighed. Pointless to worry the matter any more, they still knew nothing of how the mountains would receive them and she was, suddenly, very tired indeed.

'You used nothing, it was mostly *my* strength you drew upon, girl.'

'Mostly! I still used my own, cat!'

'Huh. Anyone, even Malaeth, can still use the second level of Sight. It's the first thing any of us learn.'

'The first thing pureblooded learn,' Ylia retorted, and closed her eyes. The whispers around her slowly faded.

Nisana gazed at her, affection and irritation balancing in her thought. *Humans. They take notions, and no sense, no rational argument will dissuade them.*

The cat's head came around; Ylia sat up, abruptly awake. Marhan was attempting vainly to separate Brendan and Golsat. Brelian, who had apparently already tried, was picking himself up from a pile of dry brush and rubbing his bruised chin. At the same moment, Levren, his face white with repressed emotion, eyes and hands clenched tight, turned away and strode off to the creek, where he knelt with his back to them all.

The two men had not spoken all afternoon; Brendan had sworn dagger-oath, but reluctantly, and he clearly had in full the Northern prejudices; Golsat, usually immune to such things, had been in a temper after his fall, and Brendan, for some reason, had gotten under his skin. The younger man had baited him since their halt until, with a cry of fury, Golsat leaped upon him. They now rolled about the floor of the dell, and though neither had yet drawn a knife, it was clear that things had gone far enough.

Try, something has to work, and fast. Ylia rolled to her knees, spoke under her breath. A red spark of Baelfyr jumped from her outstretched fingers to the two; they sprang apart, one rubbing a shoulder, the other his neck. Both stared, wide-eyed.

"Fools!" she hissed, putting all the anger in her into speech. "Do we not have enough enemies that we must make enemies of each other?" Golsat opened his mouth to speak, shut it firmly and turned his gaze to a point beyond her. Brendan's eyes met hers defiantly. "What caused this?" she demanded.

"He is Tehlatt, we cannot trust him." Brendan's face was white in the light of the newly risen moon. "He will murder us all in our sleep, his kind killed my mother and sisters in Teshmor." He spun away, drove his fist savagely into the damp ground. Brelian moved swiftly to his side, wrapped an arm around his shoulders. Brendan drew a deep, shuddering breath. Another. He turned back then. His eyes were wet.

"Golsat is *part* Tehlatt," Marhan said mildly enough, but his own expression was hard. The half-caste's face was unreadable. "He is also ours. He fought with us against Tehlatt. He was raised in Nedao, not in the skin tents of the Tehlatta. He has no cause to love his mother's kin any more than we. They would have killed her for taking a Nedaoan as mate. What part would they have of *him*, save his death and that worse than any we would face? As you well know, young swordsman," the Swordmaster added pointedly.

"I understand your pain." Ylia's voice, low in the ensuing silence, caught at her throat. "I have lost—" She could not finish the thought. "They were killed by our common enemy, the Tehlatt. *Not* by my friend and arms-mate Golsat." Deeper silence. "He lost friends and family this day also, or do you conveniently forget that, Brendan?" Brendan scowled at her; the two men then eyed each other warily.

"Come!" Marhan said. "Join hands, both of you. Now!" he snapped as neither made a move. Golsat held out a tentative hand; Brendan reluctantly took it. "And swear at least, if you cannot be friends, that you will not fight each other!"

"All—all right," Brendan mumbled. Golsat made some reply too low to catch. No sign of giving on the part of either, but truce. For the moment, it would have to do.

They moved out moments later; Nisana and Ylia again led, the others followed as best they could. But now, when they needed it most, the trail occasionally leveled out, now and again went downhill for short distances, and the climbs were no longer so strenuous. The men passed Lisabetha from one to another. Malaeth somehow held out on her own for long, thought she had seldom in her life and certainly not of late walked any distances.

An hour's travel brought them to the Pass. The road, dusted with recent snow, gleamed as a long, pale gash between black tree shadows. Marhan allowed a rest for the others while the brothers scouted the road in both directions. Nisana made a search of her own. But there were none to hinder, nothing human within leagues. They crossed quickly all the same, were swallowed up in shadow on the other side.

The trail was fainter than it had been south of the Pass. It wound among huge boulders and the dry beds of ancient streams. Now it was lost in a slide, again it ran smoothly over pine needles under tall trees where every gap between trunks appeared a trail. Sometimes it disappeared completely on ground boggy with runoff, and twice it vanished beneath still melting tracts of snow. At one point, Levren and Golsat, the best trackers they had, had to cast about for some distance before locating it again.

Only the brighter stars shone as the thin moon rode higher. Grey edged the mountains and a faint pink to the east marked where the sun would rise. The trail stretched clearly before them all of a sudden, up a short slope above the water and down a gentle descent beneath thick trees. Brendan and Brelian took in turns to carry Malaeth, whose strength had suddenly given out; Levren and Marhan led Lisabetha. Golsat, more taciturn than ever, dropped back to keep rearguard.

Another hour—two. They were walking slowly, all of them, practically staggering, exhausted beyond bearing. The land took on the semblance of illusion as minds dulled, legs and feet ached, each step drove pain stabbing upward. No one spoke, but it was clear none of them wished to stop before the end of the trail. *Only so much further*, Ylia whispered to herself. *So much—good. Again. And now—that grove of trees, you can make that? Good. Through this open dell.* . . . Nisana lay in the travel pouch, sound asleep.

And then, as the company topped a long rise, the sun's first rays crept over the mountains, casting light and warmth over a long green valley: the Hunter's Meadow. They had reached the end of the known ways into the Foessa.

They were not our long kin, who made the
Hunter's Meadow home. True beings, but of
our own myths, as real to our kind as the
horrors of the Foessa to Nedao. Sensibly so:
When, last, did any of our blood see a Guard-
ian, speak with one of the Folk, touch the
green jewel of the Yderra to know his future?
—They dwelt there for long and so I knew at
once, when my feet first touched the soil.
The land alone remembers them, but it re-
members long and well.

5

They stood for some time as though not believing the clear
evidence of their eyes. Finally, Marhan roused himself, shook
Ylia's arm as he passed her, and led them down the final hill.

The sun touched on a waterfall, gave back glittering light as
they limped slowly down the trail. A stream meandered
through the scattered groves of trees, swirled in deep, clear
green pools. Cold—water that color came fresh from the
snow. But it invited: Ylia felt suddenly as though she hadn't
bathed in a year and the heavy woolen shirt was unpleasantly
damp between her shoulders.

The meadow lay shining and clear as the sun rose higher,
and a light breeze brought the pervasive smell of apple blossom. They stopped short in amazement. Clearly, the meadow
had been planted as a garden, though also clearly it had long
since grown wild. Who had lived here, and set groves of fruit
trees so and there, who had planted the little purple crocus and
snow drop, the snow roses that lay in red and dark-pink pud-

44

dles on the crisp, half-melted snow in the shade of a clutch of stately fir?

The air was wonderfully warm, even at that hour.

Marhan and Levren were already beginning to lay out a camp and clear a space for the fire. Malaeth lay with Lisabetha in the sun, eyes closed, her face drawn and white.

The Swordmaster portioned out tasks, sending the brothers to gather wood and build the fire, to fill what water flasks there were, to fill his battered kettle. Levren was given the remaining arrows. He alone could be trusted to waste none of them. He went in search of meat. Golsat took to himself the task of circling the valley, to search for sign of beasts or other men. Marhan drew forth a precious packet from his jerkin—a fishing line, one of the two hooks he always carried—and set out toward the head of the valley. Ylia bit back a smile as he vanished. It faded, then. No, not so amusing. The Swordmaster had taken terrible teasing for his insistence on always carrying such basics of survival. Time and the Tehlatt had vindicated him.

She sighed, dropped her cloak and worked to clear rock and branch from a wide sleeping sward near the fire. She hesitated then, but Marhan had left her no other tasks. She went in search of the pool she had seen from above.

It was not very far, and a stand of aspen shielded her from the camp. She undressed swiftly. Water swirled down into a bay from a short falls, carving out a deep pond near one bank. Morning sun shone full on the water. It was cold, colder than the Torth, but she took a deep breath and plunged in. She emerged shivering violently, her teeth chattered, but she was cleaner than she had gone in. She staggered to the bank on numbed feet, found a place to sit and dry in the sun while she combed her hair out with her fingers, rewove it into plaits, tied them firmly with bits of leather thong. The sun was warming; she thawed slowly, blank-minded, content to watch the tops of trees, the dark blue sky between them, to listen to squabbling birds in the underbrush.

She stirred herself finally, pulled the woolen shirt over her head, laced the heavy pants down snugly from knee to ankle. She left off her boots, carried the mail and padded surcoat with the King's arms quilted to the breast: the day was already too warm for Tower winter garb, and the protective garments were heavy, even though specially made to her small size.

And that surcoat. She scowled at it. She was cutting it short, hip length at most, before the day was out; she'd determined *that* after wading the Torth. The thing had nearly thrown her under more than once, and for most of the night it had twisted wetly around her legs, unnecessarily spilling water into her already wet boots. There were no elderly conservative household knights and City ladies to horrify with sight of her trouser-clad legs anyway. And the time for such modesty—never, the Mothers knew, her *own* modesty—was long past.

Malaeth wouldn't like it, like so many other things she'd never liked. She'd simply have to adjust.

Levren had not returned; Marhan had come back to camp once but was now at the pools near the waterfall. Golsat was still prowling the heights. Lisabetha lay curled in her cloak, partly in shade as the sun rose higher. Malaeth sat on a slab of rock, her feet in the shallows not far away, where she could keep half an eye on the child. Brendan sat on one side of her, Brelian on the other. Her slippers lay behind her, totally ruined: She had walked nearly barefoot most of the night. Ylia sank down behind her, picked up one of the battered shreds of silk and thin leather. The old nurse slewed around, shook her head ruefully.

"My feet feel worse than that slipper looks, in truth they do! Well, there is something to be said for those boots of yours, child, for I see your feet are still of a piece."

Ylia laughed. At this moment, warm and clean, surrounded by this ancient garden, the fears and battle of the day before had no more hold than a nightmare would. "Somehow we shall fashion you footgear, old woman. You cannot walk the length of the Foessa in those!"

"I should hope not," Malaeth retorted. "I should have feet as black and rough as Nisana's." A round head on Brelian's far side popped up at mention of her name, sank sleepily back out of sight. The brothers looked at each other uncertainly across Malaeth's white hair.

"Lady—how d'ye mean, the length of the Foessa?" Brendan finally asked. "Where is it we go?"

"Ylia," she reminded him blandly. He eyed her doubtfully. "We swore dagger-oath," she added, even more blandly, and held back a sigh with main force: the man was as humorless as the rocks around them. "As for our path, we are bound for Aresada and so remain perforce within the mountains. I hope," Ylia's eyes mocked, "you have no fear of them. Marhan and I felt danger known must be counted greater than that unknown. The Tehlatt were a more certain death than anything spoken of in the old tales." Sarcasm, however, also seemed to pass him by. Brelian gave her a grave wink; it wasn't lost on *him*.

"That is true, Ylia." However his brother felt, Brel seemed to share none of his doubts—or his prejudices. "I have no fear of the Foessa. Nor has Bren—did he fear anything, that is!" Brendan transferred the dubious look to his brother. "We have heard the tales also, of course, who has not? But we have hunted within the mountains, near enough the Caves, in fact, and seen nothing to give shape to the tales."

"How could such a place as this harbor evil?" Malaeth was sufficiently awed by their surroundings to put aside werebeings, fear-bringers, odd footprints and invisible rollers of stone.

"I am for the Caves," Brendan said soberly. "We can hold out long there, if need be. And—and many of the folk may be there." Brelian leaned across Malaeth to grip his leg.

"I, too, am for this way. After all, I risked my life to drag Brendan from the walls at the last, that some of our family live. I saw no reason then to throw my life senselessly away, nor will I now. There is nothing for me in Yls or Nar."

The four of them joined hands on that. Brendan's hesitation was so slight that this time, Ylia thought, she might have imagined it. *Sensitive, overly so*, she chided herself. At that moment, Marhan and Levren returned, bringing with them rabbits and a quail.

The fire took time to bring to proper heat: The only wood to be found was damp at best, and rigging spits was a matter of trial and error. When the meat was finally shared out, it seemed days since any of them had last eaten, and the fact it was not as done as most Plainsfolk preferred made no difference at all.

Nisana held Lisabetha to eating and drinking, then allowed her to sleep again. 'I can aid you in what you must do, all you need, but the action must be yours, girl.'

'I know.'

'Good. Sleep first, then.'

'She—won't thank me.'

'No,' Nisana replied with her usual terse directness. 'Foolish, but she won't.'

Ylia eyed the sleeping girl unhappily. She liked Lisabetha, even though they had little in common, dreaded the scene sure to come.

Golsat had returned while they were occupied with Lisabetha, and was giving Marhan a report before he ate. He had traced a way around the meadow at its upper edge before descending to the valley floor along the westerly ledges. "No other folk have been here this year, probably not for many years. I saw tracks of a cloud-cat on the heights, but they were over a five-day old. There were others near the waterfall, but they were even older. There were—" he hesitated, frowned, "odd little prints crossing those of the cat, not much larger than a fisher's, but they were nothing I had seen before." He accepted his portion of meat with thanks and retired to a sunny spot on the creek to bathe his feet and eat. Brendan watched him go, tensely; even more tensely, Levren turned away, determinedly set his gaze to the waterfall.

Lots were drawn for the watches, even though the Meadow seemed safe; the first fell to Marhan and Golsat. The rest of the company settled on whatever dry ground they could find.

'Ylia.'

'Now what?' She pried open one eye, gazed at the cat.

'Search, of course.'

Ylia yawned, closed the eye. 'You can manage without me—'

'That is not how you learn. Now.'

Ylia mumbled under her breath, but rose to her feet; impossible to win this particular argument, they'd had it often enough over the past several years. Easier to give in. 'Here?' She glanced at the Swordmaster, back at the cat, whose tail twitched once. 'I *know* I can, Nisana, same as you do,' she added, her mental voice sharp with irritation. 'I just don't *like* to.'

'You ought—oh, well, it doesn't matter.' Tail high, she turned and strode off. Ylia repressed a sigh, and any thoughts Nisana might hear and find offensive, and followed.

They followed the stream back up to the grove where Ylia had bathed. It was shaded now, pleasantly cool. She found a seat near the water, propped herself against a tree; Nisana climbed nimbly onto her lap, one delicate white foot across her forearm.

'Join.' It still required concentration; several moments passed before the thought faltered from half-AEldran human to AEldra cat. Nisana shaped the link between them, a part of each, now a thing of its own, sent it forth.

As they had at the Torth, they scouted the land around them for some distance, with considerably better strength and concentration on Ylia's part. Golsat was right: No humans here, none had been within a ten of years, at the very least. There the cloud-cat he had mentioned. Other small animals—plentiful. Fish—small but in great numbers.

Ylia cried out and shivered; the contact was abruptly severed. A fear to chill the bones lay near the waterfall—Golsat's fisher-sized prints were filled with it. It was old and faint, yet still so strong she had to swallow rapidly, breathe deeply or retch. Nisana's fur hackled down her back; her eyes were black.

"By the Mothers, what was it?"

'Beyond my knowledge.' Nisana shook herself, hissed. 'A thing to perhaps lend truth to Malaeth's tales.'

"No." *Do not think it!* "The tracks are old—"

'That means nothing! If the makers return? Or we meet them elsewhere? No. The Swordmaster must be told.'

Ylia shuddered, wrapped her arms around herself. "I—all right, Nisana. But—against such a thing as that—what could we do—what could I?"

'You are your mother's daughter,' Nisana replied shortly. Ylia's head snapped up; anger pushed terror aside.

"Is it necessary to argue this again? We have done so, I swear, cat, at least once a five-day since I reached my sixteenth summer! I am *not* Scythia's, save that she bore me! Scythia of the Second House," she went on bitterly, "counted among the AEldra great, and for a daughter she must needs have me, who cannot sweep dirt from the floor with the Power in her." She shook her head. "Enough of it! We have spoken of this before to no point. And this is neither the time *nor* the place for it!"

'Oh? If something befell me, what then?' Nisana was in no good mood herself.

"What do you want of me? I have *tried*! My mother tried! Look at the result!"

'Scythia, may she walk now in the Meadows of Overworld, was a fool, and so are you! Look at me—*look*, I say!' Nisana wriggled free, dropped neatly to the ground. The full spectrum of the Power played around her dark head. 'I am more of mixed blood than you!'

"So?" Ylia retorted. "I am not nearly so blessed as you, and I can wield little and in few ways."

'Because that is what you believe. You convinced yourself of that, stubborn girl, and will listen to nothing I try to tell you! Scythia was of the Second House, yes. And her skills were undeniably great. But yours,' she snapped, her mental voice throwing sparks in all directions, 'is no less a gift. One day you will be grateful that is so!' Her thought was suddenly gentle. 'Ylia, *listen* to me. Just once. The AEldra blood in me has been mixed with that of cat-kind more often that anyone can tell. I am as you see me, and my mother was accounted among the greatest of AEldra. Of any kind.

'The Power exists, that is all. It cannot be lessened, or broken, or divided; only improperly used. It takes forms, like talents. Your mother could heal; I can't. But she could not bridge greater distances; I can. Perhaps Scythia—no. She was wrong. You are wrong. The Power is in you.'

"Perhaps." Ylia was clearly unconvinced. "To what point, if I cannot use it? No. I am what I am, and if there is a way to change things, I cannot see it."

'Nor can I.' Nisana clambered back into her lap, leaned against her hard. 'And I have none of the Plainsfolk's Sight. All the same, I know.'

"Good," Ylia replied dryly. "Hold that thought for me, cat." Nisana sighed heavily, moved to the girl's shoulder as she rose. "Marhan," she added flatly. "This will not be amusing, we had better get it over."

It was not particularly pleasant. The old Swordmaster believed none of it, eyed the AEldra cat with open mistrust the entire time. A thing only to be sensed by sorcery? When all he could see was a small, harmless looking print in the wet ground? But he had been armsman too long not to take heed of possible danger, whatever the source of his knowledge. "No point to sift the tale for fact until we see this thing," he said finally.

"No. We have more than enough troubles. But we had better keep close watch."

"We would anyway." Reproof was in his voice, though milder than Ylia expected. *Don't lesson the Swordmaster, fool!* "We will speak of this at evening meal," he added. "Yours is the next watch after Lev's, go sleep."

"I—yes." She hesitated. "Marhan—another thing—"

"Well?"

"Golsat."

The old man eyed her thoughtfully. "You like him well enough, or so I thought."

"No, not my meaning. Brendan—"

"The lad's young and he hasn't spent much time outside the barracks." Marhan considered briefly. "He'll learn. If he lives so long."

"Well—"

"He's an odd package, the lad," the Swordmaster went on. "Brave as a company, and skilled. Well, you saw him at Fest last winter, didn't you?" She shook her head. "Skilled. Took on two of your father's best and disarmed both of them. Not once, but twice; they thought it a trick the first time, y'see."

"Oh." Helpful, perhaps, to know he wasn't all stilted talk, and that there might be ability behind that wooden mask.

"Lev, though." The Swordmaster sighed. "He tries, our Lev. And it's not Golsat himself, or even that he's half Tehlatt. You know he was born in the North?"

"In Anasela." Her father had told her, some years back, when there had been trouble over training a handful of Ylsan lads.

"Even so. He's told me about it, now and again. First things he remembers are the raids. They left the North when he was perhaps four, moved first to Teshmor then Koderra. There was other trouble after his father took to merchanting, took Lev with him once or twice. Sea-Raiders. He hasn't said much else, ever."

"It—must have been bad."

"I'd say so. He tries; he managed the Narran embassy last fall without a visible twitch, even gave some of their guard training when they asked for it.'' Marhan sighed again. ''It's just a thing—''

'Like your fear of height.'

'Thanks, cat.'

''—he can't control. At least, not totally.'' He shook his head. ''He'll stay away from Golsat; there'll be no problem. And Golsat knows to avoid him—probably learned that at the same time he learned where the bowmen's mess was located. As for Brendan—'' He cast a meaningful glance at her hand, chuckled. ''He has enough sense not to start a fight with *you* around, I'll wager. Go on, go sleep.''

How simple, after the truth came out, to say I should have known at once what had walked the valley before us and left terror behind. Perhaps I should have. That it was the Lammior's fear cast into some walking form, I knew, of course. Pointless to share such a thing with a half-trained child, or with the old woman. In that, I had become more like those I dwelt among so long—putting aside an unpleasant thought in the hope that it would thereby vanish. I was wrong—though even I could not have foreseen how horribly wrong.

The Nedaoans do not believe as the AEldra, in the One and his chosen representatives, the Nasath: They pray instead to the Mothers, whom they believe made the world and all that dwell therein. They are weavers, the Mothers: Inniva, who chooses the threads for the pattern; Noteyen, who lays the warp and the woof, which is how a man or woman shall go in life; Lel-san, who ties the knots when the weaving is complete. It is their way, not mine. Yet sometimes it does seem that there are patterns.

6

Nisana set out on her own to hunt. Ylia rested. She couldn't sleep, still shivered now and again as her nerves remembered the shock of discovery. She took her watch with Brelian at midday. Some time after she lay down again, and exhaustion took over; she fell into such a deep and dreamless sleep that she was several moments remembering where she was and why, when Nisana roused her at dusk. She stretched cat-wise, laughed quietly at the cat's amused thought, and made for the stream. Chill water felt even colder against her overly warm face, but it brought her fully awake.

Everyone else had found seats about the fire: There was fresh meat, and Malaeth had gathered liontooth to make a pale tea in Marhan's blackened old kettle. A shadowy shape well across the clearing was Golsat, perched on a boulder to keep watch. The brothers tended the spits.

Swordmaster and Bowmaster were bent over something near the fire. Ylia rubbed her eyes, still couldn't fathom it and finally moved closer. The ruins of Marhan's ancient jerkin lay between them, they were fashioning Malaeth boots. She stood watching them.

Delaying. You know it. You and Nisana both. It was true; anything at the moment would have held her attention, kept her from the task at hand. But truly, she dared wait no longer. Lisabetha came willingly, docilely away from camp, sat where placed on smooth, dry granite, a tree at her back. Her eyes, dark blue, overly large in the thin face, were open, glazed. Ylia sighed, closed her own eyes, took a deep breath, and began to prepare. Nisana sat between them, waiting.

They could continue to lead her. And feed and care for her. Tempting thought. But it was unfair to the others, particularly the men who must carry her when the ground was rough, and though they pitied her now that pity would turn to dislike and anger, given time. No. No alternative. Nisana's thought touched her. 'If you're ready—'

She sighed. 'As ready as I'll get, cat.'

"She is beautiful." A quiet voice spoke behind them. Ylia uttered a choked little sound, whirled around, dagger half from its sheath. Brelian stood behind her, an astonished look on his face. "I'm sorry, I startled you." His attention was all for Lisabetha, though; he was already on one knee beside her.

"You—" Ylia bit back the rest of her comment, met the cat's eyes with astonishment. 'He loves her.'

'He has for some time, even I can see that,' Nisana watched him thoughtfully. 'Odd, such compassion in one so young. He has fewer years than you, and he's male.'

'Mmmm.' It was unusual, to say the least. Boys of Brelian's age were far more likely to think of swords, horses and dogs; to think of women, if at all, as something to be sought and paid for in ale houses.

He sat still for a moment, then reached and took Lisabetha's hand. He bent swiftly, kissed the fingers, and without another glance strode back to the fire.

Once again—as she must, always, and never mind what Nisana, what her mother had thought!—she joined with Nisana, borrowing heavily of the cat's considerable Power as she took hold of the girl's shoulders, reaching at the same time with her thought, this time to will her forth. Lisabetha stirred, struggled briefly, went suddenly limp.

"What have ye done?" she whispered. "Why could ye not let me die?" Tears coursed down her face. But before Ylia

could answer, the girl's eyes went to the fire, the treees, the
mountains which stood clear even against the black sky, and
she twisted frantically. Ylia rolled her eyes, exasperated,
shook her fiercely. *By all the Mothers at once, did any of us
hold terror of the mountains, why must it be this one*? Lisabetha slumped weakly against the tree, but the horror was still
in her eyes, ready to swallow her whole.

"We are within the Foessa, yes." Ylia surprised herself; her
voice was level, inflectionless, showed none of the distaste she
felt for her present task. "We are north of the old Pass, and
we make our way to the Caves of Aresada, which your father
prepared against such a time as this."

"Way." Lisabetha closed her eyes and moaned. "There is
no way here which is ours, we had done better to die in Koderra. Better die now, all of us, than face what awaits us."
Her eyes came up then, and with a look so bitter Ylia knew full
memory had returned. "Ye have done me no favor, Lady. I
chose death, ye had *no* right to gainsay me."

"So you say now," Ylia replied gently, though in fact she
was furious with the girl. How dare she carry on so? And
however much she had lost, how could she seriously prefer to
die? "Would Lossana your mother have willed you to such an
end? Your father? Do you think Gors held to life as long as he
did so that *I* might escape the Tehlatt?" Stubborn silence. "It
was for *you* he did that deed, and with his death he laid upon
you blood-price, that you live and prosper. You are the last of
your line, it is for you to see that the House of Planthe goes
on!"

But it was no good. Lisabetha raged and wept alternately
and ever pleaded to be let alone, to be allowed to die as she
had chosen. Such a horror of the mountains was upon her that
the assurances Ylia offered—their strength of arms, her own
AEldra power and that of Nisana—made no impression at all.

At long last, Ylia's patience snapped, and she sat back on
her heels, her voice cold and commanding. "You have one
choice, Lady Lisabetha, and one only. Come freely with us,
on your own two feet, and cause no more trouble than you can
help. Or I will return you to that state in which you walked to
this meadow. That would be an unnecessary burden on all of
us, but if that is what you wish, so be it, and I can and will do
that if I must!"

Lisabetha recoiled, and a fear-born blast of hatred drenched
both AEldra minds. "Ye would do this. And I had thought

ye different. They were right, *he* was right, ye would make
trained beasts of us all, ye with the witching!''

Ylia jumped to her feet, her own eyes darkly furious.
"Someone will bring you food when it is ready. Eat and prepare yourself for the journey tomorrow. Malaeth will aid you,
if you need her. Remember what I have said!'' And with that
she left the girl, stopping only long enough to ask Levren to
take her meat when it was ready. She practically ran from the
fire into the night to ponder Lisabetha's last words.

Brendan sat now on Golsat's flat rock, gazing toward the
north, though the moon would not rise for several hours and it
was too dark to see much. He ignored her. She cast him a bale-
ful glance, kept going. Some distance on, she found another
rock and clambered onto it, pulled knees to her chin and
thought hard.

Lisabetha had been Lady to the Princess Royal for less than
a year, having just come from Teshmor the past fall. Ylia had
not particularly wanted her. Had, in fact, wished no Ladies of
any sort, since she took no pleasure in the formalities of the
inner household, and spent as little time as she could in
needlework and gossip.

Of course, what Lord Corlin had asked of the King was not
unusual: Service in his household for the Duke's daughter
would give her greater stature when it came time to bargain
her a husband, even though Lord Corry was counted near to
the King himself and second to no other Nedaoan Lord. And
they were close friends, Brandt and Corry, and so Ylia's father
had accepted the girl, and Ylia had perforce gained another
Lady.

But Lisabetha had been a pleasant surprise, and Ylia found
herself liking the girl in spite of herself: Lisabetha was pleasant, amusing, enough use to the Queen that the Queen's
daughter was not embarrassed by her, and, unlike many a
young and fair maid, had caused no jealousies in the ladies'
apartments, provoked no untoward gossip.

But her thought, just now, had reeked so strongly of Vess
that one less skilled even than Ylia could not have failed to
catch it.

Vess. Causer of trouble for so long as Ylia could remember.
Seven, eight summers older than she, son of her father's
youngest sister Nala, he was—or would have been—fifth in
line for the succession behind the Koderran Prince, later behind the Princess Royal, had he not been born, as Nedaoan

old women say, on the wrong side of the blankets.

To Vess, of course, that was no matter at all, for he coveted the crown, and to his mind, if a female could aspire to it, so, clearly, could a bastard.

There had been incidents in the North, attempts to turn the people against Brandt and his witch wife, his half-witch son and daughter, and after Beredan's untimely death, against the thought of a woman sitting on the ancient Nedaoan throne, as no woman had held it in the past 500 years. It must have come as a great surprise to Vess that the folk loved Brandt; even, in their own, slightly disapproving fashion, loved the fair Scythia and were proud that their King had stolen the White Witch from her own kind. And so, thereafter, there had been incidents, culminating in the assassin at the City gates.

When that failed, Ylia had assumed, childishly, she was beginning to think, that Vess had simply given up. Perhaps, after all, he had not.

She shifted. The rock was cold. Of course he had not! A stubborn man, Vess, and unlikely to relinquish an idea until what he wanted was in his grasp. Though how he thought the folk would accept one like him! Not only bastard, but by the look of him, less Nedaoan than she, though Nala had never said. She had entered the Citadel and taken the robes of the Chosen when he was a child and died of fever not long after.

Vess. Her mouth was dry with frustrated hatred. *If I had killed him two nights ago! His blood on my sword—the Tehlatt had no right to him!*

She remembered him as she had seen him the time before that: Midwinter Fest in Koderra, surrounded by his personal guard—a calculated insult to the King, which Brandt had ignored with ease. His clothing had outshone that of everyone present, including the King's, and he had only watched the sword competitions, had not entered any of the crossings, lest he rend his fine garments, Ylia had thought at the time. But she was not the only one there who looked upon him with open contempt. Though even she could not honestly deny his skill. He had learned, and learned well, from Marhan.

And now—*what to think?* Lisabetha was other than the innocent maid she seemed, but—but what? A spy for Vess? Put so, it sounded foolish. But was it?

And if so, had Corlin been in league with Ylia's despised cousin? She nearly laughed aloud at that thought; humor restored a measure of sense. No. Lord Corry would no more work to her ruin than—than Marhan would. Than her father would have. If there had been scheming, then it had been all Vess'.

But it was unimportant now, Vess was dead. She slammed one fist into the other. He'd returned to Teshmor, or so the guard had said. *All injured innocence, that was how Gramad had phrased it*. But, was he really dead? Hope never made anything so, and had only one person escaped the walls when the Tehlatt attacked, that one would have been Vess. Presuming, of course, that he had reached Teshmor at all, or that Teshmor had been his goal when he left Koderra. *If he lives, his death to my hands*.

'So.' Nisana leaped abruptly to the rock. 'We harbor a grain-serpent in the threshing house. Is it safe to take her to Aresada awake and under this burden she carries?'

Ylia shrugged. "We have no choice, we cannot leave her. And we really cannot return her to her former state, can we?"

'Well—' Nisana considered this. 'It would be impractical, of course.'

"So. She will come to cooperate because she has no choice. Eventually we can persuade her we mean her no harm."

'Hah.' The cat pushed her chin over Ylia's fingers. 'I cannot read futures, unfortunately. But I will keep an eye on this Lady of yours, that she does no harm to you.'

"Me?"

'She might see your death as a way out.' Ylia considered this in blank astonishment. That had not occurred to her. 'You are too trusting,' Nisana went on accusingly. 'You humans. When she is asleep tonight, I will read her.' So firm her thought that there could be no argument. Ylia opened her mouth, shut it again. She must strongly feel the need, for as a cat, she would consider such an invasion of thought thoroughly contemptible.

"As you wish," was all she finally said. Nisana rubbed a last time against her fingers, jumped down and padded back to the fire. Ylia followed.

The others were sharing meat directly from the spits, sipping hot tea in turn from Marhan's pot. Lisabetha and Brelian alone were not in sight.

"He's gone to take food to her," Malaeth said. Old she undoubtedly was, but her eyes were keen and at the moment bright indeed. Brendan laughed.

"A moon-calf, my brother, ever since Dame Malaeth

brought her from the tunnel," he said dryly. "But his moon-
ing goes back years; he has nursed a soft spot for Lord Corry's
pretty daughter since she wore short robes and his sword was
a wooden plaything. And when she came to Koderra, he
stopped wenching with the rest of us." He reddened, turned
hastily to the old woman. "Uh, your pardon, Lady." Ylia
turned aside to smother a grin; Malaeth looked scandalized.

"Enough of your gossip, brother," Brelian growled from
the shadows. "She asks for you, Dame, if you are free to aid
her." Malaeth rose with the help of his proffered hand,
limped into the darkness. Brelian pulled the spit from his
brother's fingers and fell to.

Lisabetha approached the fire a short while later. She had
plaited her hair and appeared physically, at least, ready for the
next day's journey. But her expression was sullen and cold.
For that reason, Ylia kept her mouth prudently closed when
Nisana returned to the fire during their second watch. It
seemed a long time she walked about the meadow alone. Suddenly the cat returned, her thought open, and Ylia read of
Lisabetha.

Fear, yes; that lay overall. But underneath, a hatred of the
Inner House of Ettel, of the AEldra strengths—the witch-
Power—forged with cunning and skill. Again and again,
thought of Ylia's cousin, and there was almost as much fear as
longing. Fascination, weakness—it was as though he had
woven a drawing spell, as though he were a snake, she a field
mouse. Fear, a greater fear, of what she had given, fear that
Vess would spread that knowledge, as he had threatened, to
her father.

"My watch." Ylia started. Golsat had come quietly up behind her as she sat. She nodded, gripped his forearm briefly
and got a genuine, if faint, smile in reply. The fire was warm,
the cloak not, at the moment, necessary. She drew it lightly
across her shoulders. *Ugh.* Too much to think about, and she
was tired, and the watches near dawn were hers. She sent Vess
and Lisabetha from her mind with effort, resolutely closed her
eyes.

One thing I will say of humans: They manage to get along better in large numbers than a grouping of cats would. Even those who traveled north with me from Koderra, with all their petty disagreements, sulks, miseries and clashing egos. Of course, there came times—all too frequently—when I thought I would go mad, listening to them bicker for hours over some trivial point. But then, as any of our kind knows, traveling with an equal number of cats—as I did only once, when I was young and reckless—is not simply irritating; one puts one's life at serious risk doing so.

7

The night passed uneventfully. Nisana and Ylia shared last watch with a most aloof Brendan. Apparently he had no desire to push the relationship of arms-mate, though whether because his watch companion was witch, swordswoman, or because she had defended Golsat, she could not decide. After a short period of intense irritation, she refused to let it bother her further, and she and the cat chose a portion of Meadow well away from him.

Only the cry of owls and other night birds broke the silence; the last watches ended as the sky lightened eastward. Ylia built up the fire, Brendan went for water as she woke the rest of the company. First sun had to see them well on their way. None of them wanted to spend more time than absolutely necessary on the journey, and none of them knew how the land might lie beyond the Meadow.

And there were the footprints, though none knew of them but Nisana, Ylia, Marhan. Perhaps, Ylia thought over and over during the cold early morning hours, the makers were like other wild creatures; perhaps they would flee when so large a company approached. *Perhaps the sky is green, the trees yellow.*

Shortly after sunrise, they waded the stream and set out northward, using a faded, narrow trail that followed the water. Trace of deer was heavy; there was no sign of Golsat's strange prints.

By the third hour they had climbed several dozens of lengths up the steep, rocky shelf and could nearly see back to the Yls Pass. Noon hour found them in a boulder-strewn cut between two peaks, and though the sun was high in a cloudless sky, the wind cut chill through even the thickest of garments. Malaeth and Lisabetha huddled together on the ground; Marhan paced rapidly back and forth as he ate, trying to keep his blood awake. Ylia and the brothers remained on their feet, shifting now and again from leg to leg, fearing to let sore calf muscles tighten since they must go so much further before dark. Every one of them ached miserably from the rough climb. After too short a rest, they moved out again.

But the trail that had brought them from the Meadow vanished among snowbanks and rockslide. Across this uncertain terrain they moved cautiously, the brothers scouting out the most stable footing, the others in a line behind. A long scramble down a narrow cleft brought them back finally to the timberline, and to a gentler downslope.

They had crossed a series of sharp ridges and so come to another valley, this at least four leagues in length and two wide. An emerald of a lake snugged between the tall fir that swept from slope to slope. Water cascaded from the sheer rock face directly across the valley; the lake reflected trees, water, clouds, now and again was ruffled by a sudden breeze.

A long rest this time. They were sheltered from the wind by stunted trees of the upper slopes. It was quiet, intensely so for Koderrans who were used to the noise of City. Here, the few quiet words spoken by any of them, the occasional high, whistling cry of the birds wheeling across the lake seemed to echo.

The sun was low when they resumed the downward trek, and by the look of the high rock walls to the west would drop from sight early. But they only needed now to reach that lake before full dark. By the water would be game, shelter from the wind. Only Lisabetha had not spoken in favor, saying flatly that she was of the party against her will, that the others should all do as they liked, since they would anyway. Brelian would have spoken then, but she turned away.

But she had walked the entire day without aid, had showed more strength than any of them thought possible, though she fell more than once. 'Pride.' Nisana's tart comment, her first of the long afternoon. Ylia considered this, nodded. Not that it mattered, so long as the girl kept up with them.

Malaeth was limping again, but it was only when level ground was reached that she finally accepted help.

The land about the lake was thick with old bracken and pine needles, the ground dry. Levren cleared a wide space, dug a shallow pit for the fire before going to see to his snares, and Marhan set out close behind with his precious line and hook. Golsat had left the company near the tree line and now came in with two rather thin-looking ground birds.

"My fingers ache," Malaeth murmured, holding her small red hands to the fire. "And my feet. And my legs. And—and everything." Brelian nodded feelingly.

"You are not alone in that, Dame." He winced as he made contact with the ground, cushioned as it was. "Even a full day horsed has never left me so stiff as this."

Ylia closed her eyes, adjusted the folded cloak under her head. Her whole body hurt, she was chilled, tired and hungry. Thirsty, also, but too tired and stiff to take the ten steps to the stream. Tired, though: that was the worst of it, she could have wept of tired. Nisana sprawled at her side, insensible.

Lisabetha nodded where she sat, one hand cupping the elbow she had badly scraped early in the day. She would still have none of any of them, had brushed aside all others of aid and even those small kindnesses Brelian would have given. He now sat with his back to her.

Evening meal was a gloomy, silent affair. Finally Levren stirred. "I will check my snares at first light. We must have food for morning. Do we push on tomorrow?"

"Aye." Marhan nodded unhappily. "We walk slow, better

walk long to make up for it. Best hoard the bread, though, we'll need it later." The brothers eyed him miserably. Golsat nodded somberly. He had not spoken all day, still sat well away from the others, and the fire. Ylia gazed at him a while, cast an irritated glance at Brendan, who caught it but seemed merely puzzled. 'Don't waste sarcasm on him, it's lost.' Nisana rubbed against Ylia's arm, closed her eyes again.

"So." Brendan shook himself, stretched cautiously, wincing as muscle protested. "We knew this was no Midsummer picnic when we slunk from the Plain. We push on."

"Do not look so disheartened, brother." Brelian grinned, clapped him across the back. "No monsters have descended on you yet, have they? And—if they do, that is work for your sword, if Ylia and her cat have not shriveled them before you can free your blade." He winked across the fire at her, and in spite of herself, she laughed.

"Well—maybe," she replied. "I would probably be of more use with sword than the Power. I wouldn't count on magic, if I were you."

"No? Why not?" Brelian asked frankly, then reddened. "Unless one may not ask, of course," he added hastily.

For some reason, she was not as tongue-tied as usual. "Why not? After all, we are arms-mates, it is only fair you know what guards your back, or not, as the case may be." She leaned back, collected her thoughts. "What do you know of the Power—anything? A little? Well, many hundreds of years ago, when Nedao was still an island kingdom, the AEldra were seafarers, and no more witch-kind than—well, than you, Brelian. But a call for aid went out and they came to what is now Yls, to aid the people then living there in their way against the Lammior."

"Lammior. I have heard that name, somewhere." Brendan rubbed at his chin, finally shrugged.

"A wizard. One who could create storms, could make creatures from air; if the tales are true, create evils to slay for him. When the AEldra came, the fortunes of war changed, the Lammior himself was slain. As reward, the AEldra were given the Gifts of Power. How much real truth there is in the tale, I cannot tell you. The Power itself is the only possible proof.

"A gift and a talent both, the Power. It does not show itself equally. Many of Yls no longer have it, or have little, for like a talent it must be exercised or lost. And it manifests itself differently in each of us: Just as Lev has greater skill with bow than most, while Marhan is better with sword and dagger, so it is with the Power. Some AEldra can heal, as could Scythia, my mother. Some can build a *seeming*, again as she could, so real you could touch it.''

"The bowmen," Marhan whispered. He looked, briefly, as unhappy as he must have when he first learned of the battle plans.

"The bowmen," Ylia agreed. She caught at the corners of her mouth with her teeth; a smile, at this moment, could only enrage the old man. "Some can fashion such a thing real to the eye, not the hand. Some can see in their minds distant places, as though they stood in that place, while others such as myself can only reach with an inner sense more like touch than sight. Some very few are able to bridge—to be in one place, and then in a distant other place they have forechosen in the space of a quick breath. This I have never seen done.

"My mother had many of these skills, as has Nisana. I have few, and such as I have are not strong."

"I," Malaeth volunteered, "have little besides the mind-touch myself, and that has grown capricious the past season or so."

"Some AEldra, like Nisana," Ylia continued, "have different form. As you see. I have heard there are AEldra among the great sea animals and the larger hunting birds, but if so, they are rare and were never really plentiful. Certain of these are said to shape-change. Another thing I cannot swear to, since I have never seen it."

"I have," Malaeth put in. "Nisana could, when she was much younger. I was but a girl then, and she—"

"Wait." Golsat had moved, unnoticed, closer to the fire. He cast a swift, cautious glance in Levren's direction, but the distance seemed to serve; the Bowmaster ignored him. "Your pardon, Dame, but you are clearly of long years. And you say that—" He gazed down at the sleeping cat. "Their kind do not live so long," he said flatly. Malaeth shook her head.

"AEldra do," she replied. "I have long since passed three score myself, long enough that age is a matter for boast rather than concealment. She was born in the fall, Nisana, the same year I was born in spring." Golsat regarded her in blank astonishment, the cat with a stunned kind of wonder. There was a brief silence, broken by a light wind soughing through the trees. Ylia took up the tale once again.

"I do not clearly understand all Nisana's uses of the Power. She is cat, I am human, and there are places within each of us closed to the other. But we have in common, she and I—and Malaeth—a strength of will. That is trained in all AEldra from early childhood." Even Lisabetha was listening closely to what she said, though to all appearances she was staring disinterestedly across the lake.

"I have few of the talents, as I say, and what I have are weak. For I am half of Nedao, and therefore of mixed blood." 'Hah.' Nisana had wakened. Ylia ignored her. "I can use the mind-search, you have seen my use of the second level of Sight, which is a way of seeing in the dark with both eyes and mind. Also, I have the small weapons of the Baelfyr, though not the great." Brendan grinned suddenly, rubbed his neck. "Of course, AEldra can merge thought, and Nisana and I do so, to speak or to strengthen each other. We can search for enemy at greater distances.

"But there are things none of us can do." She gazed around the fire. Interest among her companions, and a little fear, still. "None of us can read thoughts. I cannot read minds, though if it is strong enough, I can sense emotion. The same way, I think, as a dog senses fear. I cannot speak into anyone's thought if that person is not AEldra. And we cannot foresee the future; at least, I cannot. And I have never met anyone who could, though the High Lord in Yslar is said to *dream*— and what he *dreams* frequently comes to pass." Lisabetha started. Ylia turned, but the girl had closed her eyes.

She turned back to the fire, held out her hands. Small, too small to properly grip a standard hilts. Strong, though. The Mothers knew she'd worked them long and hard enough. "Poor by AEldra standards, certainly. Enough to be of aid here, perhaps."

"No weapon should ever be discounted, and certainly not in our present placing." Levren stretched. "Well. Interesting. I do not think I knew the half of that. But my blood froze, I admit it," he added with a laugh, "when those other bowmen appeared among us!"

The Swordmaster shook his head. "Magic," he muttered unhappily. "We had better set the watches," he added brusquely. "One or two at a time?" Levren shrugged.

"Ylia, what do you think, is it safe enough for one? We could all use the extra sleep."

She met Nisana's eyes, briefly touched thought with her. "One. There is no need for more, there is not even a bear to hand that I can tell."

"Those would avoid us," Brendan said. "Shall we draw lots, then? If the first is not mine, I would like to prepare for sleep properly before it catches me sitting."

"I will take the first," Ylia offered. "And search better. Portion the rest how you choose." Lisabetha gazed at her with dark, unfriendly eyes, rolled into her cloak with her feet toward the coals. Conversation lagged, as first one and then another slept. The two AEldra-gifted were alone.

It was truly a black night, for clouds had come from north and west as darkness fell, and now covered the entire sky. Cat and girl moved down to the edge of the lake, listened a few moments to the gentle lap of water against the narrow, pebbly beach. A search showed nothing at first, save those animals one might expect: deer, rabbit, squirrel. Beaver and marmoset. The elusive fisher, a bear. High on the slopes behind them, goat.

'Nisana, if that's all we find—'

'Another try, when we haven't the responsibility for them. I'm not satisfied.' She trotted back to the fire but seemed unable to rest, spent the next hour pacing in and out of the shadows. When Levren took the watch, they went back down to the water's edge, made a wider search that left Ylia exhausted, drained. But again—twice—they came across those footprints that shivered the blood. Old, yes. Old, but so strong, even as old as they were.

'I do not like this.' Nisana's thought was edged with fear of her own. 'They are old, faded. To meet the makers, to come upon that in full strength!'

"Shhh." Ylia shook her head. "I refuse to think upon it, particularly tonight. I would sleep."

The moon sailed from behind ragged cloud, briefly turned the lake to silver and glittering gems. They returned to camp.

But sleep would not come. *Mother. Father.* Grief suddenly pressed upon her with a terrible weight and would not be denied. Men and armsmen she had known her whole life—comrades, dagger-sworn, Father—did they lie cold and dead leagues away? Or had the Tehlatt burned their bodies upon those great fires? She swallowed, hard; tears coursed down her face. She curled into a tight ball of misery and wept.

'Ylia! Ylia?' She was, suddenly, no longer alone; Nisana came from the place she had chosen near the fire, fought her way between the folds of dark heavy wool to lie with her small head hard against the girl's throat. The cat's own grief was palpable; still, she tried to sooth her human companion, nudged at her, washed her cheek with a rough tongue. Nothing helped.

At length, worn out, Ylia slept. She woke at first light with a small, furred body pressed hard against her face, small paws twined in her plaits.

Odd—but then, I have lived my life among humans, and carry within me attributes of a Power fashioned for humans. To grieve for my sweet Scythia—I missed her, I had known I would. I had not thought I would so mourn her loss.

*We have tales in plenty, ourselves, of the
Foessa and the things once hidden among
their treacherous heights. Few of these did
Nedao ever know, and those they heard they
most often chose to disbelieve. For they are a
common-sense folk, and the tales of their
Black Well, their Harvest-Fest bogies are all
an amusement to them, since they are things
no man has ever seen or touched—or slain
with good steel.*

8

It was sunrise when Ylia staggered to her feet, clumsy and
stiff with cold and the previous day's exertions, but daylight
was doubtful. Clouds covered the sky and it looked likely to
rain within the hour. Brelian was tending the fire and there
was a little warm water for washing, which she gratefully accepted. Levren returned to camp while she was still replaiting
her hair, bringing filled snares, and Golsat was not far behind
with two speckly trout which, when pressed, he said he had
caught with his hands. Brendan was so astonished by this he
forgot his quarrel with the half-caste.

"No—no one can do that!"

"No?" Golsat shrugged. "If you doubt, come with me and
I'll show you how it is done." Brendan leaped to his feet,
waved Brelian to join them, and the three vanished in the direction of the stream. Marhan gaped openly after them.

Levren's catch was already spitted and he pushed the trout
into the coals with a long stick while the Swordmaster roused
the last of the company. Malaeth yawned, sat up with an

amazing vigor; she seemed to have regained much of her strength with a good sleep, but Lisabetha was white and drawn, and Marhan had to take washing water to her where she lay.

They saved Levren's meat for noon-stop and ate the trout, since it would not keep as well. They were a kind unknown to any of the company, though similar to many found in the Torth. Small but tasty, these, and there were enough for everyone to have his own, for Golsat brought more. The brothers gravely verified he indeed caught them with his hands, and he had even shown them how, though neither had caught anything but buttom grasses. In the process, however, Brendan had largely lost sight of Golsat's hated heritage, and they spoke together with little of the stiffness that had marked their few previous words.

'Gods and Mothers, cat, I had not thought it possible.'

'Well? Marhan said it first; he's not totally a fool, and it wouldn't take much to let him see sense.'

Ylia nodded. 'If Lev—'

'No.' Nisana gazed across the fire to the Bowmaster, who still sat carefully, so he would not catch sight of the darker man. 'It will take more than hand-caught fish to settle Levren. Perhaps your Mothers can rearrange his brain some night.'

The view that greeted them as they broke from the trees was awe inspiring. They stood in a deep, wide cleft between towering, jagged peaks, the heights covered with snow. Many were hidden in masses of swift-moving cloud. Before them, the water stretched for two leagues or more, forming a bowl at the base of the surrounding mountains. Waterfalls plunged down from all sides, vanished in the trees or dropped directly to the lake. A distant roar of falling water, the cry of a scavenger bird high overhead were the only sounds.

To the north, the wide spill of water they had seen the day before. It dropped from a saddle between two rugged, red-rocked heights to split on a pile of rock and tree, fell thence in two slender, shimmering lines. As they stood watching, the saddle was obscured by a thick mass of cloud that foamed down over the heights. The air was cool and damp. Marhan nodded as though his fears had been confirmed.

"Three leagues, perhaps more. We'd better stay yonder tonight, make the climb tomorrow. Take an easy day after yesterday. My feet hurt," he added.

"Whose," Brendan demanded, though mildly for him, "do not? I would not mind a second night in this valley; at least I slept warm last night."

The sun filtered through momentarily thinned cloud cover; the saddle was again visible. Brelian stiffened, peered intently. Ylia's eyes followed his gaze; Nisana, alerted by that tension, climbed from pouch to shoulder.

"Marhan, have you your glass?" Levren held out a hand. The Swordmaster dug through his belt pouch, brought out a small Narran seeing glass. The Bowmaster squinted through it, nodded once, passed it on. When it came to her, Ylia peered, caught her breath: There, plain to see with the device, was a trail, a maze of sharp-cornered switchbacks leading up the saddle just east of the falls. She handed the glass on to Brendan.

"Well? What do you think? Does this continue the trail we had yesterday?"

Marhan shrugged. "Don't know. Not important, if it goes north."

"It was not made by animals," Golsat said. He handed the glass back to Marhan, who returned it carefully to his bag. "It is definitely man-made, though it seems old and uncared for. Of course, there are mountain-hunters within the Foessa," he added, "and they could have made it."

"Well." Marhan gazed thoughtfully across the lake. "It is certainly ready made for *us*. If no one else minds, though, we won't make that climb today."

"Agreed," Brelian said quickly, and even Lisabetha nodded. The company turned away from the lake's edge, stopped at the creek to fill water bottles and set out to skirt the mere.

This day's march went easily, for all that there was no one not painfully stiff. But the way was flat and forested, the ground underfoot thickly carpeted with pine and leaves. Often the way Marhan led was through knee-deep fern, and Malaeth occasionally moved away to gather plants for evening meal: liontooth with its shaggy yellow flowers, bracken, cresses by the edge of a trickling stream, flat plantain and flowering elder for tea.

Marhan led, since he had a good idea of where he wanted to finish for the day, and he set a slower pace than any taken to that point. Even Lisabetha was able to keep up, but Malaeth still limped, and Nisana rode the entire distance, for her pads were cut and bruised.

Noon-meal: they sat or lay in a clearing barely a length from the water's edge, watching as the sun came from behind heavy clouds, more frequently than it had earlier, to turn the water briefly to dancing silver and emerald, the waterfalls to glittering diamonds that brought tears to one's eyes for the brightness of them. As they moved on, however, the clouds drew in closely and a wind blew cold and damp from the heights, driving grey-black masses ever more swiftly across the sky, so that one moment the peaks stood out against cloud, and the next vanished under a billowing curtain. Once rain fell, but the trees sheltered them from the worst of it.

It took Marhan some time to find a place he liked for camp; even so, no one was particularly worn when they stopped. The place the old Swordmaster chose was well within the trees, and so sheltered from what rain might still fall, not far from the lake. A creek tumbled noisily down a steep cleft; one of those from the twin waterfall high above. The water was nearly too cold to drink, but there were deep pools under overhanging rock and bushes that had Golsat rubbing his hands in anticipation. He dropped cloak and weapons-belt near the firepit, and took the brothers with him.

Marhan tended the fire while Levren went to set snares; Malaeth went down to the lake to bathe her sore feet, Lisabetha with her. The girl, while still not speaking with anyone, had stayed close to the old nurse the entire day.

'Ylia—'

'I know, cat.' She sighed heavily. Tired, still, despite the ease of the day's walking. 'Search.' She nodded, caught up Marhan's empty kettle. 'Not here, though.'

'Of course not.'

'—you needn't mock me, Nisana,' she added stiffly. 'Uphill. Perhaps we can find a patch of groundberries. Mothers know we're high enough.'

Nisana had little interest in berries of any kind, but had no objection. They moved quietly past the fishers. Golsat's voice reached them: "Damn-all, Brel, not like that! Ye must move

fast—did you never grab a maid at Fest!'' Brendan laughed,
Brelian snorted in disgust. Nisana's amusement filled her companion's mind briefly.

"If we are going to search, let us do it first." Ylia set the
kettle on a flat rock, dropped down next to it. The clearing
was small enough, but she could see the flat white flowers that
preceded groundberries. Too early for fruit, then. "We leave
this valley tomorrow, cat; I am afraid what we will find when
we do.''

'*You're* afraid! How do you think *I* feel?' Nisana eyed her.
'But it's too bad. If you had more to add to this, we could
search further—'

"If we had the strengths of the Nasath, we could search
Yslar," Ylia retorted. "Or bridge to Aresada tonight, all of
us. If, if, if!''

'Join,' the cat replied shortly. They searched, shivering as
the sense touched lightly on the fear they had found the previous night, across the lake, still, there. West, then. Nothing,
not even the least trace of life of any kind. Nothing but snow,
heavy snow and bitter cold.

'Not for us, that way.'

'For once I totally agree with you, Nisana.' The cat sniffed
in reply, directed the sense northward.

A howling tore through them—a cry of warning! AEldran
the language, yes, High AEldran, unused in hundreds of
years: "Beware, ye of the Folk! The south is no longer safe to
us! Beware of the Fear-That-Follows! Beware, ye of the—''

She was cold, gasping for air, and her palms slipped damp
and shaking down her pants as Nisana abruptly severed contact. "Great Mothers, *what was that*?'' The cat made no
reply, only shook. Ylia pulled her close, held her until the
tremors subsided. Her own heart thumped painfully. "A
warning—but what was it?''

'Against the thing we have already found. But the AEldra
have never spoken of themselves as the Folk!'

"Malaeth's stories.'' Ylia could not force her voice above a
whisper. "The fear that sets upon a man at night, so that he
runs until he goes mad. But—but, I—they are tales, ancient
children's tales, nothing more!''

'They *are* more,' Nisana replied grimly, 'as we two are finding. We will watch, you and I, and guard as best we can, being
warned. And pray as well. To the Guardians, to the One of the

Chosen—to the Mothers of the Nedao if it will aid, that the message no longer has purpose for us!'

Ylia nodded. Her hands still trembled. If she could have recalled that search—but to not know what came against them—*which is worse*? She swallowed hard, tasted bile, started back to camp.

The fire crackled cheerfully. She stopped to warm chilled fingers, strode back into the near dark to fill the kettle at the creek.

Golsat was solemnly wrapping fish in long bank grasses—unlike those of the previous day but still trout by the look of them—and had shoved a third into the coals moments before. Brendan, next to him, was almost insufferably pleased with himself, for he had managed, by great perseverance and even greater luck, to catch a fish himself. It *had*, he admitted when pressed, slipped from his hands at the last, but fell onto the bank instead of back in the water. Brelian finally rolled him over and cuffed his ears.

They were comfortable for the first time: The wind was gone, the cloud cover broke not long after sunset. There was almost enough to eat, something warm for everyone to drink, if only a mouthful. Comfortable, too, in another sense none of them really noticed: They were adjusting to their surroundings. The silence was no longer so terrifying, the lack of familiarity less unnerving.

Levren had first watch. Ylia's last glimpse of the sky before she slept was a frost of stars.

The night passed uneventfully. Once during her watch, a number of deer splashed down the creek, and much later all of them but Malaeth were shaken awake as a bear crashed through the brush not many lengths from camp. But neither bear nor deer paid attention to the humans in their valley, and nothing else seemed aware of their presence at all.

I did try, once, to explain to the girl the difference—how she senses evil, as a thing separate from her, and how it pervades my body with certainty of the thinness of the barrier between it and all that is me. She does not understand; how could she? I do not intellectually understand it, either; I only know it, and that is more than enough.

9

The morning sky was a pale, rain-washed blue over the valley. First sun lay upon the lake, mirroring surrounding peaks with their fresh snow. Hard against the west shore, near the twin waterfall, a fire burned, and the smell of baking fish drifted with the faint blue smoke.

Golsat had taken the last watch, thereafter sought the stream, so there was breakfast, and plenty of it. Fortunate, since some beast or other had stolen Levren's snares and any game they had held. Marhan wrapped what was left of the meal in grass and leaves, folded it into a sling torn from one of Malaeth's pettiskirts and hung that from his belt. Levren drowned the fire, pressed the turves back into place over the blackened hole, and turned to lead the day's climb.

And climb it was: in the light of day, the cliff was dauntingly steep indeed. A short walk over springy leafmold brought them to the base of the ancient trail; it took two easy, near-flat turns, then began to ascend through thick forest. Faint, clearly not used in years, the trail never faded, not even when it emerged from the trees and tilted up in earnest. Once in the open, it worked back and forth across the slope.

Roughly dressed stone held against the down-slope side of the trail in places.

The morning wore on, still they climbed—slowly, for it was tiring work and warm, and the air was growing thin. By noon-hour, however, they were even with the ledge dividing the waterfall. A fitful breeze blew cold spray across the trail, and the noise was deafening. Another thirty paces, however, and the trail took another wide swing to the west. They rested there, ate, gazed back over the way they had come.

The scree across the valley looked impassible, they could not tell where they had come down. Ylia turned away from the view; *heights. Brrr!* Foolish, and it embarrassed her, angered her, but she couldn't help it. Long drops made her dizzy and ill.

They rested only an hour; the saddle still towered above them, and they might well have to go some distance after that to find shelter for the night. And they could travel only as fast as poor Malaeth, who leaned on Marhan and Levren in turns. Her feet hurt, her lungs labored in the thin, chill air. But her spirits held, and she traded chaff with the men, laughed at their jokes, argued with the Swordmaster. Life as usual, save that now and again a shadow crossed her face.

Ylia stayed to the front for the most part, well to the inside of the trail. Once, when it widened, she dropped back to speak with Marhan. Malaeth, again at his side, ruffled Nisana's head. The cat leaned perilously out of her pouch to grip the old woman's hand with soft paws and chew at fingers. Ylia shook her head. "Children, both of you," she laughed.

"Well, at least *I* am walking on my own feet," Malaeth retorted tartly.

'Because no one will carry you, that is all,' Nisana replied, her thought lofty. Malaeth ruffled her head again. Ylia rolled her eyes, moved, with a caution she hoped unnoted by her companions, back to her place in the lead.

Lisabetha kept her eyes to the ground in front of her for the most part, but now and again gazed wistfully at Marhan and Levren, at old Malaeth joking with Golsat. She was beginning to regret her harsh words, but was too shy and uncertain of herself to speak to any of them. Levren had been watching her, though; before long, he was walking with her, carrying on an animated conversation, and if she did not quite hold up her end of it at first, he carefully took no notice.

It was nearly the fourth hour from midday before the last of them staggered onto the saddle and turned to look north. Marhan eased Malaeth into a cleft in the rock, decreed another full hour of rest.

"It's cold here." Lisabetha pulled the dark wool high around her throat, tilted the fur-lined hood over her head and turned her back to the wind.

"Nasty cold," Levren agreed. "If you'd rather move down a ways and wait there—"

"No. Thank you," she added, and gave him a small smile. "I'm too tired to move just yet."

"Mmmm." Levren nodded, eased himself down against a pile of rubble next to her and closed his eyes. "Marhan? You've an eye to the sun, I presume."

"Aye. It's late enough. We'll do better if we take a decent rest, though. I'd not mind water," he added. Brendan pulled his bottle free, passed it over.

Silence a while; the last lengths of trail had been nearly straight up, and the air was so thin, so cold it burned. Brelian stood, caught at rock until he could see straightly, moved far enough up the trail that he could see down again.

"Ugh. I thought I liked mountains."

"Oh?" Ylia hitched her cloak a little tighter around her shoulders, walked over to join him. Chill air reddened her cheeks, caught at her throat. She stared out north, nodded. "I see what you mean. To look at, maybe one or two to climb. That—that's not a pleasant sight." Before them were mountains as far as the eye could see. East and west, rough peaks cut off any view either toward the Plain or toward Yls. Ahead of them, the ground dropped rapidly but the descent was considerably shorter. The trail showed pale and thin down the slope, vanished in a huddle of dense, stunted fir, wound through a narrow ravine. Another grove some distance beyond that, wider, filled the cleft from wall to wall. And then the ravine pinched abruptly in and took an eastward turn. Rock walls pitched up beyond that, and beyond them, more mountains.

"There, I think." Marhan came up between them, pointed to the second stand of trees. "Firewood, there. Likely water. Shelter from the wind, anyhow; that's important."

"More important," Ylia replied, "it's as far as I intend to walk today."

"I agree," Malaeth leaned against her. She was still breathless. "That is, if my poor body can drag itself on! To think," she added to Lisabetha, who held onto her other arm, "of such a climb as that, and at my age, too!"

The descent proved much easier than the ascent; the trail was less precipitous, though slides had wiped it out in several places and the slope was unstable. But the last of the sun was fading from the trail as they passed through the first grove; only the peaks to the east still shone golden with the end of day. It was dusk in the ravine by the time they reached the place Marhan had chosen from above; darker still under the trees, even though few of them stood man-high. A deep, narrow stream wove between them and bubbled downhill.

"Good enough," Marhan grunted. He dropped his gear, began clearing for a firepit. "Lev. Bren, Brel. Wood. You women, kindling." The company scattered. Golsat squatted by the stream, shook his head. Too shallow, too cold. He began pulling rock from the bank to line the firepit. Lisabetha, Malaetha and Ylia gleaned handsful of dry twigs, fir needles, small sticks. It was rapidly growing dark; Marhan had to light his fire by feel.

But for the noise of the creek, the silence was total: no birds, no chattering of small beasts, not even the faintest whisper of wind. Uncanny, the dark and silence together; even with the fire built, no one could see beyond a pace or two into the trees.

Levren staggered in not long after with a load of dry, rotten branch in the turned-up hem of his cloak. "I see no point to hunting here," he cast a wary glance over his shoulder. "If we have enough to share out, we should. Marhan?"

"Perhaps. Golsat? You've the last of it."

The dark man considered, nodded. "I think so. If we're careful."

"Well then." Levren unclenched his hands with visible effort, sat with feigned ease where he would not have to look at the half-caste, "unless you think, Marhan—"

"Huh. There's no game here, not any close. I'd stake my blade on it."

The fire set shadows to dance against the red cliff face

behind camp as they ate and night deepened. Black darkness
and a heavy, pressing silence.

Marhan looked at them with a practiced eye: *he* was exhausted, he could admit that, to himself, at least. None of
them looked any less tired than he felt: Malaeth was holding
herself awake by main effort long enough to eat something,
Lisabetha chewed slowly, eyes closed. She and the old woman
slumped against each other for support. *Good; the girl's coming out of herself.* Even if she spoke to no one but Lev and
Malaeth, she'd be less irritation than the sulky creature they'd
dragged along the two days before. Levren raised his brows
as Marhan's gaze crossed his, smiled faintly. He and Golsat
looked tired but not completely done for. *First watch, those
two,* the old man decided. *No—damn. Lev and one of the
lads. Nuisance. But I'll need sleep before I take guard.*

Ylia leaned toward the fire, elbows on knees, her forehead
in her hands. The cat braced itself against her leg, washed one
dainty forepaw. *Cat. Huh.* It had, he grudgingly admitted to
himself, been less problem than he'd thought it would. As for
Ylia. Well, she was never any trouble, she took whatever hard-
ships came her way uncomplainingly; all the same, he still
wished her in Yslar and out of this. *If trouble comes, and I
lose my King's only child. . . .* He couldn't complete the
thought.

"This is uncanny," Brelian murmured. Marhan jumped at
the sound; low as the lad spoke, his words seemed to echo
across the rock. "It was quiet below, but not like this!"

"You imagine things, brother," Brendan replied firmly.

Brelian shook his head. "*I* do, eh? You've eyed the ground
behind your shoulder often enough the past hour."

Malaeth stirred. "Ylia."

"Ma'am?" She came awake with a start.

"You and Nisana had better search, even I can sense something wrong here."

"Wrong—" She closed her eyes again, forced exhaustion
aside. The old woman was right, something was wrong. There
should have been *some* sound, somewhere. "All right." She
twisted, gazed out into the dark. "I—" She could feel color
mount to her face. *Damn.* "I'd rather stay here, if no one
minds." No one appeared to. "I'm not—not really good at
this, it requires all the concentration I can give it. If—you
could keep quiet—" She closed her eyes.

East and north first, in a tight circle about the camp.
Nothing within arm's length. A wider circle, and still nothing.
Slightly reassured, she relaxed a little as she and Nisana
searched further northward. Nothing still—nothing at all.
'Odd,' Nisana remarked. 'No fear. But no beasts, no birds,
not even insects. That cannot be normal.'

'No. West, now, but carefully. I would rather not trigger
that warning again.' The back of her neck prickled, as though
someone stood, half-sensed, directly behind them. She put it
down to those around the fire, pushed the stray tendril of fear
firmly aside. *The Power will sense anything amiss.* Certainly
anything that close.

"*GORS!*" A high, wailing cry tore the AEldra bond. Ylia's
eyes snapped open. Lisabetha struggled wildly in Levren's
grasp, reaching with two shaking arms toward something
across the fire. *At my back, oh Inniva.* It took all she had to
turn and look.

A light, slender and wavering; a dull, brownish-red thing
danced against the western rock wall. So much she saw with
the clear Sight that still held from the mind-search. Viewed
directly, however—

"By the Black Well," she choked. "*NO!*" Brandt stood
there, his arms outstretched, his lips forming her name—at the
same time a drawing caught at her, so strong it had her halfway to her feet before she was aware of it. Evil! Thrice evil!
She tore her eyes from it, leaped to her feet, held both hands
out in warding: "By the Guardians, I adjure thee, by Eyaliase
the pure, begone!" A ball of red-orange Baelfyr crackled from
between her palms, arced across the distance toward the *seeming*. She stared, stunned and half-blinded.

But the thing was gone, gone as though it had never been,
and the rock wall flickered with the light of fire only. Lisabetha, with a despairing cry, tried frantically to hurl herself
after, but Levren had her. Ylia fought air into her lungs, spun
back. Every one of them stared horrified into the night where
the foul thing had been.

"You! All of you! Turn away at once, do you hear?" Her
voice was ragged with loathing, scarcely recognizeable. "What
Lisabetha saw, that is nothing for any of us to look upon and
live!" She sprang across the fire, caught Lisabetha and shook
her fiercely. The girl's head rolled loose on her shoulders.
"That was not your brother, girl, that was a *seeming*! It would

have slain your body and devoured your inner being had you
followed it!'' Lisabetha stared at her blankly, collapsed in
tears on Levren's shoulder.

Ylia was already back around the fire; her voice was still
harsh with fear, anger at that fear, at herself. ''Brendan,
Brelian, what did you see there?'' Nisana stood at her feet,
whole body bushed, her ears flat to her skull. Brendan drew
back in sudden fear. *You'll get nothing if you terrify him so,
fool.* She fought for control, knelt and gripped his arm. ''I am
not crazed, Brendan, I swear it. I must know what thing you
saw against that rock. *Tell me!*'' But he could only shake his
head. With a heroic effort, he tried to force calm upon himself, and failed utterly.

Brelian wrapped an arm around his shoulders. ''I cannot
tell you what was there; Lisabetha drew my attention, I saw
only her.''

''I—saw it,'' Brendan gasped. He was shivering, ill with
fear. ''But it—but it—'' he shook his head angrily, swallowed.
''But it was not my friend Gors that I saw, no. My—my
mother—'' His voice faded. Brelian's arm tightened.

''No,'' Marhan said sharply. ''It was Brandt, as I have
often seen him on the practice grounds, weapons ready for a
crossing.''

''As I feared.'' Great Mothers, how did she deal with such a
thing as *this*? ''That was a *seeming*, an unformed seeming—a
wraith, if you will. We must not look from the fire again
tonight. An unformed *seeming* has no real shape of its own. It
takes shape from your mind. That is why each of us saw one
dear to him or to her, and not the same person—or thing.''
Marhan shuddered. ''It would have drawn Lisabetha from us,
as it nearly did, over a cliff. Or it would have possessed her
body, cast out her inner being and taken to itself her outward
shape.'' She swallowed hard, tucked her hands under her
cloak, held them hard against her sides to keep them from
shaking.

''I saw it,'' Malaeth whispered. ''I saw it.'' What she saw,
however, she would not say.

Ylia knelt to gather Nisana close. The cat's fur was flat once
again but her mind was still turmoil. ''They say,'' she went on,
''that a *seeming* can draw you once you have looked upon it.
That it calls to you. It may be, then, that one or another of us

may try to leave the fire tonight. Will you believe me when I say we must not?''

"But—but you slew it!'' Brendan protested.

"No. I struck at it with a warding. It is gone, but I doubt I had sufficient strength to kill it. It may only be banished, and if so, who can say for how long? I do not know; how should I? *I* have never dealt with the black powers; AEldra do not, have not in so many years that the only writings are tales. I know only that if any of us is moved to go into the night, we must *not!*''

"What of wood?'' Levren's normally easy voice cracked. "We have not enough to keep the fire burning all night.''

"No. Nisana and I will go for more; we alone have any protection against such an evil as that.'' 'I hope, girl.' Ylia closed her eyes briefly. 'Thanks, cat.' "Swear to me you will not look away from that fire!'' She swallowed, strode into the trees.

Not so terrifying, once she forced herself to move. Even without the second level of Sight, this near the camp she could see well enough, could of course see the rest of the company huddled together around the now high-burning fire. 'An unformed *seeming!*' Nisana was stunned, still scarcely coherent. 'I have only heard of that kind of thing, it is among the most vile uses of the Power—who would set an unformed *seeming?*'

"And who could expect it to catch prey in such a deserted place as *this?*'' Her voice, she was absurdly pleased to note, was steady once again. That, at least. "Fear—an unformed *seeming*—Mothers, what else walks these mountains, Nisana? Lisabetha may have been right, we may have done worse for them than if we all died in Koderra!''

'Nonsense!' the cat retorted crossly. 'Do not speak like that, poor, foolish child; you banished the thing, after all. *And* alone, when *I* had no wit to aid!' What she had seen, what had shocked her so deeply, she would not say. Ylia decided she had no desire to know.

"And—and if I had *not* banished it, and it had invaded me?'' It smote her, suddenly, just what she had faced. Her knees nearly buckled. She bent to wrap shaking hands around a dry chunk of wood, forced one deep, slow breath after another. The sickness passed.

'Why think on it, since that did not happen?' Nisana demanded reasonably. She was nearly her normal, cat-practical

self once again. 'And we take overlong with the wood; they
worry back there.'

"Of course," Ylia replied dryly, but there was affection
there, too. She freed a hand, rubbed soft, dark ears.

They made four trips altogether, until a stack of thick
branches and one long log lay just outside the camp.

The others still huddled together, staring intently into the
fire. All save Lisabetha, who lay, eyes closed, in the comfort
of Levren's arm. Ylia dropped exhausted between Marhan
and Golsat, warmed chilled fingers. She could not bring herself to meet what must be angry looks. She'd shouted at them,
bullied them. However necessarily. "I—I'm sorry, all of
you."

"Why?" Marhan demanded sharply.

She shrugged. "For my harsh words. I was afraid, and there
was great danger. For all of us. But I was afraid, mostly, and
fear overrode sense. I shouldn't have shouted. I'm sorry."
Lisabetha raised her head, gazed at her with dark, tragic eyes.
"Lisabetha." She met the girl's eyes with a visible effort.
"That was not your brother, I swear it."

"I know it," Lisabetha whispered finally. "Gors is dead.
But—but it *looked* so like him. I forgot all, save that."

Ylia eyed the rest of the company. "There, you see? That is
how a *seeming* is." She sighed, then. "So much for a decent
sleep tonight, for any of us. Tonight, of all nights. However,"
she added, forcing a little life into her voice, "Nisana and I
will take first guard. We'd better watch in pairs tonight." No
one argued.

"That thing—what if it returns?" Brendan wanted to
know. "Can it be touched with steel?"

"No. You wouldn't in the guise it had for you, though,
would you?"

"I—no. But you and the cat cannot watch for the entire
night!"

"No. I do not intend to. As for protection—I know of nothing, I fear. With other evils, well, you must know as well as I,
which fear steel or iron, which fear fire or light of sun, the
burning of certain herbs, or the circle and silver triangle of the
Mothers. But a *seeming*—no. And the warding I used against
it is an AEldra thing.

"You could not see it as it truly is, my friends. It has no
form, no being. It is Power, raw force, like a snare triggered

when a small beast blunders into it. There is no protection against an unformed *seeming*, save not to look upon it.'' She paused, tried to think.

'Ylia.' Nisana pressed a suggestion of her own.

'I don't think I could—'

'My strength, of course. Try it.'

'Well—' She closed her eyes, concentrated, bolstered her strength heavily with Nisana's. "Do you see it?" Marhan's eyes went wide as the pale colors of the AEldra Power danced around her plaits. "I can stretch this to surround us all— at least, I can if we stay very close together tonight. It's not complete protection. But it will warn me if anything evil approaches. And it may well frighten such a thing away, thinking us better armed than we are." The light flickered and died. "I will rekindle it when I waken you and Brelian, Marhan."

The Swordmaster heaved a sigh of relief when it vanished. He and Brelian exchanged unhappy glances, but neither said anything aloud. Levren built up the fire and rolled into his cloak. The rest followed suit.

It is my considered opinion, having crossed the terrain we traveled that day, that the folk of Nedao have there a perfect model for their Black Well. A more hellish, cold and miserable land I have never seen, and hope never to again.

10

The night stretched; watch followed watch under a cold, moonless sky. Of all the company, only Nisana truly slept. Ylia tried, knowing that for the sake of her companions she must appear confident of their safety. Brendan feigned sleep after his share of the watches, his body relaxed against the hard ground; only his breathing gave him away. No one else seemed able to close eyes at all. Brelian and Brendan had the fire built high and water heated at first light.

There was little to eat—only a few terribly dry pieces of biscuit, a little cold bird, some stale fish Levren shared out. As soon as there was sufficient light to make out the footing ahead, they were gone.

But the trail was lost in scree before day properly broke, and they wandered in a world of biting wind, narrow gullies and ravines, where footing was hard and treacherous, where rock bruised feet even through heavy boots or rolled treacherously from underfoot. A constant chill air flowed across the ground. Lungs burned. Hands clawed at rock that too often tore loose from crumbling yellow dirt, frozen fingers slipped across rough granite and bled stingingly.

They took it in bits; necessary, since it was impossible to see any distance at all, and because no one could bear to face longer stretches. Cut into pieces, it was still not easy, only easier: another distance, that pile of red and grey rock—so.

And now up and across, and down again. Halt in what little shelter a narrow cut in the cliff gave. On again—remember to stand slowly, for the air is still thin and a blackness teases the eye and mind of those who rise too quickly. Sway, grasp at cold rock with chilled, aching fingers, try not to cry out as the icy wind strikes again, tearing through cloak and mail alike. On once more.

It was impossible to choose any kind of route here, for there was no place from which they could oversee: At most, they gained a ridge from which they could see more rock, another ravine or two, and from that, take a direction. Left unspoken was the dread that they blundered toward a place unpassable, that they would need to retrace their path.

During the second hour, Marhan ordered a longer halt. His maps, and Golsat's fine-honed sense of direction were useless. *Damn.* He didn't like his options at the moment, but nothing else presented itself. They were going to have to send a scouting party ahead to find the best trail—*any* trail. And the two best trackers among them—Golsat and Levren. He could send one of them, but two would be more than twice as efficient. And they needed *out* of this foul high country, and that before dark.

Malaeth and the girl could clearly go no farther without a prolonged rest. *Damn, and damn again.* No help for it. The old Swordmaster sighed, walked away from his huddled companions, caught the Bowmaster's eye, drew him after.

"Marhan? You don't look pleased. Anything else gone wrong?"

"No—just what might," the old man growled. "Listen, our odd lad there, I know you've a problem, and I know it's not only him—no, listen first, will you? If you had to, could you deal with it enough to work with him?"

Levren gnawed at his lip; he'd gone pale. "Marhan, it's not a thing I chose, you know that."

"I know that. You've done well this far, and I know it's much to ask of you. You're the only decent scouts among us, you and he, and you're the only ones with enough energy for what we need. Someone has to go ahead, make certain we're not heading for a box canyon, find us a proper way, and get us down among the trees again before night."

"I—I know. No food, no reserves, no firewood, even. But I—"

"I'll send young Brelian with you; you needn't even talk save to him." A tense silence. "Look, I don't ask you to make friends. Just—deal with it, if you can. Can you do it?"

Levren drew a deep breath, let it out slowly, let his gaze travel back to the chilled, exhausted company. He forced himself to look directly at Golsat. A lump like fear or sickness formed in his throat; he swallowed, closed his eyes until it went away. But the knowledge he'd do what Marhan wanted was already thick in his mind. He had to; the old man was right, all around. "I—I can try, Marhan. I can't promise anything, but I'll try."

The Swordmaster clapped him on the back. "Good; I knew you'd never let me down. And he knows to avoid you."

"I know." *Mothers, what a thing for one man to need know of another.* He drew another deep breath, let it out even more slowly as Marhan walked away, drew Brel and Golsat off in the other direction.

Levren swallowed, hard. *All right. A man does what he must—you dealt with those Narrans, a year past, at Brandt's request, and they never knew how even sight of their foreign faces curdled your guts.* Once again he forced his eyes to dwell, briefly, on Brelian and his darker companion. No easier this time. Likely it never would be, not at his age. *He is of use to us, of use to Nedao. You need not talk to him, just to the boy.* That helped, a little. Enough that he could bring up a small smile in the general direction of the three men when Marhan, Brel and Golsat came toward him.

Golsat, they decided, would lead, since he had done the most pathfinding, and his sense of direction was near infallible. The others gave them a rather anxious send-off.

"Give us a full hour before you follow," Golsat advised, "lest we need to retrace any of our way. We will leave rock stacked—so," agile hands made a familiar pattern of four rocks, "or branches where we can—" He broke off, grinned at the Swordmaster briefly. "I certainly need not tell *you*, need I?"

"No," the old man replied dryly. "I know how to mark a trail also. We will see you by evening meal."

"Mind it *is* evening meal, too," Malaeth began with a heroic effort at her usual bantering tone, but she broke into harsh coughs.

"We shall indeed, Dame, by the Mothers' favor," Golsat

replied gravely. He motioned to his companions, then; they climbed into the wind. Brelian's cloak flared out wildly above his head as they dropped down out of sight.

"And may we see them again," Malaeth whispered. Lisabetha closed her eyes, pressed further back into the slight shelter of two uptilted slabs of black rock.

"Of course we shall, Dame," Brendan said firmly. "They are the best we have for this sort of thing, and doubtless this foul place is merely a small field which we shall see an end to before the sun drops from nooning." Malaeth smiled at him, but it was a forced, exhausted thing, and she leaned back against the Swordmaster, closed her eyes once again. "We'll see them, if only at the bottom of the Black Well," Brendan finished grimly, so quietly that only Ylia, huddled in her cloak behind him, heard his last words. She stirred, touched his arm.

"The Mothers would not send *us* there, do you think? The Black Well, instead of the White?" *Anything* to take her mind from the white-faced Bowmaster following Golsat up that rock-strewn ledge.

Brendan considered her question gravely, and with more attention than it would have merited in another place and time.

"Perhaps," he said finally. "But why would a warrior choose the White Hall, and the eternal feast? King Wergn, they say, did not, but when Lel-san tied the threads of his life she gave him choice, and he took the road to Hell, that he might yet confound his enemy." The faintest of smiles lit his normally somber face.

She edged nearer, gave him a tentative smile in reply. "I had not heard that tale, and I am well versed in our history. I know how the Great Isles were taken from us in siege—"

"By the Sea-Raiders, who hold them to this day—"

"—and how Wergn made the bargain with them, that the folk who could or wished to might go hence—"

"—and so many did that the sea was ablaze with the many-colored sails of their ships—"

"—that did, but only if Wergn and his Council remain as surety against treachery." She was taking fire from the conversation, could see the answering color in his face. Cold, Lev and Golsat, the night's terrors were temporarily forgotten: From childhood, she had loved best the tales of Wergn and his brave Queen Leffna, she who had led the folk to the Plain, who had fought personally, sword to sword, against the

Tehlatt. ''And when his Lady would not leave, he ordered her
bound and taken aboard the ship perforce. But he never came
to the Plain.''

''Slain by treachery,'' Brendan said. His speech was almost
a minstrel's chant. He must also, she realized with a kind of
wonder, truly love the old tales. ''By the treachery of the Sea-
Raiders, with the aid of one of his inner council who saw him
as traitor to Nedao—but by treachery in any case, for no other
way could serve against such a man.'' He met her eye then,
and flushed. When he spoke again, his voice was more normal. ''Well. It is said in the North that when he came before
the Mothers and they judged him, the bargain was then
made.''

Silence. ''Inivva,'' Ylia murmured finally, ''she who
chooses the thread; Noteyen, who lays the warp and weft; Lel-
san, who ties the knots when the weave is complete—''

''Mothers of the sacred Well of Life, guard us now.'' Brendan touched his fingers to his lips. He smiled then, rather diffidently. ''Many of the North follow the ways of the Chosen,
but as you see, I do not.'' Lisabetha, an ardent disciple of
those same Chosen, scowled at him indignantly. Brendan
shrugged. ''Their god is no warrior, is served by no warriors,
how should *I* understand such a god? Why, they do not even
have tales of a single hero—if they have any, that is!''

Ylia clapped a hand across her mouth; above it, her eyes
were merry. ''Do not look at *me* to gainsay you,'' she said,
''you know what I am. The Chosen look upon AEldra as servants of their Evil One, even such a blameless creature as Malaeth, or an unskilled, such as me.''

''Well, then,'' Lisabetha demanded suddenly, ''what *do*
you believe in, you AEldra?'' She stopped short, her face red
to the ears.

Malaeth touched her arm. ''It is a fair thing to ask,'' she
said mildly, ''though not of this one,'' she added, waving a
hand toward her charge. ''Ylia mouths the prayers of Nedao
and Yls both prettily, but she believes in nothing but her
steel!'' Ylia opened her mouth indignantly, closed it as Malaeth went on regardless. Brendan caught her eye, winked
gravely. ''The AEldra do not have gods. We look upon the
One or the Mothers as a way of putting a face, a being, to that
which cannot have such a thing, a way of understanding that
which cannot be understood. To the AEldra, there is good and

evil. There are also the Nasath, the Guardians; they who gave power to the AEldra. They are not gods, though many worship them and call upon them as if they were. For we have not seen them in many hundreds of years, not since they laid upon us the Gifts. They watch, it is said. But none know for certain, and none of Yls have seen a Guardian.''

Marhan roused himself with a huge yawn. "All this talk of gods is putting me to sleep," he grumbled. "It has been long enough, we had better set out after them." Malaeth closed her eyes briefly, but held out a hand for Brendan's aid and staggered to her feet. They set out in the direction the foreguard had taken.

"Well, I cannot see a thing!" Marhan's temper, never even in the best of times, had given way long since, and he was in as foul a mood as he had ever been. Brendan set his lips in a sour line.

"Shall we stop here, then?" he demanded sarcastically. "The women will thank you! There is less shelter here than where *I* suggested we stop, but you would not listen—"

Ylia stepped between them. "Stop it, both of you; my head aches, I'm cold, hungry, wet and *tired* of all this snarling." She shifted her shoulders, felt a trickle of water slide down between her shoulder blades where the seams on her cloak had been imperfectly lanolined; bits of hair stuck to her forehead. Brendan returned her scowl, glared at the old Swordmaster, stalked away muttering. Marhan rolled his eyes skyward and started out again. "I cannot see any great distance, either," she added, "but it seems to me—"

"Do you wish to lead, lead," Marhan cut in nastily.

Only long-instilled caution kept several tart remarks behind her lips. She pushed past him in the direction where it seemed there might be a pile of stone. The second level of Sight was useless, regular sight not good, and Nisana of no aid at all. She, when it began to rain, had crawled determinedly down into the travel pouch which hung at Ylia's breast, under the cloak. *At least one of us is dry*, she thought miserably. It wasn't really any comfort.

The stack of four neatly piled rocks pointed right. She glanced over her shoulder, but maintained that same careful silence as they passed it. *Blind old man, why he can't admit it instead of stubbornly trying to lose us all. On a day like this,*

*he might as well wear an eye cloth and carry a stick to feel his
way.* She waved an arm overhead, caught Brendan's attention.
He'd moved westward across the open field in hopes of finding the marker. Relief was in his face as he rejoined them and
took up rear guard. They plunged into a narrow cut, followed
its twists and turns. Ylia stepped aside to let Marhan go ahead
once more. In such a place, there was only one direction and
no danger he would lead them astray as he had done in the
open.

"A ledge, just ahead," he called out suddenly. He bundled
Malaeth and Lisabetha out of the rain, took the bits of wood
they'd gathered over the past hour or so and built a fire. It was
necessarily small and didn't last long, but it warmed hands
and feet.

At Brendan's suggestion, they heated and drank plain
water. "The warmth pushes hunger aside, for a little while."
Surprisingly, it did. Ylia rummaged through her bag, added a
pinch of rosemary to a second pot.

The rain feathered around them, threatened to become
snow, gradually moved south. A vague sunlight pushed
through the clouds to lighten the afternoon. Marhan scattered
the last bits of charcoal. "Go, now. Who knows what's on its
way." He helped Malaeth to her feet, took up the lead once
again.

They were sheltered from the wind for some time; the ravine
deepened until rock walls pressed in and towered to great
heights on both sides. The stream ran down the middle; now
and again, it poured down an opening in the rock; finally it
vanished underground.

Slowly the way grew wider; the bank to the right gradually
fell away, giving a view of distant peaks and a wall of black
cloud, a sharp drop to more rock and wash. But the west wall
still held off the worst of the wind, and now rose to even
greater height, until it was a solid mass of overlapping slabs of
stone. Here and there it hung out over them. Malaeth cast frequent nervous glances upward, moved with surprising haste
past such places.

Ylia stopped. Her mouth went dry, her stomach turned
over. Something—something *wrong*. Horribly, terribly
wrong. Brendan turned as he realized she was no longer with
him, and some distance ahead Marhan motioned them both
impatiently on.

"What?" Brendan had caught her mood, if not the cause, and was already at her shoulder, hand to his hilts, eyes studying the back trail.

She waved a hand for silence. Deep in her pouch, Nisana was stirring. "A scent? No—not—even that," she whispered, scarcely aware she spoke aloud. "A sense of a scent?"

"What are you talking about?" Brendan demanded. She waved him to silence again.

"Don't know. Something, somewhere, near—" As though her mind had conjured on its own the scent of death. Old, old death.

"Something *wrong*," she whispered. A noise moved across rock and the sparse, weedy grasses, a faint hissing that was neither wind nor grass. The thinnest of shadows moved between sun and ground and fell across them.

Ylia threw back her head. A thing like an immense bat glided overhead, banked and soared directly at them. Evil pulsed from it, rooting her in horror to the rock as the deep pits that were the thing's eyes sought hers. Its mouth opened, revealing rows of tiny rasping teeth and eight long fangs.

An unclean touch moved with a stealthy, feathery caress across the edge of her mind: *come.*

*Backward, the Nedao by our standards—
but they are not stupid folk, as many of our
kind say. They are keen-witted, skilled
traders and bargainers and appreciate
Osneran fine silk and other Narran-traded
goods from Oversea as well as their more
civilized neighbors. A conservative folk altogether, however, and I often wondered how
they would meet peril, or even sudden
change. In the Foessa, where peril and sudden change were an hourly occurance, I
found my answer.*

11

A redness blurred her vision; less than a whisper, that voice: *come. No!* She wanted to cry that, to scream aloud, but no sound came; she tried to move, could not. A wild, painful scrabbling against her chest that was Nisana fighting to free herself from the confining pouch. The shadow overhead halved as the thing drew in its wings and fell. A blast of hot air blew across the swordswoman's face, bringing with it the full stench of a thing long dead and rotting.

"To me, foul thing!" Brendan's voice cracked like a boy's, but his sword was up and out, his free hand sent her sprawling. A deafening cry echoed across the rocks, tore at her inner being. She shuddered, swallowed several times, pushed resolutely to her feet. Nisana wriggled free, dropped to the ground, moved forward to sniff, long-necked, at the creature. It had fallen to the path, wrenching Brendan's sword from his hand, and lay nearly across his feet.

Marhan gulped audibly. "What monster is that?"

Brendan shrugged, went back to retrieving his blade. "A thing beyond my ken, Swordmaster," he replied cooly, thought not at all steadily. "Lady Ylia, what do you know of it?"

"Nothing." She was still swallowing rapidly, desperate that she should not be ill. Marhan reached out and caught hold of her arm as she staggered. Her vision cleared. "I—it resembles a bat, but—"

"No. Not of any kind. Too large," Marhan grunted. He glanced over his shoulder; Lisabetha and Malaeth were not far ahead. He motioned them to stay where they were: unnecessary. Neither one of them would have come another step. Brendan, his sword once again his, poked gingerly at the thing. Too large, indeed. It lay, wings spread wide, across the trail and partway up the western cliff, fully a man's length and half again from tip to tip. Its body was covered with a very short, dark brown fur, save for the face, which was black and wrinkled.

Nisana took a cautious step forward as Brendan poked at it again, held her ground when it twitched. Ylia bit her lip.

And it was gone, gone as though it had never been. Lisabetha cried out. Marhan retreated, caught his heel on a snag of rock and fell back into the cliff.

Nisana leaped onto Ylia's shoulder. 'What a monster! Like something of a nightmare!' Her thought was more blazingly curious than frightened.

'But it was there, cat!' Ylia's thought, her whole body, shook. She hugged herself, hard. It *had* been real, it had touched her inner being, had fouled her thought, and Brendan had slain it with good steel. 'Nisana, it was there!'

'Of course it was!' Nisana snapped. 'Did I say otherwise? It *was* there, it no longer is. And why?' she demanded, as though she was teaching.

'Why?' Ylia echoed blankly.

'Because, having failed, it has returned to the one who sent it.'

"Sent?" She whispered the word aloud, forgetful of the armsman at her side, but Nisana had already returned to her pouch and her thought was closed.

Brendan wiped his blade on a handful of dry grass, glanced from the now-empty spot at his feet back down the trail.

Marhan and the other women had already started forward. "Whatever it was, it is gone," the armsman shouted after them. "Let us leave before another comes!" Marhan scarcely slowed at all, waved them imperatively on.

Ylia drew a deep breath, started after, was arrested by Brendan's hand on her shoulder. "All right. What was it?" His face was darkly determined.

"I told you, I don't know what it was." But he looked unconvinced.

"I understand why you will not say the name aloud to the Swordmaster," he said testily. "And I am sure Malaeth and the girl would rather not know. But—"

"Do you think me a liar?" she demanded hotly. "I have no idea what it was! None! And I do not *want* to know! It is gone, that is enough. I do not wish to be reminded that it ever was at all!" There was a cold silence. "Sorry," she said stiffly. He had it coming; hard to fight the words out, all the same. "Not the thanks you deserve for saving my skin."

"It was my skin as well. Remember?" Brendan's manner was suddenly reserved.

"Well, I *am* sorry. Truly." She drew a deep breath, let it out with her mother's calming charm. "I was afraid; I froze."

"And it made you angry. It would anyone." Another silence. "We—have all been afraid, some time or another." He hesitated, stole a sideways glance at her. "*I* was last night. Had that thing wished, it could have stolen my life with its bare hands, for I was as helpless as a child."

The quiet was not so stiff this time. "I thought you feared nothing in this world," she said lightly. Brendan smiled. Shrugged.

"I once thought I never would." The smile remained, answering lightness, a self-effacing smile. *Odd, that I dare tell her the thing I dare tell no other. Not even Brel.* "The old heroes, they were all brave. And I wanted—" he cast another doubtful glance in her direction, "I wanted, when I was a boy, to be one of them. Because—well—I realized young that much would be denied me when I was grown because I am not of a noble house. But heroes—they come from all classes, don't they? And not much is required of them, really—skill with weapons, which I have. And bravery, of course."

"Of course." There was no mockery in her voice, and within her only awe. *How can he dare tell me this, as though he sought my understanding—as though my understanding mattered*? But—but he was wrong. "Brendan, no. None of the truly great heroes were fearless." Again that doubtful glance. "Think. They were brave, the ones you admire from the histories, but of necessity. Think!"

He shook his head, unconvinced. "Merreven, Kilderes' brother, when he went against the Mathkkra, the cave dwellers, they who had slain his brother, when he drove them from the Plains and put the last of them to the sword—"

"He feared, because he knew what he must face, but his path was before him and he had no choice. The thing needed doing, lest the innocent suffer, lest more die as had Kilderes, a blood-sacrifice—"

"But—"

"Brandt, my father." Dark pain pressed against her throat. "He feared, I know he did, when he chose to remain behind, forming a rearguard in Koderra, so that the barbarians would not press on south and the helpless might reach the open sea. I saw the fear in his eyes, Brendan, and I know it now for what it was—to face death so clearly, to know there is no chance you will see the next day.

"But long years from now, when the Tehlatt themselves are dust, the tales will tell of the hero Brandt and the White Witch his wife who fell with the great Flames upon the enemy. Do you think she, also, was not afraid?"

"You believe this."

"Because I know it. Because it is true."

Brendan smiled suddenly, a genuine, warm smile. "Perhaps so. I have never thought much about such matters. In truth," he added with a brief grin, "I have seldom in my life thought at all, merely acted."

"For which I have reason to give thanks," Ylia replied. "I acknowledge," she added with the least of bows, "the debt of my blood."

Brendan shook his head. "As you wish. But it was my life as well, you know. But—I thank you. For everything you have said. You have given me considerable to think upon." Again that warm smile.

His attention was suddenly drawn to the fore: Brelian had returned, and with him was a strange man, a tall weed of a creature, clad all in skins to the fox's pointed muzzle and red ears that bobbed above his head.

They caught up with Marhan, who stood guarding the serving women from the old man—a mountain-hunter, he could be nothing else—with one hand on his hilt. Brelian had interposed himself between Swordmaster and hunter. "Marhan, it's all right! We met him on—"

"You'd trust to—"

"Marhan, if you'd just listen—!"

"Stay your hand, Swordmaster," Ylia shouted as they came up. "You've plenty of time to murder him, if that's needed. I doubt he'd outrun even you!" Brendan winced; Marhan glared at her but released his sword. Old but alert brown eyes stared widely into hers from around Brelian's arm. "Who is this, Brel, and where did you find him?" Marhan spared her another hard look, shrugged and stomped off.

"He found us. We were lost. Not far ahead there is a place we thought we might have to climb, but even that proved impossible."

"Climb?" Malaeth whispered, aghast. Lisabetha patted her shoulder reassuringly, but she looked no less anxious.

"No climbing," Brelian assured them quickly. "This is Verdren, who once lived in Esmalda west of the river, but he decided there were too many folk breathing his air, so he came here. What, fifteen years ago, Verdren?"

"About. A man loses count when all the years are alike." The old hunter's voice was creaky, as though he seldom used it. Quick eyes studied them in turn.

"He set us upon a proper trail," Brelian continued. He cast a brief scowl at the Swordmaster, who was clomping back toward them. "We would never have found it. It is not far ahead, but somewhat east of us."

"Where did you leave Golsat and Lev?" Marhan growled.

"Less than a league from where we join that trail, there is a valley and a small lake. There was sign of game even before we reached a point where we could see the lower ground. They went ahead to find us a place to sleep and have meat for us when we arrive." Marhan glared at him, transferred the glare briefly to Verdren. "They—chose to, Swordmaster." But Marhan had more things to worry at the moment.

"Handy that he chanced to be there, wasn't it?" Brendan remarked dryly. The old hunter met his eyes indignantly, though he must look up a goodly distance to do so.

"You had better think it was!" he snapped. "I seldom

travel anywhere abouts *here*, I can tell you that! But that my pack animal wandered last night, you might have spent another cold night in the rocks, instead of warm and fed below!" He spat. "Think on that, young lordling, and put aside your fool's doubts!"

"Oh." Ylia bit back a laugh. "And *you* never doubt anything you find here, I suppose? You have lived here for long years, and seen nothing in these mountains, Verdren, that you are so open-hearted?" A line deepened between his brows. *Shhh, don't tease the old creature.* Her next words were more placating. "If we have spoken to you with little gratitude or trust, then we owe you apology, and you shall have one. But we have spent three nights in the Foessa, and what we have already seen—"

"Do not tell me. I will not ask." He eyed her curiously, cast a brief glance in Lisabetha's direction, went back to a frank appraisal of her mail shirt, breeches, short-torn surcoat, and the young woman who wore them. "There is only one female that I have heard tell in all Nedao who wears the uniform of the Koderran Guard. But—"

"Ylia," she said. "Myself." To her intense embarrassment he dropped stiffly to one knee and bowed his head. The furred headpiece bobbed gently back and forth.

"My—My Lady. Forgive me, I did not know you. If I spoke any disrespect—"

She pulled him back to his feet. "It's all right." Out of place here, the formal trappings of high station. And she was not used to full obeisance. "There is no need for ceremony, we are too few and our need too great. It has taken the skills and strengths of every one of us that we stand here at all. But if you would have my thanks, the thanks of all of us, aid us now! We are bound for Aresada, for the Caves. Do you know them?" A nod. "Can it be done?"

Verdren gnawed at his under lip. One hand tugged at the fox paws again, and he finally nodded, reluctantly. "It can, if it must. But let us move on. This is not a good place, anywhere hereabouts. You need maps and I have no hide about me, but there is a place not far ahead where I can draw them in the dirt."

"I have a map," Marhan began, but Verdren merely turned and set out at a swift pace. Malaeth and Lisabetha fell in with Brelian; the rest followed.

"You will need it," the old hunter said. "But we will move anyhow, for this place is not good. I have seen things near to here—and the Foessa *are* haunted, you know." Ylia caught Malaeth's dark, accusing eyes on her. Marhan snorted. Verdren regarded him with a level, disapproving expression on his old face. "Do not scoff, Plainsman. They do not lie, who say that! I would not for all the bounty of the Mothers walk the way you have come!"

"You have seen—" Brendan hesitated.

"I *have* seen. Shadows across the trail, but none to cast them. Battles fought under the trees, all in silence, until a fog shrouded them or the sun banished them. Things which stand and call, looking most like my old mother—"

"*You* have seen that thing?" Marhan breathed. "But how did you escape it?"

"How not? It was not my mother, you know. She is long since dead. And, if not my mother, what should it be in the Foessa? Why, a thing of evil!" he finished triumphantly. "I have not gone that way in a long time, and shall not, ever again. But there is more," he went on, dropping his voice until it was a mere silibant whisper. "Have you heard of the Fear-That-Follows?" He cocked his head to one side, scratched his jaw. "It dwells here, the Fear does. I can direct ye around one such place, where it is—or was. It moves about, you see, and is seldom two seasons in the same place. But you must take great care," he added earnestly, "the Fear will eat your bones!" He gazed anxiously at the Swordmaster, but Marhan was beyond scoffing.

"That tells us little enough," Brendan said finally. "Can it be slain?"

"Can it be slain? What, with steel?" Verdren laughed, a high, thin giggle. "Now, how would I know that? I have never seen it. When I could smell it out, I never remained to see how it looked! I am old, boy, but my legs have not failed me yet!" Brendan favored him with the odd little look he usually bestowed upon his brother, and asked no more questions.

"You have never seen this Fear, and yet you know of it," Ylia said finally. "How?" None of them, save she and Nisana, had been aware of the Fear, and this old man was purely of Nedao.

"Ye can—smell them out, Lady. No—" he frowned. "Not precisely that. Something about 'em, ye can tell when they are to hand. When they wish, or so it's said. Tell me, did the hairs on your neck never stand for no reason?''

"Did—" They were, right at the moment, as she remembered the flying thing and shivered.

"That," Verdren finished grimly, "is how I know."

The ravine opened out suddenly, leaving them on a high, sloping meadow, gazing out across thick forest far below toward a long, narrow valley. There was a glint of water through the trees, a thin trickle of smoke which rose as high as the tallest trees before flattening out to drift north.

Verdren dropped to the ground with a pleased grunt, held out a hand to the Swordmaster who reluctantly produced his map. Ylia stayed with them a while as they huddled over the parchment, Verdren's fingers moving rapidly this way and that as he kept up a constant discourse. Marhan pointed to one place; Verdren shook his head, drew lines and marks in the dirt between them. She was already lost. Easier to leave them to it. She crossed the turf to stand with the rest of the company.

Brendan and Brelian gazed out toward the smoke; Malaeth sat hunched against rock, her back to the wind, Lisabetha at her side. "How much further, Brel?" She was tired, suddenly. *Reaction.*

"Perhaps an hour," Brelian said. "No more. And the way is easy once we come off this height. But I would rest as well as I can now, Dame," he added to Malaeth. "I fear it is steep and narrow at the first."

Malaeth fetched a sigh, huddled deeper into her cloak. "Well, at least it is down and not uphill we must go."

Brendan turned back to watch the mappers. Marhan had returned his precious oil-wrapped packet to an inner pocket, and was now speaking earnestly, gesturing back the way they had come. Verdren paled visibly, stumbled to his feet. "What are they talking about?" Brelian demanded generally. Brendan and Ylia exchanged glances. The three of them started back down the trail. But Verdren drew back a pace, another, and as they approached, sketched a hasty bow in their direction.

"My Lady, I must go, I have not yet found my horse. Perhaps I'll see ye again, northwards of here; fare well, all of ye!" He turned and sped past Marhan at a pace that belied his years and skinny legs, was lost in a clatter of falling stone downhill and to the east.

Marhan turned, his expression blank with surprise. "All I did was to ask the old fool what he knew of that flying thing," he growled, "and you saw! He would not even give me an answer!"

"Why did you do that?" Brelian demanded irritably. "We could have used his aid. I was so careful, we all were, to mention none of the things we had seen, since he was so skittish —and now *you—*" He broke off. "What thing? Bren?"

"Oh. A bat. Something large. Unlike the old man's Fear, it could not withstand an honest blade." Brelian scowled vexedly at his brother.

Marhan chuckled. "Heh. Bat. If a bat flies by day and is two manlengths in wingspan, then it was a bat!" He, too, eyed Brendan sourly, then brushed past to join the women. Brelian regarded his brother another long moment, transferred the appraising look to Ylia. No, no joke. From Bren, anyway; *he* wouldn't know how to form one. But Ylia's face was pale enough for freckles to show tan across her cheekbones. He glanced across his shoulder cautiously to make certain Lisabetha and Malaeth were still out of hearing. Glanced at the sky. Late.

"Tell me of it tonight. We had better move, we will be long in getting Mistress Malaeth down from here. It is steep, but not beyond us. That old man," he added defensively, "was a *lot* of help!"

"Huh." Marhan had caught that last. "He would have talked us all to death before dark set in tonight. Come on. It is cold here, and I can see there is at least fire!" Ylia moved out to take the lead, and as Brelian and his brother followed, overheard the latter say, "An odd old fellow, wasn't he? Now, did *I* come upon this Fear, I would at least see what it looked like!"

Brelian laughed. "And wrestle it to the ground!"

Ylia glanced over her shoulder, smothered a grin. Brendan was watching his brother with grave doubt. Brelian clapped an arm across his shoulder.

"No, of course not," Bren said finally. "I would use my blade on it. What else?" He spoke so seriously, that none of them dared to laugh.

There was little light in the chamber, for no torches had been lit, and the sky had been darkly overcast for much of the day. Even the tall, narrow windows lining the north and west walls could not dispel the gloom. The tiled floor was dark, polished, bare of rug or decoration, save for the winged horror sprawled near the flight of shallow stairs. One wing nearly brushed worn, brown boots. One toe came forward, nudged the thing thoughtfully.

"I told you it would not suffice." A woman's voice, low and husky. The toe prodded the inert shape again.

"It could have. *She* had no protection against it."

"She had the swordsman. Protection enough, my Lord."

"So it was." A distortion blurred the floor, the thing was gone. "A test. That is all."

*There is this we have in common, all of us,
of whatever kind: We will come to the aid of
family, and often dare more or chance more
for family than we will for others. Though I
met one or two, on a time, who did not have
this loyalty to kindred; perhaps this is a
guide, by which one might begin to gauge
them, the good and decent humans from
those who are not.*

12

Brelian, if anything, had carefully understated the difficulty
of the path before them. Hunger drove them all; hunger, and
the sight of that wisp of smoke rising above the trees, nearer
every time any of them looked up. Malaeth, older than any of
them, softer, unaccustomed to travel of any sort, let alone to
scrambling across wild country, scarce clad for any journey,
held grimly to the way, walking where she could, lips com-
pressed tightly as she must sit on the cold ground to slide until
she could again stand. Through it all, she neither complained
nor asked help.

Ylia, who had always loved the old woman, developed an
awed admiration for her.

The roughest of the trail was, fortunately, a short distance
indeed, and they came out of a narrow cut into forest. Thereafter the trail wound around rock and thick stands of trees,
was thickly padded with pine needles and dead leaves.

The sun was nearly down before they reached open woods
and level ground. They could smell the fire long before they
saw it, the odor of burning fir mingled with—Mothers be
praised—roasting bird and trout baking in the ashes. It was

not long thereafter they passed the last of the trees and Golsat stood to wave them on.

The fire was several lengths from the water, well away from the trees. Levren emerged from the forest as the exhausted company reached camp. "You have timed things rather neatly," he said pleasantly. "It's not Plains-done but edible."

"Good," Brelian grinned and tipped Golsat a wink. "I'd rather not have had to fight the barbarian for the raw stuff."

Golsat merely smiled, not at all perturbed. He and Brelian had come to a good understanding of each other by the time they'd come within sight of the valley. And he had now an abiding respect for the Bowmaster, who had handled himself well in the circumstances. "Only *half* barbarian, boy. And if the fish is warm—isn't that cooked?" Brelian hooted; Golsat turned back to the fire to rake several bundles of blackened water-weed from the heat with a branch. "I would wait a few moments, if I were you. This is done, but hot to the bone." He eyed them, gravely anxious. "If there is not enough, I could catch more—"

Lisabetha giggled weakly. There were twelve bundles, the largest as long as her forearm.

Levren took Marhan's kettle and went for water as Golsat began cutting the grasses away from the fish, dropping them onto scraped lengths of clean bark he had pulled from some of the dry logs. There was a profound silence around the fire for some time after that.

'Ylia—'

'I know, cat.' The pain in her middle set to rest so she could again think, she followed the cat away from the rest of the company and down to the lake. 'Search.' They caught the edge of the warning, faint with distance if no less terrifying; there, a rapidly receding thought which must be Verdren. Nothing else. Here it was quiet, though not unnervingly silent. As full dark covered the sky, night birds cried back and forth across the upper end of the valley, something yelped mournfully from the ridge they had come down earlier. There were soft splashing noises from the lake that promised more fish. A bat—normal size and with no aura of any kind—sailed quietly overhead, was lost in the gloom.

Pretty. Marhan and Levren both had argued that they should halt a full day to build some supply of stores, to rest. Malaeth was white and worn, Lisabetha's face smudged as though she had wept and wiped her cheeks with grubby hands. She had turned her ankle earlier and walked as though it hurt her. But the two women weren't the only tired; even Golsat, when pressed, admitted he was exhausted.

'Well?' Nisana demanded finally.

Ylia shrugged. "I could weep, I am so weary. My legs ache, I feel as though I haven't slept in days."

'Well, then,' the cat urged. 'You have searched, we both have. Safe?'

She pressed aside memory of the horror that had fallen upon her earlier in the day. Nodded. 'Safe.' It didn't, entirely, *feel* that way to her for some reason. But if Nisana could find nothing. . . . *Nerves*, she told herself sharply. *Leave it be.*

It was very quiet around the fire. Brendan's eyelids drooped. Marhan was grumpily nursing a blister and had retired to the far side of the fire.

"It is safe," Ylia announced as she and the cat came back into the light. Nisana sprawled out across Malaeth's lap. She had eaten an astonishing helping of fish; had, in fact, barely been able to hold herself awake to complete the search. Ylia eyed her affectionately, gazed around the fire at her companions. *Safe*, she reassured herself, and hoped she could remember to believe it.

But she followed Levren down to the lake later. "Lev. It's —it's probably foolish, I know—"

"Why? And when have you done anything foolish, girl?" His smile warmed her, as it always did.

"Lisabetha."

"Mmmm." He squatted, splashed water over his face, rubbed it on his cloak hem. "I see. No, not so foolish as all that, Ylia. Since dark, she's not looked well at all."

"No." She squatted beside him to fill the bucket.

"Just reaction, I expect," Levren said sympathetically. They looked back toward camp: Lisabetha stared into the fire with an unnatural concentration, hugging herself. "It takes you that way."

"I know." She did, too; it had taken her that way.

"And she was doing so well." He sighed, thought a moment. "I will mention this to Marhan also, Ylia. She trusts him."

"Good." She still felt a little foolish. "I—do not know what she might do, or that she would do anything at all. She would not leave us. Where would she go?"

"If she is really that afraid, logic would go to the wall, girl. You know that."

She didn't, not of experience, anyway. Blind fear—before the bat-creature, she'd never felt it at all. She caught at his arm. "Lev, she would not harm herself, would she?"

"I—no." He shook his head. "She follows the way of the Chosen. But she is strung tightly, and it is hard to say for certain what she might do. To watch and be prepared, the three of us, that would be best. It is certainly too bad," he added, "that she saw that thing last night. And this other beast you and Marhan spoke of." Ylia shivered; he gripped her shoulder. "Frightened you, didn't it? It is all right," he added blandly, "I won't tell anyone."

"Pooh." she laughed weakly. Sobered. "It did frighten me, Lev. Terribly. And it infuriated me, to be so frightened."

"So it would. But it must have been quite bad," he added, even more blandly, "to frighten *you*. Hmmm?"

"Levren, stop it!" It was a genuine laugh this time.

"Quite seriously, girl, you astonished me last night. One thing to train a child to handle weapons and all that entails, another to see the training put so well to use. Your mother," he added gravely, "must have taught you well at the same time. But as for Lisabetha—"

"I know. She is highly fanciful, Lev; and I think she senses evil almost as though she were AEldra." He nodded.

"She is Northern, you know." He shook her easily. "You know who she reminds me of? My Lennet." Ylia giggled, clapped a hasty hand across her mouth. Levren's volatile eldest daughter was as unlike the brittle Lisabetha as—as Marhan was. "Truly," Lev insisted. "She is certainly every bit as dramatic and hysterical of mood as my dragon of a daughter."

"Any of your daughters," Ylia grinned in reply. Levren shrugged, spread his hands wide.

"Well, they're certainly nothing like me, that way, or Ilderian, their mother."

"And your sons—"

"Laydik isn't—"

"You spoil them shamelessly; Ilderian rides close herd on them and tries to undo your indulgences, no wonder—"

"But they're good children," Levren broke in flatly. It was

possible to push him too far on the subject of children—particularly his own eleven, though he'd have stood up for any of his small Koderran friends as loyally.

"So they are," Ylia replied, and was rewarded with a warm smile. "But how did you get Lennet out of Koderra?"

"Not hard at all; she left willingly when she heard *you* were sailing for Yls also."

"Ah."

Levren grinned. "I don't envy you meeting up with her once again, girl. She won't be pleased."

"Ha. *I* did not give her the lie, my friend!" He merely chuckled, not in the least concerned. That was part of his strength, of course, that he took nothing seriously unless he must, that his emotional keel remained firmly under him. "But I am getting chilled out here, and they are waiting for that water."

Only Malaeth slept; everyone else had gathered close around the fire, as much for the companionship as for warmth. Marhan was regaling the brothers with tales of his first years in service, giving weapons-training to the boy Brandt. There was a silence; Golsat then broke his usual reserve and began a tale of his own, telling of his escape from Anasela ten years before.

"I was still a boy," he began, his voice low, even more expressionless than usual, "and my father and I worked the fields together, for I was eldest. Life was hard but good; in the fall, there was the Harvest-Fest, in spring, folk gathered to aid each other in the planting. We had good neighbors and often I went with my father to Conrasy, the village half a day's ride from our farm. Though I was yet too young for proper sword-training, Father trained me himself. And he served under the Duke. Erken.

"It was late in the fall, and we had worked a long morning harvesting the last of the corn when we saw a great smoke to the north and we wondered. The folk of Anasela burnt off the fields in the fall also, but we had never seen such smoke. And we looked at one another then and saw that same fear in each other's eyes. We dropped our bags and cutters and ran back to the house."

Golsat hesitated. "My—my mother, as you all here know, was Tehlatt. She had been third wife to a minor chieftain, but had fled their camps when he beat her for overcooking his meat. My father found her two days later when he went to get feed for his cattle." He paused, stirred the coals with a slender branch, threw it into the heart of the fire when it began to smolder and took up the tale once again.

"Father was a good man," he resumed, even more quietly. "And he took pity on the woman, though many Anaselans would have killed her without thought. But he took her back to his cabin and tended her until she was well. He thought, you see, that she would prefer her own kind. But she would not leave, and offered instead to care for his house, to cook his food, and he, wishing to bring no shame upon her, wed her after the fashion of Nedao, though many of his friends protested such foolishness.

"Between them grew affection and friendship, and then more. And she bore first me, then my sisters both together, and my brother, who was little more than a baby when Anasela fell.

"We ran from the fields that afternoon, Father and I, and smoke darkened the northern sky. My mother was within the house, gathering bundles of food and warm clothing, while my sisters readied our three horses. My mother, you see," he added simply, "had the Sight, and she *knew* what we feared, that the Tehlatta had invaded Anasela and were firing farms and villages as they came.

"Still she did not falter, nor did she weep as many might have done, for she had great strength, and fear for her family drove her. Well she knew the Tehlatta would burn her alive, as example, did they capture her. More: that they would treat my father the same, for having given her aid. And we children, for we were of her blood as well.

"Within the hour we rode out, the ponies carrying double, and we rode until full dark, pushing the animals until it was clear they could go no further. And all day the smoke followed, but now it seemed to draw nearer as we came down to the Planthe, many leagues east of Teshmor.

"We abandoned the horses when we reached the Planthe. Foolhardy, perhaps, but we had no choice; our sturdy little farm beasts could not outrun Tehlatta war-mounts. We unpadded them, wiped them down, hid the gear so they might be taken for strays, that perhaps, if they were found, it would not be suspected any of Nedao had come so far. We took then to the River.

"For several hours we slogged through the shallows, returning to the bank only when the water became too deep or too swift, reentering always as soon as we dared, so we would leave no trace of our passage. At length we were forced to carry the smaller children, and at daybreak we, too, could go no further. We found a willow thicket near shore where we could hide until dark.

"It was midday when the first war company swept past us, a small one, no greater than ten. Other bands passed thereafter, once so near we feared to be run over, and I covered the mouth of my little brother lest he cry out and betray us. My sisters had evil dreams for many years after, but my mother sat quietly through all those long hours, and her face showed nothing.

"It was nearly dark and we readied to go on again, when once more riders came into sight. Perhaps they saw us from the first—" Golsat shrugged, his face darkly somber, "perhaps not. It does not matter. They fired the brush where we had hidden, and as we fell back into the river, they attacked.

"My father pushed my mother and the children into the water before setting himself to my shoulder, that we two might hold rearguard for them. I knew that I would die there, yet my pride in my father's trust was so great, I could not fear." Brendan's head came up; he stared at the half-caste in astonishment. "And so we stood at the edge of the bank, swords in hand, and we vowed together to kill as many as we could of them, before they slew us.

"My father died beside me, a Tehlatta arrow through his throat, even as I killed the last of those who opposed us on foot. I dragged him back into the water with me, but as the current pulled at my legs, another arrow, guided by whatever gods favor human wolves, pierced my forearm. I fell into the water and knew nothing for a time.

"When I opened my eyes again, I had drifted onto a sandbar some distance down-River and the pain in my arm had pulled me awake perforce. I cut the shaft close to the skin, since I could not remove it and could not bear the pain whenever it moved. Once again I went into the Planthe; the banks were dark, the moon down. I had no idea how far I had come."

He paused, his normally impassive face grim and sad. "I found my mother the next day, in a cave along the River, at a

place where the shores rise to great height. Not far from Teshmor. She had been unable to keep all the children together in
the dark and so had clung to the youngest and most helpless,
but my brother drowned during the night. My sisters reached
the City before us; a fisherman found them down-River of my
mother's cave, on an island, and brought them on. They lived
in Teshmor until—" He paused, went on in the same flat,
emotionless voice. "We never found trace of my father's
body."

A heavy silence fell. A night bird screeched sharply overhead and several of those around the fire started; Lisabetha
cried out faintly, pressed a fist against her mouth. Marhan
stirred. "Well. Perhaps your luck will hold for us, eh?"

Golsat raised his head. "Perhaps. I own we fared better
than most. I certainly did—a green boy with his father's cut-
down sword, his black hair marking him to the Tehlatta as
clearly as stripes tell chipmunk from squirrel. And we are
more here than an old man and green boy." Of fears or hopes
he might have for his remaining family, Golsat said nothing.

Brelian roused himself and volunteered to take the first
watch; Golsat stirred, offered to aid. The two men strode into
the night. Brendan gazed stricken after them. "Inniva's
breath, what I called him—" He set his jaw, leaped to his feet
and vanished into the dark. Levren gazed after them, closed
his eyes. Beneath his cloak, his hands slowly unclenched. It
seemed not as hard to manage, quite, this time.

Marhan was already half-asleep, Malaeth snored softly.
Lisabetha lay close to her, wide-eyed and pale. Nisana slid
away from the old woman, yawned widely, leaped neatly
across her. Lisabetha started as the cat rubbed against her
shoulder, stretched across her arm. Silence. One slender hand
moved tentatively to stroke the soft fur.

'Thanks, cat.'

'Mmmm.' Sleepy response. 'She's warm and she has nice
hands; I like that.'

Ylia stood, stretched hard, strode off toward the lake.
Lisabetha would sleep, and sleep deeply. Nisana would see to
that. One less thing to worry, but something else was working
at the back of her mind, had returned after Golsat ended his
tale. It worried her, the moreso because she could not label it.
If I knew—think, girl. She walked partway around the lake,
retraced her steps. Finally she sat on a shelving slab of rock

that overhung the water and listened to night noises: the distant drone of bees, the little rustling sounds of small, shy, beasts; the occasional bark or shrill cry from the distance. She watched starlight glitter on the lake.

"My mother, would you were here to guide me now," she whispered, and the bitterness of the thought was alarming. She pushed it away; it returned. *I should have saved her; she should have come with me. I swore it, I promised my father, myself, and what came of it*? And, angrily: *How dared you to leave me so, Mother? I'm alone, I'm frightened*! She had sought death, what could anyone have done to restrain her? "Well?" she demanded of herself. "What could *you* have done, half-blooded, unskilled—powerless as you are—to restrain a full-blooded AEldra of the Second House?"

The water rippled with a light breeze and she gazed at it gloomily, drew her knees to her chin, let her thoughts float.

At first, she was not aware of the change in the faint light. But it danced; how had she not noticed? And such patterns, such beauty. She fought a yawn, suddenly had to fight to hold her eyes open. *How could I have thought myself unable to sleep*? The light rippled across the water, dazzling, swirling—shaping—a form, a person—Mother. Scythia, clad all in white and silver, stood before her.

'Ylia.' The voice belled through her inner being, rainbow-shimmered arms reached. 'Daughter.'

"Mother." A knot loosed in her throat. Tears smeared her vision. She blinked them furiously aside. *Mother. See how her arms reach for me, I must go to her*. She stood, wavered light-headedly, her foot came down on a loose branch and twisted, throwing her to the rock. Pain in scraped palms and knees brought her to herself in an instant: *No*! She rolled, raised arms in the AEldra warding, too late.

With a shriek that burned the mind, the thing was on her, clawing at her inner being, pressing against her will. Its thought, horribly, still retained a semblance of Scythia. *Do not resist—daughter*.

"No!" She cried that aloud, or thought she did. No! But it was a battle with cobwebs, nothing upon which to fix a grasp. She clenched her teeth, held even as she realized *I cannot hold, I am lost*.

Gone. All gone. She lay as she found herself, sprawled face down on the hard rock. Nisana's small head filled her blurred vision. She tried to reach, had no strength.

Nisana radiated fury. 'Fool! To come away from the fire and make yourself a target! Have you learned nothing these past days?'

"I—" She cleared her throat. "I have. Now. And I am glad you are here to tell me so." She closed her eyes. Tears edged down her cheeks. "And I am very, very glad that I am still here to listen."

The cat rubbed hard against her shoulder. 'Mph. We need you. I cannot speak with your Swordmaster, and he would never listen to Malaeth!'

Ylia eyed her in astonishment. Laughter bubbled up; she silenced it. There was nothing humorous in any of it. "You—did you see?" she asked finally. "A—another *seeming*. And yet we sensed nothing of it—"

'No. Not like the other. It was not unformed, it was made to resemble Scythia, and so set to have *your* inner being.' Ylia shuddered, closed her eyes again. 'Or mine, of course. Likely, though, yours. After all,' the cat continued remorselessly, 'the bat-thing chose *you* over the two helpless females we had with us. And think—'

"No. I will not, not tonight." She leaped to her feet, turned to look back at the water only when they were very near the fire indeed. A shard of moon topped the eastern peaks. She breathed properly only when she gained the relative safety of firelight. She warmed herself at the fire: her palms were scraped, her knees were sore. Fortunately the heavy cloth of her trousers hadn't torn. *Be sensible, you're safe now*, she ordered herself sharply, and moved to lay near Malaeth. Nisana crawled under her cloak.

'Sleep, girl. You will be safe, I'll see to it.' Nisana soothed, as she had Lisabetha, pressed against Ylia's shoulder, purring gently, until the girl's steady breathing told her she slept indeed.

She slept, my Scythia's child. I did not, the whole night: It worried me. How had I not sensed the thing which nearly had her? Or the unformed seeming of the previous night? Ylia would likely not have found it, but I should have, and that was not a false pride such as our young hero bore, merely clear knowledge of my strengths. No. I feared even then that Ylia had the right of it. Something wrong, she had said. Something about the mountains—or in them.

13

It was late; she knew that by the warmth on her face even before she opened her eyes. There was no one else in camp. She sat up, stretched. At first, she could not even see anyone else; finally she picked out Lisabetha and Malaeth down by the lake. Somewhere back in the trees, then, Marhan shouting at Golsat.

The fire had burned down to coals; one leaf-and-grass-wrapped packet sat among the hot edging stones, close to Marhan's kettle. Pleasant odors came from both.

A wash first. She rolled to her feet, brushed dried grass and dirt from her pants, shook out the heavy cloak.

Malaeth smiled as she neared. "Hoo. Sleepy thing, you looked like a baby, all curled up like that."

Ylia laughed, blushed. "Baby! *Malaeth!*"

The nurse laughed merrily, patted her shoulder. "Well, as near as I remember, it's been so *very* long," she teased. Ylia cast a glance heavenward—*if anyone ever won such a contest of words with her, I would love to hear it!*—and smiled at

Lisabetha, who had tucked her skirts high so she could gather lily root and fresh cattail greens in the knee-deep water of the marshy shallows. Rather surprisingly, the girl smiled back, shyly, but a genuine smile, as she started back to the fire with her thick bundle.

"Nisana sent her sleep last night; I think she has not slept well since we came into the mountains," Malaeth confided as soon as she was out of hearing.

"Mmmm. She sent *me* sleep last night, too."

"I had no need of help," Malaeth admitted ruefully. "But that was a bit more walking than I am used to."

"By the way," Ylia grinned at her, urchinlike, "when did you begin to snore, Malaeth?"

"I?" the old woman drew herself up indignantly. "I, snore?"

"It wasn't Nisana. But don't take my word, ask anyone at the fire last night."

"Pooh," Malaeth replied comfortably. She pulled her feet from the water to eye them critically. "You'd all lie; you think I don't know what your Swordmaster calls fun?"

Ylia laughed, bent to wash face and neck. The water was cold where it entered the lake, but not as cold as she had thought the night before. "If the sun stays out, we could actually bathe."

"Well—" Malaeth cast a doubtful glance toward camp, an even more doubtful one at the water. "I suppose so." She didn't sound terribly enthused. Ylia dragged her boots off, washed her feet and went barefoot back to her breakfast.

The day was mostly given over to rest, to drying the fish and bird Golsat and Levren brought in. Marhan improvised a rack of green branches to hold the meat and turned it over to Malaeth. For the rest of the afternoon, he sat hunched over his map with a purplish liquid of the old woman's distillation, incorporating Verdren's changes and landmarks into its faded surface.

The light wind dropped away in the early afternoon; Lisabetha and Ylia took a swim, washed those few items of clothing that would dry over the fire, kept watch for Malaeth after she found a place sufficiently secluded for her taste. She washed down with warm water from the kettle, spread her underthings on low bushes, out of sight.

The evening passed pleasantly. The party might have been

a pleasure expedition instead of flight. In her wanderings
around the meadow, Malaeth had found young chickory and
set Brelian to digging the roots for her; there was a proper tea,
finally, not merely hot water with herb flavoring.

Lisabetha was weaving a carry-bag from the tough lake
grasses; she'd completed one for Malaeth earlier in the day,
another for Golsat.

Marhan belched loudly, drew out his map and glanced up
with a wicked gleam in his eye. "C'mere, boy. Double-check
tomorrow's trail with me." Brendan raised his head indignantly, but his anger gave way to bewilderment when Ylia
sighed heavily and moved around the fire to the Swordmaster's side. Marhan grinned evilly. "Thought I meant you,
hey?"

"Well—" Brendan spread his hands, shrugged.

"It's a habit of his," Ylia was stiff with irritation in spite of
all intentions not to let the Swordmaster get under her skin.
"He has called me 'boy' for years."

"But—boy?" Brendan looked at his brother, back across
the fire.

"If you really want to know," she pulled Marhan's hood
down over his eyes as he opened his mouth to cut her off, "he
thinks it a great joke. After all, how many Nedaoan swordswomen do *you* know?" She tapped her chest with one finger.
"But my father knew I must have it when it was clear I was the
last of his children and the one to succeed him. Of course,"
she added diffidently, "*I* wanted it. Swordplay has always ap-
pealed to me more than—oh, needleplay, and the other diver-
sions permitted young noblewomen." It was Malaeth's turn
to sigh; poor woman, she had tried! "And when my father
brought me to Marhan to train, he flatly refused."

"I did not!" Marhan protested as he pushed the hood back
to his shoulders. "I only said—"

"That you had never tried to teach a maiden—heir or no—
and were not about to begin at your age," Ylia overrode him.
"I was only a child of thirteen summers at the time, but I
remember every single word you uttered that morning, Marhan." The old man eyed her sidelong; some of his language
had been strong indeed. "But Father wouldn't listen," she
went on, laughing at the memory, "fortunately for me! He
just told Marhan he would have to adjust, old age or no, and

that if he was too damn-fool stubborn to teach a girl, he could pretend I was a boy." She leveled a black scowl at the old man. "And so he has called me boy ever since. *When* he remembers," she added sweetly.

"Huh. Memory's all it ever was." Marhan rattled his map. "Anyway, *boy*, what say we go this way and then—" a weathered finger traced across new, purplish landmarks. "Now, that hunter said it was *possible* to go this way, but I think if we came down further east—see, like so—and then he said there was—" Ylia followed him with all the concentration she had; it took that much to understand maps, and she admired the Swordmaster for his easy grasp of them. Not that she'd ever tell him so, of course.

Watches were kept singly to allow each as much uninterrupted sleep as possible. The next morning they were afoot before the sun topped the eastern ridges. They skirted the lake, forded a narrow brook and crossed the valley, bore north and a little west. They were deep in forest once again before they were twenty lengths past the far edge of the lake.

"Trail." Golsat came back to join them. "Deer. It holds near the waterfall. Hear it?" Impossible not to. "It veers west near the top of the ridge, turns back north. Faint, but better than none, I'd say."

"Mmmm." That was the way Marhan liked it; a true path of some kind. It irritated him when, as in the open rock field, he was forced to admit to himself that his eyes weren't what they should be.

The water remained within hearing all morning, but stayed out of sight. The trees were wide-spaced, the forest floor open. But still, they could not see any distance at all. For the first time in days, the snow-covered peaks were invisible.

Two days they traveled through heavy forest. The deer trail petered out early in the first afternoon, leaving them to rely on Golsat's sense of direction once again. The forest floor was thick with old needles, dead leaves.

The quiet was with them, the breathless hush they had come to associate with the Foessa, but never that unnatural silence encountered in the high ravine where the *seeming* was. Here were flowers on the berry bushes; a meadow thick with new yellow and lavender blossom, shoulder high, the heady drone of bees, and game, though they seldom saw anything but prints.

With no sign of anything unfriendly, even Nisana and Ylia began to relax, a little. Ylia spent most of the second day with Brendan, Brelian and Golsat, each one trying to top the others with outrageous old jokes and tales. Lisabetha, not far ahead with Malaeth, turned now and again to smile or laugh, though she still would not be drawn into conversation, and spent all of her time with the old nurse and the Swordmaster.

The next day saw them once again climbing through loose rock into a region of wind-twisted, gaunt pine, and then above even those. Just above tree line, they rested and took a long-overdue noon-meal while the foreguard searched out the easiest way down.

Marhan brought back the good news: "There is a trail, not far ahead." He dropped to the ground, gratefully accepted his share of the food and Brelian's water bottle. He was a little short of breath. "It leads to a ledge—wide and grassy—looks about two leagues long. But smooth and level." He swallowed. "There is another valley below that; I think we can reach it before dark. With luck." He chewed, washed down a rather tought bit of cold rabbit.

Malaeth fetched a relieved sigh. "This roundabouting is wearing. Come, Brel," she held a hand out to him, "help me up."

"If we can make better time there," Marhan began apologetically.

Malaeth sighed again but nodded. "If the footing's better, I can try, Swordmaster."

He flushed, a rare thing. "It's just—"

"Just," Brendan put in, "that we'll be until first snows at the rate we're presently walking. No, Malaeth, it's not your fault," he added, "But—"

"Never mind, lad." Malaeth patted his shoulder.

Far overhead, a raven cried harshly. There was shelter almost immediately from the ever-present high-country wind as they dropped down into a field of snow and ice-moved boulders. On the edge of hearing: water; the faint hiss of wind through the forest still well below them. Human footsteps rang loud and foreign.

Marhan led, followed by Lisabetha and Malaeth. Brendan,

Brelian and Levren then, together. Golsat. Ylia brought up the rear, Nisana's travel pouch now slung, much more comfortably, across her back.

She halted abruptly. A slithering of rock that did not belong to them, behind but a length or more to the right of the way they had just come. She listened intently—nothing. She shrugged, hurried to catch up. A sharp, thin "click!" rang in her ears as something struck hard against her left shoulder. She fell, more from surprise than the force of the blow.

"Golsat!" she hissed, and spun back around, crouched. Nisana was already on the ground, testing the air. No one to be seen *or* sensed, though there was certainly proof someone had been there. Golsat reached down to scoop up the glittering object near the swordswoman's feet: a black, hand-chipped and polished knife, its handle inlaid with tiny bits of shell. The tip was broken. He searched further, gathered up another finger's worth of blade from between two rocks.

"That was foiled by my mail." Ylia glanced across her shoulder cautiously. The others had stopped but were not close enough to hear. Good. She waved, smiled reassuringly. "Nothing important. Go ahead!"

"All right?" Levren demanded.

"All right!" she shouted.

Golsat balanced the knife on his hand. "Well. This is interesting."

"Interesting," Ylia snorted. "You might call it that."

"Mmm. We have a friend, it appears."

She laughed grimly. "No friend of *mine*." Her fingers closed around the broken shard and she pressed it into his palm as she stood. "Who might a knife like that belong to?"

He turned the knife over, ran a thumb gingerly along the edge. It was sharp, would easily cut to the bone. "I should know of this. Stone knives—well, no matter. I will think on it." He scanned the strewn boulders. "The one who threw this could be anywhere. We had better leave."

"Before Marhan becomes impatient."

Golsat laughed, pocketed the knife and pushed her down the trail before him. "When is he not? But for the safety of your four-footed friend, I think we'll give them another target. Whoever they are." Ylia picked up Nisana, let her climb into her pouch again.

Mothers. He takes these things so calmly; that's bravery for you. It didn't occur to her he thought almost exactly the same thing.

Matter closed. She strode forward, put on as much speed as she dared with such treacherous footing, so as not to hold them up. But she had a battle a while later when she confided to the brothers what had happened, for nothing would do but that Brendan must return and find the thrower of the knife.

"I would let it be, brother," Brelian said lightly, though even he looked, finally, a little irritated with Brendan's single-mindedness. "We may need you later—alive, please—and there is a long way to go before dark." But Brendan was determined, and Ylia's patience, tenuous at the moment anyway, finally snapped.

"All right, where do you intend to find him?" she demanded. "Do you think he is waiting there still, for you to come and slay him? By the Black Well, Bren, you could hide a barn in these rocks, let alone a man—or anything else! Have you eyes all about your head? And an inner sense to tell you when you need them behind you?" He hesitated. "I already *told* you I could sense nothing, human or animal, for leagues around us. What, then, does that leave you?" Brendan paled noticeably, though his eyes were still set. "Forget the thing, and keep your eyes open. I wager you will not need to go in search of it at all. The way our luck has run of late, it will find us!"

*Of all the enemies one might encounter,
the greatest is fear. So had I heard most of
my life. They who tell you this fail to add
that none believe it until chance places them
in the path of terrors. I know the truth of it
just so, and more than once even I was
nearly defeated by awaiting horror before I
saw the physical enemy. In this, young Ylia
and the child Lisabetha knew more than I—
or, in any event, learned it harder and
sooner.*

14

It was no great distance at all to the narrow ravine. Footing
within was treacherous, for there was loose rock and brush,
and much of the flat inner surface was taken up by a swift-
moving creek. But it was short, and they emerged without further mishap onto Marhan's ledge. A narrow trail, the merest
depression in the surrounding grasses, led nearly due north,
holding close to the western cliffs. The land to the right was
level for perhaps a dozen lengths, then fell smoothly away,
sloping gently for perhaps another five lengths. It sheared off
abruptly then, and the opposite wall of that canyon reared
high, a few ragged trees clinging to sheer walls and ledges. The
hollow roar of a great waterfall at some depth between the
stone walls echoed across the clearing.

There was a brief halt, only enough to allow Golsat to catch
up. Ylia, moved by some odd, nervous prickling, took a few
hesitant steps to the side, let her gaze wander. *We would be
fortunate to reach the far end of the ledge before dark, never
mind the valley beyond it.* But she could see Marhan's valley,

119

a pale green blurred by distance and a mist of ground fog. And the way between was straight and flat.

To the west, cliffs sloped raggedly up. Beyond them, snow-covered peaks were already shrouded in thick cloud: the sun would be setting early. A few clutches of black pine dotted the sward; heavy forest held the northern slopes. A flight of small birds swooped low, vanished across the southern ridges.

A profound discomfort nagged at her inner being. 'Search,' she whispered to herself. Alone—she *could*, given a little time, though not very thoroughly. Nisana slept heavily against her back, didn't stir at her weak mind-touch. "I mistrust this place, Marhan." The words were out before she realized she intended to speak at all. She bit her lip.

The Swordmaster turned on his heel; his mouth was set. "Mistrust." He heaped sarcasm onto the word. "Well, then, I hope you have another way for us to go! Or shall we stay here the night?"

"You—do not sense anything, do you?" Brelian asked. Reluctantly she shook her head. Nothing she could lay a finger, or a name to. But—

"Vapors, damn it, boy!" Marhan snapped. He had limped most of the afternoon and was in a surly mood indeed.

"No such thing, this is *me*, remember? I only said—"

"I say we move on," Marhan overrode her rudely. "Now. Before the weather blows up, as it looks ready to do. It is cold, it is getting late, we have perhaps an hour of sunlight. But I need not tell *you* that, need I?"

"Have you seen trace of game? Anything at all?" she asked, not without qualm. Bad to press Marhan when he was in such a foul mood; the moreso when she knew she could give no cause for fear. *What is wrong with me*? A nice, clear trail, the ending in plain sight—*have I reached the point of vapors after all*? She thrust the thought aside angrily. Damn the man! She glared at him.

Marhan was shaking his head impatiently. "Of course not, I wasn't looking for game! I was looking for a way *off* this damned plateau and into that valley for the night! Unless," he added nastily, "you would rather sleep on rock again?"

"Touchy old fool!" she mumbled to herself.

"*What*?"

"Nothing," she snapped aloud. "I said nothing!" Levren stepped neatly between them.

"Come, you have set us on guard, eh? We will be all right. It is still daylight, after all."

Ylia caught a grip on her temper and held it. Whatever was wrong with her, there was no cause to alienate the Bowmaster. "Levren, it was daylight when that bat-creature attacked us." She drew a deep breath, expelled it in a rush, adding, as he patted her shoulder, "Do not speak to me, please, as though I had lost my wit. I haven't!" He shrugged, stepped aside.

"That stone knife—are you certain it is not that which has you—" That was Brendan at her shoulder.

"Stone knife? *What stone knife?*" Lisabetha jumped to her feet and pushed past Marhan. Ylia spared Brendan a hard look as Golsat drew the blade and held it out. Lisabetha gazed at it intently; she would not touch it. "Where—where was this found?"

Golsat gestured with it. "Yonder, just into the stone field." He caught her arm, then, for she had gone dead white.

"There are tales of—no." She shut her mouth tightly, turned and tore loose from his grasp. Golsat frowned at the knife, restored it to his inner pocket.

Ylia scanned the trail, the land to both sides of it, the ravine behind them. Her own face was almost as pale as Lisabetha's, but her mouth was set, her eyes still dark with anger. "I have not lost my nerve, Bren, if that is what you think." Her voice barely carried to him, near as he stood. "There is something. Here. Something wrong, though I cannot put a name, or even a *kind* of wrong to it. But there is something." She swung around to face him, gazed in turn at her companions. "And I warn every one of you, right now. Watch! Since we go on—" Marhan nodded grimly. "Then let us go! As the Swordmaster has so kindly reminded me, we have no time to waste!"

Marhan mumbled something, glared at her one last time— she matched his glare with one of her own—and started out at a goodly pace. Malaeth squeezed the swordswoman's shoulder in silent sympathy as she and Brelian passed.

'Nisana.' 'Mmmph.' Mind-speech had finally made contact, only to encounter a thoroughly asleep cat, one not at all pleased to be wakened. 'Nisana!' 'Mmm—what?' *Mothers, is it something in the air, or are they kin*? Ylia wondered sourly. *Touchy creatures*! 'We need to search.'

A pause. Then, sharply: 'Why? I sense nothing. We searched in the rock field, again at the head of the ravine. I was asleep, Ylia. Make your own search!'

'I have. I can find nothing. But—'

'And so you woke me. You are as bad as Lisabetha,' she grumbled, and stretched, hard. 'Have you considered there might *be* nothing?'

'That is the third time I have been accused of cowardice,' Ylia stormed at her. 'And there *is* something—'

'There is nothing!' Nisana was worse than Marhan, given the right circumstance, and being roused from her afternoon nap was certainly one such. 'I sense nothing. This is not like the other places, where things were.' Silence. Ylia could feel the effort it took for the cat to get control of her anger. 'Ylia. By your own Mothers, I never implied you coward. But— *there—is—nothing—here*!' Her mind-speech reverberated.

Ylia's hands curled into fists. 'Oh—go back to sleep!'

'I intend to.' She mumbled to herself as she turned, seeking a comfortable position. Not far ahead, Marhan was still grumbling under his breath.

Chill air brushed her face; she pulled the cloak closer as a shadow obscured the sun. The upper peaks were buried under cloud, taking the sun under. Marhan's valley was rapidly vanishing in feathery drifts of mist.

An hour's steady walking brought them halfway down the ledge. The sun was gone for good; the world had turned a dreary, damp grey. Sheer streamers of fog floated over the ground, blown by a fitful breeze.

Marhan stopped, motioned the company close. "I daresay you'd like a rest. But—"

"No." Malaeth was winded but determined. "Not here." She glanced in Ylia's direction, but the girl's eyes were closed as she concentrated, oblivious for once of the reactions of those around her. Marhan rolled his eyes.

"No." Brendan shook his head. He stared at Ylia. *What has frightened her, who fears no more of anything than I do*? It worried him, both her odd reaction and the fact that he could do nothing about it. "Let us go on; there will be plenty of time for rest when we reach lower ground." He moved to Ylia's side, roused her with a touch as Marhan started off once again.

They had barely begun to move when thick cloud draped down the mountainside: one moment they could see, if not any great distance; the next they were enveloped in a moist, impenetrable curtain.

Seven hells! Marhan stopped short. *It's going badly, the fool girl*—no, he really couldn't blame it on her, things didn't go bad for thinking them. All the same, he was far from happy at the moment. *Quit fussing, old man; think instead*! "Ho, Levren!" he called out finally. His voice rang overloud, he hastily lowered it. "We had better walk in file here. All of you, hold onto the person before you, lest we lose one another. This should thin below but we must get there first."

"I'd think so." Levren's calm voice reassured him. They'd get there; of course they would. And the fog *would* be thinner.

Someone gripped his shoulder; Ylia. Hard to tell features, even so close, in this soup of a fog, but the plaits gave her away. "We will lead, Marhan. Nisana and I." She eased past him before he could agree or argue, ignored the dubious look he gave her and started off. Marhan sighed, caught at her shoulder, felt a reassuring tug on the hem of his cloak.

Not as useful in fog as at night, the second level of Sight, but better than a pair of normal eyes. Better, certainly, than Marhan's eyes. Ylia forced herself to a slow, reasonable pace: faster or slower and the old man would think her nervous or hesitant. Nisana climbed to her shoulder to aid her with cat's vision—her own inner strength bolstering the girl's use of the Sight.

Their progress slowed; the fog thickened as the sky grew dark with coming night, and now there was rock underfoot where small slides had come down. For the most part, however, the trail remained clear. Ylia scowled at it, at the scarce visible rocks and trees they occasionally passed. Her mistrust was growing by the moment. But there was no other way; without the trail as guide, they'd be hopelessly lost in moments.

She smiled briefly, humorlessly. Could anyone have seen their progress, they'd surely have laughed: She in the lead, a small black and orange cat teetering on her shoulder, both peering uncertainly into the fog, she calling aid to those behind; Marhan, limping, scowling and chewing at his moustaches, holding firmly to her free shoulder. Golsat holding to his; Malaeth behind Golsat, clinging to the ties of his jerkin and Lisabetha holding the edge of the old woman's cloak.

Brelian with a hand on her arm, Brendan holding the edge of his brother's cloak, and Levren at the rear, one hand holding Bren's cloak, and his free hand, like Bren's, holding a drawn sword. *We must resemble a company of blind mummers.*

'Ylia.' A soft murmur in her mind. 'There *is* an unwholesome feeling to this mist. Although—I cannot precisely say why.' As close to an apology as she'd ever get from Nisana, but at the moment more than welcome.

'Search, then. *Please.* I will be more glad than you could guess if you prove me wrong. But I think—' The words died away; she gagged, stumbled, nearly unseating Nisana, as a gust of pure Fear struck, fresh and close at hand! It was gone in the same instant, leaving her to wonder what she *had* sensed. Marhan's fingers tightened on her shoulder. "Sorry, Marhan. A rock."

"What—was—that?" He hadn't even heard her: his voice was hoarse, unsteady, but he had the presence of mind to keep it low.

How did he, of all people, sense that? Mothers and all the gods at once, was it clear to more than me? " 'Ware, Swordmaster!" A tickling of it stole across her mind, raising the hairs on her neck. Nisana growled low in her throat. To the left—no—right? 'Nisana?'

'I cannot tell!'

'It is here. With us.' *Damn the fog, I can barely see a pace before me and it's not yet dark.* 'We—we'll have to stop— we'll have to—' Her thought was a wild babble; somehow, half-ill with terror, she caught it and forced it still.

'Where, girl?' Nisana's thought was no more controlled than her own. The Fear nudged at them, stealthily. 'Keep moving, leave it behind—if we can.' Rock clattered down across the trail not far behind.

'Nisana, if we—' Ylia's breath caught in her throat. The Fear struck again, hard, just in front of her.

"Draw sword!" Marhan *had* felt it. "Something unclean walks this ledge with us!" Nisana sprang to the ground. The screel of several swords drawn at once was drowned by a terrified scream and sounds of struggle.

"Lisabetha! Lisabetha, no! I will keep you safe, I swear it, do not fight me!" Brelian's voice overrode hers. Ylia pushed back past the Swordmaster, who crouched a little to the left of the path, blades in hand, peering near-sightedly into the fog. He was swearing under his breath. Lisabetha, a dim shape in a thinning patch of grey, struggled with Brelian like a mad thing. A blur of movement—she threw him across her body and to the ground as though he were a child, turned and sped under Levren's arm, hared back down the trail. The rest of the company stood rooted in shock.

Ylia was the first to move. Marhan's shout reached her; she slowed only to call over her shoulder: "Guard the others, I will get her! She is not worth two lives!" But as she ran headlong after the girl, boots thudded after her. Brelian.

"You cannot deny me. I lost her, mine to regain her!"

"With my aid," she panted. "You cannot see five paces in this!" But the fog was thinning, drifting across the trail in swirling eddies as a cold air blew down from the heights. Clearly, all at once, they could see the girl not far ahead—a slender, flying form, her cloak twisting wildly behind her. But, with each step, they were gaining.

Lisabetha—and what? Small, pale, spidery things leaped and fell from the ledges and overhanging rock, more sprang from the trees and she was surrounded. Then, with a horrid shriek, she was down. At that moment, a massive shielding dropped away. Ylia staggered back into Brelian, who had stopped as though struck. The Fear-That-Follows! She gagged, would have fallen, but Brelian grabbed her arm and shook her fiercely.

"There is no time for that, we will lose her!"

She swallowed, fought terror. It receded, a little, at least to the point where she could again move. Lisabetha had risen to her feet once more, but could not break free. Brelian drew his sword, slipped his dagger from its arm sheath and cried: "Lisabetha! To your aid!" and he was gone. *Go, don't think, just do it*! She gripped her hilts hard, ran forward to meet the horror that was already turning on them.

For a space, then, she was fighting for her life and could take no stock of whether Lisabetha still lived. Brelian fought with savage determination an arm's length away, but could make no headway. Thrust, parry, duck as a rock hurled at her head crashed into the ledges behind. Lunge. The Fear was a constant pressure against her inner being. How many of the foul, many-legged things she slew she could no longer recall.

But slowly they were being driven back, she and Brelian, back up the trail. And sounds of battle behind told her the rest of the company was already beset.

Time ceased to have meaning. Then her head cleared a little, and she found herself standing against the western wall of the ledge, a narrow stone shelf behind her heels marking the end of any retreat, from there fighting an enemy to which there was no end, though the bodies of their fallen littered the trail, and the ground as far as she dared look. Brelian —there, a length away, dangerously in the open. Lisabetha—perhaps. And Brelian was still trying to cut through the foe that way. Levren and Golsat stood together, shielding Malaeth, who crouched in terror under a slab of rock, while Marhan fought grimly away to the left of them. Brendan, somewhat to her surprise, had taken a position hard against her left shoulder and was wielding his blades with cool skill, crying encouragement to the others: "Ho, Golsat, that was a good thrust! Brother, to your right—hah! A fine play, if a trifle shorter than I like them. But a good height for removing heads from shoulders, eh, my Lady?"

"Perfect, my Lord!" she shouted back, trying to match his banter. But it was hopeless. *Hopeless as any chance that we might win free of this place. That any of us should live to see the sun rise. But—but to die at the hands of these. . . .* The Fear clung to her like the cloying smell of death; she shook her head in a vain attempt to clear it, fought even harder.

A moment's respite; the creatures withdrew. Not far enough so they could escape, but enough to allow them to breathe. Ylia looked over her companions. No one badly hurt yet, but—*Nisana?* Realization smote her, hard. She had not seen the cat—since when? 'Nisana!' The inner voice was shrill with fear. 'Here, silly girl.' Familiar, reassuring pressure against her leg. 'You scared me, cat!' 'Worry for yourself, girl; I'm well enough.' 'But, Nisana—' 'But.' The cat gazed up at her. 'We'd better have an end to this soon. Stay here, watch only.' Before Ylia could even open her mouth to protest, the pressure was gone and a shimmering lit the ledge, her sword, Brendan's. Power surged across them.

And a mountain cat stood where Nisana had been: a snow-white cloud-cat, twice the size of any real cloud-cat. The colors of Power played about its head and shoulders; its eyes were twin suns. It yowled, exposing long teeth; Baelfyr touched the canines. Its cry echoed, etched itself across human eardrums, vibrating through the ground. The cloud-cat snarled then, leaped from the rock.

The creatures shrieked, scrambled madly aside and fled down the trail, leaving their dead behind.

And then, there was only a small, tortoise-shell cat crouched on the damp ground. Brendan drew back, the breath hissing between his teeth. Ylia's sword and dagger clattered to the rocks, she leaped down to gather Nisana up. 'I—I did not know you could do that!'

'Well, I was not certain I could, not anymore.' Dry, but so weak!

Human arms tightened convulsively, forcing a faint squeak out of her. 'Nisana!'

'Shhh. Don't worry. And don't *hold* so tight!' she added tartly. 'I am weary, I must rest. It—it is demanding, a shape-changing.' She sounded apologetic, rather embarrassed. 'What happens, when you do not use what you have.' Ylia fumbled with the straps of the riding pouch one-handedly. She was shaking. Levren pulled the thing free for her; Nisana crept inside, her movements slow, cautious.

"Lev?" For the first time, Ylia became fully aware of their surroundings. It was quiet, dark. Dead creatures all around them; none, that she could see, alive.

"They are gone." Blood trickled down his sword hand and he favored his left leg. "But so is Lisabetha. And I fear," he glanced over his shoulder, cautiously lowered his voice, "that Brelian is badly hurt." Brelian caught the look if not the words, shook his head.

"No, I am fine. Honestly." He was not. His voice shook, his face was white. "They have taken Lisabetha, I saw them, I must go after!" Nor would he be dissuaded.

Ylia handed Nisana's travel pouch over to Levren. The cat slept so soundly already that she was not aware of it. "Guard her well, Lev. She saved us, and will not be able to fend for herself for some time. Keep the others here until Brelian and I return."

Boots scuffled up behind her. "Boy, if you think you're going anywhere, let alone after those—"

"Marhan, would you rather let Corlin's daughter die, at the hands of those things? Or maybe we should let Brelian go after her alone? He will, unless you tie him; *look* at him!"

"I'm not talking about Lisabetha, *or*, Brelian," Marhan snapped. "I'm talking about *you*, going after that hoard of nightmare beings!"

"All right. You know what they were using against us, though, don't you? Sorceries, black sorceries. If *you* go with Brel, how do you plan to deal with them? I haven't much Power, and little enough to cope with that, but I'm all we have." She met his glare unflinchingly. "There is no time to argue, Marhan. I *have* to go." Silence. "Do you think I *want* this?" Silence again. "It does not matter." She turned away. "You trained me, you know my skills, turn loose of me as you would any of these men!" She took her blades from Golsat, waved Brelian to follow. He shook off his brother's restraining arm and came resolutely behind.

Once again they took the back trail, but slowly now. In spite of his reassurances, Brelian walked as one stunned or sorely hurt, and Ylia needed to cast about with a mind-search to find where the enemy had gone. They had vanished, in those short moments, as though the earth had swallowed them.

As, in a sense, it had. Before and to the left, down the long incline, there: a strong accumulation of Fear, strong as a beacon. *How, how did I not sense it earlier*? The answer to that was easy, frightening. *Because it had need for secrecy. Because it can shield against AEldra power when it has need. Because it has no fear of being followed, horror that it is, to its lair.* It has greatly misjudged its prey this time, she thought grimly, and the thought steadied her. A little. Enough.

A tight copse of a dozen or so trees; in their midst a tall jumble of stone and slabbed rock. And at the center of that jumble an opening into the earth, leading down and in, at a height not much more than a man's, wide enough for two. Just within the entrance lay one of the creatures, dead and pale in the starlight. A short sword was still clutched in one of its forelimbs.

Carefully, hoarding her pitiful strengths against future need, she knelt to probe the black opening. Brelian leaned against the rock, guarding the rear. She could hear his labored breathing, sense the pain in it. There, the Fear that said they had gone this way, that they were not far ahead by straight measure. There, also, another fear which radiated like a madness, and she knew Lisabetha still lived. Though for how long, who could say?

"Brelian." Silence. She glanced up. He leaned against the rock for support, hunched over a little, and his breath was coming in gasps between clenched teeth. "Brel. They have gone this way. But you—"

"No. I cannot leave her." His voice shook. "If my Lisabetha lives in that place, I swear I will bring her forth alive, though I perish myself." He choked, swallowed hard. Ylia caught at his arms with suddenly chilled fingers.

"Brel. Listen to me. If we go—in there, we must both be strong. If you—Brel, are you all right?" Fear gripped her at sight of his face. To lose him, and the girl. . . . But he shook his head.

"I am winded, that is all."

It wasn't true, anyone could see that. But she knew she could not convince him to wait, could not leave Lisabetha, either. *No choice. Mothers guard us!* She drew a deep breath, let out a little of the fear with it. "Then you had better live as well, my friend. One of us may need to carry her, and I would rather it were not me!" He smiled, a mere ghost of a thing, and plunged into the tunnel without further word.

The darkness was absolute at first, and without the second level of Sight they would have come early to grief: The tunnel twisted and the floor was uneven, strewn with rock and dirt fallen from ceiling and walls. Not far from the entrance, however, the cave suddenly widened and a thin, yellowish light came from the walls and floor, not unlike gaslight over the southern swamps. There was a cloying odor that coated her mouth. *Dead things.* It was disgusting, but there was no room in her for further fear. She glanced at her companion, increased her speed now that he could see as well.

Silence, save for the muted plop of water dripping somewhere. Ylia stopped, caught at Brelian's arm when he would have gone on. The light was fading, a little; directly before them was a sharp bend. "We're gaining on them."

"Good." He closed his eyes briefly, nodded. He started forward, paused as her hand caught at his sleeve again. His face was greenish in the evil light. "They are beyond that corner, Brel; another moment, we'll be on them." Her voice was steady, low-pitched, muted by the stone and dirt all around them.

"Then—"

"I will create a diversion with the Baelfyr and thereafter

take rearguard. You must grab Lisabetha, retreat as quickly as
you can. Will you do this?''

"I—but you cannot—"

"I can," she hissed fiercely. "Do not be another Marhan. I
am protected in a way you are not, either of you, remember
that!" He nodded reluctantly. "*She* is your concern, Brel. If
you stay to aid me, we will all die!" That, finally, reached
him. "And I am not Brendan. I will take no unnecessary
chances, believe that! Do not waste the ones I must take." He
nodded again, this time in true agreement. "All right, then."

Her heart lurched, painfully. His cloak had fallen aside, revealing a dark, damp stain on his breeches, just below the belt.
Even as she stared, it spread, ever so slightly.

*Oh, no. That's a killing touch. How far has he come with
that? And, how far can he still go?* "Brelian?" He gripped her
arm reassuringly, even dredged up a smile. Tears blurred her
vision, she dashed them angrily away. "Damn you, you lied to
us!" His gaze followed hers, the smile faded. He shrugged
then.

"It doesn't matter, Ylia. Don't worry, I'll get her out."

She wrapped an arm around his shoulders, kissed his cheek.

"I know you will." It was a real smile, however blurred
with tears. Brelian briefly tightened his grip on her arm,
turned to start down the tunnel. "Go when you have her, and
go quickly, swear it!" She wiped her eyes on her sleeve;
gripped sword hilts with a hand that was beginning to shake.

"I swear it," Brelian said quietly. They moved together,
rounded a turn directly into those they pursued.

There were fifteen of them milling before a black cleft in the
rock; Lisabetha stood bound in their midst, clearly visible, for
she stood a full two heads taller than they. The last of the
yellow light turned them an unwholesome grey-white.

Lisabetha's eyes widened; her lips moved, but no sound
came. Then: "Brelian!" A breathy, shrill little sound.
Enough. The creatures whirled about. Some turned to fly and
one or two vanished through that narrow slit, but others
brought forth swords and knives.

This is it. She stopped, leveled both hands at them and cried
aloud. The draining left her faint, but Baelfyr leaped forth as
it never had before, spreading green-edged flame among them.
Pandemonium. She cut through those still standing, hurled
Lisabetha behind her, freed her sword. "Take her and *go!*"

She sensed, rather than saw, Brelian draw the terrified girl up the passageway, leaving her alone with the Fear.

She was blocking the tunnel, and only seven of the fifteen were still alive and willing to fight. *If—no.* The Power was gone, at least for the moment. *But so much of it—I did that, I did.* She thrust the thought aside as the creatures, seeing she made no further use of the horrid flame, eagerly leaped forward.

A sudden calm washed through her as she slowly gave way up the passage, holding back as long as she dared so that Brelian and his Lady could reach clean air. The Fear pressed at her, but it somehow didn't matter.

Thrust, parry, parry again. A rock, awkwardly thrown, glanced off the wall and into her shoulder; she pivoted, drove her blade through the thrower. Lunge again; parry with the dagger as yet another of them tried to slip to her blind side.

Pace by slow pace she retreated toward the outer world, leaving a trail of dead and dying. *Have I taken a wrong turning? It could never have been so far.* The thought chilled her; she thrust it aside. More of them from below—*like ants, without number or end.* That thought, too, had better be squelched at once. And then—

Darkness. She stumbled as rubble caught her heels and the light faded. "Nearly there," she whispered. To use any of the Power at all made her legs tremble, but the second level of Sight was absolutely necessary. Worth the drain. Her sword arm ached, her fingers hurt.

Movement to her left—she whirled, lunged. A side tunnel; one of them had come from it. Another opening to the right—she started as cooler air touched her face, stumbled hurriedly past it. Empty. Was that fresh air behind? She drew a deep breath. Perhaps. Another step—another, *oh, Mothers, almost, almost—*

A stunning blow crashed against the side of her neck, something hurtled against her legs. She fell.

Breathe deeply, for the Power must have calm and assurance to work; believe, and you drive out fear. So the Training Manual in the First Uses of Power tells us. And so I told the child all the years I trained her. For all her denial of the skills, the Power and the greater strengths themselves, it is rewarding to know that once, at least, she must have listened to me.

15

She did not completely lose consciousness, but she could not force her eyes to open. The Fear pressed upon her, filled her, and there was no strength of will left to fight it away. Cold, boneless fingers brushed her face. A long silence, followed by sudden movement; her arms were bound, her feet. A bandage was dragged across her mouth, tightened.

Move! Don't let them. . . . She tried to raise her head, subsided as the movement threatened to make her ill. Her body was jolted up, onto hard shoulders, moved. Down, further into the tunnels.

It was a long, slow journey, all in the dark, and the way twisted constantly. Always downhill. After what seemed a very long time, they dumped her onto a stone floor. *Move.* But other hands caught at her shoulders before she could, pulled her to sitting, retied her arms to a heavy post set in the rock. Warily, cautiously, she opened her eyes.

Gloomy, not entirely dark. The cavern was large and low-vaulted, its far end lost in shadow. Several entrances were visible from where she sat, dark holes leading into darkness. *Lost.* It smote her like a blow. Any of them might have been the en-

132

trance they'd bundled her through.

The only light came from an enormous firepit not far away.
A flat, dressed stone lay near it. Within a length of the firepit
sat a huddle of the silent, spidery horrors. More entered from
one of the passages.

*Did I take enough time . . . did they get free? If Brelian's
strength held. . . .* She held her thoughts fiercely away from
herself. What would they do now, her companions? One lost,
another near to death. . . . She closed her eyes, probed the core
of the Power, but it was cold and dead; even the use of the second level of Sight was denied her. *Time. If there's enough of
it, enough for the Power to rebuild itself.* But it frightened
her, a little. *If I used all I had, more than I had right to. If I
used everything, all of it in that burst of Baelfyr.* Not a good
thing to think of. She twisted her hands, worried the bonds
that held them. Tight, not unbearably so; with care, they
might become loose. *And then?*

Weapons. If she could pick one or more of those nearest
her, take them unaware. Perhaps. Worth a try. Worth the
thought, anyway. She studied those grouped near the firepit.
Verdren's warning—the one she and Nisana had triggered—
Fear. Fear-That-Follows. What manner of thing was it? But
when the inner voice would have answered, she hastily silenced
it.

They were not truly spiderlike, for they had six limbs instead of eight—two for standing, a third some were using to
brace themselves upright, three with handlike bifurcated tentacles. Most of them wore a weapons-belt slung across the
roundish body, and these had short swords—iron, by the look
of it, and not well-forged at that. Those without the belts carried spears tipped with chipped stone blades. One or two held
bows, though these seemed poorly crafted and could not have
had any great range. Many of them were naked under hide
cloaks roughly pieced together, the fur still hanging in ragged
patches from the inner side; a few wore a longer tuniclike garment woven from grasses and hair.

The faces—she could hardly stand to look upon them. Eyes
large and nearly round, giving them the intense look of owls.
They did not blink. Eyes the color of blood, without white,
without brows, though on some a semblance of brows had
been painted or tattooed, along with lines on the backs of the
primary tentacle-arms. They had hair, lank stuff the color of

the skin, so that from any distance they appeared to have
none. Boneless narrow faces, with the merest of noses: thin
slits between the eyes, above the mouths.

The mouths. Things of nightmare: Pale tongues, long
pointed teeth, no lips of any sort. *Whatever I have slain by the
tens this night, I will call down no disfavor of the Guardians
for taking human life. These—they are not human*!

The thought struck her funny, she could almost have
laughed at it. *Well? Go ahead, call upon the Guardians, why
not? And—and yes, the Mothers—why not the One of the
Chosen? See which of them will aid you from this hell!* She
flexed her hands again—the rope was looser, but not loose
enough.

The chamber was suddenly and painfully lit as wood was
thrown on the fire, torches lit and jammed into clefts in the
walls. Those near the firepit crept away as another entered,
surrounded by attendants: chief or shaman. He wore some
kind of dark red robe that left only his head and primary arms
exposed. An obsidian dagger hung from a strap around his
neck. He moved to the dressed stone, sat, gestured to those
who guarded the prisoner. One of them caught at her plaits,
tore the gag free.

She worked her aching jaw back and forth, spat. The shaman watched with those impassive, expressionless eyes. But
when he spoke, the language he used—haltingly, and with
many ancient and long-unused words—was the speech of
Nedao!

"You are of the Plain. Why do you come here, to slay my
folk?"

"I—you ask this of me?" Her voice cracked shrill, out of
control, but the creature took no heed that she had spoken at
all.

"You do not belong here. Is it not enough you drove us
from the warm lands to these high places? This is our home
now, the home of Mathkkra. You do not belong here."

He waited then, but she was stricken dumb. *Not Mathkkra,
no*! Terror momentarily blinded her; a roaring filled her ears
and she would have fallen over had the post not kept her
upright. She had never listened when she was a child to those
tales; she still avoided them, those that told of the cave
dwellers, the blood drinkers, the Mathkkra. Pale as death
itself, it was said, they stole into the Plain on dark nights, kill-

ing, drinking the blood of whatever kind of thing they killed. Until Merreven ha'da Wergn had ridden against them, slain them all. In hundreds of years, none had been seen, and they had become figures to carry at Harvest-Fest, creatures in tales to frighten imaginative children.

She bit her lip hard. The shaman watched her with those red, near-round eyes.

"You killed many of our kind this night. Also, you took away the one they would have brought here. You take its place." There was an obscene grace in the movement as he wrapped opposing tentacles around the haft of the knife, held it aloft. A murmur of many whispering voices filled the chamber. The blood drained from her face.

"I would not attempt it." Somehow her voice came steady. "I carry the ancient sorceries in my body!"

"That cannot aid you. It has aided none of those who come here. Those brought to this place die by the knife, as you will." The chipped blade glittered in the torchlight.

"Then free my hands and give me my dagger," she said through suddenly dry lips. "It is not fit that a warrior die so!"

A strange gurgling noise—the creature was laughing! "No. You are of Nedao, human. Not fit. Any of my people would know shame to fight you."

"And those who lie dead above?" But the horror was rising in her again; she caught her lip between her teeth, hard. *Do not beg, do not show fear, do not! You shame yourself to no purpose.* She lowered her gaze, wished in that instant she had not. At her right hip, a shallow depression had been chipped into the rock. Its interior was dark-stained, dark splash marks surrounded it.

Round, red eyes stared at her from all sides; she closed her own, commended herself to the Guardians and the Mothers.

With that, somehow, came a measure of calm. A death such as this—but cleaner than that she had already faced twice over. Better than that her companions might yet face. Grief tugged at her, tightened her throat. *To never see them again.* . . . Worse, that she could not warn them, could give them no aid—grim purpose pushed that aside. *I will take some of these with me when I die, and it will not be like a tame pig with a knife in my throat!* So faint a thing—but the Power was stirring, returning sluggishly to life. She formed the words her mother had used upon Koderra's walls at the last. *I command the manner of my own death, and that of any within this chamber.* It was comfort of a kind.

Whispering. Those about the fire fed it again; sharp-edged shadows cut along the walls, pressed across the low ceiling. A chanting began somewhere beyond the firepit, was spreading, now rising, now fading as some took it up and others ceased. Words she could not understand. But there was no need, the meaning was all too clear.

"Daughter." She jumped, jarring her head against the post, stared wildly around the red-lit cavern. Whose voice? No Mathkkra; Power had vibrated through the single word, setting her blood to humming. "Your life is not asked this night. Take your birthright and go from this place!"

Take my—she could have wept. *My birthright! Look to what pass it had already brought me, sword and half-blown Power both!* Silence, inner silence, and the sensation was gone, her heart thumped erratically but her blood no longer sang. Foolish hope. No. *What I am*, she whispered to herself, *and what I have, that I shall use, and woe to these who have driven me to such a pass!* She felt warily within; relaxed. The Power was her own, as it always had been: weak, useful in its own way. Useful enough now. She withdrew into herself, only vaguely aware that the shaman had risen and cast aside his blood-red robes, that another, bearing a stone bowl, had moved to his side.

Breathe deeply, for the Power must have calm and assurance to work; believe and you drive out fear. How many times had Scythia spoken those words, how often had Nisana pressed them upon her? Time hesitated; those around her were moving at a dream's slow pace. Calm. One deep breath. Another. *Ready.* She reached into the center of her strength and drew upon it as she had never dared before.

And it responded! Her cheeks burned as it surged through her body: So much, more than there had ever been, more than she had ever imagined, as though the true Power, unsullied as it had come from the Nasath was filling her inner being, spilling out through her fingertips, her hair, exhaled upon her breath. She vibrated with it. *Mine, ah mine!*

Her eyes had misted, suddenly cleared. The shaman stood naked before the dressed stone, holding the black knife in one forelimb. Another stood at his side, a rough stone bowl clasped between two forelimbs. First blood to the gods, she thought, and shivered. But those around her were wrapped in that mesmerizing chant which now echoed through the low chamber; none of them, certainly, were aware of the change in their prisoner. She drew her knees in, braced her back against the post.

A sudden silence. The fire burned higher, the air itself seemed to have taken on the red that was only the reflection of fire. What was it—something—something foul, something unspeakable. Or—were there only these? No, something had once been here, had left behind a sense of itself that was all too clear to her newly awakened senses. Something worse, much worse, than these—

A shadow fell between her and the fire: the shaman and his acolyte had reached the sacrifice post. She could not look. One of them caught her plaits, pulled hard; her throat lay open, exposed to the knife poised overhead. In that moment, she acted.

One low word: The bonds fell from her arms and legs, the knife flew back, clattered to the stone floor and was broken into shards. She knelt, cried aloud as she brought her hands up against those who surged forward. Baelfyr rolled in great balls around the chamber, crackled and danced from the ceiling. Those nearest fell dead, the rest fled in howling terror.

All save one—for she seized the acolyte, forced her way into his mind and ordered him to lead her forth. He turned blindly, stone dish crashing unnoticed to the rock, scuttled for one of the entrances. Just beyond, she turned back, cried out once more. The ceiling fell in with a roar, trapping within dead and dying alike, shaking the tunnel. Rocks and dirt fell around her, the ground shook.

She hurried on, urging the guide to greater speeds as the desire for fresh air and clean light became a driving need. Left. Right. Right again. Straight a distance. Another tunnel to the left, and a certainty that Mathkkra fled this way. She shouted out: the ancient words shaped themselves; the entrance collapsed. Moments later she reached familiar ground and struck down her guide. On. On and up.

She plunged full speed into the darkness of the upper tunnel, sweating and cold at the same time, a sudden sharp pain in her side, her breath coming raggedly. First light was on the trees; the boulders surrounding the entrance were a pale grey. There Marhan, Levren and Golsat waited, swords at the ready. She staggered, spent, into the open, and Lev caught her as she fell.

She blinked at him. "You—you were coming after me." He had to bend close to catch the words.

"Of course. You didn't think we would leave you, did you? We had to see the others were safely bestowed first." Golsat knelt at her other side, gripped her shoulder. Metal in his free hand glinted red in the light of the newly risen sun. Her sword, her dagger.

"I found them five paces within the tunnel," he said. *So close. I knew I was close.* She stirred, pulled herself to her knees. Marhan reached for her then.

"Bad?" he demanded, gently. His eyes were darkly worried. She nodded. "You are not injured?" She shook her head. "Swear it?"

"Swear it. Worn, not hurt." Difficult to concentrate enough to form the words. "This—Lev, help me up, this place must be closed."

He eyed her doubtfully, cast an even more doubtful glance at the slabbed, deepset rock. "We can try. But—"

"No. Not that way. Help me up."

"Well—" But he pulled to his feet, bringing her up with him. She walked back to the opening easily enough but had to lean against the rock for support. Whispered, then, the words of destruction. The inner ceiling shattered well down into the tunnel. *Not the only way. There must be others, find them.* Gods, it hurt to think. She shook that off, clutched at harsh rock, probed. There—the Fear. She spoke the words again. And again. Until only a *seeming* of it remained, as it had in the footprints. Nothing else.

"Brel. Lisabetha. Did they—are they with the others?"

Marhan's face was grim. "We moved south again after you left us, to wait. It would have been folly to come after you when we were spent, senseless to throw away lives if there was no need. The trail led here, we knew where you had gone. And there—there was hope you would win free." He wrapped an arm around her, led her up the slope.

"Not long after we came, Brelian staggered forth, leading the girl, and he fell. She is with Malaeth, and has not spoken or ceased weeping since he brought her, but—"

Ylia gripped his forearm so tightly he winced. "No, he is not dead. Or he wasn't when we came back for you, at least.

But—it will not be long. How," he added furiously, "were we to know he was hurt so?"

"He would not let us stop him, you know that," the Bow-master assured him. "Not that it makes things better for us. But—his choice." She could see the smoke now, among the rocks to the left of the trail.

"I didn't know myself until too late, do not blame yourselves." She was short of breath; hard to talk, still, from events, as much as physical weariness. "Marhan's right. He knew, he accepted the consequences." She forced a quicker pace; bruised and stiff muscle protested. "Take me to him, if he has not fallen into the last silence, I may be able to save him." Marhan wasted no time with questions for a change. Levren and Golsat moved out ahead of them, and she wondered at that but was too blank of mind, too concerned with other more important things to pay much heed.

If I could heal him—I can try. Even if the healing is not mine, I can do him no harm. The Power sang through her inner being.

Malaeth and Lisabetha sat away from the others; the girl leaned against Malaeth's arm, her eyes closed. Malaeth patted her hair absently, but her attention was for the bundle of rags near the fire. It was with a shock Ylia realized that bundle was Brelian, wrapped in his own cloak and his brother's. Brendan hunched on the ground beside him.

She knelt. The boy's face was white and cold, his eyes were closed, brow puckered with the pain he had denied in the tunnels. Brendan looked up; his face was haggard, his eyes red. Chilled fingers caught at her arm. She pulled the coverings away, laid a hand against Brelian's throat. The pulse was rapid, weak, like his breath. She probed the wound with a delicate mind-touch. Not deep, no. But he had lost too much blood: His desperate rescue of Lisabetha might well have cost all he had to give.

"Brendan." She touched his hand where it still clutched her arm. He gazed at her blankly. "Go and bring me water, and then leave me. I will need quiet if I am to try to save him."

"You—" Sudden hope brought him to his feet.

If I fail now. . . . She didn't dare think it. "I will try. I don't know what I can do. I'll try."

He swallowed tightly, walked as though this was the first he had stood in long, cold hours. But as he went around the fire, he passed the women and he stopped to look down at Lisabetha. Unwillingly, she gazed up, shrank from what she saw in his face.

"You." His voice was flat. "Unworthy as ye are, for all your great House, my brother looked upon ye as the only woman in his world. And ye would none of him. Well." He drew a deep, shuddering breath. "See where he lies!" More he would undoubtedly have said but he choked and turned hastily away. Lisabetha hid her face in her hands, and her shoulders shook.

Brendan returned the other way around the fire, and would have dropped back to the place he had held. But Ylia took his hand, willed him a measure of calm. "Go, Brendan. Keep lookout for us. If I can save him, by the Mothers I swear I will." At first she thought he hadn't heard; he gazed blankly between her and his brother, his lips moving. Then he turned, suddenly, and strode hurriedly away.

She sat back on her heels, put the water aside, studied the dying Brelian. Once—once only had she seen anyone attempt the healing of one so far gone—*and Gors died anyway*. She closed her eyes, then, laid both hands on the boy's brow, withdrew into her new strength.

The words—those, at least, she knew. Silence, total, inner silence. Focus Power through the hands: There was a sudden warmth in her fingers. Her pulse quickened. 'Shhh. Shhh.' Silence all triumph; silence, too, the inner speech that distracts. Light filled her; the warmth spread up her arms.

All at once, she knew what to do. *Mother was right, Nisana was.* They'd told her how, patiently instructed, put aside her protests she'd never have use or need. She was smiling as she traced the sign of healing over Brelian, willed strength back into his body, felt it knit under her fingers, traced the wound lightly as skin and muscle rejoined. A scar he might have, yes, but even that impossibly faint. Nothing worse. A deep inner peace washed through her, the body under her hands stirred as Brelian drew a deep, even breath. Another.

She blinked. There was already color back in his thin face. Brendan approached hesitantly, caught at her hands as she stood. "It's all right, he'll live, Bren. He will sleep a while, that is all." He drew a ragged breath and fell to his knees at his brother's side. Tears ran down his face.

*A gift and a talent, the Power, so they tell
us; a thing which must be constantly used,
or lost. Or, at the very least, a thing which, if
infrequently used, takes dangerous
amounts of one's strength. As I well knew;
had I not so instructed Scythia in her time,
my own young, and later young Ylia?
Embarrassing, to say the least, that I proved
unable to act as I taught.*

16

Ylia sat for a long time, staring blankly into the tiny fire;
they all did. *We look like death.* Her clothes were matted with
dirt from the tunnel, stiff with sweat; hair stuck to her cheeks,
strands of it wrapped around her arm: one of her plaits had
come unbound somewhere during the night. The men were all
unshaven and unkempt; Lisabetha's hair had fallen from
its high crown of braiding, her face was black-smudged,
streaked; Malaeth's eyes were dark and heavy-lidded, her face
slackly pale. Levren's cloak was torn across the shoulder,
there was dried blood on his upper arm. He limped. Marhan's
sleeve was sliced from shoulder to cuff, and the creases around
his eyes and mouth were deep shadows in the morning light.
Even Brendan looked as though he had rolled in mud, his dark
red-brown hair and beard were tangled wildly together. Golsat
stared at the rock ledge, toyed absently with the obsidian dagger; a long, ugly cut ran down his temple, blood matted his
beard and had spilled in thin dribbles onto his shirt.

They were near to collapse, every one of them. But they
dared not stay where they were, even if any of them had
wished to. For the moment, though, no one had the energy to

move, to begin the preparations that would lead to their going on.

Ylia tested their surroundings cautiously. The Fear was gone, save for that vaporish holdover among the rocks. But that meant nothing—it had hidden from her before, likely it could still do so. "We had better move on, soon." She formed the words, could not put sound behind them.

Only luck or the will of the Mothers themselves had spared the company from complete disaster this time; another such incident might prove their undoing. But—no, she dared not count upon the new strength that danced through her veins, even though it clasped her inner being as Nisana's fur fit her body.

"Swordmaster." Golsat thrust the Mathkkra knife into his jerkin. Marhan roused himself. "We surely do not wish to spend another night here?"

"If I must carry Lisabetha myself, I will not see the sun set from the ledge again!" Malaeth declared fervently. Marhan studied Brendan, who had not moved from his brother's side.

"The lad *will* mend?" he asked. His voice was pitched low, even though Brendan looked unlikely to hear at all. "You are certain?"

"He is healed, Marhan," Ylia replied, as softly. "It will do no harm if he is carried from here. He sleeps, that is all, and will sleep for some time. To regain his strength."

Marhan studied them one after another, measuringly. "All right. Lev. Golsat. If we carry Brel on his cloak—what do you think, can we?" Levren nodded, rose slowly, frowned as he put weight on his left leg. Ylia scattered the fire and struggled to her feet; aching bone and muscle protested fiercely. She drew Nisana's pouch, with its still-sleeping cargo, over her head, took sword in hand.

Brendan and Levren each took a lead corner of Brelian's cloak, Marhan and Golsat the other two, and they started off slowly. Malaeth was stiff, unsteady: cold and lack of sleep had left her weak and ill. Lisabetha held to her feet grimly and was walking unaided, though her eyes were vague and she seemed to take in little of what happened around her. Ylia came up to wrap a supporting arm around her old nurse as they moved out.

A slow journey, but uneventful, and already warm. 'Cat?' Silence. Nisana was still sunk far into herself.

The ravine down to the valley sloped gently and they emerged at length onto a springy carpeting of thick grasses and yellow bellflower. The stream that ran down the canyon had a tributary here—nearly a river—that flowed down the long, narrow valley before turning sharply against the base of the bluff and dropped down to join the torrent below.

The men deposited Brelian in the sun; Golsat and Levren set out separately for meat while Marhan built a fire. But Brendan would not leave his brother's side—and Lisabetha gazed at them.

She turned as Ylia came up behind her. "He will live, Lady? This truly?" Icy fingers gripped at the swordswoman's arm. "This is not—is not just a thing you have said?"

"He will live, Lisabetha." Lisabetha closed her eyes; she was beginning to shake; Ylia caught her by the shoulders, drew her away from the camp. Next to the water there were large boulders, already warm. The heat felt good against her back. "I would not have said it for Brendan's heart's ease. Such a tale would be quickly proven false and cause greater pain than the truth. Also," she added sharply, "I do not lie to any man, nor to any woman either!" The girl met her eyes very briefly indeed, turned to a study of her fingers.

"I—I know." She swallowed tightly. "I—no; I did know." Her words suddenly came in a rush. "I—when I first came to Koderra, I knew so little of you, I had seen the Queen three times, just to meet and give courtesy to, when she came to Teshmor, and you only once—at tourney—but—" She swallowed again. "But—but what I believed, what they said of you—"

"I can guess," Ylia began, but the girl swept on, not even aware the other had spoken.

"That you were witches, you and the Lady Scythia—AEldran, possessed of the Ylsan Power, dedicated to the destruction of all who serve the One. That—that one day the King would die, and that Nedao would be ruled by magicians, as Yls is, and the land would be ensorceled, the true faith prosecuted. So—so many of the Chosen say, those who were my tutors—so my nurse and many of my friends said." She stopped, frustrated for lack of the right words. "I—it was what I knew, I never knew any of the—any of Yls, any—there was only one side to the coin, until I came to Koderra. Father—Mother—*they* never said such things, but, then Father was a good friend of King Brandt; they would not have said such things to me, even had they believed them. I—'' She hesitated again, went on rapidly: "And so did another tell me.'' She added no name, but she had no need; Ylia could, with a face to go with it. Vess! *Foul cousin, a death at the hands of the Tehlatt is too clean for you. May we meet again, and you will know fear*!

"You believed this of us, my mother and me? Old Mala-eth?''

Lisabetha looked unhappy. "I—I didn't *know*. And those who taught me—Jers, my father's scribe until two winters ago, my tutor, he is a wise man, a devout follower of the One; how could I dare gainsay what he said? He knows good from evil and the kinds and ways of each; I know nothing of such matters. And—and yet—I was confused, afraid, when I came to Brandt's Court. For what they said of you, of the Queen —how could it be true? To heal, to save people from pain and death by magic—how could such a thing be evil?''

Ylia pressed her hands. *Patience*. Difficult, at the moment, to achieve, and yet, absolutely necessary. "How could you be held responsible for what you were given to believe?'' How could Lord Corry have permitted such narrow men to form his only daughter's mind? "And—there is no need to tell me this, it pains you.''

"There *is* need,'' she said flatly. "I have been more than a burden to you and these others, and you had better know the worst of it. All of it. I was a spy in your chambers, I would have been your death. I was to have been.'' She glanced over her shoulder to where Brelian lay and then for the first time met her Lady's eyes squarely. "Your cousin, the Lord Vess. He came to Father's Court this last winter. I had seen him before, of course, though seldom near to hand. But—but all at once, he seemed—oh, amusing, and he spoke me fairly, his manner was all courtly around me. Now and again a rose, still wet with dew, would lie on my morning table, or a width of lace from Oversea would appear in my chambers, or a kerchief with scent from Nar.''

"Yes.'' Ylia tried to keep the loathing from her voice. "They say he is fine-spoken with the ladies and has gallantry that serves him well.'' She could not resist adding, "He has never used it on me.''

Lisabetha nearly smiled at that. "He would not. He fears

you, for you have the AEldra Power. Though—though I have heard it said, also, that he finds you fair. He feared your mother.

"But *I* was an easy mark for him, I know that now; I had only begun to feel my woman's blood, to enjoy the flirting, the bandying of words with boys, when it before had seemed only silly. Vess was—he was like a hero out of the old tales, with his weapons-skill, his songs, his fine gifts, his pretty speeches. And I was a fool," she added bitterly.

" 'Betha. Could you tell Lossana, your mother, what you tell me now? Or Lord Corry, could you tell him?" She shook her head, and a dark flush spread across her cheeks and throat. Ylia once again fought down anger. "Never mind. The shame is not yours, girl. Vess has had the virtue of women older and more world-wise than you and I together will ever be. No, I can hold no blame to you."

"I—I had no excuse. I was carried away at the time, I told myself that. But I gave to him willingly. And—and if my father knew—"

"He did not?"

"No, no of course not. Vess arranged it that I be sent to the City; a suggestion through my mother or her women— through the council, I don't know—"

"Never mind. I know how my cousin works."

"That a suitable husband be found for me. Or that my position in the Queen's household might make me worthy of an Osneran noble. But it was a lie; for me there was none but Vess. Even after—even after he made me the bargain."

"Silence on your loss of maidenry in exchange for my death." *Foul cousin, live yet, that I may find you*! Lisabetha nodded miserably.

"A—a powder to put in your drink. And so much time to —to accomplish the deed. But," she swallowed, blinked hard. "But I could not."

"Of course you could not." She lowered her voice; Levren and Golsat had returned to camp and both had cat's ears. "And you cannot think how glad I am!" That won another near-smile. "But you would not have done it, Lisabetha. Whatever Vess thought of you. You take too great a burden upon yourself, little sister."

"But I—"

"No. Enough. Do not worry the matter further, 'Betha.

Please. And do not worry over Brelian. He will probably waken later today, as well as any of us. Probably better, for all the rest."

"All right. I—thank you." Lisabetha met her eyes, smiled tentatively. "I must look a sad sight," she added, "if I am half as dirty as you, my Lady."

They both laughed, a trifle shaky, more than a little nervous. "Ylia, same as everyone else. Please. There will be time enough later for the formalities. I don't care for them much anyway, you know that. And if I am half as dirty as you, I am surprised you recognized a Lady at all!"

"It wasn't easy," Lisabetha admitted. Her eyes were warm.

"Well, let us eat first. Golsat has something over the fire. And then you and I will do what we can to find women under all this grime." Lisabetha hugged her hard, and they walked back to camp arm in arm.

Marhan stared at them over the spits. *Women. Make sense of them, try it.* But Lisabetha's gaze was once again anxiously on Brelian and the hunched shape of his brother beside him.

"Would—would he let me keep watch, do you think?" She would not name Brendan. "I owe Brelian blood-debt."

Ylia considered this, finally shrugged. "Perhaps. I will do what I can. Eat as soon as Marhan has something ready."

Brendan sat with one hand on Brelian's cloak, his eyes staring blankly across the valley. Such was his preoccupation that he was not even aware of her presence until she touched his shoulder; he started, whirled around. "Bren. I told you he is well." *Gently, Ylia, he will crack into shards.* There was a terrible tension to the set of his body, a wildness in his redrimmed eyes. "He sleeps, but he must, to repair his strength. He is healed, though, I swear it. Or can you not believe what I say? Would you see where his wound was, and no longer is?"

He turned away, shook his head. "No. You would not lie to me, one arms-mate does not lie to another." He shifted; a little of the tension seemed to go from him. "I watch, that is all. We are the last of our father's line, he and I, and so—and so I watch."

"If that is so, then *you* must take care, Bren. Brelian is out of danger, but I am concerned for you now. We move again tomorrow, early. This place is safer than the ledge, but not safe enough."

"You are concerned for me." Brendan turned back to face

her; his face wore that bemused expression that went with Brelian's sallies at his expense. "For *me*? Why?"

Why indeed? On a sudden impulse, she laid a hand against his cheek. He started, but did not move away. "Another attack will be the death of all of us, if we do not eat and sleep. You already look like death itself, Bren. You need food and rest. We cannot afford for you to be unready, should we be attacked again; you are the strongest fighter we have." She leaned back, burrowed both hands under her cloak. "Lisabetha," she went on, "has asked to watch while you sleep." His head jerked up at that, and his eyes were hot. "No, do not glare at me! He would have died to save her, and she has acknowledged blood-debt! Do you think it was an easy thing for her to ask, knowing how you feel? Would you throw such bravery back in her face?" Doubt was on his drawn face. "No. Such as you are, I know you will not. And how would Brelian say?"

Brendan gazed down at his hands. Shrugged finally. "So be it. Blood-debt, that is a serious thing. And—and Brel will be pleased. But I swear to you," he added darkly, "I swear I will not see him hurt again by this wench, no. That I will not."

She caught at his hands. "Thank you, Brendan."

"Thank my brother, when he wakens." But his hands tightened, briefly, on hers.

Marhan and Golsat had already portioned out some of the meat, and Lisabetha ate quickly, finishing almost before anyone else began. Then, stopping only long enough to wash her hands and face at the water's edge, she timidly approached Brendan. Perhaps she had feared what he might say and wished to get it over with, but he merely glanced at her, stood and walked over to find a place near the fire.

Watches were chosen, and Lisabetha insisted on her share. "I have shirked long enough," she argued, and Marhan reluctantly gave her the first with himself. Ylia searched once again before sleeping, and stretched the personal shielding to encircle the campfire. *How easy this time*. She pulled the still sleeping Nisana close to her shoulder, and was asleep in moments.

But dreams kept her from full rest. Once again she fought against the horror in the tunnels, or ran, ran along twisting and turning underground ways that had no end, that narrowed, shrank until she must crawl, and all the while the sound of running feet echoed from behind and ahead both.

She was almost pleased when Levren roused her to share watch with a silent, withdrawn Brendan. She woke Marhan, fell back asleep then, and slept deeply and without dream. That she remembered.

She woke late in the afternoon to find Nisana gravely studying her. 'You have grown.' There was awe in her thought. 'What chanced last night, to bring this?' Ylia opened her memory; the cat sat a while, pondering. 'Well—I *said* you would—'

'You needn't be so smug about it. But how can it be mine? I, who never had much at all, and then, suddenly—all *this*?'

'Whose else? Do you think the Power can be lent, like a comb? I told you, it simply is. There was a need such that you pushed beyond your own stupid arguments to take it.'

'Well—perhaps.' She wasn't really convinced. 'But then, whose was the voice? That was *not* my imagination!'

'One of the Guardians. Obviously.'

She laughed, she simply couldn't help it. Nisana glared at her indignantly. 'Nisana. Nisana, I am sorry, truly! But—but the Guardians! Listen cat, I love the tales, you know that. But to believe in Mother's Ylsan folk tales—'

'You did not believe in Mathkkra until last night,' Nisana objected huffily.

'No. Not until I saw them. Nisana, I am truly sorry. Perhaps I am too much like my father, but wishing to believe in something is not enough.' They sat silently for a while; Ylia held out her arms finally; Nisana, with a mental shrug, climbed into her lap and allowed herself to be hugged.

> *As stubborn and prejudiced in her way as the Bowmaster in his—though a change had come over the man since my kittenhood trick scattered the Mathkkra. And so, one could, I supposed, hope for eventual sense in the girl.*

The sun dropped behind the mountains and the wind, which had blown fitfully through the afternoon, abated. The silence was total, save for the crackling of the fire. Marhan had meat on the spits and Golsat was pushing small fish into the coals.

"Food?" Ylia demanded wistfully as she came into the light. Her stomach was beginning to hurt, she could not remember the last decent meal she'd eaten.

Marhan grinned. "If you like it cooked the way this wild man does, there is food! For the rest of us, however, it will be a little longer."

Golsat cast his eyes heavenward. "I never said I liked it half-raw," he protested. "Only that I *can* eat it that way, if I must. Or raw," he added thoughtfully, "if it is fish, and fresh . . ." his voice trailed away.

"Ah? Ah?" Marhan laughed. "You should have seen him. No, perhaps you should not have. The fish were barely warm."

"It was hot enough," Golsat replied, shoving the last of the fish into the red coals with a bit of stick. "It's these cities of yours. They soften you, turn you into old women—ah, eh, your pardon, Mistress Malaeth," he added hastily. Malaeth made a primly disapproving little noise.

"Well, I think our old woman has done very well." Ylia dropped down next to the old nurse. Malaeth had Marhan's kettle boiling and a soothing odor was wafting across the fire. "And never again will I believe she led the refined youth she has always told me." She ducked, giggling, as an elderly but still accurate hand swung and a blow glanced off her ear.

"Never did think to come to this," Malaeth said. She sounded perversely proud of herself. "Climbing rocks like a lad! Next I'll probably be climbing trees, or fighting with one of your swords!"

"Now, you know," Levren began earnestly, "that might not be such a terrible idea." He was interrupted by a muttered comment from Marhan, but the Swordmaster would not repeat himself aloud.

'Malaeth.' Ylia leaned over to sniff at the kettle and laid a hand on the old woman's shoulder to strengthen the mind-speech. 'It might not be amiss to add chamomile to that tonight, later. Perhaps a little dried lettuce also, what do you think?'

'If I had it.' Malaeth's thought was thin, faint. 'I have plantain, elder flower, raspberry leaf; but no soporific.'

'I have a little in my pack, I was holding it for such a time as this. Here.' She undid the strings, handed it over. 'That is all we have, use it as you think best.'

*Often I wonder—to myself alone, since the
girl would be scandalized if I shared the
thought with her—how long it would have
been, under ordinary circumstance, before
Brendan and Golsat would have become
friends? Or before Levren could gaze eye to
eye with the Anaselan and not turn white
and sweat? Battle and near-death brought
them close where nothing else could ever
have.*

17

Levren made room; she dropped down between him and
Marhan. Brendan, on Lev's other side, made no sign he was
aware of any of them but studied the flames as though he were
a seer. Lisabetha alone was not at the fire.

The swordswoman inhaled deeply. "I would have starved
before now on my own, Marhan." The Swordmaster nodded
absently, but his eyes were fixed on his hands. "Are you
asleep?" she inquired sarcastically. "You should have done
that on your watches, old man!"

Silence. Then: "Go ahead, Marhan," Levren prompted
across her shoulder. "*You* said—"

"I know what I said," Marhan snapped. He brought his
head up reluctantly, met her bewildered eyes. "Meant it too.
The girl has her mother's blood, like that cat's. AEldran."

"I can't really help that," Ylia said dryly. "Or an apology
might mean more. *Now* what have I done?"

"You?" He was genuinely astonished. "Don't you mock
me, boy! You warned me loud and clear up there, and I ignored you! Same as if—as if Golsat had seen tracks and I'd

150

ignored *him*. If you hadn't returned when you did," he continued, "Brel would have died, and I would have been to blame."

"We were all dead when we entered the Foessa," Brendan said bleakly. "Do not take Brelian's harm to yourself, Swordmaster. It was his choice, where and how he fought. And why."

"Not entirely his choice," Ylia reminded him. "And there is no need to lay blame." Marhan shook his head unhappily. She caught at his shoulder, hard. "Stop it, Marhan! Why *should* you have believed me? What proof had I? I could scarcely believe myself!"

"If I may suggest," Golsat cleared his throat. "You cannot agree on that subject, so let us have another, shall we? I would like to suggest we move north in the morning—not far. But there is a ridge just yonder, through those trees," he gestured into darkness, "and another valley beyond that. There is game, a lake. I would feel better myself, I admit it, with a height between us and that ledge."

"I suggest this also," Levren said, "that if it is a reasonably safe place, we stay there a while, a full five-day at the very least, to dry meat. We have been so far fortunate, between our hunting skills and the quantity of game in these mountains, that we have not truly gone hungry. It is not wise to trade on luck, though—not here. We may come again to a place where nothing lives, or chance may separate us." Golsat surreptitiously made the Northern warding sign against evil.

"I agree." Marhan nodded. "We have had fools' luck so far. And we all need rest, not just Berlian." His voice dropped so low that even Ylia, close by, could barely hear his next words. "And this pace will be the death of Malaeth."

She opened her mouth; closed it again. He was right, of course: distance, cold, poor food and scarce. No rest. Malaeth had borne up wonderfully so far, but she was old. Old and soft. She could not take much more of their present pace; they dared not ask it of her.

"Such counsel follows my own thought." Brendan looked up abruptly. "What do you say, though, Ylia? Are there more of the things that attacked us? And—and what were they?" Eyes still black with his brother's near-death held hers.

"We are safe for now." She avoided his last question. "There are none alive of those who attacked us. That much I know. But I had better go and see to Brelian," she pressed to her feet, "before the meat is ready." The last, rather wistfully, to Levren. He laughed.

"Almost," he promised.

Lisabetha sat with Brelian, a darker shadow among the overhanging trees. Ylia felt the pulse in his throat, touched his forehead. His face was cool, his breathing normal. But the girl at his side was drawn and anxious. "Have you eaten or slept, 'Betha?" She shook her head. "He laid blood-debt on you, and you acknowledged that. So it is not right that you lay one on him in return, that you are haggard and worn when he wakens."

"I—"

"Go wash, eat. If he wakens, I'll call you. Go on." She watched the girl walk toward the fire, and gingerly ease herself down next to Malaeth. She leaned back then, watching as the stars slowly became visible in the night sky. A bat flew overhead, vanished into the trees.

"Ylia?"

She started. "Bren—Brendan?"

He took her hand, dropped to her side. "I have not given you proper thanks for saving Brelian's life," he began hesitantly. "I do not wish to seem ungrateful in your eyes." And he brought her fingers to his lips. She stared at him, totally caught off guard, astonished. "And now," his grip tightened painfully, "tell me what secret you hide from me, what secret you have hidden since I slew that bat-creature!"

"I? Secret?" She pulled to free her hand but his grip tightened again.

"Secret, my lady. Sent, you said," he stated grimly. "I asked of that, and you put me off. You put me off a while since over the stone knife. I will not be put off any longer. *What are they?*" His voice was low so it would not carry to the fire, but harsh with anger. "What was that bat-creature, and who sent it? How can I aid you when you tell me nothing?"

"Brendan, give me back my fingers, that is my sword hand you are crushing." With a startled oath, he let go. "I—all right. Perhaps I should have told you. Events have intervened, though. And just now, I would have had to tell everyone. I would rather not." A silence. "But I meant to tell you, believe that."

"Then do so, now. *What was that thing?*"

"I cannot say exactly, because I have no idea myself. I swear it." She met his eyes. "You want to know all of it? All right, then, listen!" And she told him—the footprints in the Hunter's Meadow; the Fear; the warning. "Of the *seeming*, you already know."

"As much as I care to. Go on."

"I know nothing of the thing you slew. I have never heard of such a thing, anything like it. But—" She hesitated, sought words that could, perhaps, explain. "I was aware beforehand that something was wrong, though I couldn't tell what it was; do you remember? Well, I know now. Someone of the Power —of *a* power—bridged a night-creature to us. It was that I sensed, the surge of power that accompanies a bridging. Though I did not have enough Power of my own, then, to know what it was."

"Bridging." He scowled at his hands. "It was somewhere else, and then, instantly, with us."

"You pay good attention. It was sent to us. To *us* in particular. We are not alone in these mountains."

"It was bridged to us, and then, when I slew it, the body was bridged back." Brendan was following his own thought. "Who did this?" he demanded.

"I do not know. I wish I might never need to know. But there is still more *you* do not know." She told him then of the *seeming* by the lake. "Unlike the other one, this was meant to look as it did. Like the bowmen in Koderra. It was set to snare one who held Scythia dear."

"And I dared accuse you of fear because of a knife." Brendan gazed at her unhappily.

"No, it is past. Do not worry it, Bren."

"But—but how could anyone know—?"

"Know to choose that likeness? How else? Someone knows that I am here. And Nisana. Probably that someone knows something of each of us, by now. And do not apologize again, please, Bren, because I *was* afraid. I still am. Someone knows a great deal about us, about me, and I know nothing, except that he—or she—exists."

Brendan was silent for a while. "And those things last night?"

"Mathkkra."

He laughed. "No. They—they are only legend!"

"Then," she replied dryly, "You have slain legend, my Lord."

"But—no!" He shook his head, rather wildly. "They had no weapons, the Mathkkra. I know the tales, as well as any man. Merreven and his followers, they slew every one!"

"That was never likely. Think! It makes a good ending for an ancient tale, that all died, but how could we trust to the truth of such a thing? And Merreven's bards sang of it, but *they* could not have known for certain. And as to weapons, well: It has been five-hundred years. Merreven fought with a single-edged sword and a greatshield—what man has worn such war-things in Nedao for over three hundred years? Why should the Mathkkra not change as well? It is not as though they were *well* armed, you saw the temper of their blades, didn't you?"

"But—Mathkkra!" He considered this in silence for some moments. "Mothers guard us! What will you tell the others?"

She shrugged. "The truth. I must, don't you think?"

He nodded reluctantly. "We must know what we fight. But —Malaeth and the girl—"

"Stronger than you think. Stronger than I think, even, probably. They will not be pleased, but they will deal with the knowledge. I find it amazing," she laughed, "how easy it is to accept knowledge when there is no alternative. Don't you?"

Brendan laughed softly then. "We give ourselves airs. Why should a Mallick ascend from the Black Well to wreak havoc against such as us?"

"One does. Or a semblance of one. Something as evil as a Mallick. See, though, Bren, I am as much in the dark with such things as you. More, maybe, for the AEldra are blind to the black uses of the Power. It is said evil use was denied us by the Nasath." She laughed again, but there was no amusement in the sound. "It frightens me, because I cannot understand it."

"I thought," Brendan said, gently mocking, "that there was nothing at all you feared." His hand caught at hers again and held it lightly. She started, turned as Brel moaned. She freed herself from Brendan's suddenly nerveless fingers and, faint though the sound had been, Lisabetha came running.

In the dim light of fire and stars, Brelian's face was a mere blur against the ground; they sensed more than saw this eyes open. His hands sought Ylia's where they lay against his arm.

"Who—?" A mere hoarse whisper. He coughed. "Who—?"

"Myself, Ylia."

"Where are we? Bren—Lisabetha—?"

"Well. They have kept watch over you."

"The—Lady." An even fainter whisper. "How does she?"

"Ask her. That is she to your left." But Lisabetha backed away hastily and practically ran back to the fire. "She is well and unharmed, only she has not eaten or slept much today. Here, speak with Bren, I will bring you food shortly."

Lisabetha sat close to Malaeth and her face was white; she did not look up as Ylia returned to the fire. The swordswoman ate quickly, scarcely tasted what was put into her hands, swore as she scalded her lip on the kettle. She took a portion of meat and the tea back to Brelian. He was sitting, wrapped in his cloak, his back against a tree, and hungry.

"And now," he said finally, "if someone would only tell me what has chanced. Bren will not tell me a thing—I swear to you, brother," he added testily, "there is nothing wrong with me!"

"I think we might piece it together for you," Ylia said. Brendan cast her a reproachful glance. "If you feel well enough to join us at the fire, that is."

Brelian considered this. Shrugged. "I—certainly. Never better. Your arm, Bren." And with his brother's aid he stood, but refused any further aid and walked alone to the fire.

There was a deep silence as he came into the light. Lisabetha glanced up, let her eyes drop back immediately to her hands. Marhan gaped openly, but Lev was already on his feet, clapping the boy on the back. He and the Swordmaster made room for the brothers between them.

It was a jumble at first, with all of them, save Lisabetha, trying to tell the battle from a different vantage. Ylia went on, then, to tell him, and the others, what had passed in the caverns. She glossed over the sudden astonishing change in her AEldra Power, said nothing of the voice. "It—I suppose it was the fear of death, the threat of—of such a manner of death. For one moment it was the weak thing it always had been, and the next—" She shook her head, brought her portion of the tale to a close. Marhan picked up the last of it.

Brelian broke the ensuing silence. "I remember, I think." He closed his eyes. "The battle in the fog, the sudden pain that nearly tore consciousness from me; I knew I was badly hurt, but somehow, it didn't matter, not like—like other things did. The tunnel—it wound on forever, like the pits under the Black Well. Witch-fire—Lisabetha. The way back was—so very long.

"But mostly the pain, and then its lack. Time seemed to hold, then, and I remember Bren's face, uncertain whether I saw it in truth, or only thought it, and I knew I would die. And yet, I have wakened in health, and where there was a wound I can feel nothing, nothing at all. And you tell me less than a day has passed." He bowed across the fire. "I will pay the debt of my blood."

"I thank you," Ylia replied formally. The ancient vow acknowledged the saving of one's life at risk to the saver's own. *I risked so little—almost nothing to save him.* But she would not dare speak that.

Levren stirred. "I did not know you had the healing. Well that you do; Brel was hurt to the death when we found him."

Ylia shook her head. "I did not have it until last night. Not the healing and never enough strength to use it. I am reminded, though. You," she added pointedly, "limp. I will see to that tonight, Lev. We need you whole."

He smiled. "You have no argument from me. I twisted it in the rock. It's not badly swollen, but it hurts."

"And you, Golsat?"

He smiled faintly, touched his hairline. "You might have had to reattach my head, or at very least my scalp, had it not been for Levren. It isn't bad."

If it hadn't been. . . . She pulled her mouth closed with an effort. The Bowmaster shrugged. "It wasn't—"

"Not much, it wasn't," Golsat broke in bluntly. "I was down and at least five of those creatures were on me; I couldn't even get my sword up." He inclined his head. "I hadn't thanked you for your aid, but not for lack of gratitude," he said quietly.

Levren drew a deep breath, let it out in a rush and extended his hand. It cost him; not as much as it once would have. There was a time—not many days before—he'd no doubt have hesitated, and Golsat would have lain dead at his feet. His action on the ledges had been automatic, his fear that he might be too late as deep as it would have been for any of the rest of the company. "No need, friend."

Golsat took the proffered hand, gripped it briefly. It was damp, tense. Not friends, not really. Not yet. "Mathkkra." It still amazed him. "Who would have believed it?" He stirred the coals, dropped more wood onto the new flames. "I never thought them other than legend." Brendan's suddenly amused eyes met Ylia's. "They are carried on poles at the Harvest-Fest, but I deemed them one with the other such things. Were-wolves. Vampyres. You know—made up by folk who would then frighten themselves with the very things they create. Real terrors are enough for me!"

"Are you so certain the other things are make believe?" Levren inquired dryly. "Anything we meet hereafter will not surprise *me*!"

"But, what are they?" Malaeth demanded. Brelian laughed.

"And you lived in Nedao—how many years, Dame?"

"I had my hands full with Scythia and then with this girl," she retorted. "I never had time for tales, and never time for the sort of tales that would rob me of sleep!"

"And yet you told *me*—" Ylia began, a wicked gleam in her eye.

"Things in the mountains, yes," the old woman broke in sharply. "Nothing like that!"

"*I* know of them." Lisabetha leaned forward and gazed self-consciously at the hands she held to the fire as they all turned to look at her. "I have heard most of the old tales, like you, but I have also read many others no longer told in the land. Father gave many of the ancient writings that were kept in the Tower to the Chosen to recopy." Her voice gained strength as she spoke. "They were never numerous, the Cave-folk. That our long kin could tell. They hunted in small bands and went abroad at night, preferring to avoid even light of moon, if they could. Mostly they ate small animals such as they could catch by snares, or pits, or thrown stones. But they found sheep easy prey and were not above killing the herder as well, if they could. They—they drank blood, and left the kill behind if it was large. Drained."

"Ugh." Malaeth shivered.

"But there is nothing in the old tales of Fear, is there?" Ylia demanded. Lisabetha shook her head.

"No. Nothing. And such a thing would have been recorded.
Even though no accurate description of them survived, I think
mention of the Fear would have." She glanced at Golsat.
"Small wonder you could not recognize them as Mathkkra.
The figures from the Harvest-Fest bear no resemblance to
what—what was on that ledge, do they? At Teshmor," she
went on haltingly, her eyes going back to the fire, "in my
father's halls, there was a room where ancient things were
kept. A chair of Bergony's, an old sword or so, painted
shields, woven breastplates. Other old-styled weapons. Were
you never there?" Her eyes met Brelian's; both of them
flushed.

"I knew of it."

"There was a knife. Black, smooth stone, with a leather
thong threaded through its handle, its blade chipped into a
sharp cutting edge. It was called a sacrificial knife, though
that was conjecture, really. It was said to be Mathkkra, was
said to have come from the Lord Merreven's raid, though of
course this could not be known for certain. But—when I saw
the one Golsat had, I knew, I knew what awaited us. I mean,"
the high color left her face rather alarmingly. She stumbled
on, "I knew what—had attacked you." *Mothers*, Ylia
whispered fervently, *had I known what the weapon was,
would I have borne up as well as Lisabetha did*? Silence, which
Marhan finally broke.

"All my days," he said heavily, "I have held to my
weapons, and they have served me well. Magic, and creatures
out of myth, and again magic." They had never seen him so
unhappy. "I no longer know *what* I should trust."

"Marhan. Look at me, old man." Ylia could, suddenly,
have wept for him; she moved to his side, gripped his arm as
he looked up. "Nothing has changed overnight; things have
only been added to what we already knew. Strange things, I
grant you. Nisana saved us from those on the ledge, but we
killed many with steel, Marhan. To each thing its place." He
tugged at his moustaches impatiently. "*Listen* to me! I have
AEldra Power—the full powers of my mother's kind, I think,
and unless there is a thing I do not know of AEldra Power, it
is mine forever. But that is *not* my only safeguard. When a
sword is needed, then I shall use that, but if the Power is called
for to aid us, then that. To each thing its place, Marhan."

"There is this, also," Levren added matter of factly. "There will unfortunately be more need for fighting before we reach Aresada. So much is clear, even to me. And so is another thing: need for sleep, and as much of it as we can take. In pairs, for the watch tonight. Two together are less likely to doze. But the rest of us had better take what rest we can get. Now."

Brendan and Ylia drew the third; Levren and Lisabetha garnered the first, to be followed by Marhan and Golsat. Marhan would have argued against Lisabetha, but Ylia came to her side and, in the face of two determined women, he gave up.

"On your head, boy," he finally said, "be it."

"I cannot fight, I admit that," Lisabetha said flatly. "But my eyes are good and I can rouse the camp quite speedily if there is need. What else do you want, sir?"

Brelian laughed suddenly. "Trust her, Marhan! You have heard her—she could wake a drunken Tehlatt!"

"Huh."

The Power itself is inborn; its uses require long and hard hours of instruction and longer and harder hours of practice. To know precisely how much strength is needed for a certain task—that may be the difference between saving three lives and only one; it may be the difference between bridging to safety, or not bridging at all. I cannot think which was more irritating: that the girl once insisted she had little so that I must push her to use it, or that she now used it so lavishly that I must bully her to hold back something of her strength against other need.

18

By the time the sun topped the eastern ridge the next morning, they were halfway down to Golsat's valley. Wide at its midpoint, it pinched off sharply to north and south: hours of sunlight would be short here. But it was a sheltered place, and there was game.

Another stream came out of the north, dropped rapidly across the valley floor to a small lake, out its southern end to disappear finally in a boulder slide. Here were pools deep enough to cover the tallest of them, shallows easy for even old Malaeth to wade. Here were the red groundberries, bright against the pale, thick grasses; here, also, on the northern shore of the lake was a flock of the great geese that winter in the southern marshes. These were so unused to people they remained on the water and even allowed approach within a few lengths before they swam unconcernedly away.

They dropped packs and loose bits of clothing: Cloaks in need, all, of repair; Marhan's blackened and oily kettle, which needed not only a hard cleaning but a patch of some sort, for it had recently sprung a leak; Ylia's tiny healing pouch and the food bag—empty—she had filled in the great kitchens in Koderra a lifetime ago.

Even before they reached level ground, Levren was busily appointing tasks: Malaeth to begin gathering herbs—those that could be used for cooking as well as the healing varieties; Lisabetha to aid her in that if needed, but otherwise to weave more of the tough grass bags. The brothers with Golsat, for fish, unless Brendan would rather gather wood. He and Marhan would go for game.

"What of me?" Ylia demanded as they separated.

"You search," Levren replied tersely. He and Marhan vanished northward. She sighed, dropped to the ground and pulled her boots off.

Malaeth gazed around at the tattered bits that were all their belongings and shook her head unhappily. "I am going to bathe my feet first; they are hot and dirty, and they hurt. 'Betha, Ylia, you had better do the same. We will get more done thereafter."

Brendan glanced at Ylia, mumbled something she couldn't quite catch, and strode off toward the woods. Golsat stretched, yawned hugely. "That was pleasant sleep I got last night, and I wager I could match it today. However." He yawned again. "Ah, well. Brelian? What do you think—there, hm?" Brelian followed his companion's finger. Shook his head firmly.

"Full sunlight on that pool, you'd never get near them, even if any were there." Golsat grinned delightedly and clapped his companion on the back.

"You learn! Slowly, but you do learn! Come then—*you* choose the place, and we shall see! There are interesting kinds of fish in these high places, I find. Always a little different. Lady," he added formally as Lisabetha returned to camp to drop her boots, "you might come with us. There are plenty of reeds along the banks for your satchels. Hmm?" Lisabetha looked at him in surprise. Golsat, moreso than the rest of the men, seldom spoke directly to her.

"Me?"

Golsat smiled deprecatingly, shrugged. "I could use a net to carry the fish." Brelian stood a little to the side, unmoving, scarcely breathing. *Golsat, no, if she does*—if she did. He could feel the color mounting his face. "Of course, if you have another thing to do—"

Lisabetha capitulated with sudden grace. "Whyfor not, Golsat? I won't try your game with the fish, if it is all the same." Golsat bowed in reply, a sweeping, formal Teshmoran gesture that lacked only the plumed cap. She, Ylia and Brelian stared.

"After you, then, my Lady."

"Nonsense! 'My Lady' indeed!" Lisabetha laughed. "You call *her* Ylia, and she's your Queen!"

"As you please, then, 'Betha. After you." he caught the startled Brelian by one shoulder and propelled him forward, immediately after the unsuspecting girl. That done, he turned, winked gravely, and hurried to catch up to them. The three vanished downstream. Ylia gaped after them.

A low chuckle brought her around: Malaeth had seen it all and was enjoying herself immensely. "He'll have them pledged before sundown, see if he doesn't! That man," she laughed, "has all the wiles of a Narran card-reader!"

The sun was sliding down from midday when the fishing party returned: Golsat came first, four long, red-speckled trouts wrapped in his jerkin in place of a carry-net. Lisabetha and Brelian wandered in over an hour later, hand in hand, totally engrossed in each other.

Second day. Marhan and Levren had the good fortune to fell a deer. Having given the company a welcome change from bird and rabbit, and also having assured full packs when they set out once more, they left further hunting to Golsat and Brendan and turned to repair, to cleaning and mending their few weapons, and lastly, surprisingly in Marhan's case, to working with Lisabetha and Malaeth, trying to give them at least a little self-protection. Marhan dressed the older woman a long staff that would aid her in walking; also, it could be used as a weapon and she could at least hold a single attacker at a distance, as she was willing to attempt the simple Köderran striking maneuvers he showed her.

Lisabetha had had a little bow-training from her brother and his friends when she was younger; it was, of course, not

enough that she could be entrusted with Levren's few precious
arrows, even if she could have bent his bow. But she showed
a quickness with sword that surprised all of them. Unfortunately—again—there was only one light sword, and that was
Ylia's.

But it was a thought to save for a later time, and Ylia promised herself to remember after they reached the Caves. In the
meantime, Golsat gave her his long Northern dagger, set the
Mathkkra knife in its place. With this weapon—the blade was
nearly forearm length—Lisabetha proved astonishingly deft,
at least in practice. But she had, also, other protection.

As Brelian learned when he offered, half-jokingly, to teach
her Teshmoran wrestling skills, a form of fighting using kicks
and throws, rather than the Koderran style involving fists and
open-handed striking. He was flat on his back almost before
he finished speaking, Lisabetha's knee against his throat, her
hand wrapped hard in his hair. It was some time before he
could stop laughing long enough to cry quarter. Lisabetha
moved gravely aside, held out a hand to help him sit.

"You cannot have forgotten the last time I threw you, upon
the ledges," she said soberly, but her eyes were merry.

"So I had, but never again," Brelian assured her. He was
still laughing. "When did you learn all that?"

"I had, I thought, lost most of it. Gors taught me a few
years ago; he and Galdan—you know, Erken's son."

"Oh. I'd forgotten him. He's something older, of course. A
good man, but odd, too, if he taught *you* wrestling."

"If—oh. Because I'm a girl. Erken is terrible, isn't he?
Worse than Marhan. 'Maidens'—he says the word as though
it were, oh, dragons, or some other mythical being. And he
has narrow ideas, to say no more, of how the nobles should
be—"

"Well, from what I remember, his son certainly never—"

"Not like that. Erken isn't a snob, like he'd just earned his
rank. You know *that* kind." Brelian nodded. "It's the respon-
sibilities, how the people expect their rulers to be—I express it
badly."

"No. I understand. I think. Anyway, I was enough younger
I didn't have much to do with Galdan. And then when he left
Teshmor—"

"I remember that well enough." Brendan had been sitting
in the shade polishing his dagger, rather owlishly watching his

brother and Lisabetha. "A good fighting man, as good as I."
But when Ylia glanced at him, he winked. "Went to Yls,
didn't he, Brel?"

"Don't know, brother. They said also Nar, that he was aiding the traders against the Sea-Raiders. No one knows for certain except Erken, because Galdan simply—went."

The dagger slipped unnoticed to the grass; Brendan was
studying his fingers. "At least one of them is alive." That so
quietly only Ylia heard him. She moved to his side as Brelian
slipped a finger under Lisabetha's chin.

"I have it, dear Lady," he said solemnly. "I shall disarm
those we fight, and you can throw them and sit on them!"
They were still laughing as they wandered back toward camp.

Ylia laid a hand on Brendan's arm; his pain and grief were
suddenly so strong she could not bear it. "Brendan—Bren, my
friend. Do not think on it, that way lies madness. *Stop it!*"

He shook his head sharply, but the brooding look was still
in his eyes as he looked up. "How do you not think? My
mother, my brothers. My little sister, she had only four summers." He turned away again. "How do you stop thinking?"

"Force it away," she urged. "Grieve, weep if you can.
Shout, throw things! But do not brood that way! You cannot
take their pain, Brendan; do not even try! You imagine too
much; do not! *You must not!*" She pushed onto her knees,
moved around to face him again, took his shoulders hard between her hands. "I have a loss like yours, Bren; I know what
I am speaking of. Grieve, but do not imagine what pain they
suffered, how they might have died. It does no good, to them
or to you. And we need you, Brendan." She sat back on her
heels, let her hands fall to her lap. There was a long silence.

Brendan looked up again, then, and some of the terrible
blackness was gone from his eyes. "One forgets. You lost.
Lisabetha. . . . We all did. Family, friends, arms-mates." He
studied her face. "You know—there is more to you, Ylia of
Koderra, than is readily apparent. Do you realize that?"

She shrugged, abashed by this sudden, personal turn to the
conversation. *Well, you invited it, speaking to him like that,
didn't you?* "There is more to *you* than meets the eye, Brendan."

"Oh?"

"I thought of you as—well, at the first, as a swordsman.

A good one, of course. But—well—" She fumbled, embarrassed, to a halt.

"Say it. Go ahead." With another sudden change of mood, he smiled warmly, the smile crinkling his eyes. *How comely he is*; she flushed, turned hastily away. "A narrow-visioned and shallow fighting man," Brendan went on, mockingly, "whose only thought revolves around his blades, the Midwinter-Fest crossings—which of course he would win—and ale with his mates. And wenching. A man without humor." Ylia shook her head. "All true, unfortunately."

"No," she protested. "I mean—well—there *is* that to you, but there is a side you conceal, Bren. You are perceptive, though you hide it. You are a warm man. And a kind one, under your hero's armor. Capable of reason and deep thought when it is least expected."

He laughed quietly, laid a hand briefly across hers. "One might say as much of you, of course. Nedao's Lady Princess, who shocks the villages and the city matrons with her man's clothing and man's weapons. Who wields well on the practice floor, but is unlikely to use her skills against enemy, whose blades are unblooded and likely to stay so. Figurehead; not a true fighter. Ylia the Unreachable, for it is hard to speak with her, for shyness or coldness of being, who can say? An oddity. And when she becomes Queen, she will wed by the council's choosing and her sword will rust away while she provides Nedao with heirs. Which," he added, his color suddenly high, "by the look of her, will be many."

"Hah!" she retorted. And then, curiously: "They can't *really* say—all that of me?"

Brendan laughed. "Some. Not everyone, of course. But those who went to the alehouse with me, or—uh, the other places we went—"

"Manazena's house. I know of it." He glanced at her, surprised. A king's heir, particularly female, shouldn't know about such places. Particularly, he thought in some confusion, this one.

"I—uh—well, we were young and mostly non-Koderran. Few of us had ever really spoken with you. And you were a novelty."

"I daresay," she said dryly.

"Well, you were," Brendan insisted. "And, of course, it

has been lifetimes since Nedao had any swordswomen at all:
Leffna, of course. A few since. Not many in five hundred
years.''

"You could count Hrusetta, who ran from her father's
holdings outside Teshmor to join the Sea-Raiders.''

He waved the legendary Hrusetta aside. "There is more to
you than that!''

"I like to think there is." She shifted so she could pull her
knees up and rest her chin on them. "Odd, how wrong a first
impression can be.''

"It is. And I would—'' Brendan leaned forward, his eyes
warm. A call from the fire brought him around.

"Bren!'' Brelian waved a demanding arm. "Lev needs you,
now!''

"—well—''

"Go on. We'll—talk later.'' He gripped her hand, jumped
to his feet. She resisted an urge to turn and watch him; got to
her own feet and walked firmly and swiftly in the opposite
direction: Cresses for the evening meal, that was what was
needed. Perhaps mint, if it could be found; possibly more
plantain, though Malaeth had picked that over fairly well near
to camp. Chickory, maybe, or yarrow. There were things to be
done, no time to waste.

Nisana came in search of her a short while later, however,
and the plants went ungathered. The cat was in an uneasy
mood, and nothing would do but that they immediately ex-
plore Ylia's new uses of the Power, test its extent. 'And there
is much you need to relearn,' she added sharply. 'You have
grown sloppy, you waste strength. You overspent by at least
half again when you healed Brelian.'

"I was less concerned with that than saving his life,'' Ylia
retorted. "And you were asleep.''

'Next time there might be more than one of us badly hurt.'
Nisana regarded her with impatient green eyes. 'It felt good,
didn't it? The backlash of Power after the healing was completed? I aided your mother often enough, though I cannot
heal myself. If you need to aid more than one, there is no
backlash. Only the draining.'

"You know full well—''

'I do not criticise, you did well. But you must learn to hoard
your strength, however much you have. Look what I wasted

when I shape-changed! And how much use was I for the rest
of that night?' She became brisk, all business. 'Now, what
have you done with this, have you tried the far vision yet? And
use mind-speech, please. Even that needs practice, you know
that.'

'Well—'

'Well?'

'Since—no.'

'You must use it, if you have it. It is a great deal of trouble
to me, and the touch works as well. And I can sense at greater
distances than I can see. That holds true for most of us. But
there are times when I find only the vision will do. And you
are human, which makes it different. Try!'

Ylia closed her eyes obediently. Nisana's thought rumbled
through her head. 'Yes—more strength than that to start. And
yes, go ahead, close your eyes if you must, if you find yourself
distracted. Later, of course—however! Now. Have you a goal
in mind? Then reach—no, not from there, from *there*, and not
so much of your strength as that!'

'Less and I cannot use it at all!' she complained. The cat
butted her arm, hard.

'Have you the feel of the inner place? No, not *there*, either,
no wonder you are so wasteful—' And then, crossly, 'Very
well, try it that way!'

She did—and, suddenly, she had it. They sat, she and the
cat, beneath the trees in a sheltered glade of aspen near the
western edge of the valley, but she seemed to stand at the same
moment in the midst of the camp: There, Brelian and Lisabetha scraping at the deer hide together and giggling, Marhan
and Levren turning strips of meat over the fire so it would dry
evenly. Brendan, toying with his dagger and looking about,
rather casually, as though he had misplaced something and
would prefer to find it without calling attention to himself.

'Now,' Nisana commanded, 'less. No, do not argue again,
just try it! You see?' Not as much of a drain, and yet it held.
Less—less again. Finally the whole blurred, darkened. She
opened her eyes to find Nisana glaring at her accusingly. 'Is
that the best you can do?'

'My first try—!'

'Not good enough,' she insisted firmly. 'Again!'

No good arguing with Nisana, particularly when she taught.
She closed her eyes obediently, tried again. The sun was nearly

down when the cat finally allowed her to quit, and the grove
was in shadow.

'Your command of the Baelfyr is good. The healing—
I think you will have no trouble, if you learn to pace yourself,
to remember what else you must do that will require the
strengths. Your far vision—acceptable. Possibly better than
my own, since you are human.' Grudging, but then Nisana
was never free with praise.

'Bridging, now,' she went on. 'Have you ever tried that?'

Ylia shook her head. 'No. Mother made me try once. I
don't think I can.'

'You could not heal then, either,' the cat reminded her
tartly. 'One last thing, then, and we will truly be finished. Try
it. It is—no, not like that, bridging comes from *here*! I—join!
Now—pay close heed, it works—like this!' There was a nasty,
falling sensation in the pit of Ylia's stomach, as though she
looked from the very unprotected edge of Koderra's highest
tower. In that instant, they moved from the aspen grove to the
middle of the meadow, thirty or more lengths away. Almost
before Ylia could realize they had moved, Nisana bridged
them back again. *Oh gods and Mothers, stop, I'll be ill*—she
fought rising sickness, swallowed rapidly. The nausea receded.

'*You* try it, now.' If Nisana was aware of her reaction, she
didn't show it.

'No. I can't.'

'It is not—'

'No. I cannot, please, Nisana. I—And do not tell me,' she
added fiercely, 'how easily you can. I won't do it!'

'You are afraid.' Nisana was deliberately contemptuous.
*She's seeking to goad me into trying it again, and I can't, I
can't*! Frightened? Yes, she was that. Bridging was worse than
the worst of heights she had ever faced.

'If you—'

'All right, I'll try! But—' She sought the inner place where
the bridging came from and fixed a destination—nearer than
the one Nisana had chosen—firmly in mind. Nothing. Again,
harder. She fell forward, sheltering her forehead against her
shins. Her brow was slick with sweat.

'No. I cannot. Look, read me if you don't believe what I tell
you.'

The cat's delicate, apologetic joining brushed against her
inner being. 'Odd. I have never seen such a thing, that it

makes you ill. Forebear then. But—if you can, try it now and again. You may be glad one day you did.'

'That had better not be foresight,' Ylia replied caustically. Her stomach hurt and her hands shook. She stuffed them between her thighs, clamped them tight. Nisana rubbed against her, leaped up the ridge to hunt.

Ylia's gaze followed, but she lost her almost immediately in the dusk. The sky already was that velvety dark blue that holds in the high places after sunset. The air was pleasantly, rather surprisingly warm; the wind had died away, at least for the moment. She leaned back, gazed across the intervening meadow to the campfire and the shadows of her friends.

One of these detached itself after a while, started across the open ground. Brendan. Brendan beyond doubt. She stood and moved out of the grove so that he might see her, for she was suddenly certain she was the object of his search.

It was Bergony who first permitted the Osneran Chosen—with their narrow, hide-bound religion—to inhabit the King's old summer dwelling within the foothills, half-way between Koderra and Teshmor, in exchange for their writing skills. For it was Bergony's fondest hope that he would be remembered in Nedao as the King who brought literacy to his common folk, and who caused the oral traditions to be set down. Foolish to wonder if he would have permitted the Chosen their foothold if he had known his eldest son would wed one whom the priests term witch—and that their daughter would carry—again, for the Chosen—that same curse. Then again, the Chosen in Nedao are a small, if vocal, cult. Even among the folk of the North, where the religion is strongest, few would deny their well-loved Ylia her place.

19

"I thought I might find you here—I saw the cat leave you a short while since." He hesitated. "I—I hope you did not remain for solitude, since I have broken it."

"No. Nisana was helping me—giving me instruction, really. But we are long since done."

"Instruction?" He dropped down to sit cross-legged on the turf. Near, he decided, but not near enough to be considered forward. She could see *him*, of course—*magic*, he whispered to himself, and wondered a little: In all his life, he'd never seen magic, scarcely thought of it. And these past days, he'd seen little else.

She smiled; her face was a paleness against the shadow, the dark cloak. "I do not understand what I have, what I can do now, that I could never before. How to work the Power. Nisana is helping me to sort it through." Silence. "Bren?"

"Ylia?"

"Does—does it bother you? My blood, my mother, Nisana —the Power itself?"

"Does it—" he considered this for some moments. "I see. Because I am Northern, you mean?" He more guessed at than saw the nod. "No. I do not follow the Chosen, I told you that. And even if I did, even a man of narrow mind would see on this journey that there are more sides to magic, to this Power, than the evil the Chosen prate. But you. . . . There is nothing you could ever do that would bother me, I swear it. Save not to ask my aid when you need it."

Silence. She gazed at him, astonished. He cleared his throat, transferred his gaze from her face to his hands, to the tops of the trees that were rapidly merging with the sky. "I must tell you this." He spoke quickly, bringing the words forth before he could change his mind or lose courage. "I—well—you must see that I—you are more to me than arms-mate," he finished in a rush and added then, formally, "I wish to say only—only that, if it is an inconvenience to you—"

"To me?" She was glad for the dark, glad he could not see her face clearly, for it burned, and tears touched her eyes. She caught at his hands. "Brendan, are you blind? Are—do you think you are any less to me?"

He gripped her fingers tightly. "I had not thought to look upon any woman as I do you. But I do not know, not for certain, *how* I feel."

"I know." She did. "Because that is how I feel. More than arms-mate, more than friend, though you are those things to me also. But I never thought beyond duty to Nedao. If this is how Brelian loves his Lisabetha—or another thing entirely—"

"Whatever it is, we shall know in time." Brendan pulled gently at her arm and she leaned against him. It was a while before either moved. Brendan finally stirred. "They will be calling us, we had better return to camp. Which reminds me," he added as he helped her to her feet. "I brought you this. The first of the jerky." He pressed a narrow, oily strip of meat into her hand. She worried a bite off one end.

"Tough. Not quite dry enough, of course. Not bad. Needs salt, though."

"It is rather bland, isn't it? Mistress Malaeth is soaking some in one of her teas, she thought it might help."

"Mmmm. Sage might work. Well, it will keep us alive, and it does not actually taste bad." She laughed then. "Come, you are right, we will never hear the last of it if they must call *us.*" He laughed.

"I also meant to ask if you would cross swords with me in the morning," he said as they neared the fire. "I have a new trick I think you might like."

She nodded. "Of course." Brendan inclined his head formally, but his eyes were warm. Brelian hailed him from the other side of the fire; Ylia went to aid Malaeth with her greens.

The morning was grey and chill and swordwork welcome, for it stirred the blood. They were far from perfectly matched, and Ylia, excellent at her own level, fought frustration, certain she could never hope to equal his casual brilliance, which owed as much to flair as it did skill. But she had an edge on him, however slight, in speed and lightness on her feet.

Frustrated or not, she learned much that morning: The quirk twist by which he had disarmed the King's two swordsworn simultaneously at Fest the past winter; the heel-pivot-sidestep combination, which gave him greater control of a change of direction; the means he used to pull an overeager adversary off balance and onto his point. And lastly, he had shown her his new trick: A dagger throw more accurate than the common underhanded sling. This called for an across-body, back-handed movement of hand, wrist and arm that was painful if practiced for very long at a time, but it gave back such speed and accuracy as to make it well worth learning.

"You could take the coin at Fest with this," Brendan said eagerly, and she was nearly as excited, for though she had barely passable ability with thrown knife, she had already buried the blade two fingers from the mark, twice in a row.

"It's wonderful," she laughed, exultantly. "Has Marhan seen it?"

"Well—I hadn't shown him; not yet. I was still working on it yesterday." He retrieved the two blades, his and hers, handed them to her. "Try again. More snap to the wrist. You

really have to *think* the motion at first, since it is so unlike the
old way. Oh, yes, that has it!'' The knife was less than a finger
from the mark this time; his thudded in a moment later between the mark and hers. She retrieved them both and
dropped to the ground, leaned back against the tree.

"Enough. My arm feels like it will break off at the wrist if I
try that once more. If I quit now, I might still have a hand in
the morning.''

"Good idea.'' Brendan squatted on his heels next to her.
"*I* wasn't quite so sensible yesterday; mine still hurts.'' He
smiled. "You know—you're good!''

She tilted her head back and laughed. "And you're surprised, aren't you? No, don't try to hide it, everyone is. But
why shouldn't I be good? Marhan made a lot of noises, but he
trained me just as thoroughly as he trained any of Father's
dagger-sworn, any of Corry's men.''

"Well, it *is* a surprise. A pleasant surprise, of course,'' he
added hastily.

"Of course,'' Ylia mocked gently. He reached out to brush
stray bits of hair from her damp face.

"I never had a chance to train with Marhan when he was in
the North. I was a little too young. Most of what I know
comes from Erken. And, of course, I got in what practice I
could with Galdan, his son. He and I were nearly of an age,
though he seemed older, and usually he was away, tending to
things for the Duke. But I learned a lot from him—Galdan.
More than from Erken, I think.''

"He must be quite good then.'' She blotted her brow
against her sleeve. "I have seen Erken, and he is one of the
best Nedao ever had.''

"He is all of that. But Galdan has a flair I admit I copied
shamelessly.'' He drew a deep breath, and the light went out
of his face.

"No. Don't, Bren. Here. Now. Nothing else.''

"I'm sorry.'' He caught her fingers, held them in both his
hands. "Somehow, I'm reminded—I fenced a few times with a
cousin of yours.''

"Oh?''

"Nala's Curse—sorry. Vess.''

"No cause to be sorry. You do not insult *me*.''

He hesitated. "He's skilled. Vess. But if I may say it, a
sheep louse otherwise!''

Ylia leaned back against the tree laughing. "Oh, Mothers,

you could not have named him better!''

"Whenever there was trouble among our officers—we were only commons and young ones at that, Brel and I, but Father knew him all too well—whenever there was trouble, you could usually find Vess at the bottom of it. And—women—'' he hesitated, glanced at her dubiously. One didn't really speak of such things among ladies. But then, Ylia was not the velvet-cased darling one thought of when one thought of ladies. She caught his eye and, apparently, also his uncertainty.

"It's all right. I've been around the creature a good deal of my life. So far as I can tell, he only began attacks on my life when the attempt on my virtue failed." She smiled up at him. "Now you're shocked."

"No—''

"Never mind the lie. This is me and I can tell, remember?''

"Oh.'' He laughed, embarrassed. "Anyway,'' he went on. "Whenever there was trouble—of *that* kind, involving a girl, he was in that up to his pretty, embroidered collar, too. And he nearly killed some poor tinker—the gate guard broke that up, I think, barely in time to save the old fool.''

"I heard about *that* one,'' she said. "Poor child hadn't known how to repulse him, and when he spread the tale around her father caught up the sword he'd hardly ever used and went for him.''

"I wonder,'' Brendan said finally, "that he'd attempt closeness with you—'' This time he stopped and turned red to the ears. "Not my meaning; hush, woman. He'd have gone for Brandt's heir if she'd been pimpled and cross-eyed, to gain the throne. But with your mother, your AEldran blood—''

"I know. He always talked loudly enough about that. Nedao falling prey to a plague of witches, led, no doubt, by Mother, with me at her side and a hoard of demons on our heels. If you ask me, he babbles Chosen very nicely in Northern company, but believes less of it than I do. And he's so hungry for the King's circlet, he'd do anything to have it.''

"Oh?''

"He is, you know.''

"Is?'' Brendan shook his head. "Not any more, he isn't.''

Ylia considered this gravely. "You think him dead? Really? Well, I can only hope you are right.'' She lay back on the cool grass. Brendan dropped down beside her.

"What do you know that I do not?''

She shrugged. "Nothing. I cannot foresee. Just a feeling. He was not on the walls."

"I do not recall him, but then—"

"No. I was in a position to know, and I would have seen *him*, if no one else." Silence. "Not on the walls, certainly not amongst—not with the horsemen." Pain darkened her eyes briefly; she pushed it away. "He could not have gone to Yls, the boats had left long before Father's Council was done, and he—well, *I* cannot picture him taking a rowboat down-River and out into the open sea. And if he returned to Teshmor, then I'm a Tehlatt!"

"He's dead, then. Has to be."

"I hope so." Doubt nagged at her. "But Vess is better at taking care of himself than anyone else I ever knew. I cannot imagine him dead, somehow."

"Well—" Bren considered this gravely. "Anything is possible, I suppose." An idea struck him. "Vess—*he* could not be behind these attacks on us, somehow, could he?"

Ylia stared at him blankly. "I—*what*?"

"It's not likely, I know that, but think on it, try!" he urged.

Silence. Her eyes glazed, stared through him. "I—there has always," she said finally, "been *something* about Vess. As though Nala, his mother, lay with a Mallick and then brought forth Vess. Something beyond simply—unpleasant, though he has none of the Power; he is certainly not AEldran. But there was always—" She closed her eyes, shook herself. Shook her head. "It does us no good to guess at these things, Bren. I—I would say, not likely. More likely that some—thing—already here sets things at us, don't you think?"

"Likely. Probably. But unliklier things have happened to us already, remember that!"

"All right." She smiled. "This will all seem like a dream, won't it?"

"When we reach Aresada? Perhaps. If we ever get so far."

She nodded. "We will. No," she laughed, laid a hand across his mouth as he opened it indignantly, "*not* foreseeing: stubbornness. We are so determined, all of us, nothing will dare impede us further!"

He laughed also. "Or face your wrath, is that it? Look you, we are wasting time here. Or so Marhan and Levren will see it if they come looking for us."

"They," Ylia replied firmly, "will get nothing from me

until I have at least bathed my face and my poor feet. Come,
help me up, I am worn out and it is entirely your doing.''

"Oh, you are? Look at me, if you think *you* are tired." He
fell back flat, puffing and gasping. She giggled, jumped up
and pulled him to his feet. They wandered down to the lake,
splashed themselves, each other. Brendan combed his beard
and hair with his fingers, kissed her fingers gravely and went
in search of his brother. Ylia struggled with her boots, finally
managed them off and plunged her feet and legs into the
stream, above where it joined with the lake. *Ahhh. Bliss beyond comparison.*

"Ylia?" Not Lev or Marhan; Lisabetha had found her. "I
need to speak with you. Now, please, if you will."

"A good time. I am going nowhere until my feet feel like
they are feet once again. Brendan wore them out this morning." Lisabetha smiled, rather absently. "And how is it Brelian has left you to yourself for so long?" The smile widened,
briefly warmed her eyes.

"Oh—he and Brendan had things to do. They went to cut
me a staff like Malaeth's. But I think Bren wanted to talk to
Brelian alone, anyway."

Her face felt suddenly warm. Lisabetha grinned at her, sus-
picion confirmed. "You wanted," Ylia said pointedly, "to
speak with me."

The smile slipped; the girl nodded. "I must. I—promise you
will not laugh at me. But—I—I have *dreamed*."

"Dreamed," Ylia echoed blankly.

She nodded. "I have never, ever spoken of it. But I think I
can tell you; you will believe me. And not despise me for it.
But—also, it concerns you." The swordswoman's hands went
cold as she began to see what Lisabetha was skirting. *Mothers,
the child has the Sight. She can foresee.*

"All of us," Lisabetha went on unhappily, "but you
mostly. You see—" She sat abruptly on the bank. "—it is a
thing I have always done, since I can remember. That I dream
a thing and it happens. Not often. But sometimes. And I can
tell when it is that kind, when it is only dream." Her hands
twisted in her lap.

"You can foresee."

"I can," she admitted. The hands tightened on each other.
"Not as the Northern women do, but in dream. Last night, I
could not sleep right away, for I—well, I was happy. Excited.

But I knew, all of a sudden, that I was asleep for I was dreaming—one of *that* sort."

"And the dream?" Ylia asked as she hesitated again.

"We were in a place; there were rocks and twisted, stunted trees. I saw you—you and Nisana—you were standing alone, a distance away from me. A redness filled the air and you were both gone." She drew a deep, shuddering breath. "There was such fear, such a horror, I could not breathe. Swords, the clash of weapons. Cries. And I woke. I—dared not close my eyes again, after that."

"Foreseeing." Unnecessary to ask, the truth of it rang clear to her bones. "But, Lisabetha, a foreseeing need not come to pass! Any deviation from a chosen path can avert the thing foretold." *Or so they say.* "Tell me what you can recall of the dream; try and remember." Silence. Ylia touched her shoulder. "What did you see? Enough to recognize the place? And that fear—was it Mathkkra?"

Lisabetha forced a smile. "Well; at least you believe me. But I am certain of nothing. I was too frightened to retain anything but what I told you. But it happens, now and again, that a dream comes more than once, or that I remember more of it later. I might recognize the place, though it could be anywhere high within the Foessa. And it frightened me so badly! I am sorry, Ylia. Perhaps I—should not have told you."

"No, and don't be sorry. I greatly prefer being forewarned to being surprised. Particularly the kind of surprise the Foessa hand us. But, why did you never tell me of this before?"

"You must ask?" Lisabetha fell into a bitter contemplation of her hands again. "Since childhood, all I have heard of such a thing is that it is evil, a gift of the Dark One. No good person, no true child of the One *dreams*. But I never wanted it!" she cried out. Ylia caught at her hands; she clung to strong fingers. "Would—would you know what I saw last? Teshmor's fall and my brother's death!"

Ylia detached her fingers gently, wrapped them around the girl's shoulders. "Lisabetha. Little sister. Listen to me. I do not wish to undermine what you believe, your Chosen religion. Truly. I have no right. But I swear to you by everything *I* hold sacred that your foreseeing is not evil. No more evil than the healing I used on your Brelian. You never chose it, it chose you; how could that make *you* evil? They misinterpreted the teachings of their One, those who told you such things. They must have!" Mothers, how *could* Lord Corry and the Lady

Lossana ever have countenanced such teachers? Or were these
Chosen that insidious, presenting a pious and humble face to
the parents while they sought to turn the child?

"But it is a poor gift, Lisabetha, one I am glad I do not
possess, to see that which you cannot cure. And," she added,
"it is odd indeed that you dream. That is how an AEldra
would foresee, in dream. But you are not AEldra."

Lisabetha shook her head. "No. I can trace my lineage back
to the Isles; there is no Ylsan blood in Planthe." She drew a
deep breath, let it out slowly. "I—I do not know. *You* have
been called evil; I was taught your mother, the Queen, was
evil. Because of your blood. But I do not believe it, not anymore. If you say—"

"I say," Ylia replied firmly, as she hesitated. "Do not tor-
ture yourself for a thing you cannot alter! And *you* are not
evil, Lisabetha, we all know that!" That brought another faint
smile. "Listen, Brelian is calling you. Go on, go to him. But
try to recall anything you can of this dream. And remember
this: You have warned us. We have never before had that
much aid since we began this journey."

The girl ran back to camp. Ylia shivered. *Foreseeing. By the
Nasath, why did I never see it? I should have realized.* It was
no comfort at all that what Lisabetha saw paralleled her own
fears: Someone in the Foessa was aware of them, and sought
to work to their undoing. Someone was aware of *her*, Ylia,
personally, and wanted her death.

> *Those of our own AEldra kind who dream true say
> that any deviation in the chosen path will permit one to
> avoid the thing dreamed. I do not dream true; none of
> our cat-kind do. Nor are we generally of a fatalistic
> bent. But there are no set rules, no things which are
> always so or never so. Perhaps we were fated to the path
> we walked from the first day we entered the Foessa. Or
> perhaps—as became increasingly more likely—our path
> was chosen for us.*

There is a Nedaoan saying: Trust nothing
you cannot both see and touch. And then
trust only half of that. And there is our own
saying: If it is unknown, make absolutely
certain fear is truly unnecessary. And so I
put no trust in the child's dream, but did not
fear it either. I was cautious—as I had been.
It was not, unfortunately, enough.

20

The sun topping the ridges on the fifth day looked down
upon a swarm of activity: Eight people gathering belongings,
snuffing the fire which had become a deep, blackened pit;
donning roughly patched cloaks and food pouches which now
bulged with provisions, reluctantly beginning the northward
journey once again. A tortoise-shell cat wove in and out of
their feet, sprinted ahead to wait on a sun-warmed outcrop of
rock and wash one white forepaw.

The valley was a short one, and before the air began to
warm the company was among the trees, starting up a narrow
rift close to one of the streams which flowed into the lake.
Over the years it had cut through solid rock to a depth of
many lengths, carving it as a sculptor works soft wood, and
through this tortuous, moss-covered stony canyon the water
boiled a deep, clear green, frothed with white. They stayed
clear of the rock whenever possible, since it was scoured
smooth at best, treacherous where spray from the depths had
made it wet.

Perhaps an hour's slow, cautious climb brought them out
into level forest: Dusty, dead pine needles covered the ground.
Here and there a low, scraggly bush, light-starved and dry

looking. Mushrooms projected from tree trunks near the ground or pushed up through the mold of the forest floor. The trees towered, cutting off most of the sunlight. Fallen, rotting logs were numerous, making straight travel difficult.

Once again they were dependent on Golsat's wonderful sense of direction, for often there was not even a ray of sun slanting through the trees to show which way they went. It was still: They could hear the creek long after they moved away from it, now and again the harsh chattering of squirrels, the distant chirp of birds from high above, the whisper of wind through the distant tree tops.

Gradually the tall, dry forest shaded into cedar; by mid-afternoon they were surrounded by the stately, red-barked trees. The ground was thick with fern and berry bushes with flat, furred leaves. Now and again a long branch of wildflower reared its delicate lavender head above thickets of fern; more than once a cloak snagged on thorns. Here they went straight through the undergrowth, holding to Golsat's instinct.

Throughout the day, Ylia held rearguard with Brendan. "Bren, this is between us." She had argued with herself for days; finally, at long last, persuaded herself to speak. "There may be danger. Lisabetha has foreseen it."

He frowned. The message took several moments to sink in. Then: "*Lisabetha*?" His eyes went wide.

"Lisabetha. Do not let her know I told you of it."

"But—" He shook his head, opened his mouth to speak, abandoned whatever thought he had. Thought again. "Danger. No more?"

"That there is Power in it. Be on your guard."

"I am with Marhan," Brendan said gloomily. "I want an honest enemy who carries weapons like my own, and when I fight him, that is all he has to point at me. And when I slay him, he is dead and stays there!"

"I would prefer none, if I could choose," Ylia retorted.

He laughed at that, held out a twist of jerky. She worried the end off it with her teeth, offered her water bottle. He caught at her fingers, carried them to his lips, held them against his cheek. "We are warned; at least there is that. That is more than a warrior dare ask, isn't it?"

"So it is. And we shall win out again, if we are beset." He smiled. They stretched out their pace to catch up with the others.

• • •

They descended from the trees near the halfway point of a long lake late in the afternoon, camped near its gravelly shore and were on their way at first light.

A second night; a third. They made dry camps well after dark, stopping only when footing actually became hazardous, for Marhan was becoming impatient with their slow pace and wished to press for as much distance a day as he could. He got little argument; the company was becoming nervous with thought of the long journey still before them, increasingly uncertain of what they would find at its end. There was wind, the air was chill and the sun hid behind clouds two days running, but they slept warmly both nights: the first in a thicket, the second in a shallow cave.

Nisana kept her own counsel for the most part, making such searches as she felt necessary, though on one or two occasions she held Ylia to aiding her with the far vision so as to strengthen the swordswoman's use of it. Twice they sensed the Fear, but at a great distance. Beyond that, only those animals native to the Foessa.

'Perhaps the girl dreamed false,' the cat grumbled. It was late in the third day, and she had been restless for most of the afternoon, twisting and moving around in her pouch.

'Do you really believe that?'

'I would rather. Then it would be that I sense nothing because there is nothing to sense! As it is—I cannot tell. Huh. Let it go at that.'

Ylia reached under her cloak to rub the thick fur. 'So I shall, cat. Because if something is there to be sensed, you will know it, my Nisana.'

'Huh! As I knew of the Mathkkra in time to avoid them?'

'That was different.'

'It is *all* different here,' she snapped.

'You,' Ylia snapped in reply, 'are as bad as Marhan! Do not plague me with guilt, cat! If there is anything to be found—or not found—you will know it.'

'Perhaps.' But she was mollified and lay still for some time after that.

The fourth day out from the valley brought them once again to a place of heights and sheer drops, of great falls of rock and ledges, waterfalls and the ever-present wind. The land fell off swiftly to the west, and they could see down into tree-filled valleys, see jagged, snow-and-ice-clad peaks beyond them.

Ylia shivered, pulled her cloak close, fastened it with the bit of sharpened twig Golsat had fashioned for her two nights before. It helped some; though not enough. But they walked quickly to keep warm, and managed nearly two leagues by midday.

"Ylia?" Brendan had spent most of the day with Golsat and Brelian at rearguard. She caught at the hand he held out.

"Brendan?"

He smiled. They walked together for a while. At length he roused himself. "You know, it is just possible—I am not certain, but it *is* possible!—that that peak yonder, the tallest of them, is Yenassa."

"The—"

"No, not that one." He caught at her shoulders, turned her to face more north than east. "There. It sits just south of the village Malfor." She squinted, finally shook her head. "It is pointed enough to be Yenassa," he went on. "Unfortunately, I have seen it from only three angles, never this fourth. But if it is Yenassa—"

"Malfor." Hard, really, to remember another life and the great map in Koderra's Hall that showed even the least of villages, such as Malfor, with its twenty-odd huts. "That would put us beyond the halfway point to Aresada, wouldn't it?"

"So it would." He wrapped a would-be casual arm around her shoulder as they set out again. "If so, we could make the Caves by midsummer."

"Certainly that. If not sooner." She leaned against him. "Though—these past few days have been pleasant."

"I could say as much," he replied gravely, and set a light kiss on her brow. "More pleasant for me than most, in fact." He gazed thoughtfully across her hair. "I think I will go get my brother's opinion. But that *must* be Yenassa."

"All right."

"I won't be long." His fingers slid across her shoulder; he dropped back. She smiled, caught at the warmth that bubbled across her inner being, the warmth that had radiated from his thought, and hugged it to her.

The silence was broken only by the wind and a crow that followed them for most of the afternoon. Eventually it flew off west, dropped down into one of the hollows far below and was gone, leaving them alone with the whine of wind through rock. Slides became more frequent, often blocking whole portions of the ledge. Marhan and Levren, who had been scouting well ahead, came back to confer during one of the longer rest breaks.

"There isn't much ahead, except perhaps a stand of trees or so. It may be a cold night," the Bowmaster said. "We couldn't see any way down off this ledge yet. Unless—" he eyed Ylia, carefully avoiding Marhan's cold scowl. "Unless there is a way you and the—and Nisana could find—"

"We can try," Ylia replied doubtfully. When they set out again, she and Nisana led.

The land was becoming more rough by the length: flat, water-worn sheets of rock, covered with forest debris from the ledges above, alternated with huge huddles of boulders. A few wind-twisted trees, rooted precariously in the steep cliff face to the right, stayed the wind a little. Slides, and more slides.

Late in the afternoon they came to the widest such pile of rubble they had crossed all day; it dropped from high above, covered the ledge, straggled out to a sheer drop on the left. There was no way around, only across. Treacherous footing here: Rock slid underfoot, clattered down the ledge to drop in silence to the valley a hundred lengths or more. Ylia savagely forced her thought away from this as she threaded a way across to solid ground. Nisana bounded lightly from rock to rock, waited impatiently on the other side. The rest followed, slowly.

'Ylia. Come here. Now!' Nisana padded to the very edge. Ylia swallowed, followed unwillingly. *Gods and Mothers, not an overhang, and it goes down to—no, don't think it, don't dare!*

Tall, broken rock walls still lined the eastern side of the ledge, but to the west the ground dropped away sickeningly, and to a terrifying depth. A bowl-shaped, thickly forested valley lay far below. Here and there tall, broken trees stood above the rest. There had been fire here, though a long time since.

She tore her eyes away with an effort; she was dizzy, ill with it. Horrible, horrible heights. 'No,' Nisana snapped. 'Not that. Look—with your mind, do it!'

No. Her body would give way, she knew it, would pitch her over that ledge and down . . . down. . . . She managed, somehow, to stumble back, to turn away.

Breathe, gods and Mothers, do it! A deep breath. Another.
But the strangely unbalanced feeling remained. In fact, it was
growing stronger by the moment. A strangeness, a threat—
ambush—Mathkkra? What lies in wait for us down there? For
there was *something*.

'Ylia/Nisana, join!' They demanded simultaneously, driven
by a sudden, dire urgency. Ylia drew on her own strengths, felt
the reassuring, bolstering power of the AEldra cat strong in
her mind. They probed at the land below: Devoid of life,
unless one counted owls and—and no. She was certain, suddenly; the last of the height dizziness, the terror that accompanied it, left her as her mind snapped around something.
'It's not right, cat. Not what it seems!'

'No. All wrong.'

It hid *something*, the notion teased at her like a half-noticed
fragrance, something seen from the corner of an eye. 'Hold,
cat,' she commanded, 'and aid me!' She drew a deep breath,
launched hard at the landscape below them with the full
strength of both.

"Ah, no!" Lisabetha was free of the slide. Her eyes were
wild, her face the color of parchment; her words echoed off
the rock around them. "Ylia, no! This—that place—!" The
sense of the words penetrated; Ylia tore free of the *sending*,
again stumbled back from the ledge.

Too late! The emptiness behind them was shattered, and she
screamed aloud in terror and pain, for suddenly they were no
longer alone: Something within the valley was also upon the
ledge, within her mind, pressing savagely upon her will, burning against her inner being. She braced, fought, called upon
her inner strength. There was a roaring in her ears, a cry that
was hers, an echo or reply that was Nisana. A surge of power.
Then: a redness blared across her eyes, momentarily blinding.

Men stood there, men and Mathkkra, surrounding the
others. Ylia staggered. *A step, just one step*. She *must* break
free! But it was as though her legs were frozen in place. Her
right hand touched her hilts, fell limply away. The roar of
Power dimmed all other noises; only faintly now could she
hear the sounds of battle. Lisabetha fell; Brelian.

Pain. There was only pain . . . as though her body were
afire, her mind being torn asunder. A whimper: Nisana. And
Brendan, surrounded by enemy.

Their eyes met as his blade sliced a clear place between them, and she heard his voice above the noise of battle, the inner clamor that was threatening her sanity: "Ylia! I am coming, beloved; hold!" She moved, then, somehow—a step, a second. *Brendan. My Brendan needs me, he needs my aid, I must go to him.* Her fingers groped once again toward her hilts.

Then all was drowned in a waterfall of blood and death. With a strangled cry, she pitched forward into welcome darkness.

They say the dark uses of the Power are denied us who are AEldra. But there are those of us who have studied the histories of Yls, the traditions handed down from the beginning of AEldran history, and we wonder. If the Power is, if it is ours, then how should any side be denied any of us with the strength to take what we want of it? I have never myself wanted such powers as they say the Lammior bore within him—none of them. Nor have any of cat-kind. But—among the human of us—who is to say?

21

Pain. So much pain. Her mind shook with it; a high, whining hum filled her ears. She attempted the sign of healing —*hold, cease, do not breathe, do not move*—so little concentration, but it set her head pounding. Slowly the ache lessened, the scree died to a whisper of sound at the edge of hearing. Only then did she become aware that she lay at full length, and not upon the ground, but upon a cool, tiled floor.

Pressure against her ribs—*boot?* It withdrew. Light feminine laughter echoed across a vastness of chamber. "My Lord, this is not my cousin's daughter, it is not even woman, and surely not AEldra! It is disgustingly dark of skin, it wears men's clothing—and it smells." *Smells?* She sniffed cautiously. An exotic perfume teased her nostrils.

"Not so, Marrita, my own." A man's voice, this time: resonant, distant. *Whose?* "AEldran, nevertheless, it is. Half, at least. And kin. And woman, though I forgive your doubt on this count, at least!" He laughed. The laughter ceased suddenly. "And," the voice was hard, "it is aware once again, are you not? Do not dissemble, not to me, Queen Ylia of Nedao."

Nedao? I am Ylia. She forced her eyes to open. Swallowed. A sour taste filled her mouth.

Light filled the chamber, reflecting against high windows, blinding her. She blinked rapidly. *Who spoke?* Small feet —woman's—cased in cream-colored boots, the toes edged in deep blue, were momentarily all she could see. Then—robes of a paler blue dragged the floor, the hems edged in cloth of silver, much broidered; the velvet gemmed here and there as though precious stones had been flung carelessly across the fabric, like stars in the night sky. She who stood there neither moved nor spoke.

Ylia rubbed a hand across her brow, wiped it on her breeches. *We were assailed*. She remembered that—but—*we*? There was a blank, a terrifying blank. An effort to force it set her head pounding again. *Up. Whoever they are, do not grovel before them*. For whatever cause. She rolled to hands and knees, gritted her teeth, finally tottered to her feet.

AEldra tall, the woman who confronted her. Pale golden hair was piled in elaborate curls, held here and there with delicate silver clips. Dark blue stones gleamed at her ears, matching the wide cornflower blue eyes under narrow, finely arched brows. The generous, rouged mouth smiled, revealing neat little teeth; but the eyes did not smile. A face as young as Lisabetha's, as innocent of line—*Lisabetha? Ah—my Lady of Chamber*, she suddenly knew. *But she fell, I saw that*—it was gone.

She caught her breath as her eyes focused on the thing only half-seen as she stood: a ring of that rare, translucent green stone, worn on the right hand, little finger. Suspended from this, a tissue-fine kerchief, broidered in a maze of delicately, intricately couched threadwork.

She stared stupidly at the gauzy thing. Longer than wide, draped, one end fastened to the ring, the other to the wrist of the AEldran's robes. This hand, it effectively proclaimed, is too fine for common labor, for anything save decoration. But that bit of personal ornamentation could only be worn by a female member of one of the Ylsan Great Houses, and in fact was seldom worn by any but a member of the Sirdar's own family!

AEldra, beyond doubt, but unlike any Ylsan she had ever met. A gainsaying of everything she had ever known or believed of Power. *Unclean! The ancient strengths can only be used for good, but somehow she has not been held to that*!

Ylia met her eyes, unwillingly. The AEldran gazed back with cool amusement, as though she knew the Nedaoan's thought, allowed her own glance to wander from plaited hair to the toes of worn boots. She withdrew then, as though she had suddenly lost interest, and Ylia lost sight of her in the glare of light coming through the windows.

Silence. The dread which had hovered behind pain plucked at her thought as new bits of memory smote. Lisabetha—she remembered suddenly, truly. Lisabetha had fallen and so had Brelian. On the ledge—where? And—were they all dead, all of them? Silence. She reached within. The Power lay intact, and she drew a ragged, relieved breath at that. But she could not reach beyond herself with it. *A shielding—whyfor? That I think myself alone? That*—she staggered as her legs threatened to give way. *Do not dare be weak, this is no time for weakness*!

She shook her head in a desperate attempt to clear it, blinked against the light that was making her eyes tear. How long had she lain there? And—who approached?

Slow click of boots on the tiled floor, an outline against the tall windows. The other—the man's voice—the strength upon the ledge. He stopped a bare arm's length away. He—man, by his shape—*man's form, but who to say what dwells within*?

There was a wrongness about him, radiating from him. AEldra Power; recognizeable as AEldra Power, though stronger by far than any she had ever seen or heard tell of—and turned, corrupted.

And suddenly, she could see him much too clearly.

He was tall, even for AEldra, and pale skinned; his hair was a coppery gold, like his brows. Reddish freckles scattered across high cheekbones, the back of the hand that stroked his clean-shaven chin. His eyes, unexpectedly, were dark, the color of smoke and difficult to meet. He was clad all in somber red—breeches, a close-fitting tunic, both plain and serviceable. The only ornamentation of any kind about him was a Narran short cloak of deeper red than his pants, casually tied across one shoulder and under the other arm. No visible weapons, though he had the unmistakable look of a swordsman.

They studied each other; his eyes were unfathomable, his face expressionless. Ylia felt the first edge of anger pressing aside pain and emotional numbness alike.

"Ylia, Brandt's daughter." His voice was coldly mocking, resinous. An unpleasant smile turned his lips. "Ylia, daughter to the fair Scythia of the Second House. You do honor to my halls, Lady of Nedao." He paused, awaiting response; she made none. He smiled, gestured imperiously to someone behind him. A chair was brought—by Mathkkra. They retreated toward the darker side of the chamber as he collapsed into the seat, sprawled his legs.

She caught her breath; so faint a sound, but he raised his brows, and laughed. It was not a nice sound. "You wonder at them, I see. They serve me." She tore her eyes from him with an effort. High peaks, out the window barely visible against the yellow light of late afternoon. *Where am I*? "I am Lyiadd. You may call me that. Or cousin. We are distant kin, after all."

"No." Her voice threatened to give way; she coughed, winced as headache flared. This—this aided the Cavefolk, and called them servants? "No. Even if your father and mine were the same, I would not call you kin!"

He raised sand-colored brows and laughed again. "Marrita, did you hear that? And you doubt she is Scythia's?" Marrita, wherever she was, made no answer. "That was always *her* way with a compliment," he added, his attention once again all for his prisoner. Ylia drew a deep breath, let it out slowly. *Anger is what he wants, do not give it to him.*

"Yours is the Power the filthy things have taken."

"*I* would not call them filthy, were I you," he replied, casting a fastidious eye over her torn and travel-stained clothing. "They serve me; of course I have armed them. Do you any less for those who serve you, Lady of Nedao?"

"When the High Council learns what you have done—!" she began. He overrode her.

"But who will tell them—Lady? *You*? Your four-footed AEldra companion, perhaps?" He snapped to his feet with a snake's grace and speed. The stench of turned Power sent her reeling back: one long hand, wrapped in her hair, prevented further retreat. "They will learn *nothing*," he hissed against her ear. Fear surged through her body, her mouth went dry and her legs would no longer hold her: when he released her plaits, she fell.

Up! She forced her terrified body to obedience, rolled and struggled to her knees, then stopped abruptly. *Nisana*? The cat lay not two paces from her, still. Lyiadd was forgotten. She laid a hand on dark fur, but for one shaking moment could not tell whether she lived, so slight was the rise and fall of her small ribs. Alive. Still unconscious. Ylia slewed around, suddenly furious, rose to her feet.

"It may be that you are stronger than I." She could not force her voice above a choked whisper; the sound caught in her throat. "That what Power is yours is greater, and no longer AEldra. But I vow this, who calls himself Lyiadd and cousin, and heed well what I say: If any of my friends have taken harm at your hand, or at your bidding, I will have your life in return. By the Guardians I swear it!"

But he only smiled. "You threaten? *You*?" Laughter grew, echoed. And he vanished.

No trick of her vision, no—he was there, a presence, a horror, an enormous red shadow against the windows, and the light from them was dimmed, as though the sun had dropped behind blood-stained cloud. Red—the air was red, as red as old death; she could not breathe. It pulsed through her inner being, pressed against her will, bringing with it a knowledge that should she give in this time, what remained would no longer be Ylia. She caught her lip between her teeth: Sudden pain and the taste of blood brought her to herself, a little. And somehow, she held.

Gone! She staggered, fell to hands and knees. Tears blurred her vision, it hurt to breathe. Gone—no. Reverted. Lyiadd's boots, dark brown, nearly as worn as her own, hove into her line of vision, and from far above, he laughed.

"You cannot fight me; only a fool would try." There was no strength in her for speech: she spat. "Like your mother, you are impulsive. Clearly, you need time to think how best to act. That I can give you, even if I can give you neither manners nor looks." She dragged herself across the floor to clutch Nisana to her breast as he turned and rapped out an order. Men gripped her arms, dragged her to her feet and from the chamber.

Many flights of stairs and long corridors later—she had long since lost any sense of direction—a door was opened and she was thrust into a small, windowless stone chamber. She clutched Nisana still. Dark was total as the door slammed into place. It took her several moments to remember the second level of Sight, several more to recall how to use it. A clear, if not very clean floor; there a heap of branches, straw and worn blanket against the far wall. One hand touched the wall and she moved as slowly, as cautiously as an old woman. She sighed with relief as she dropped to the odorous pile, set her furred burden on it.

Nisana stretched, blinked.

'Nisana?' How long had she been aware?

'Shhh. Guard your thought. He is listening, do not doubt it!'

'He?' The chamber blurred; she scrambled frantically for support.

'Close your eyes, lie back. Do it!'

She fell limply; the blanket was prickly against bare hands and neck.

'Breathe, girl! You will faint otherwise, and I cannot aid you! Lie still, breathe deep!'

She drew a deep breath, let it out slowly. Another.

'The Power will not obey if you are not calm, you know that. That is right—again—better—'

The tightness in her throat gave way suddenly; she curled into a ball and shook. Silence. A long silence.

'Nisana?'

'Shhh. Relax. Take the time to do it properly.' *Great Mothers, what did I do*? 'Shhh. You did well, do not worry what you cannot alter. Shhh. Relax.' But it was some time before she could control the shaking. Nisana leaned against her arm, a reassuring weight. 'You did as well as any of us could have. Do not worry it. Sit, if you want—not so rapidly!' Ylia dropped back onto one elbow and the nausea faded, slowly.

'How—long were you aware? You frightened me, I thought you dead.'

'A while.' Noncommittal and terse, even for Nisana. Dark-green eyes met hers, the thought in them clear: *He is listening*. She had said that. 'Are you with me again—fully?' the cat went on, in a clear change of topic. 'Body heat, pulse, are they normal?'

'Mostly.' She let her head fall forward, concentrated. The last of the headache flitted across her mind, was gone. Dread surged back to the fore. ''Where are they?'' she whispered aloud. The sound was muffled by thick stone.

'I cannot say.'

'I—'

'No. We are screened, you and I. I cannot sense them.'

'Lisabetha—Brelian—'

'They fell, Ylia. I saw that much. If badly hurt or dead—I don't know.'

She swallowed. Forced herself to go on. 'I—I think—I am afraid that—'

'I did not see Brendan,' Nisana answered.

'I did. He was trying to reach us when I was taken. He was fighting—'

'Against such odds? The fool!' But her fury vanished as abruptly as it had risen; she rubbed against Ylia's fingers. 'I am sorry. I know you are—but against so many!'

"He would not tamely give over," she whispered. *If he died, trying to come to my aid—but I still live; he must!*

'We are shielded here, you and I.' Nisana broke into her thought. 'Are you properly aware once again?' She nodded. She was aware, aware, suddenly, of what she had done and said in the upper halls, challenging—*why did he not merely kill me and have done*?

'Why? Why did he not kill us both, you and I—or all of us —when we first entered the Foessa?' Nisana was silent a long time. Then: 'Lyiadd.' She was musing, sharing her thought as she rarely did. 'You of Nedao, I have always been amused at your fatalistic attitudes. But after today I can no longer laugh. For it is certainly fate of some kind that brings together Scythia's rejected suitor and Scythia's daughter!'

"*What?*"

'Not a serious one, not by my Scythia's seeking! Only of the Fifth House, and that nominally, Lyiadd. Not kin to your mother's House, either, though he always pretended it was so.' Her thought trailed away into an inner silence from which she roused herself with obvious effort. 'Ambitious, Lyiadd. Lacking even then in scruple. Not notably imbued with Power, but of course those of the Lower Houses are not, particularly. Skilled with the weapons of hand.

'He sought your mother eagerly, to better his standing. And of course—Scythia was a lovely maid.' Another silence. 'She was also kind-hearted, unwilling to hurt, but even she finally became angry and drove him away in a fury. He would have pressed his suit even after she had chosen the young Lord Prince Brandt.'

"Self-centered." Ylia caught at bits of Nisana's tale. "In that I doubt he has changed. But—not notably imbued with the Power?"

'He was not.'

"Was—not." She slammed a fist into her open palm. "I do not like this, cat! Why is he here, where are we? And *what does he want of us*?" She caught her breath, forced herself to silence.

'Ask this of me?' Nisana replied irritably. 'But he brought us from that ledge with purpose, even you can guess that much.'

'Else we would all have died.'

'Exactly so. I know that more of us live than you and I.'

'You *know*!'

'That much. Nothing else.'

"Purpose." Ylia rolled the word on her tongue. Caught her hands together to stop them shaking. "What purpose can we serve such as that? He cannot need *us*! What possible worth have we, other than to ourselves and to each other?"

'I do not know.' Nisana's thought brushed gently across her mind. 'I am sorry, girl; would that I did know.' Ylia pushed fear aside, a little, stroked the cat's fur and kissed the place between her ears. She rose to pace the room—four steps by five.

'Doubtless we shall learn of it, in time, then.'

'Doubtless.'

They held silence for what seemed a very long time after that. They slept in turns, resting as well as they could in the stillness and total dark; though, after so long out of doors, Ylia felt as smothered as Nisana did. They drank from Ylia's bottle, rationing its contents carefully, shared strips of dried meat.

Nisana's mind-touch finally alerted her, dragging her back from a long blankness. Feet whispered across the stone floor beyond the door, Fear licked the chamber. A rattle of bolts. The door slammed against the wall, a torch was thrust within. Before her eyes could adjust, cold, flexible digits wrapped around her wrists and arms to pull her from the chamber.

I did not tell the girl all I remembered of Lyiadd; there was no need to upset her in such a way, and it was clear to me that she would know him all too well before we were done with him. There was much about him I chose to forget myself, in our present plight, so that I could look at him with my fur smooth. He knew me, beyond doubt, for I had always been with my sweet Scythia when he came to court her. He hated me then, for my clear Sight, my knowledge of what he truly was. More, though: Cat-hater. He was that, one of those with an uncontrollable aversion—not, I suppose, unlike the Bowmaster's for foreigners. I own I had used it against him whenever there was opportunity, and I did not look for my life to stretch overlong if we remained within the Lammior's walls. Lyiadd was not one to forget a grudge, not of any kind.

22

The return to the upper levels was longer and more tortuous than the route which had taken them down to the dungeons: A long, dark corridor, its walls seeping a foul water, its floors dangerously damp and slicked, led away from the cell to a flight of stairs, oversteep in its angle, the steps cracked and chipped. Another hall, lit with a single torch, half-gutted, flaring in the breath of cold air gusting through a sagging doorframe. A chamber, great holes in the walls and partly fallen ceiling, a long table marching down most of its length. Moonlight fell between blackened beams, caught at the spiderwebs which hung with gossamer precision across empty windows, between a staff that still bore traces of a rotting standard and the dust-strewn table. Down a corridor whose walls were deep-piled with rubble, around a corner, through two doors into another corridor: This one was wide, well cared for, its floors polished, torches set every ten paces in shining brass brackets. Candles in protected niches were neatly trimmed. Fine hangings covered most of the walls; an occasional polished shield gave back light and movement in twisted patterns. They stopped abruptly before one of the many doors. It opened into a darkened chamber.

The Mathkkra whose appendages had held her—she could not think of them as hands—stepped back. What had been dim movement within was revealed by the second level of Sight to be her companions. *Marhan?* The Swordmaster stood there, blinking against the sudden light, his face dazedly blank. She ran to him; behind her, the door closed with a resounding slam.

"Marhan. Oh, *Marhan*." She clung to him and shook. His grip was momentarily crushing, then, suddenly, gentle. The fear that had nibbled at her inner being returned in full. She pushed free; he would not meet her eyes.

Malaeth—she was there; Lisabetha came from the dark corner, wrapped her arms around both. Ylia gazed over her head: Golsat—there, his back to the wall. Levren—he had been sitting with Golsat, but was on his feet. Brelian knelt near the wall, not far away. No one else. She pulled her hands free from Malaeth's, pressed Lisabetha gently aside.

"Ylia—come—" Levren had an arm around her shoulders. She twisted free.

"Brendan?" The name caught in a suddenly dry throat. Brendan lay at her feet, hands folded across his dagger. She knelt, laid a trembling hand against his face. Warm, he was still warm. But he no longer breathed. "Brendan—beloved—"

"He died only a short while since," Lisabetha whispered. "We could not save him."

"Brendan—" *Oh, Bren. No!* Pain and madness tore at her. *I could have saved him! I could have, but I was not here and for that he died. I could have—could have.* . . . Levren's hands caught her shoulders; she fell against him and wept.

She was weak and ill when she finally pushed away from him again; one hand clutched at his arm lest she fall. The other hand reached, fingers slipping across Brendan's face, to his shoulder. A dreadful gash had torn through his mail there; his blood darkened the steel rings. But there were others—many of them. She went cold. It would not have been easy, no. But she could have saved him. *My Brendan. He* had known this, had kept her away until it was too late. 'Lyiadd will die for this, my Brendan, by the Mothers, by the Black Well, by your body I swear it!'

Nisana pressed against her arm, hard. 'He will hear you! Do not think such things!'

'Let him hear.'

'He has done this so you may know the kind of being he is, what kind of thing he could do to all of us. Ylia, beware!'

'I am not afraid of him.' Nor was she—she had gone numb; there was only deadly purpose left.

"Ylia." Marhan's voice was husky. She turned to look at him properly. His shirt was torn and bloody across the forearm. *My Swordmaster is hurt.* She stood, swayed, gratefully accepted Levren's grasp on her shoulders as she reached; as light as her touch was, he winced. "I dropped my guard when you and the cat vanished," he said.

"I will heal it. No, do not protest, please Marhan. Let me do what things I yet can." Her voice held no emotion. Like the rest of her it had gone cold. But the healing remained. *Lyiadd has allowed me this, too: Brendan is dead, but I can heal scratches.* Marhan stood with closed eyes, felt gingerly where the wound had been.

"Lisabetha. They hurt you, little sister, I saw that much. Come here." She brought Brelian with her, his hand caught tightly in her own. An ugly bruise spread from her hairline and temple, and clearly pained her terribly. Ylia dealt with that, cupped her hands around Brelian's face, for he was in shock, nearly as far gone as Lisabetha had been in Koderra. She swayed, subsided gratefully against the Bowmaster: Nisana had been right, the healing *could* drain.

The door slammed against the wall, one of the human guards entered, dragged at her shoulder. "You, woman. You

are wanted." Marhan stepped between, tore the man's hand
away.

"This is no filthy commoner such as you!" he snapped.
"This is Nedao's Queen, and that is how you will speak to
her!"

The guard's hand was up to strike the old man when Ylia
moved. The dagger blade in her hand gleamed red in the reflected torchlight. "I *am* Nedao's Queen. Keep your hands
from me and mine. I will come when I am done speaking with
these my friends." She met his eyes levelly; his fell. "Do not
dare touch me—*or* my armsmen—again." She turned her
back on him. "Lev. Marhan, all of you. We have found that
which aided the Mathkkra, which sent the bat-creature and all
else that has plagued our steps through the Foessa. Why we yet
live, I cannot say, and I commend you each to the Mothers or
to the One, as you choose. For we may," she swallowed hard,
"we may yet wish we had fallen with Brendan."

"We knew we lived on stolen hours when we came from the
Plain," Golsat replied quietly. Black, expressionless eyes held
hers, as though he was trying to tell her something beyond his
words. He turned away. She gazed at them one by one—for
the last time, perhaps—then turned, and without so much as a
glance at Lyiadd's armed, strode from the chamber, Nisana at
her side. She heard Marhan's angry words, Levren's reply.
Both were cut off as the door closed.

They walked no great distance, all of it through inhabited,
well-tended halls. At the end of a short, carpeted corridor the
guard pushed open a double, deeply carven door. Ylia stepped
into near-darkness once again. Nisana jumped briefly to her
shoulder, down again as the door closed. The guard remained
in the hall.

No torches, only a fire, near the door, which had burned to
embers. Against the far wall, a candle wavered half-heartedly.
Moon shone full upon ruins beyond the windows: Columns
sagged at crazy angles, lay in broken rubble, leaned against
walls that stretched away into the trees. A tower stood alone,
blue-white, mounds of debris obscuring its base, a cave-
pocked cliff behind it.

The chamber was larger than she remembered it, and she
could now see that, between the windows lining the north and
west walls, the entire corner of the room was raised. Two steps
ran the length of this dais, and two chairs stood in its midst:

oversized, high-backed, wide-armed, canopied. One was empty. Lyiadd sprawled in the other.

His hand cupped his chin. He stared somberly, disconcertingly, at a point well above her head, and when he spoke finally, his voice was expressionless, almost absent-minded, as though he were not only unaware of his prisoners, but unaware that he spoke at all.

"I sense it—I know it is there—no. Again, no." A gemmed dagger, a noble's conceit strapped to the back of his hand, caught the moonlight. He shrugged, the hand dropped back to his side. "Gone. No matter, it always returns." *To whom does he speak?*

"You wonder why I am here, don't you, Ylia of Nedao? Or more important to you, why *you* are here." Silence. His eyes caught, held hers. "Answer me, damn you!" His hand cracked against the chair arm; she jumped, but the fear that had gripped her at their last meeting was no match for the cold that sealed her inner being. "Say or not, then, as you please." He sank back in the chair; his expression was speculative now. Another, even longer silence.

He rose, paced down the room to face her. "Some of you is Ylsan. You will understand, then, why I inhabit these halls if I tell you they were once the Lammior's?" A wordless, shocked sense of Nisana, abruptly cut off. "For a thousand years or more, they stood empty. But they are mine now, and his the strengths I have gained, the greater strengths that were denied the AEldra. I do not have all of them, yet. Though I shall. But the secrets that hold the walls from turning to dust do not reveal themselves so easily." He turned to gaze out the window. "And why, you wonder, do I tell you these things? Because I find it amusing—you have the stupid AEldra fear of the greater Power. For your knowledge, for though you hold obstinate silence, I sense your curiosity. And, because I would have your aid. No, spare me any words you would say, I sense your derision also. I would have your aid. Lady of Nedao." He laughed. "What is Nedao? A handful of ragamuffin followers *you* have led into this peril! A miserable clutch of peasantry crouching in caves a host of leagues from here. I can offer you better than that!"

"No."

"No?" He laughed again. "You still speak without considering. I can offer—"

'She is not her mother, Lyiadd. But even Scythia could say *no* when it was necessary.'

"Small one of the AEldra." Lyiadd turned, smiled unpleasantly as Nisana leaped once more to Ylia's shoulder. "I had not forgotten you." She gazed down her slender nose at him as only a cat is able.

'I was certain you had not. Nor have I forgotten you!' Lyiadd moved back a pace, his expression that of a man who despises cats, and a dislike beyond that.

"No. You can offer nothing I would have," Ylia broke the ensuing silence, her voice flat.

"You do not know this, since you do not know what I would offer."

"No."

"I do not *need* you, of course. But I dare not let you go free, any more than I dared chance letting you go your way in the hopes you would remain unaware of *me*." He began to pace; she watched him warily. Nisana yawned, disinterested, leaped down and padded away to stare out the windows. "It would be easier for both of us if you accepted my aid and gave me yours, freely. Better—not only for you." Silence once again. "Your companions, did you find them well?" His voice was suddenly silken with malice. "My folk were to capture only, know this. It was no fault of mine any of them were injured."

"Liar."

The single word, so flatly uttered, infuriated him; he caught at her plaits, drew back his free hand to strike. "Let me go!" she flared. "Do you think I fear your blows? My dagger-sworn is dead, two others injured, yet another in shock! Strike and yours will not be the only blow!" Her face was as pale with anger as his. He lowered his fist; the other hand remained firmly twisted in her hair. The air in the chamber was thunderstorm thick.

He laughed suddenly, ran a light finger down her throat. "It is a violent creature, a product of its kind. Perhaps you prefer a more gentle form of persuasion?" The laughter gained volume as disgust twisted her face and she closed her eyes. "I should be offended! But I prefer Marrita, who is shaped like a woman and smells like one, who comes to me willingly and knows my needs and likings." He traced the line of her lip. "But then, some of my guard might find you amusing. Everyone has a breaking point of some kind, Ylia of Nedao."

"Beware then," Ylia whispered, "lest I find yours." Only a stubborn pride kept her from gagging.

"And then? Why do you think you would have that chance? I could tear your inner being with no effort at all, now. I could yoke you to my will, if I chose. For as long as I chose." *As I did with Lisabetha, but without waking. Or, would I be aware, aware of what I had become? Unable to stop*?

'You cannot.' Nisana's cool thought broke in on Ylia's. 'Such things cannot hold forever, however strong. We both know that. But you cannot subdue *me* in such a way. My inner being is beyond your reach, human. Try, if you dare!' Ylia glanced at her, back to him. It was true, it had to be, for the look he gave her was murderous. *Nisana, tread cautiously, he will slay you out of hand in his anger.* The cat eyed her briefly, then turned back to her study of the landscape, her thought once again shuttered.

"Well, it doesn't matter, does it? Because I would prefer your willing companionship, your free aid." He let go her plaits, moved back up the stairs onto the dais, past the chairs to the windows. Moonlight formed a nimbus around his pale red-gold hair. "And so I will make you—one last offer. Think well before you speak, not only your life rests on your choice." Silence. "A trade. You and the cat—for your company of followers."

"Trade?"

"Even so. Pledge freely to me, and I will allow them to go on."

She turned away. Nisana was still aloof: *my choice.* But—when she could not even think?

She started, her heart jumped painfully; Lyiadd had stolen up behind her, a red-clad arm pulled her back against him. His voice was soft against her ear. "But *you* are brave," he whispered mockingly. "What is it to you if I give the old woman as a sacrifice to my Mathkkra? You know how sharp the black knives are; she would never feel it, would she? When they cut her throat and let it bleed into the stone bowl?

"And the girl. Under all that dirt, those common garments, she could be pretty. A present to my inner guard after I have taken her—the boy would not mind overmuch, but if he objects to watching, we could remove his eyes."

"Stop it." Her voice was barely a whisper; her mouth had gone dry.

"And your Swordmaster, he is old, he has lived his years. I could put the Baelfyr to him, a little at a time—or perhaps a Thullen; he feared the creature, he fears magic of all kinds. He would beg for death."

"Stop it!"

"Yes, the Baelfyr would be more fitting to the half-blood, since the Tehlatt were cheated of him. I have wondered often how long a man could be persuaded to live, if the Fire is put to him, a little at a time—"

"Stop it, stop it, *stop it!*" Hysteria tore at her throat, and only his grip kept her on her feet. Evil—how could one human body hold so much evil? His hand moved lightly across her shoulder, was gone as he strode back toward the windows. A less-than-thought fluttered across her mind, the gauzy, winged half-hope of a madwoman. She thrust it away from consciousness.

"You would prefer that they live, these companions of yours." Ylia nodded. "A trade, as I have laid it before you?" She nodded again. "If I bridge them a distance from here, to a place where they can resume their journey north?"

"I cannot trust you."

"The three of us will join in the bridging; we can place them a distance where, alone, I cannot reach to return them. Marrita has none of the greater uses of the Power. You would have that for surety."

"I cannot trust you."

"No. But it does not matter, does it?" And he laughed. "Because you have no other choice."

'He does not lie.' Nisana broke her long silence, padded back to Ylia's side and jumped into her arms. 'He has no use for them, once you have sworn.' Lyiadd cast the cat a dark look, and Ylia, with a sudden chilled certainty, knew she had spoken truth. And that, because of it, she would die.

Not soon, no. But he could not use Nisana, or frighten her; he could not turn her to his. *How long will he hold her as surety for my conduct?* "I have no choice: the trade is yours. But—" Her voice broke. "Ask nothing else tonight, I beg you. Not now. I am ill." All the pain and fear flooded back; she suddenly shook with it.

"That much can be amended." He made no call of any kind, but the doors opened and one of the guard stood there. Lyiadd moved with a swordsman's grace to speak with him, waited as the man vanished down the corridor. He returned shortly with one of Marrita's women. "Go with Losora, she will see to your needs." The triumph was gone almost as suddenly as it had come when she capitulated; black gloom settled around him as the chamber emptied and he was again left alone.

Losorra led up-hall, down a side corridor and to a small, plain room. A bar dropped into place behind them, scraped aside when she returned with food a while later, slammed down behind her with finality.

A roughly furnished chamber, this, containing only a table flanked by two backless chairs, a simple tapestry covering a windowless wall. The bed was missing its hangings, and a stuffed and tied overblanket was its only cover. Ylia dropped to one of the chairs as Nisana sniffed cautiously at the tray.

'It is safe, girl.'

'He would not poison us, Nisana; he has what he wants.'

'No. I thought of his woman! And there are poisons which do not kill, merely alter. There are none here, I would know.' Ylia gazed at her, stricken. 'Do not fear for me, Ylia. I can take care of myself. Eat.' Nisana nudged her, hard, as she eyed the food without appetite. 'Eat! Need I force you?' Cat's eyes met human, carefully un-thought understanding in them. Ylia nodded; ate. *Food—strength. Eat.* 'He means us to stay here the night. Dangerous to allow us to go to them.'

'Why?'

'For what you might tell them.'

'Does he think me a fool, cat?'

'I cannot say. But he takes no chances. Now, if we bridge them far enough tomorrow—'

'Tomorrow?'

'You do not think he will wait any longer? He is anxious to be rid of them, do not doubt it!'

'No.' Ylia pushed the tray aside. Nisana picked daintily at what was left.

'If we place them far enough, they will be well past the half-way point.'

'Half—way—' She stared blankly across the room. Brendan had spoken of that: Yenassa. Halfway to Aresada. It was the last thing he had said to her before. . . . She bit her lip, blinked rapidly, but it would not be pushed aside this time. She burst into tears.

'Ylia. No. Do not! It was not your fault, listen to me! Do you think—even if we had not come to that ledge, if we had not searched and so broken the shielding, you and I, Lyiadd would have taken us, and Brendan still would have fought! Whether you had heart-sworn to him or not, he would still have fought!' She couldn't believe it. Even if it was true, it didn't help at all. She had cried out, he had heard her, had tried to come to her aid. Lyiadd had known what would cause her the greatest pain, and Brendan had died because of it. *Brendan—my Brendan. My fault, all of it!*

Nisana's rough tongue rasped against her cheek, her neck, her ear, dragging her back from inner blackness. 'Ylia! Come —come sleep, I will send you sleep! Ylia, by all the gods at once, listen to me!' Ylia choked, drew a deep, shuddering breath. Another.

"Sleep," she whispered. "Give me sleep cat; give me dreamless sleep!" She pushed away from the table, staggered and fell across the bed. Nisana was at her side; the candles went out as the cat willed them. Ylia dragged the covering across her shoulders, remembered nothing else.

The great hall was bathed in moonlight. Window frames and columns cast long shadows across the tiled floor. Half in shadow, Lyiadd lay back in his chair, stared moodily at the opposite wall. An enormous winged shape floated over the ruins beyond the window, its inky shadow following across the chamber.

"Have I done it rightly?" he whispered. "Yes; she has no choices, save those I offer." A humorless smile touched his face, was gone. "Nor, any longer, have I. Catalyst—" His voice, scarce loud enough to disturb the nearest shadows, trailed into nothingness. *Catalyst. That such a child could serve as a turning point for so many matters, and she not even fully born to the Power!* For that, more than fear of discovery, he must keep her, though he still did not fully understand what It had meant, when he delved into the Heart of the Night and was so Answered.

Catalyst: Alive, she could be the means of his destruction, that much was clear, if not the why of it. Dead—dead, the forces channeled through, or by, or because of her would fall upon him now, while he was still ill-prepared, still in search of what It still withheld from him. No, it made little sense. But It did not lie to him, never, however obscure Its Answers might be. Altered, fully his, she would still be Catalyst, but *his*: his to mold, to shape, to utilize against his future subjects and any foolish enough to ally with them. As for the cat—his eyes narrowed. Not long; he'd suffer the creature as he must, for the moment. But—no, not long.

He leaned forward, suddenly intent. *There—almost at my fingertips—gone again.* He rose, strode to the edge of the dais. *No matter. It will be mine in time, and then Yls will be mine. And Nar. And thereafter—thereafter, who knows what may follow?*

> *So many humans speak of their griefs, they share them—now and again, they take the pain and cast it into songs, such as "Edetta's Lament." And while it is not a thing I often do, to recall their songs, my fair Scythia sang that one often. "Ask not of thy beloved, lady; for he is dead and gone; Across his head, a bramble grows; and at his feet, a stone." True love, another common subject for song: Young, of course, thwarted by fate and cut tragically short. Perhaps, in a day long hence, there will be another like song, and they will call it "Ylia's Lament."*

Not my choice—though I cared, in my own way, for each of our company, it was Ylia who would rule them, who knew and loved them as kind to kind, Ylia's decision for both of us. I knew that the boy's death colored her least movement, her least thought that night, and I knew she planned, so far within even Lyiadd could not read her intent. But even I could not have guessed the direction her vengeance would take her.

23

Nisana woke her in the cold, grey hour; food had again been brought, the door stood ajar. 'He intends to send them hence as soon as may be. Eat,' she urged. Ylia ate what she could, knowing she must, but it had no taste. She was disoriented from waking in such a strange place, lightheaded from enforced sleep and not enough of it. *It is not real, any of this.* But the table was hard under her fingers. *I will wake—or perhaps I died when the bat-creature fell upon us.* She swallowed; a tear coursed unnoticed down her cheek. *But Brendan is dead.*

Nisana rubbed against her arm, bringing her attention back. 'Are you well?' Rare, true concern edged her thought. Ylia forced a bleary smile, nodded.

Movement beyond the chamber: guards stood in the hall, waiting.

The hall was crowded: Two full companies of armed lined the walls. There were no Mathkkra. A dozen or so more men stood at the foot of the dais, drawn swords in hand: The rest

205

of the company had preceded them. Ylia moved toward them, stopped hard against the sword of the captain who had brought her to Lyiadd the night before.

Before she could so much as speak, there was a commotion; the outer doors opened and Lyiadd entered, followed by a household guard, Marrita directly behind, surrounded by ladies. With only the briefest glance at the prisoners, the AEldran woman took her chair on the dais.

Lyiadd crossed the chamber, stopped at Ylia's side. She tapped the sword that touched against her breast. "Tell him to move. I must bid farewell to them." Lyiadd frowned; she sighed heavily. "Do you think me a fool, that I will say anything to prevent their leaving? I know you can read what I say to them; I will act in that knowledge." She turned back to the guard. "Tell this to move." Lyiadd gestured; the guard returned her look of distaste in full before he stepped aside. The remaining armsmen made an opening for her.

"What d'ye think you're doing? What chances here?" Marhan demanded furiously.

"Shut up," Levren snapped. "You waste time." Ylia gripped his hand, Marhan's shoulder. Golsat, two paces away, met her eyes levelly but turned away before she could speak. Malaeth clung to her; she kissed the old woman's brow. Brelian knelt, back to her, oblivious to everyone and everything. Lisabetha stood behind him, hands tight on his shoulders.

Brendan lay upon a dark, inlaid pallet. His mail shone, his hair and beard were neatly combed, his eyes closed. Pale hands clasped the hilts of the sword that lay upon his breast.

Tears blurred her vision as she knelt at his side. *This is not real, cannot be real.* But the face under her fingers was smooth and cold as the tiles. She drew a shuddering breath, kissed his brow, turned to clasp Brelian tightly, stood and embraced Lisabetha. "Care for him well, 'Betha," she whispered against the girl's ear.

"You—do not go with us." Levren caught at her arm.

"No." The word came past a tight throat.

"What have you done, lass?" Malaeth whispered.

"What I must, Malaeth. I had no choice; none of us have choice. But you will be safe hereafter. Safer than we were, for he will no longer pursue you."

"Ylia—"

"A trade, Marhan." He stared at her, aghast, shocked into silence. "Reach Aresada. Do that for me, and please do not hate me. I had—there was nothing else I could do, I swear it." Golsat turned back from his study of the distant landscape. Cold eyes met hers, the words she would have spoken to him died on her lips. She turned back to Marhan.

"Take what I have, it will be of no use to me here." She undid the belt, drew off her water bottle, her depleted healing packet, the pouch of provisions. Malaeth took them blindly; tears ran down her face. Ylia bit her lip, turned away.

"Are you ready?" Lyiadd was there. "You of Nedao. Note, please, that you have your weapons, your stores—all you brought with you. She has bargained for your lives; I hope you are as grateful as you should be. She and the cat remain with me, of their own free choice. In turn, you live. A reasonable trade, at least to her mind, since she made it.

"We three will bridge you far from here, as many leagues to the north as we can, by means of my Power. I strongly suggest you resume your journey and forget this place. There is no point to your returning here, is there?" Silence. "You who are warriors, you appreciate the odds against you: should you do something so foolish? The old woman, she can explain to you, perhaps, what other things you might face, were you to act so stupidly as to return." Silence again. "Leave me alone, you Nedaoan barbarians, and I will do as much for you and yours. Complete your journey to Aresada, and find another ruler for your kind."

"There is nothing here for *us*, since we have learned the temper of her steel." Golsat spoke with such loathing that she went cold and sick. "Why should we return for such a traitorous, ill-gotten heir to Brandt's throne?" Levren leaped, dragged Marhan back; the Swordmaster's blade was halfway out and his face was murderous. Lyiadd laughed as he wrapped a possessive arm around Ylia's shoulders. She closed her eyes; Golsat's words rang through her inner being.

"Nothing here for you, as he so nicely puts it. Let us go!" Marrita swept out with her women. The guarded Nedaoans and Lyiadd, his arm still across Ylia's shoulder, followed.

A wide porch gave onto vast ruins: three broad steps led down into the open. The air was chill, for the sun had barely cast its first rays across the trees on the western slopes high above. She stood where Lyiadd left her, barely aware of

Marhan's furious gaze, Golsat's cold one, Marrita's hot-eyed
glare. Lyiadd was at his consort's side now, conversing with
her in a low, earnest voice, but her expression remained furious.

Ylia stepped back; her heel caught in a shallow ditch cut
into the turf, sent her staggering. She eyed it dully, turned on
one heel to follow it around a large, uneven rectangle. A light
breeze cooled her face.

Odd. As though a cloak had dropped across her inner being,
suddenly she could no longer sense Nisana—not even Lyiadd,
though she could readily see him. *Sword-field.* Something
Scythia had told her son once, long ago, and Beredan had told
her—a place where men possessing AEldra strengths could
learn swordplay without relying upon the Power. A sudden ex-
ultation gripped her; she tamped it, hard, as Lyiadd scowled
over his paramour's shoulder.

"Come now! I would have this done." She walked back
across the demarcation, back onto rubble-strewn pavement.
The muffled sensation was gone. Gone, too, that horrid chill
that had gripped her since Brendan's death. There was grief,
pain—but they had been pushed aside. Anger, purpose—she
was properly, fully aware again. And ready to catch at the
chance when it presented itself.

"Join!" He caught at her fingers; Nisana jumped onto her
shoulder. The air around him shimmered, seemed to catch the
red of his garments as he raised his hands. Ylia's own hands
tingled as the joining caught; her ears hummed. Her friends
were enfolded in that redness, gone. She turned from emptiness as the contact was severed. Sweat beaded Lyiadd's
brow, hair clung damply to his neck. "I have held to my end
of the bargain, but of course you would see this, since," he
added mockingly, "you cannot trust me."

"No. I cannot." Flat answer. He took her shoulders, turned
her to face north and a little west.

"There—perhaps twelve leagues. If you are capable—"

"Capable enough." 'Nisana?' The cat leaned against her,
joined. Her companions sat on a high, grassy ledge, and tears
were spilling down Marhan's face. She blinked rapidly; the vision was gone.

'You saw, Ylia?' She nodded. 'He has kept his word, they
are beyond the reach of any, save a strength equal to the
threefold one that placed them there.'

"Good," Ylia whispered. "What we do hereafter is for us, not out of fear for them."

"You begin to bore me." Lyiadd's words were edged with exasperation. "You speak of fear, always; whyfor? If I had wanted you dead, you would be dead already. And you gave up the ruling of Nedao, such as that might be, to remain here; I will not be ungrateful. Perhaps one day I may find a substitute for you. Nar, perhaps, or another."

"Why?" It took effort to face him, to meet those opaque eyes.

He shrugged, laughed briefly, began walking back toward the staircase. "Why not? Let us say for your aid, for your assistance, when I take Yls and make her mine."

Ylia shook her head. Paced casually, or so she hoped, back along the way she had just come. "You speak of war and death, and then ask my aid." *Ten steps—nine.* Less than a thought, lest he hear her.

"Well? What is the Sirdar to you? And—who spoke of war? I will have no need of war. Not once I have gained that I seek."

"Do as you will," she replied flatly. "I am here because I have no choice. But I will not dabble in evils, as you do. I will bring no further dishonor to the House of Ettel than I have done already, nor to my mother's line." *Four steps—three.* Her boot turned a little on the trench as she stepped onto the sword-field.

"So you say—now. But I will persuade you eventually." No threat, merely calm assurance. He pivoted neatly on one heel, crossed the trench with a long stride.

"Nisana, leave me, *go!*" she whispered fiercely. The cat dropped neatly to the ground, sprang away. "*Lyiadd!*" Her voice echoed through the broken columns. Dead silence. Lyiadd turned. They stood, both, in the very midst of the field, ten paces apart. "I claim blood-price for the life of my arms-mate! And I challenge you, here and now, that he be avenged!" The renegade AEldra closed the distance between them, stopping only a hand's distance from her face. *He did not suspect, not even the least!* "How—dare—you!"

"I dare." Her voice was pitched to reach the farthest of his men. "Did you think I would bow tamely to your bidding? You let Brendan die to no purpose! Save only to daunt me! And Nisana—how long do you plan to hold her life as surety for my behavior? Until my actions are no longer my choice at all and I am your creature entirely? No. It is my right, by the law of Nedao *and* by AEldran, to cry you challenge, and before these, your armed, I do so!''

Men looked at each other. "Or are you afraid?" she demanded in the now heavy silence. "You have dealt with evil and worked horrors with the Power for so long. Do you fear to cross blades, here on your own sword-field—with *me*?"

His eyes never left her face as his hand caught at the strings that held the Narran short-cloak in place. He slung the flare of blood-red cloth from him, spread his arms wide. "I wear no mail."

She dragged her own cloak loose, tore Nisana's travel pouch over her head, undid the shoulder clasps that held the mail shirt in place. The armor hit the ground with a dull clank; she pushed it aside with her foot. The leather under-jerkin followed; she shivered as the cool breeze cut through her shirt.

"Nor do I."

Marrita launched herself across the open ground, caught at him frantically. "She has tricked you; she plans, I read it in her!"

"Of course she does," he replied quietly. "She plans my death, Marrita, love. But she will not have it." He pushed her gently away. She sprang at Ylia then, nails ready to tear. Lyiadd dragged her back.

"I will not exchange scratches with you, Lyiadd's trull. I am a swordswoman—I do not sink to what your kind calls fighting." Marrita's eyes were icy with hatred. Ylia turned away from her, dropped to one knee. Nisana met her gaze, understanding in her eyes that neither dared voice. "You are not bound by anything I do," she whispered. There could be no answer; they were held apart by the sword-field. Dark green, impassive eyes held hers, a small paw touched her fingers. It was answer enough, though not the one she'd wanted. But she'd known already: a vain hope that the cat bridge away while she and Lyiadd fought. Ylia kissed the thick fur between her dark ears and stood.

The sword-field was already ringed about, empty within. She gave her mail another shove with her boot, pushing it outside the field, stepped into the open. Some distance away, one of Lyiadd's men held Marrita. Nisana padded off the field, sat on Ylia's cloak. None of the armsmen would stay near her, and those who had been close to the outlander's mail, cloak and jerkin moved would-be casually away.

It felt strange. Even though she never had much of the AEldra Power, there was always some. And now, cut off as she had never been, unable to sense outside her body, unable, as she had done since babyhood, to touch thought with Nisana. Fear flared briefly, then ebbed. If it was unnerving to her to be trapped within herself, dependent on steel weapons, how must it seem to this creature, who had depended on nothing save his warped power for so long? She drew sword, snapped the dagger free, checked her grips, tested the balance. The familiar actions were steadying.

Lyiadd was several paces away, testing his own arms: one of his men had brought him a Nedaoan sword and a serviceable, plain dagger. His voice was raised, suddenly, as hers had been, to include his following. "Dost wish," he called out, "to assuage thine honor with first blood?"

"Nay," she replied flatly. "I seek thy death here!" He laughed, said something to one of his guard which she could not hear but which left the man grinning. "I foreswear, by the Guardians, all use of the Gifts," she went on, completing the formula, "that the outcome be of the weapons of hand only."

"And I so foreswear." Movement behind him: Marrita twisted to free herself, subsided abruptly as hands tightened on her wrists. Lyiadd strode forward, sword extended. She studied him as her blade touched his, aware that he in turn was studying her. A broader blade, his—longer also. And his reach was longer, too. She would not dare cross at the point, lest her own sword snap, but she was used to that. He was stronger, of course; most men she had fought were. But she was younger, more agile, steadier—she hoped—of wind. The first clash would show more.

"You make an uneven trade, my blood for that of your liegeman. Even if—ah, if he were an amusement for you as well." The softly spoken words broke into her thought. *He means to anger me.* "I merely offer you a better trade. Consider this: mine the urgings to Kanatan, mine the knowledge allowing the attack of the Tehlatt at a time unexpected and unforeseen." His sword came to ready as his voice dropped away: he had expected her to throw herself at him.

"To thy hands—the lives of my mother, my father, my folk." She stared at him. *How calmly he speaks and thou-*

sands die, and it is no matter to him. "I dare believe nothing you say. But that you claim it is enough. I will avenge this, also, upon thee, Lyiadd!"

"Pretty." Elaborate distaste. "You are unworthy, like all of your kind. I would offer you a world above any you could grasp alone, and you would throw it all on a funeral pyre of vengeance. So be it." He turned to walk away, leaped in the same motion, twisted and was upon her, his sword a down-slashing blur.

An ancient trick—startling but old. She barely flinched, her own weapons were already poised and his sword struck against hers, slid down to the hilts. She twisted away. A quick, ferocious clash and they were suddenly a length apart, circling. Measuring each other.

He fights as he talks, with treachery. He feinted, dropped his dagger hand, sidestepped, leaped forward again. Ylia turned sideways after the Northern fashion, to present as small a target as possible, concentrated on her sword; a sharp pivot, another. A leap in, a sudden backstep as the dagger slashed and he pulled away. She *did* have an edge on him in speed, but she would need all of it, for he was skilled and he had played this game to the end before. She had not.

So she wove about him: a slash here, close crossing there, another slash—parry—leap—draw him out, wear him down. But still neither had drawn blood. Once she saw Marrita's pale face, once Nisana—otherwise, nothing but Lyiadd. A murmuring among those watching, suddenly hushed.

Her blade slipped through his guard, hit on his dagger, but he was not quick enough. He stood still, as though rooted. The shoulder of the swordswoman's shirt was torn where he had cut moments before, and only a quick drop and twist aside had saved the arm under it. But she had sliced the front of his shirt and a bright ribbon of blood ran down his breast. Not dangerous, it would not even slow him. But—*first blood to me*! She balanced on the balls of her feet; he drew a deep breath as his points came up again.

Another close and furious clashing of steel on steel; they were once again circling at arm's distance. First one, then the other feinted, trying to draw an unwary response. She was beginning to tire. He was already tired. *Now*! She pressed forward; he gave way, one slow, reluctant step at a time. She pressed again, renewed the attack furiously, baring her teeth in a mockery of smile as he moved back another pace and another; those who had held to the eastern end of the sword-field cleared hastily away.

He must not leave this safety! She leaped forward, circled. They moved back toward the center of the field. His face was pale with effort, his breath came in gasps. She closed, beat at his sword, pivoted to follow the opening her dagger had made —too soon! With a snake's speed he sidestepped, his dagger slashed across and up, and she fell.

A wordless roar went up from those watching. She gazed dumbly at Lyiadd, at his sword held steady against her throat, at her sword arm that was both numbed and afire. She tore her eyes from that last hastily: dizziness washed through her. His dagger had run a long, deep course from forearm to elbow, and even if she dared take her attention from her opponent, she could not heal it; not on the field. Strength of will—that, alone, she still had. The bleeding slowed, became a trickle. The fingers—she forced them to wrap around the hilts again. Her dagger hand was empty; the blade had spun high and was a full length away, silvery on the grass.

"Will you continue?" Cold satisfaction edged his words, though his voice was uneven with his ragged breathing. "Your companions—know that I will deal with them, somehow. After I have finished with you!" He drew a deep breath, let it out slowly. "That is ugly, it must pain you."

"No," she replied flatly. "I can manage it."

"Perhaps. Were it the only—" He laughed. Fear, pain threatened. His point moved from her throat, tugged at her shirt, ripping through the fabric, drawing blood as she had drawn his. She caught her breath, bit her lip. Another touch, crossing the first.

He hesitated only briefly. The blade wavered, held her eyes, moved downward to press hard against her side. "Strength of will," he murmured. "How much have you, I wonder?" A blackness swirled across her eyes, by the shock of it she knew he had cut deep, though she could not yet feel it. The twin cuts at her breast burned with sweat; her arm throbbed.

"Did you take so much pleasure from Brendan's death? Even your Mathkkra slay more cleanly!" He bared his teeth, drew the sword back; as suddenly, he brought it back to rest against her throat.

"I underestimated you. You nearly provoked your death,

and that was what you wanted, wasn't it? No. You will not die, though you will wish you had. I dare not kill you. But how long do you think it would take you to die here, alone and unaided?"

"How long did it take Brendan?" Hot anger released her from the paralysis that had held her terrified and hurting under his blade.

"Long enough." His blade pressed hard against her throat. He laughed as she involuntarily closed her eyes; the pressure was gone. She blinked. Sunlight glittered on the point hovering just above her eyes. *Mothers no, he will blind me!* Horror stopped her breath. But it moved again, sliced her cheek open from temple to chin, and she screamed with the pain of it, a shrilling that echoed across the silent watchers. Blood ran down her arm.

"You are losing the game. Concentrate, concentrate. Will time aid you? A minute—two, perhaps? Ask of me, beg. Perhaps I will give you more." His sword was gone; she watched through a haze as he leaned against it. *Concentrate.* She must, somehow. She caught her lip between her teeth, hard. The bleeding slowed.

"Ask—of *you*?" she whispered then. And she rolled, crying out again as full weight bore down on her sword arm, clawed for her dagger. She threw it, backhanded across her body, hard.

No long throw, and no great one, for he stood so near she could scarcely have missed him. But true. It flew straight, caught him high in the breast, buried itself in his body to the hilt, and he fell without a cry.

The child never failed to surprise me, but in this thing she gave me one of the greatest shocks I had ever had: that she defeated Lyladd and not by the Power common to both, but by her father's strengths. That she had planned it so, hiding her thought from him and even from me—though I knew she intended something against him, chauvinistically I presumed it to be yet another attack with the Power. That she could take a formal sword crossing to its lethal conclusion, planning that, also: There were still things about this child I had known all her life, that I did not know.

24

"*LYIADD*!!" His men stood rooted in horror; Marrita tore free to fly across the sword-field. Her scream roused the stunned watchers, but too late: as she flung herself down, Ylia caught her by the sleeve. Off balanced, Marrita fell against the wounded Nedaoan, whose sword was already at the woman's throat.

"He is not dead!" Ylia's voice cut flat across the babble. *A lie, gods and Mothers, grant me it's a lie!* "And let the first who moves pay blood-debt to Lyiadd for this female!" She pushed to her knees, to her feet, dragging Marrita with her. Lyiadd's consort whimpered as Ylia's hand tore at her hair; it fell from elaborate coils to fall across the swordswoman's arm. No pressure at all, and yet it hurt. Mothers it hurt.

Nisana behind, no one else; that much she saw in the brief

glance she risked. So near. *Go*. She caught her lip between her teeth. The arm was bleeding again. A step. Another. A third.

"Much joy may you have of your Lord, Marrita. Such as I have left, you are welcome to!" A mere hiss against her ear.

"I will have your death for this," she spat. Ylia laughed light-headedly, slung her away and staggered back. Marrita fell across the sprawled, still body just as the swordswoman's heel caught against one of the rocks that edged the western side of the field. She twisted, caught her balance, staggered again as dizziness and pain struck hard. Her foot tangled in the spill of mail shirt and this time she fell.

'Ylia! Join *now*!' Nisana's thought forced its way into her mind; she clutched at shed clothing, rolled into a ball around it as the ground tilted and dissolved under them. Marrita's hysterical, furious weeping, the sound of running footsteps—all cut off as suddenly as if a door had closed.

Ylia choked, gagged violently. Nisana's small, dark head filled all her vision. 'Join again—do it!'

'I cannot—!'

'You *can*! Would you bleed to death, after all of that? I cannot heal you. I can aid, but not here; join!' Claws sank hard into her knee. '*Join*!' Between them, they temporarily stopped the bleeding, but they dared nothing else. Ylia had no strength to spare, she would have to sleep long after such a healing. And Nisana had been able to bridge them barely a league from the Lammior's valley.

'Join—do not argue with me, girl, just do it!' Ylia whimpered, knowing she had no choice but fearing the bridging as much as the threat of Lyiadd's armed.

Two more bridgings. Nisana had to cast about some time for the rest of the company. 'I have them.'

'No. *No*.'

'This is no time for foolishness, girl!'

'I do not care! Nisana, I am sorry. I cannot face it please!'

Nisana, for answer, climbed silently into her lap, waited. A deep breath, a second—it *hurt* to breath, gods and Mothers, it did! She reached finally, rubbed at the cat's shoulder. Nisana leaned against her, silently sympathetic if not understanding. 'Now, cat. Let us do it *now*.' She gripped the bundle with white fingers. Silence, and that horrid sensation of toppling from a height. Voices, then; anxious, frightened voices. She forced her eyes open, struggled to sit. Hands aided her; Levren at her side. Nisana had bridged into their midst.

"How did you come here—you are hurt, girl." The Bow-master pushed her hair away from her damp face. "How badly?" Before Ylia could answer, Malaeth pressed forward, screamed.

"Your face!"

"Malaeth, it is nothing." She forced what little strength she had left into her voice. "A scratch—look, it doesn't even bleed."

"But—oh, no. Not that. It will scar, even with the healing, you will have a scar!" Ylia began to laugh.

"Stop it!" Levren snapped. She shook her head, tried; could not. Tears burned across her right cheek. A sharp blow across the other sobered her abruptly. Levren shook her hard.

"I—sorry."

"Don't be. How badly are you injured? What can we do? Wait, drink first." She took his bottle, drained it.

"I—can walk. I think. We stopped it bleeding."

"It? They! You do not look as though you could stand alone! Rest." A pause. "Can we rest here, do we dare?"

"I think we can. A little, anyway. Only three of us knew where Lyiadd set you. And he is dead."

"Dead?" Marhan and Levren together.

"Dead. I killed him." Golsat moved around to Levren's other side, dropped down beside her. "My friend." She caught at his hands, got in return one of his rare smiles. His left eye was swollen nearly shut, already dark purple, his lip cut. "Golsat. Your eye—what *happened* to you?" He shrugged.

"Marhan hit him," Levren replied, when it became obvious Golsat would not. Marhan scowled at the ground, sucked his moustaches.

"But—Golsat, not for what you said this morning! Marhan, he was trying to help me, didn't you know that? Golsat, why didn't you tell him?"

"You knew?" Golsat's face lit briefly. "I feared after they took you from us. And I did not know what you might do to protect us, what this enemy might do. I—only thought to aid you. When I realized what you were doing, that seemed suddenly what I had to say. Lest he change his mind and kill every one of us. There was," he added ruefully, "no point to convincing Marhan, he would never have believed."

"I know better. And it was aid, Golsat; Lyiadd was more willing to release you, believing that at least one of you was casting me aside. More ready to believe I had no alternative but to stay with him. And so he was more surprised at the last when I gave challenge to fight him to the death. His."

Marhan pressed forward. "You will be the death of me," he said finally, his voice ominously flat. "Such a fool's chance."

"No," she cut him off sharply. "Not a fool's, it worked." She cradled her right arm in the left, bit back a cry as pain knifed through her side. "He was aware of us, to our very thoughts, as soon as we came into the mountains. Long before we fought his Mathkkra." He shuddered. "There was no escape for you, but to do what I did. And none for me—but the rest of it. I fought him, I won. It is over, enough." He sighed deeply.

"The arm—is that the worst of it?" She closed her eyes, shrugged cautiously. Nothing bled, but pain was overwhelming. Levren pulled gently at her shoulders; she fell gratefully back against him. "We had better bind it, at least. But it will affect your grip."

"No." She fought speech past clenched teeth. "It can be healed, but not yet. We dare not take the time here."

"We go from here? *Now*?" Malaeth moistened her kerchief, worked delicately at the cut on her young charge's face.

"We must, and soon. We are not far enough from that place."

'And Lyiadd may not be dead after all,' Nisana added.

Ylia closed her eyes against encroaching dizziness. 'No, he is dead, I killed him!' The cat rubbed against her leg, her thought soothing.

'Lyiadd?' Malaeth's mind-speech was a mere whisper.

'You heard?'

'Not Lyiadd of the Fifth House!'

'The same,' Nisana assured her grimly. 'And now *you* know why we need such haste!'

'I—was—not close enough—to see him—his face.' The old woman's though was tenuous, faint, but understandable. 'My eyes are as bad as Marhan's, now. This is dreadful.'

'No. He is dead.' Ylia's own mind-speech was little better at the moment. 'But his armed could pursue us, and if any of them can bridge—or if Marrita can. Lyiadd may have lied about her strengths.'

'*Why* was he there?'

'Later.' The swordswoman cast a glance at Marhan's averted head where he worked over the bandaging of her arm. "Lisabetha," she added aloud. "Where is she?"

"There." Golsat pointed. "With Brelian."

"Help me up." Marhan glared, would have refused, but she insisted. She had to cling to him until the world steadied. But she could stand, and alone. She forced a reassuring smile. "I will be fine, Marhan, I swear it." He stepped aside, but unwillingly, and his eyes were still worried.

Some twenty paces away on a ledge looking out north and east, was a pile of rock, a rough, unmarked cairn. Brelian knelt there, Lisabetha at his side. The breath stopped in her throat.

Lisabetha caught at her with chilled fingers. "I knew you would return to us, I *knew*—oh, Mothers, no, you are hurt!"

"Only a little," she lied. " 'Betha, we cannot stay here. We must leave, now. As quickly as we can."

"I know it." Her breath caught on a sob. "He will not listen to me, and I do not know what to say to him. He does not even know I am here!"

"Brelian?" Sweat beaded her upper lip, prickled against her eyelids.

"Ylia?" He turned, but his eyes were not focused. "Why are you here?"

"Lyiadd is dead. Brendan is avenged." He stared blankly; the words had conveyed nothing to him. "It was Brendan's dagger trick, I killed him with that." Something of that got through; he nodded, but turned away from her. "Brelian." She caught at his arm. "Brel, we cannot stay here, we must go. We need haste. You saw the number of armed in that valley. If they pursue—"

"Go then. I—I cannot—I—I will not—" He swallowed. "I stay with him."

"No." Lisabetha's voice was a tiny anguished whisper; she turned and fled.

"Brelian, we must. Lisabetha needs you, Brel; she will not go without you." Ylia blinked rapidly; tears burned down her face. "I—what we loved of Brendan is not here—not under these stones. What can you do in this place save to grieve? Is that what Brendan would ask of you?"

"He—"

"Lisabetha needs you. I need you, we all do, Brelian. And —do you think," she added raggedly, "that it is easy for me, to ask this of you? Do you think I want to leave—" Her voice broke, one hand caught at the cairn. Brelian's arms were crushing around her shoulders.

"No, please, gods no, do not weep, do not." But he himself was weeping. "I—let us go. Now, at once." Lisabetha returned, caught Brelian's hands in hers; Ylia limped back to Levren's side. He wrapped an arm around her waist, she set her good arm across his shoulders, and they started slowly north.

*Who, knowing the tale of so much of our
journey, would have dared doubt the girl?
Brandt had said it to his Council, that last
long day: "I name her my heir because she is
worthy. And so time will prove." And so it
did.*

25

Ylia never after could remember that day's travel, save that
she was supported by one or another of the men the entire
way: impossible to walk alone for pain and lightheadedness.
Golsat moved out ahead long before noon-meal to find a
campsite and fresh meat. Nisana rode on Lisabetha's breast,
close to hand, willing her strength. Later, when she felt likely
to burst into tears, Malaeth was at her ear, soothing and en-
couraging, cooing as she had to the baby Ylia's first steps: "A
little further, my Ylia. There—not so bad, was that? A little
more, and you can rest, I promise it." Finally, Levren and
Brelian took in turns to carry her. In such a manner they covered a slow league and a half, most of it fortunately downhill.

By the time they reached Golsat's camp, it was late: the sun
was down and a cool breeze fingered through clothing. Ylia
was glad, for her skin burned. She had been hardly able, even
with Nisana's and Malaeth's aid, to eat during the midday
stop. Every step tore at the wound in her side, set her arm to
throbbing. When Levren and Marhan finally aided her to the
ground, she fell over and lay in a heap. Someone draped another cloak over her, but she could not even open her eyes to
see which of them, and the inner sense was dead.

'Ylia.' Nisana rubbed against her face. 'You've rested
enough. We must deal with your injuries.'

'No. Let me sleep, I cannot.'

'You can and will.' The cat was unrelenting. Ylia opened

one eye to regard her, wearily let it close again. 'Come, it is not so bad as all that. You can heal. I will aid you with my strength. You will no longer hurt.' A pause. Ylia sighed wearily, but said nothing. 'Just because we stopped the bleeding, you are not out of danger, girl! And the pain itself weakens you, you know this! We need you fully aware!'

Tears ran down her face; she brushed at them angrily. *Weak thing*! Nisana was right: she was of no use to anyone in her present state. Hard—nearly impossible at the moment—to find the inner sense, as though the Power itself flinched away from the physical pain in some hidden corner; it was several slow moments before she could relax enough to draw it forth. They probed the worst of it.

Lyiadd had missed the major blood vessels in both her arm and her side, she knew that even in the agony of the moment. Even so, without the healing she would have been seriously harmed by either, if she had not simply bled to death on the spot. The lack of pain was so great a relief, she could have wept again. She let her head fall into her hands, drew her first deep breath in hours. Nisana curled hard against her.

'I intend to sleep a while, and so you had better. You lost blood, and you walked too far as you were.'

'I will—not yet.' She spoke to one already unhearing. She sat up cautiously, caught at the ground as the fire and those before it blurred ominously. For that, sleep, and plenty of it, was the only cure. But not until she had warned Marhan, at least.

The Swordmaster had been watching her rather worriedly, and he now came swiftly to her side, braced her upright. "Is this wise? Malaeth needs to see to your—" His voice died away; he was staring blankly at her cheek.

"No. Gone, all of them. You know I can heal—"

"Well, yes, but—"

"Not only others, old man. It works on me as well, it just takes strength I did not dare spare before." She closed her eyes, leaned back against his arm. "I need sleep, but other than that, I am well—enough."

"Good then—"

"I need sleep, but not quite yet."

Golsat met her eyes over the fire. "You said you would tell us what chanced. I would like to know," he added with a rare, dry humor, "if this is worth the trouble I took for it." He closed his blackened eye; Marhan glanced at him uncom-

fortably, away again. "Never mind, Swordmaster," Golsat
added. "Had our places been changed, what might any of us
have done to you?"

Ylia held her hands to the fire. "What—happened on the
ledge? I remember little, and I was separated from you."

Golsat shrugged. "There was a strange feeling to the air; my
hair stood on end. We heard you scream. Marhan and I had
already moved ahead, but we raced back at that. And, of a
sudden, there was a flash of light, red light. Perhaps fifty men
and Cavefolk stood there, blades at the ready. Marhan was a
little to the side and he plowed ahead, but before I could more
than draw sword I was surrounded by at least ten." He stared
blackly at the fire. "I could not fight my way free, never
against so many."

"What else could you have done?" Levren demanded
quietly.

"I have wondered since."

"You are alive." That was Brelian—the first thing he had
said all day. Lisabetha pressed his share of the meat into his
hands, forced them upward. He ate, blankly unaware of what
he chewed.

"I am alive," Golsat agreed. His eyes sought first Brelian's,
then, when Brelian appeared no more aware of him than he
was of his food, Lisabetha's. "Brel was shielding 'Betha from
the Cavefolk. Though she was fighting, too, with the staff
Marhan made for her."

"Something hit me." Lisabetha touched her head gingerly.
"I was aware, but I could not move. When Brelian fell beside
me, I thought him dead at first. Then—I heard Brendan,
heard him shouting the way he—way he did. And someone
shouted at him to throw down his blades, but he laughed."
Ylia closed her eyes, bit her lip hard.

"I went to Marhan's aid," Levren said. "Though it did us
no good at all. When you vanished, he was hurt. Next thing I
was aware, three swords were at my throat. We had no chance
at all, any of us—let alone Bren. There were at least eight
fighting him; even so, he accounted for five at least, that I
saw, before he fell." He shook his head. "We were bunched
closely together and—and moved. One moment upon that
ledge, the next in the chamber where you found us.

"Brendan was conscious off and on for long, but he had
lost considerable blood before we could get to him. Most of
the time, he was not aware and could not have felt much pain.

He—spoke mostly to you, Ylia."

"He was aware—once." The food slid unnoted from Brelian's fingers. "When—when he—" He turned away from the fire, struggled to his feet and walked into the night.

"He spoke to Brelian, asking of you," Lisabetha whispered. "We could not tell him where you were or what had happened. He thought you dead. He—told me to take care of Brel, then. Not long after, he lapsed into the final silences, and we could not rouse him."

Oh, gods, oh Mothers—She blotted tears with her sleeve.

"Where were you?" Malaeth demanded.

She told them, briefly, of her imprisonment and her two meetings with Lyiadd. She told them what he was, and all the horror he had done and planned to do.

"But—the AEldra powers," Marhan protested, "*you* said—"

"Cannot be used for evil. No. So I was told, so I have been told all my life. Perhaps he is no longer AEldra. I do not know what he is. But those ruined halls were once the Lammior's."

"Ah, no!" Malaeth alone understood the full implication of the name and went pale at it. But Lisabetha also knew something of him.

"The Lammior, the Night-Serpent," the girl whispered. "There are tales—a few tales—in the North of this horror."

"The Lammior, the Nasath guard us!" Malaeth kissed the knuckle of her smallest right-hand finger. "How came you—Ylia, how *dared* you stand against him?"

"Because I had to. I could not stand by while he worked his sorceries on all that I hold dear. I drew him out, I fought him, I won. Lyiadd is dead; the price is not as great as it might have been. I am alive and he is dead. Nothing else matters."

"Are you certain he is dead?" Malaeth asked suddenly.

"*Yes*. Certain."

"Because I know him; he is devious."

"I know he is devious. He could have killed me, he chose instead to amuse himself." Malaeth shuddered. "I threw my dagger, struck him there." She touched the old nurse's breast. "He is dead."

"But you did not actually touch his pulse then, did you? Do not be so certain, Ylia. And his woman—that was the Sirdar's daughter, was it not?"

"Marrita."

"I thought as much. I have not seen her since she had barely come to womanhood, but she has not changed at all, and the scarf on her hand gave her away. Remember, she is of the First House and capable of much. Though she never used what she had for other than to enhance her beauty. If—if Lyiadd was still alive, perhaps she could have healed him."

"No! He is dead!" Ylia pulled against Levren's arms. *Why must she belabor this*? Malaeth eyed her worriedly, finally patted her arm.

"All right; you are right, you must be. We were not there, you were. You had better sleep girl, you are too pale still."

"We will share out your watch tonight," Levren said. "Are we safe here?"

"We have not been set upon yet. I would use caution. But I believe we are safe for tonight. Though they might bridge—no. They have not done so yet, they will not now. But I will be fine. There is no reason why I cannot take my share of the watches."

"You," Levren exclaimed sourly, "are the one who needs rest. Do as you are told this once! We move on in the morning and must make more distance than we did today. We cannot do so if you cannot walk, I do not intend to carry you again tomorrow, and there are more than enough of us for the watch, even without you and Brel!"

"I take my share." Brelian stood at the edge of the firelight, his face old and grey. Levren shook his head slowly, but Brelian would have none of it. "We are one fewer, and I am uninjured. And it will keep my thought occupied, Lev." Nor would he be dissuaded, though he finally agreed that Lisabetha share with him.

Ylia sighed, but forebore to argue any further: Levren's face was grim as she had never seen it, and she had no wish to push him to active anger. And she *was* tired, so tired. She took a deep swallow of Malaeth's tea, lay back close to Nisana. The cat stretched, snuggled back against her stomach and the night blurred and faded almost immediately.

There is a certain blind spot in those of us of cat kind, a thing we cannot and do not share with humans—love, such as Lisabetha and Brelian had, or such as Ylia had begun with her Brendan, is denied us. Fortunately, I think: it seems to bring more pain than the pleasure of it

*can be worth: though, again, I do not know and cannot
say. I ached with my poor Ylia's loss, but I could not
fully understand.*

The next morning, Golsat found a way north and east
through a low, forested valley. The footing was easy, the
ground clear enough that they made five leagues before sundown. Ylia had regained much of her strength from a full
night's sleep and insisted once again on her share of the
watches.

It had been a quiet day, with only bits of conversation, and
Brelian spoke not at all. They saw little the entire day: a squirrel, two small birds. Late in the day, a flock of geese flew over,
heading north.

They stayed near the fire that night, though, and Nisana
and Ylia made search where they sat: She could not, suddenly,
bear to close her eyes at any distance from her friends; she was
frightened, unable to do much about it save hope it would
eventually pass.

The weather changed during Golsat's watch: Clouds came
in from south and east, and by morning it was raining fitfully,
lessening now and then to a driven mist. Trees, fortunately,
sheltered them from the worst of it. They made a long stop for
noon-meal and built a fire, heated water for a tea to share out
with their cold meat.

The long valley came to an end not far ahead, and a low,
long, cloud-hung ridge blocked their way. Golsat returned
with word that another long, narrow, forested valley lay beyond it, and that the climb was not as arduous as it appeared
from the bottom. Cloud covered them within moments.

They stopped, mindful of what the last mists had brought.
"I will go first," Ylia said finally, inwardly cursing herself for
the shrinking sensation that accompanied the words. Lisabetha moved to her side; her face was anxious.

"Is this—I mean, are there—"

"Only fog," Ylia assured her. Her voice, fortunately,
showed none of the fear she felt. "I can see a little further than
you, that is all." Golsat, a dim shape behind Lisabetha, made
a warding sign. "We may come above this as we climb, or it
might lift. If not, we will probably drop below it on the other
side. It is not that far, in either case." Nisana stirred, stretched
in her pouch.

'What passes? Are we stopped for the night?'

'No. Fog. Nothing I cannot handle, go back to sleep. I may need you later.'

'Mmmmf.' She resettled against the swordswoman's spine. The company started out slowly, finally holding onto one another's cloaks as the fog thickened. For perhaps an hour they struggled on, over the top, down again. The air was darkly grey, chill, and their teeth chattered. Somewhere far behind, Ylia could hear Marhan muttering to himself, Levren's amused comments.

She stopped short: No, she hadn't imagined it, there was motion among the trees to their left. Golsat dropped the corner of her cloak, set himself against her shoulder. "I saw that also. What is it?"

She stared hard into the mists. "It—I am not certain—wait a moment." Marhan and Levren pushed past, clattered on down the rocks. Marhan peered nearsightedly into the overcast.

But she could see it now: The shape of what she watched had confused her eye, as had the fact that she could see trees and ledge through it. Two armies, many thousand strong, fought a dozen lengths away, all in silence. She squinted, switched to the second level of Sight, back again as that proved useless. Nisana pushed free of her pouch and clambered onto her shoulder.

"What are they?" Golsat demanded, in a hushed voice.

Ylia laid a hand on his arm. "They will not harm you. There is no need for quiet, either; they could not hear if you shouted. They have been dead a thousand years, these."

"This is what Verdren spoke of." Brelian, his arms and cloak wrapped around Lisabetha's shoulders, stared into the mist. "Remember, Lev?"

"It must be," Levren agreed. "Look, you can see through them, Marhan; a ghost army. Two of them." Marhan sucked his moustaches unhappily, fumbled in his pouch for his glass.

They watched as the battle waged back and forth, and though she knew the tales as well as any AEldra child, Ylia found it nearly impossible to countenance what her eyes saw: water maidens, tree maidens, the Naiads and Dryads of Ylsan legend—among them the Ydera, greenish flame spiraling from its brow; creatures that might have been butterflies of vast size, or butterfly-shaped-and-colored birds. The man-shaped among them only made these seem more wondrous.

Those they fought had woven a darker fog about them,

though now and again a misshapen form manifested itself:
once, they were certain, a Thullen plunged silently to earth.

The sun finally slid from behind cloud and disbursed the
fogs, though mist still drifted across the ground. But the phantom armies vanished. They stared across broken rock into
heavy forest. Nothing. Ylia stayed back, gestured Marhan to
take the lead again.

They camped early in a hollow amid sheltering rock and
built a roaring fire: One and all were wet to the skin and they
dared not sleep so, for the air was chill. Lisabetha's fingers
were red; poor Malaeth fell asleep as soon as they got her
properly warm. Ylia had to waken her so Nisana could hold
her to eating and drinking when food was ready.

"Well, we could not hope for good weather the entire distance. Not this time of year." Levren turned his cloak to dry
the lining; he had shed mail, jerkin and shirt, sat bare-armed
as near the flames as he could. Marhan gloomily tossed sticks
into the fire. Golsat had drawn the next to last watch and had
rolled into his cloak as soon as it was near dry. Lisabetha and
Brelian leaned against each other, eyes closed.

"My watch first tonight," the Bowmaster continued. "If
you have no objection, Marhan. I am not really tired, and I
cannot face sleep until my shirt is properly dry. I will wake you
after." Marhan nodded, dragged his cloak around his
shoulders and leaned back against a broad-trunked cedar. Ylia
pulled her own cloak from the rocks and snuggled into it.
Warm and dry both.

'Ylia. Join.' She was pulled from sleep with a sudden jerk,
pried one eye open. Little time could have passed, for Levren
sat working a bit of wood with his dagger; he had resumed his
shirt, but the rest of his outer garment were still spread across
the rocks near the fire. Nisana sat next to her ear, and an ex-
tremely rare uncertainty radiated from her. 'A thing to the
north and west, perhaps a league distant. Join. See?'

'Well—not exactly see. Sense.' Strange! *An understate-
ment, and then some.* There was something about the place
Nisana pointed out. And yet, while strange, it was not the sort
of strange they one and all associated with the Foessa. No
Fear, no revulsion. Simply—well, yes, strange.

'It comes to me to bridge there,' Nisana said finally. The
uncertainty was even stronger.

'*Now*? Cat, it is late. And cold! Are you mad?'

'No. And not now, of course. After your watch. Sleep first, if you wish.'

'I certainly *do* wish!' She shivered back down into her cloak. It was damp once again, this time with dew. 'And I would mistrust any desire I felt to bridge anywhere in these mountains!'

'Of course *you* would, since you fear it so much! But—do you think *I* feel no mistrust?' Nisana snapped. 'It is different, this place––can you not feel?'

'I can. That does not make it safe.'

'No. But it *is* safe.'

'Oh,' Ylia responded sarcastically. 'And you know this—how?'

'I cannot explain it.'

'Well then—'

'But it *is* safe. And I must go there. Alone, if you are afraid to accompany me!' And the cat started away, tail high.

Ylia sighed, levered onto one elbow. 'Come back here! I cannot let you go alone, and you know it! And you have my curiosity now; are you satisfied?' Nisana returned to her side, rather smugly. 'Golsat has the watch after mine, I will tell him where we go. You are *sure* this is safe?'

'I am certain of *nothing* anymore,' Nisana grumbled. 'This place is safe. I am drawn there; it is safe. That is all I know. For me, that is enough.'

'You reassure me,' Ylia replied sourly. 'No, all right, cat.' She drew her knees up as she shifted to her side, tucked the worn hems of her cloak around her boots. 'There had better be good purpose to this, though,' she warned.

'If there were not, I would never have awakened you,' Nisana replied shortly. 'Go back to sleep!'

> *How could I have explained such a thing to her? I had never felt such an overwhelming sense of good: It was as though I had been color-blind all my life and suddenly gained that sight amid a field of summer flowers. That I must go to the source of that sensation, and attempt to define it—there is not much I would not have faced, to do so.*

*She asked me once, long after our journey
was over, if it was as difficult for me as it
was for her, to be always right. And I replied,
of course, that I was no such thing—it was
just that she chose, so often, to not believe in
a true thing, and that merely because she
had neither seen nor touched the thing made
it no less real.*

26

Ylia's watch was uneventful, save that sometime after Marhan woke her clouds began moving in from the south, bringing ocean-damp and warmer sea air with them. Nisana, her
mind for the most part shuttered, paced edgily, impatiently
around the campfire. Her relief when Ylia went to rouse Golsat was palpable.

"We must be gone a while, Nisana and I. No cause for
alarm," she added as he looked up from feeding the fire.
"There is a thing which may aid us. I want to view it more
closely." He eyed her briefly, shrugged and asked no questions.

"Take care," was all he said.

"So we shall. And we will return before your watch is
over."

A brief smile crossed his face. "See that you do."

Nisana waited her beyond the light; Ylia walked rather
slowly, stiff from the day's walk and the damp. "This had better be worth a bridging," she said pointedly as she dropped
cross-legged to the wet grass and the cat climbed into her lap.

'I would never have bothered you otherwise. Join!' And, as

230

Ylia closed her eyes, 'The more often you do this, the less you fear it.'

'Hah.'

Nisana's meadow was wet with a heavy dew; grasses and wildflowers were bent near double with the damp. A hypnotic hum of bees; an occasional bird's warble. They stood on high ground, a slope that fell away on three sides toward the trees far below. A ribbon of waterfall dropped downhill nearly at their feet, chuckled noisily over rock. Ylia stooped for a drink. Nisana vanished into the thick, fragrant grasses.

The cat was right: there was *something*. Not frightening, no: no one could be afraid here. "Nisana?" The cat appeared suddenly, leaped to a boulder. Ylia waded through the damp grass to join her. "What is it?" The cat was staring about so intently, such was her concentration, that the question startled her. "Where does it come from?"

'I cannot tell—it seems everywhere, and yet—I cannot tell!' Her tail twitched sharply. She leaped, then, turned midair to stare back the way they had come. Ylia was at her side in the same moment, sword already in hand.

"You do not need your blade." A low voice behind them. She turned, slowly. Two stood there, where none had been half a moment before, and there had been no sensation of a bridging at all. The moon, nearly at its full, sailed from behind cloud to turn the meadow into a jeweled cushion, and shone upon those who stood before AEldra cat and half-AEldra human.

Man and woman—or so they appeared. Tall, dark of hair, pale skinned. They were not clad as any folk of the Peopled Lands, but this was proper, for they themselves resembled no folk Ylia had ever seen. Though she could not have said exactly how they were different. Her skin prickled, but not in fear. She took a cautious step toward them. A second. Nisana leaped from her place on the rock; the woman bent down to gather her close.

What is it? And then, suddenly, she knew. "You are Nasath, you are Those Who Guard." The whisper was unsteady; she caught at rock for balance. Fear vied with a deep, new happiness, an awe so great she could not contain it. How had even she dared doubt? And yet, how could belief have encompassed such as these? She sank to one knee, and her sword slipped from nerveless fingers.

He of the two retrieved the blade, kissed the hilts gravely and held it back to her. She looked up, amazed, but took the hand he extended to raise her to her feet. And, at that touch, both fear and awe vanished.

"We are of the Nasath. I am Bendesevorian, she Nesrevera." And as he spoke, a realization smote her.

"You. It was *you* who spoke to me in the Mathkkra cave!"

"Myself."

"Your Power—" she began tentatively, stopped as he shook his head.

"No. Yours, though you did not realize it. And you yourself supplied the need; without that I could have done nothing. Often it happens that those not fully AEldra have a block upon the inner strengths." A smile warmed his face, brought deep color to hers. "Had the choice been mine, I would have chosen you a better circumstance!"

"My thanks that you could aid me at all." She inclined her head, abashed. "But, none have seen you—Those Who Guard —for the space of many lives, or so it is said. Why then do you come now? And, why to *me*?"

"Because the years bring changes and new dangers with them. We gave thanks to Yls in the way we could, but we had no desire to rule that people, nor any people not our own. We certainly wished no one to depend upon us as they might have come to do, losing their own ability to deal with difficulties. Such a thing is not unknown; we decided, then, not to chance it." He glanced at Nesrevera; she nodded, and she and Nisana moved a few paces away. "My sister speaks only a little of the AEldran tongue and no other speech of the lands. She and Nisana will talk together. We must speak also, you and I."

"I—of Lyiadd." Ylia forced the name between suddenly dry lips. The years brought changes, indeed. "He is no longer a threat, I killed him." Then, for the first time, she wondered.

"We hope. We cannot search that place, the Lammior's ancient holdings. We are powerless to act there, our kind."

She nodded. "I—I know. I think."

"You do, enough to understand what I say. And I grieve that none of this could be prevented. But he is well placed, Lyiadd; he could not have chosen a better bolt-hole, had he deliberately chosen a place of safety from us. It is good that you were well matched in the weapons of hand.

"We thought that valley sealed when the Lammior was

slain, that it was hidden from the outside world, that none would dare approach it. We could not destroy it, not entirely; we had not the strength for such a thing. We did not foresee one such as Lyiadd, an AEldra unsatisfied with the Gifts, one coming in deliberate search of the evil there, to take it for his own. Though the Lammior's secrets are well hidden. A man could not take them in full overnight. And not without great sacrifice."

"No." She shook her head. "He had not found them. He spoke of them. I—" She swallowed, met his eyes. "*Is* he dead?"

"We do not know; we cannot *see*, and we dare not probe that place. It is guarded against us, and he might become aware of us, if he is still alive. But Marrita lives."

"Marrita," Ylia whispered. "But—"

"One of humankind will dare much for vengeance—did not you? If Marrita took up Lyiadd's quest, whether he lived or died at your hand?"

"And if either of them finds what he sought?" In spite of the warm air, she shivered.

"Then there will be war, as there was before. But we will not speak of that until we must. Unless we must. It is likely he was slain, that Marrita will not choose his path, that those who served them will scatter and the Lammior's valley will again stand empty. We will keep watch this time, as we should have before." His face was bleak. Moved by a compassion she did not understand—who would dare pity one of the Nasath? —she laid a hand on his arm.

"Even ye who are the Guardians could not see every chance. Who can foresee and protect against all that might ever pass?" Bendesevorian smiled and she warmed.

"We will not reveal ourselves to your company. It would not be useful or of aid to you, and there is little we actually can do to be of help. Such as we can do, we will. Strength of spirit and body—you all need that. And what we can tell you: The road before you is still strewn with danger. Lyiadd may be dead, but his servants are not! More of the folk await at Aresada than you hope, but you must come there. You have allies in the mountains, however, and we shall tell them of your coming. They, also, will aid you as they can."

"For that, my thanks, the thanks of all of us." She did not clearly understand what he meant, could not. She stored the words to parcel out later. "And for the warning. It is more

than we could have looked for, to be forewarned—and—''
She swallowed sudden tears; Brendan's words on her lips. She
could not continue.

Bendesevorian placed a light kiss upon her brow. "I sorrow
for your losses. And I know words are no proper comfort."
His hand fell away from her arm as Nesrevera came to his
side. "The blessing of the One upon you and guard you!" Ylia
cried out; they were gone in a blaze of light. She raised a hand
to shield her eyes, and saw—in that light—

"Mother. My father." Scythia and Brandt stood in a vast
hall, the light of a spring sun blinding on white garments,
flowers twined in their hair. And before them, clad in the pale
blue of the King's Guard, Brendan knelt. Brandt's blade
touched at his shoulder. The light faded, they were gone.
Tears ran down her face. The moon slipped back behind
cloud.

"Nisana," Ylia whispered. The cat leaped to her arms but
stared blankly and did not speak as she bridged them back to
camp. So dazed was she by what she had seen and heard, Ylia
was scarcely aware of the bridging, the fear it usually brought.

Golsat glanced up, startled, as they snapped into being at
the edge of the firelight, nodded as they passed. For one sleepy
moment, Ylia saw him as he went to waken Brelian, but nothing thereafter, and she slept heavily.

And dreamed: fire, battle and death. A great war raged
through the Foessa, and none of humankind fought it. Rang-
ing with the Guardians were the Wood People, against them
the Lammior and his created *seemings*, misshapen horrors of a
child's nightmare brought to life.

Another battlefield, this still under the remorseless light of a
full moon; dark shapes moved stealthily in the shade of trees,
fluttered from the sky to fall upon the dead. Again change:
flight, a few forming rearguard in a narrow cleft against
dreadful odds. Until, finally, the ill-sorted army of Nasath
and their allies stood hard against the Sea, waiting, watching
the smoke in the mountains as it neared. Signal fires seaward,
though none of those held at the shoreline believed they would
be of aid.

But they were: ships, more ships anchoring in a wide bay,
and a change in the tide of war as armed men came from the
ships to ally themselves with the Woodfolk and the Nasath.

And there—to the fore of the shipmen—Mothers, a
woman! Shelagn, she looked upon Shelagn! Wisewoman,

warrior, and a knight of the First House. Hair like a silver
helmet, close-cropped to her ears, padded armor, shield upon
her left arm instead of a dagger—she led a troop through the
Mathkkra, crying encouragement to those behind her as they
clove through the enemy, through *seeming*, Thullen, evils
more horrible than they. And the force behind her dwindled,
until she stood with scarce twenty comrades against the Lammior himself. And then even she fell.

But the thing she had opposed was brought down thereafter, his body burned, his halls torn stone from stone, closed
off from the reach of men.

The dream darkened, shifted—Aresada? The entrance to
the Caves, she knew it for certain, a company of village folk
coming across the makeshift bridge that crossed the river
gorge. A valley, then; immense and broad-floored, near tree-
less, and warm earth sliding between her fingers.

A high place, a rock-bound gorge. The red light of sunset
glanced off her sword. They fought Mathkkra, she and another—she could see nothing but his sword. Blood dripped
from his fingers to the stones below, and she knew fear for
him. Not Brendan, but who?

Darkness. She turned in her sleep, fought to waken, could
not. Moved, then, reluctantly, toward a light that ever receded. Light: fading, changing, turning. Wisps of smoke
curled red in that faint light. She was within Lyiadd's hall, a
sullen fire casting feeble, sanguinous shadows across the floor.
A whisper of noise—she whirled, horror sick, but the great
chairs stood empty. Another—*what* shared that chamber with
her? She tore sword and dagger free, shouted: "Lyiadd! I
killed you once, I'll kill you again! Show yourself, if you are
not recreant!" Only laughter answered. She cried out in terror
as it pressed against her inner being, and woke.

> *I have tried, more than once, to cast into words what
> it was to me, to speak with Nesrevera: It is not my way,
> however, and I think even the Ylsan poets fall short in
> their descriptions of such meetings. They do not tell of
> the light: I felt it, felt it course through her to me. It
> woke me to wonder, and to good I did not suspect I held
> within myself.*

It is a seldom thing, that any such as the child Lisabetha dream true, even among the Great Houses of the AEldra. Though I have heard it said that, to an extent, those fully human can take such AEldra-like Powers for short periods of time, either because they have dealt with those of great Power, or because they dwell in lands imbued with such Power. So little is known of the Foessa, of the Guardians, even of the Lammior and his halls—but it seems to me as likely an explanation as any and better than most, for the temporary change that took hold of certain of our company.

27

She shivered as she sat up; there was barely an edge of light against the eastern peaks, but there was no sleep left in her. She left Nisana pressed hard against Malaeth's side, crawled to the fire. Brelian had the last of the watches; he started as he came back into the light. "Why are you awake?" he whispered. "There is at least another hour."

"Bad dreams."

He eyed her sharply, hesitated, dropped down to warm his hands. "I—I dreamed, too, last night. I—saw Bren—" he shook his head. "You will laugh."

"No. Tell me."

"He was clad as one of the King's Guard, and he stood at the King's right hand. But it was not Koderra I saw."

"A fair hall, sunlit and white—" Her voice trailed away;

they gazed at each other blankly. "You—*you* dreamed this, Brel. You saw?"

"But—you know this—"

"Because I saw it, too." *And in such circumstance.*

Brelian leaned forward to feed the fire, concentrating carefully on his movements. A shaky smile caught at his lips, was gone again. "A true-seeing? I have had a true-seeing?"

She shook her head. "I cannot say, Brelian, I'm sorry. It's not an AEldra thing, true-seeing. But I think—I think yes. However it came about." And with that, he seemed content.

The rest of the company were surprisingly easy to rouse. Even Malaeth moved about the fire vigorously, though she had been frighteningly worn and cold the night before. *But he promised aid, I remember that now: strength. Aid of a most important kind.* And Ylia realized suddenly *she* had more strength than she would have thought likely from a poor and broken night's sleep.

Nisana spent most of the day out on her own, her thought shuttered. The meeting had affected her strongly and in some way that Ylia, as human, could not understand.

Clouds moved northward across the sky throughout the morning, now and again thinning to permit a weak sunlight to dazzle the eyes, though never enough of it to properly warm. Golsat and Levren went ahead to make a trail; the rest followed down a narrow canyon, up a wet, rocky cleft to higher ground. The sun came out as they set foot on a short-turfed meadow; clouds held in a black band across the northern and western horizons, but for a while the sky overhead was a brilliantly blue bowl. The ground steamed as the air warmed, and not far ahead they could see smoke: the foreguard had chosen a noon-hour stopping place and readied it for the rest.

Lisabetha dropped back to walk rearguard with Ylia for a while after they set out again. "Brelian has told me what he dreamed last night. And that *you*—"

Ylia nodded. "A thing very similar."

"Odd," the girl said finally, breaking a long and companionable silence, "that we should dream the same thing, we three."

"Yes." She wasn't, she found, very surprised. More surprising had Lisabetha slept the night through undisturbed. "Was that all you dreamed last night?"

"No." The girl frowned at the horizon, hesitated, caught

Ylia's eye and took reassurance. Ylia wouldn't disbelieve her or ridicule her. Difficult, still, to trust after so many years. "I cannot remember all of it. War and death—because when I recalled it this morning, I thought I had dreamed that battle we saw in the fog. It was—like that." She smiled suddenly. "It was not *dream*—but—well, an odd thing." Her glance caught Malaeth and Golsat, not far ahead. "She is better today, and I feel as though I had rested several nights, not just the one. But that was not *your* doing, was it?"

"No." *Why does she ask that?* What else had she dreamed, and what had they revealed to this Plainschild who foresaw like an AEldra?

Nisana returned about an hour before sunset. The company had not yet caught up with Marhan and Levren, though Ylia was aware of them and knew they would reach camp before full dark.

'Join,' the cat demanded. 'I would make search.'

'Now?'

'What better time?'

Lisabetha, three lengths ahead of them, slowed to let them catch up to her. "Search for what?" Ylia stared at her. "I'm sorry, I thought you spoke to me."

"You *heard* that?"

Nisana leaped to Ylia's shoulder. 'Girl! You heard me?' Lisabetha stopped cold and her eyes went round. 'Do not be afraid, it is I. Nisana.' Her astonished gaze went from cat to Brandt's heir, back again.

"You—" Ylia switched to mind-speech, 'Lisabetha?'

"I—how very strange a thing!" She touched Nisana's flank. "But I could never hear you before!"

'Can you speak so?' Nisana demanded suddenly. 'Try!'

'Nisana!' Ylia admonished. Bad enough the cat bully her, she was used to it. But Nisana ignored her, as she might have expected.

'Try it!' Lisabetha twisted her face, closed her eyes hard. Shrugged finally. 'No. Well, never mind. If you can hear, you should be able to speak. We will see to it later.' As a grudging afterthought: 'If you wish, of course.'

"I—well—" She considered solemnly.

"Lisabetha!"

"Coming, Brel!" She smiled, ran ahead. They stared after her.

'I can scarcely believe it, cat. And I would never have thought it possible.'

'That she hears, or that she does not think it another evil thrust upon her by whatever gave her Sight?'

'Both, I suppose.'

'She is growing sense. And why should not the touch of the Nasath release whatever Gift dwells within her? Though I fear it is a temporary thing only. Unlikely, even though she *dreams*, that she will grow AEldra skills; but a temporary gift such as mind-speech is not unheard of.' Nisana nudged hard. 'Come, wake up! You need not stand still for a simple mind-search. Begin to walk again, or someone will worry and come back for us. No, you cannot *still* need to close your eyes, you have been beyond that stage for days now!' Ylia sighed, but started forward. It was difficult; worse, it was disconcerting; fortunately the ground they traveled was smooth and level. 'I am worried,' Nisana admitted as they searched. 'What did *he* say to you of danger?'

'That it lay between us and Aresada. And—she?'

'We spoke of other things. Though danger was shown to me. Not its placing, for it moves about. The chance of it, three times.'

'That we might avoid it?'

'Even so.'

Ylia slowed, sorted again between the search and her footing; it was an odd sensation, akin to dizziness, to sense one thing and place and move in another. 'They fear to speak straightly, don't they?'

'Rightly so. Too easy for those who do not see as clearly, who are so much shorter lived, to depend upon them for all things, thinking themselves lesser. It is not right we lose initiative.'

'I agree. And the once a straight warning could not have aided us anyway.'

'Against Lyiadd, who was determined upon our capture. You are right. West.'

Silence. Day birds had since retired to branches or nests, the night birds had not yet begun to stir forth. 'And even such as they cannot lay the future out for us as a clear path.'

'No. But I am grateful for what they could tell us.' For what they had *shown*. Whether Nisana caught that thought, she was not certain, but the cat leaned against her cheek, rubbed it with her own.

North. A troop of deer directly ahead, a young buck, his antlers still delicately velveted, in their midst, stood at a wide pool under the thick shade of trees. A quail and her young straggled into the shelter of low brush; a skunk, still thin so early in spring and not long out of hibernation, drank from a hollow in a long rock ledge. On the far side of the pool, two lengths back from it, a fire—two men gathering the wood to feed it.

East, then. Silence and cold, and then, beyond the mountains, more silence, and the feel of old death. Ylia shivered, dragged the search away.

'We knew as much.' Nisana licked her whiskers. 'Enough. We are safe for tonight.'

Nisana spent the evening with Lisabetha, the two of them well away from the rest so they might have quiet for concentration. But Lisabetha's mind-speech, if any, remained a question mark. She could hear both Nisana and Ylia. Could even, though it gave her a headache, hear Malaeth. She could not reply in kind. She was greatly disappointed when Nisana warned her it might all fade as the days went by. 'But it cannot harm to use it while you have it.'

"No. And—perhaps—"

'I cannot promise. I hope for your sake, and for ours. It is always useful.' The cat curled up in her lap. 'And I like having others to speak with.'

The next day was much like the previous one: cool in the morning, likely to rain, but clouds drew back at midday, and it warmed. The meadow's grasses were dry, the company no longer reached camp wet to the knee.

Levren took foreguard late in the afternoon to prepare a camp, thus allowing them to walk until full dark. Nisana spent much of the day with Lisabetha and Malaeth, dropping back to rearguard with Ylia near sunset so they could make search.

'Nothing.' Ylia fetched a sigh of relief.

'Not so.' The cat was uneasy. 'Eastward, a little north.' Silence. Ylia shivered suddenly at the unwholesome, chilling silence, the familiar sensation prickling the hairs on her neck. 'Do you have it?'

Have it? Gods and Mothers! A stealthy, foul sensation crept across her skin. Nisana severed the bond between them, sprang out and down; Ylia tore sword free as Lisabetha cried out, "Brelian, 'ware! To your right!"

Black against the setting sun, a Thullen soared low, swerved from Brelian's two blades, bore straight for Ylia. She set her eyes to a point above and beyond it, knowing that if she met its gaze she would be unable to move. And this time—but Marhan and Golsat were already on their way to her side.

She wrapped both hands about the sword hilts, dropped to one knee and came up under the creature as it flew over. Her sword was nearly ripped from her hands, her shoulders burned with the wrenching, but the bat-creature shrieked and slammed into the ground. Ylia backed from it, turned and fled shaking into Marhan's arms.

"Mathkkra—near," Lisabetha whispered. Her face was white. Ylia nodded, pushed away from the Swordmaster's chest.

"I sense them, too. Keep close together, everyone," she managed aloud; her voice was more harsh whisper than true speech, "and keep moving!" Golsat pressed Malaeth between him and Brelian, started forward at the best pace the old woman could manage. Lisabetha followed, Ylia after her, Marhan at rearguard.

Twenty paces—a grove of stunted trees, there. They gave it wide berth, stayed far, too, from the rocks on the left that might hold an ambush. The last rays of evening sun were on the meadow when they came, at least thirty of the creatures, but they had no determination to match that of the humans. Some twenty fell, the rest fled. The company ran.

"Were they sent? Like the others?" Brelian demanded as they reached the safety of a belt of trees. Ylia shook her head. 'Cat?' 'Nothing here that does not belong; rest.' "You are certain of it?" Brelian pursued.

"No, not sent. They could not be, no, I killed him—" Her voice spiraled into hysteria. Golsat's hands dug into her arms, his dark face was taut.

"Stop that!" he hissed. "We cannot carry you, and we need your sword!" He shook her so fiercely her head snapped back.

"Don't!" Lisabetha caught at his hands.

"No," Ylia whispered. "I am fine, it is all right." Golsat fixed her with a stern look, seemed satisfied by what he saw and moved back to Malaeth. She felt her neck, gingerly.

Lisabetha gazed at her anxiously. "Can you walk?"

"Yes." Golsat's cure had been rough but effective; she was embarrassed, nothing more. "Let us go. We are not far from camp, and we will be safe now." She turned to Brelian. "Sorry, Brel. Their strength was their own; you could see the difference, couldn't you? They are cowards. They chose to fight only when they thought the odds greatly in their favor. Fire will protect us from the Thullen." Marhan pushed her before him, took rearguard. They reached camp not long after.

She was limp with reaction, and it was with difficulty she held herself awake at all. She wanted only sleep, but not until she had eaten; food was strength for the next day's walking. Brelian dropped down beside her, breaking in on her wandering thought.

"I had not noticed until tonight. Your dagger. You haven't one."

"No." She forced a smile. "I left it with one who had more need of it." The answering smile fell short of his eyes, too. He reached inside his jerkin, drew forth a narrow blade. A dagger: slender, beautifully balanced. On the hilts a copper ship, inset just above the crosspiece. Brendan's dagger.

"This is yours—no," he pressed it into her hand, closed reluctant fingers around it. "Who should have it but you? Would you offend him, to refuse it?"

She shook her head. "I—Brelian, I can't—"

"You can. You avenged him, you said that." She nodded then; her eyes were held by the reflection of firelight on the shining thing. "It is yours by right. Take it. Please take it." She looked up, blinked back sudden tears, aware he did the same.

"I will treasure it."

"I know it." He rose abruptly and strode into the night. Ylia closed her eyes, kissed the hilts and fitted the dagger with gentle care into its sheath.

'Nisana?' Dread flitted suddenly across her thought.

'No. They will not return.'

'Good.' She closed her eyes and was aware of nothing until Malaeth woke her for evening meal. She fell asleep again, heavily, not long after. Levren woke her for watch near night's end, and she roused Nisana to search as the sky began to grey.

'You are weary, girl.' The cat's thought was a warm thing, a rare caress.

'It fell on me in a lump last night.' Ylia yawned, laughed quietly. 'Would I could ride and sleep, the way you can!'

'Would you could,' Nisana agreed; the thought amused her. Then, seriously, 'What will we do when we reach Aresada? Have you thought on it?'

'No. Not really.' She rubbed soft ears. 'I do not know what awaits us. I know there are folk there, Bendesevorian told me that much; even Lyiadd hinted at it. More than I suspected, they both said. We will have to make choices, though, and that soon. If we remain Nedao, we will need some place to live. The Caves are no place to farm. And we will need to decide quickly, lest planting season totally pass us by. There is Yls, or Nar, otherwise. But we cannot take the Plain.'

'No. That is closed to us.' She was quiet for so long Ylia thought she had gone to sleep. Then: 'We are not walking, you can make long search. It is good to stretch what you have, to test it. And perhaps we can see the Caves from here.'

'That I doubt. But, I am willing to try.' The cat drained her inner strengths ruthlessly. Mountains—heavy forest—open marshland beyond them, thick with mist under the early light. No further. But the marshland, if she recalled the maps correctly, was near enough for hope.

South from that. Nisana backtracked along the way they would go. Meadow, a spill of waterfall. A bear at the base of that fall. A deep-pooled stream, stands of birch and oak. Human minds.

At first, neither realized what they had found. Nisana nearly lost the contact as the sense of it smote them both. Plainsfolk, Nedaoans! Women in the grey robes of the Citadel; children with lean faces, sleeping for warmth in a pile like so many puppies, for there was no fire, only a cold, grey-ashed pit. An old man in Citadel grey lay at full length a distance away from them, eyes closed. An angry red burn ran down his face, his clothes were charred.

Nisana severed the joining. 'They are five leagues away. With good luck, we might reach them tomorrow at sundown;

the way is rough between here and there. But they might not all live so long.'

'No.' Ylia thought furiously. 'I have it. I cannot bridge. But you can. And I can aid you, as you aided me to heal. If you could bridge me—and another—?'

'Well. A curious thought. Worth the attempt.' She considered in turn. 'Levren?'

'I think so.' Ylia jumped to her feet, fatigue forgotten, and went to waken him.

She had to shake him only once and lightly; he listened without comment. "Five leagues." He shook his head. "In this country, we could never reach them by nightfall. And there are children, injured?"

"Without food or fire. The Mothers know when they last ate." Ylia paused, chose her next words with care. "Lev, I swear I would not ask this of you, but there is need. If we can reach them, now, you and I—"

"Your magic. A bridging?" He paled but nodded. "Well— I hope I am old enough and perhaps wise enough to know when need must override fear." He set his belt to rights, gathered his bow, his food pack, the rough snares he had constructed, dragged his cloak around his shoulders. "All right. Let us go."

Ylia clapped him on the shoulder. "Good man. But I had better waken Golsat before we go. Nisana will remain here to keep an eye out for Mathkkra, though I do not think those we fought last night will give us trouble again."

Levren grinned fleetingly; he was still pale. "Well, *I* will say a word in Marhan's ear since you are afraid to!"

They moved away from the fire then. Ylia gripped Levren's arms, he caught at her hands, hard. "I know it sounds impossible," she murmured as she and Nisana joined, "but relax if you can. It makes it easier." One moment they stood at the edge of camp, the next not far from the refugees she and the cat had seen. Levren staggered and she nearly fell with him.

'Nisana?' The mind-touch was nearly as strong as it had been moments before. 'Nisana, it worked!'

'Of course it did.'

'Of course,' Ylia mocked. 'I will return as soon as possible, or Lev will. Alert Malaeth or Lisabetha which way you must travel to meet up with us.'

'Of course,' Nisana retorted dryly, and severed the contact.

We had been alone in the Foessa for so long, we had long since given up hope of finding other Plains refugees. So unexpected were they, that at first neither of us truly realized what we had found. It must have been a blessing on the part of their One that any of them lived at all, though to my thinking, their One might have blessed them a little better, and let them all live.

28

"Ho, Nedao!" Levren called out. No response. But a few more steps brought him out of the trees and into the clearing Nisana and Ylia had seen. Twelve ragged, hungry folk huddled there, mute with fear; the old man lay still, eyes closed. "We are of Koderra."

A gaunt woman in Citadel grey pushed stiffly to her feet. "From Koderra? To aid us? Or—or has the King's City fallen also?" She swayed; Levren caught her.

"Koderra is gone. But many of the people escaped to Yls by the River. We travel to Aresada. You are far to the west, if that was where you intended to go."

She shook her head hopelessly. Ylia took her arm as Levren moved to bundle three of the children into his cloak, pressed his food pouch and the spare into the hands of the herder woman who hovered over them. That done, he disappeared into the trees. "We had no idea where we were going. If we were going anywhere. Away from the Plain. Some of us know Aresada: Pyel and Nald, my sisters; Lus," she indicated the peasant with a nod, "who is mother to three of the children. But none of us were certain which way to go. And we could

bring him no further." Her eyes went to, remained on, the old
man. His face was pinched, white above the thick grey cloak,
and he scarcely seemed to breathe.

"We will bring you to the Caves. We are bound there ourselves. Levren will return shortly with meat; you and I had better build up the fire."

"Ours went out two nights ago," the woman said ruefully,
"and we had no means to rekindle it." She seemed for the first
time to see her companion. Her eyes caught at the sword, the
dagger sheath; a faint frown creased her brow as her gaze
touched on the worn breeches. "I am Sata. Of the Chosen."

"I am Ylia," the swordswoman replied.

There was a sudden reserve in the Chosen's manner. "There
is only one in Nedao who wears that name. And—such garb.
You are the King's daughter."

"I am."

"The King—"

"My father perished in Koderra." She caught at the
woman's arm as she would have made a formal curtsy. "No. I
am not yet Queen and this is not the place." She added over
her shoulder as she headed for the firepit, "Aid me with this
fire. We will need small branches, dry leaves or needles. There
is jerky in those pouches, chew on a piece of it now, before
you do anything else. Levren will bring fresh meat, but it will
be a while before that can be cooked."

"I—thank you." No, she had not imagined it; there was a
definite, sudden distance between the two women. But Sata
aided her, and between them they soon had a fire built; the
other women and the children moved close to it.

Ylia set about constructing a spit of thick, green branches,
studied the folk she and Levren had found. Sata alone was
anywhere near normal. Lus stared blankly across the fire and
into the trees, her arms wrapped around a sleeping girl of
perhaps three; the child clung to her tightly, even in sleep. The
oldest of the children—a boy no more than twelve—stood pro-
tectively behind the other three. The other four Citadel women
sat close together, all pale, thin and dazed. One clutched the
rags of her robe to her breast and alternately whispered to herself and whimpered.

But they were mostly cold and hungry. Whatever Levren
brought would probably go a long way toward restoring them.
Ylia turned her attention to the wounded man. His pulse was

light and rapid; he looked as though a puff of wind would carry it away forever.

"By so much only he has held to life." Sata stood behind her, expression unfathomable. "I have not the means to heal him. The Tehlatta left Inda when they fired the fields, after they used her. He brought her forth. By the second day, I had to lead him; he was in great pain and no longer aware of where he was or what he did." Ylia pressed the blackened cloak aside: he was badly burned down his right arm, both hands were scarred, puckered, the fingers curled into claws. "I laid cold, wet cloths on the burns and wrapped his hands in them. But I could do nothing else, I had nothing for his aid, nothing for our own."

"You did well with what you had." She hesitated, sat back on her heels to study the old man. There were few herbs or powders of any sort left in her pouch, and nothing for the simplest of burns, let alone such as these. But she knew full well the reason for the woman's sudden lack of warmth when she heard the name Ylia.

Witch. Even Lisabetha, who had known her, thought her powers evil because of association with the Chosen. This woman was fully Chosen. And she knew Brandt's daughter— Scythia's daughter—only as a name. The Chosen had first named Scythia White Witch, and not as compliment.

"I can save his life," she said finally.

"You—" Sata took an involuntary step toward them.

"But you may not wish that I do so. And perhaps he would feel the same."

Sata set her jaw. "You would use—" she hesitated.

"I have my mother's healing. AEldra healing. Magic, if you will. But if this is a thing against your belief, if it is so wrong in your sight—If it would be better, as your kind see it, to let him die, rather than that I so heal him?"

Sata sighed wearily, dropped down to sit on the old man's other side. "It *is* wrong." There was, briefly, iron in her voice. "But—if you could save Grewl. I know he will die without your aid." She let her head fall forward into her hands. "Lady, I cannot think. Nor, perhaps, have I the right to choose on his account, as you would know if you knew him. I give you the decision."

"Then I will save him." She paused. "Who is he, Grewl? I do not recognize the name."

"No. He was not of our fane. A scholar, Grewl, more than anything else. He is a South Osneran, of a—I suppose branch is the word, of our main house which is in the north of that land. He came just before harvest this past fall, having heard of certain manuscripts in our possession that he wished to study and perhaps to translate."

"I see." She was silent a while. This was a man of Marhan's years, perhaps more, but smooth of face except about the eyes, where fine lines gave proof that he worked long and hard hours at small and detailed things. There were deeper lines of laughter about his mouth. A scholar—a scrivener—Ylia glanced at the disastrously burned hands. "He will not die. We cannot lose any more good men, who have lost so many already. Grewl is needed—we dare not let die men of learning. Go, keep the fire burning. Lev should return shortly."

"I—"

"You need say nothing. My decision, and it shall remain between me and him." From the corner of her eye, she could see Sata urging her fellow Chosen to attempt the jerky, drawing the eldest boy to help her gather wood. She closed her eyes, then, laid hands across the old man's brow.

No easy task, this; he had been long days in the great silence that so often become final, and his inner being was slow to respond. But when she finally sat back, she found his eyes open. They met hers frankly.

"Who are you?" A mere whisper, as though his voice had forgotten how to work.

"Ylia, daughter to King Brandt of Nedao."

"Lady Princess. I have not met you before. But how did we both come here? You were not in the valley when the Tehlatt came." He closed his eyes briefly; memory was, it seemed, returning. Not pleasantly. His hand moved in the Chosen blessing for the dead.

"I have come north from the ruin of Koderra, bringing with me eight others. Many died in the City, but many also escaped. We will tell you the full tale later. For now, you should rest, and when there is food, you should eat."

He stared at the hand he had used in the blessing, brought the other up and gazed blankly at them both. One moved gingerly to touch his face.

"I used the AEldra power to heal you," Ylia added reluctantly as he turned that open gaze on her once again. "If I did wrong—but I do not think I have. You are needed, by those who follow your way. By Nedao. And by me. If it is possible, you will remain with us. If I did wrong, if I have offended you, then I ask your pardon.''

But the withdrawal she fully expected did not come. He continued to study her for a time. ''Well. I have often wondered about these AEldra ways. I have never spoken with the Queen your mother, or with any AEldra, and know little save what the tales your Lord Corlin supplied us told—or what my fellows said. I did not particularly believe all I heard, however. So much evil harbored within human souls!'' A faint smile. ''But then, I have always held that the One gave us brains to interpret the teachings according to the world about us.'' He closed his eyes. ''Do you know—of the Citadel itself, who escaped?''

She shook her head. ''No. I am sorry. It may be that others did so, and that they have reached Aresada—the northern Caves Lord Corlin prepared as siege-hold.''

''I know of them.'' He drew a deep breath, let it out slowly. ''I cannot remember much, myself. I fear that—if the Father of these Nedaoan Chosen perished—'' He met her eyes again, a rueful smile crinkling his own. ''They thought, when I first came here, you see, of setting me in Gedderan's place. As a man more suitable to dealing with Nedao and its half-AEldra heir than he. Because, I suppose,'' he added diffidently, ''I am less set in my thought.''

''Oh?'' She tried to recall. Had Brandt pressed for Gedderan's removal or replacement? She couldn't remember, it was too long and too far away. The old man recalled her wandering attention with a heavy sigh.

''I personally desire no such thing. I much prefer dealing with books and pen and ink to dealing with people.'' He sighed again. ''I will not worry the matter until I must. But I thank you, very much, for your healing. That was kind of you.''

''You are welcome. As I told Sata, Nedao cannot afford to lose more lives, for any cause. And we will need you, we will need scholars when we rebuild. If that is what we do.''

''I shall hope to aid you in that, Lady. But—those who escaped Koderra. King Brandt, Queen Scythia, you do not name them.''

Ylia shook her head, pressed her lips tightly together. Grewl made the sign of blessing but offered no word of sympathy, for which she was grateful.

He sat, slowly and cautiously and she held an arm ready to brace him, but he did not seem to need it. "I do not recall this place at all, Lady." Sata came swiftly from the fire to kneel beside him; her face was anxious.

"Grewl, are you—is it—"

He smiled at her fondly, patted her hand. "It is well, Sata." He caught Ylia's eye, including her in that warmth. "I feel no pain, save in my middle. How long have we been here?"

"Near to a month. But, if you are hungry—" Sata stumbled to her feet and hurried back to the fire, began rummaging through Levren's pack.

Grewl laughed, a wheezy chuckle as weak as the rest of him. "Small wonder I am hungry! A man of my years should not be put to the missing of meals, let alone so many!" Sata returned with jerky, Lev's water bottle. Grewl took the strips of meat, eyed them doubtfully. "Is there enough of this? I would take no one else's share."

"Enough," Ylia assured him, and warmed to him even more. "One of my companions hunts; there will be fresh meat for all of you shortly. Eat that, if you can. You need strength." She went back to build up the fire, left him to speak with Sata.

Levren returned not long after, carrying three groundbirds and a rabbit. While he threaded cubes of meat onto skewers, she moved back into the trees a distance to search for Nisana.

'Ylia.' Reply came at once, strong and clear. Still distant. 'Tomorrow at noon. That is the best your Swordmaster and Brelian can conjure between them.'

'Then I will return to you at dark and leave Levren here.'

'Good.' Nisana broke contact.

It was bound to come, that she would fetch up against serious prejudice in the form of these religious folk. Fortunate for her that she came first among those who could be swayed. Even more fortunate that she took to her side, immediately and for all the rest of his days, the Chosen Grewl. For he was to be of more aid to Ylia, and to Nedao, in the days to come than any of us might have imagined when she was moved to pity for a pain-wracked, hunger-thinned old scrivener.

Levren had set up a rough spit across the fire and was sitting among the children, speaking with them, drawing them out. A little food, a little warmth: by the time they had eaten, the torn, haunted air was gone from them. Not long after, they slept near the fire together, Lus among them, Levren's cloak over them all.

Sata and her sisters slept also, a little apart from the others. Only when she was certain they slept deeply did Ylia dare move among them, laying a hand to first one and then another, willing strength, sleep, laying the healing with a feather touch among them, that none of them waken later and realize the witching powers had been at work. *Foolish*, she could not but think. Pyel and Nald had recovered to a large extent with warmth and food, but Mirs had seen her blood sister slain before her eyes and was still in a state of shock; Sata had had to hold the food to her lips before she would eat. And Inda—Grewl had pulled her from death, but a large part of her had already died when the Tehlatt had raped her and left her in the fields.

Levren went back out to reset his snares and gather more wood against the coming of night. A warm smile lit Grewl's face as he gestured Ylia to his side. Dark, intelligent eyes glowed against the pale skin. "Sit and speak with me, Nedao's Lady, if you will. I have slept enough. And I would know what has passed."

"What I can tell you—"

"I remember nothing, really. I do not even remember bringing poor Inda from the fields, though they tell me I did." His Nedaoan was nearly without accent, unlike that of so many Osnerans, and he used the easy, idiomatic dialect of the Midlands, such as the peasantry in the vicinity of the Citadel spoke. She told him what she knew, listened in turn to what he could tell—though he knew, as he had said, little enough. Ylia was surprised to see the sun was near setting when they finished speaking. Time to return to the rest of the company.

Levren sat near the fire, conversing with the two oldest boys, keeping an eye on the spits they tended for him. Only she could possibly have noticed that he sat so he would not have to look at, or speak with, the foreign Chosen. "Lev, I am going back. You had better stay here, if you don't mind."

"If I really must," he replied dryly. "They might need my aid, these young warriors." The boys eyed him dubiously, smiled in reply to the smile he gave them. "When, do you think?"

"Tomorrow, noon-hour, by Marhan's figuring. Take

care.'' She hugged him tightly.

"Take care yourself, Ylia.'' He turned back to his new young friends and she strode into the trees, far enough away so that she could bridge without any of them seeing her vanish.

She reached Nisana and was with her less than a breath later. Unnerving. Not as unnerving as it had been, though she didn't really notice that. The smell of baking trout mingled with the sharp pine-tar scent of the fire. 'Clever of you, to return in time for a meal,' the cat remarked tartly. Ylia laughed. Nisana ordinarily preferred her own catch, but she remained in camp and close to the fire when there was fish.

Marhan gaped across the fire; Nisana had bridged her directly into their midst.

"Me,'' Ylia said aloud, unnecessarily. "Sorry.''

"Sorry? What for, boy?'' the Swordmaster demanded. "Popping up like a child's toy, scaring the old man green! Nothing much, eh?''

"Not much,'' she retorted, and laughed. He snorted sourly, went back to stropping his dagger.

"Well? How many, and who?'' Golsat demanded.

"Twelve. Five women of the Citadel, a herder woman with three children. Two orphaned. A foreign Chosen named Grewl. Lev is still with them.''

"Oh.'' Golsat considered this gravely. Ylia grinned.

"Don't worry for Lev; he's handling it well enough, and the old man will no doubt sleep most of the time. They will go with us to Aresada, of course.''

"Nisana tells me,'' Lisabetha said, and her voice carried awe that Nisana could tell her anything, "that there *are* folk at the Caves. But she does not know how many.''

"No. It is too far to touch the Caves from here, in any fashion. How has the walking been?''

"Good,'' Golsat replied. "I found another trail of some sort this morning. It has gone on flat and easy for most of the day, and in the direction I am told is ours.'' He glanced at Lisabetha and then Malaeth, doubtfully at Nisana.

"That way.'' Ylia waved a hand generally north and west.

"Even so,'' he nodded. "That, at least, is good!''

"There has been nothing bad, has there?'' He seemed unusually gloomy, leaving her suddenly anxious.

"No.'' He shook his head. "Not to say there will not be.

Who knows—but I will not speak of evil here, lest speaking bring the thing itself." And he surreptitiously warded himself.

"Malaeth, how are you faring?" Ylia moved over to her side, eyed her critically. Her color was good, for a change, and she seemed reasonably awake.

"Well. I have the strength of a goat in my legs of a sudden. The Nasath grant it not fail me!" Her eyes held a wordless communication in their pale blue depths. *What did she see, and what does she know*? Ylia leaned forward, kissed her cheek.

Golsat and Marhan squabbled throughout the evening meal. "Swordmaster, we are nearly where we go. If we can place ourselves on your map as north of the Citadel—"

"I cannot be certain we are," Marhan grumbled. "And I will not believe in the end of this journey until we take the last step of it! If you are right—bah!" He spat noisily into the fire. "Even if *I* am right, we have at most thirty leagues to go, though it may be nearer twenty. Now, do the Tehlatta not hold the Caves—"

"Silence!" Golsat clapped a hand, not gently, over the Swordmaster's mouth. "You will call down all the remaining evils in the Foessa with such talk!"

"Well, the Chosen would not have it so," Brelian said. "But then, who is to say what—?"

"Shhh!" Lisabetha laid fingers across his lips, effectively stopping him mid-thought. "I have heard enough argument in my years between those who follow the Chosen and those who set milk for the house-imp and lay the first ear of corn to the Mothers to last me the rest of my days, do I live three lifetimes! Brel, if you love me, spare me another!" He gazed at her, opened his mouth, shut it again.

Golsat laughed. "Well! I meant to start no such quarrel, certainly not between you two! I am sorry, 'Betha, and as proof of that, I will take first watch tonight." He bowed, making a good job of the sweeping Teshmoran formality, even though seated, and began to dig his packets of little trout from the coals.

"Do you know," Lisabetha remarked thoughtfully, chin in hands, as she watched him deftly peel away the grass and divide up his catch, "I would never have thought I could tire of mountain trout. But the time is near when I will never wish to *see* another."

Golsat separated his with two twigs, dropped a bit of firm, pink meat into his palm so he could blow it cool. "Find something else that suits you, if this does not please. I like it." He popped the bite into his mouth. Lisabetha made a face at him.

"I should think so; I know what a guardsman carries for food! If I had eaten such things, I might be grateful for trout every night—for five-days on end—I would not," she sighed, "mind bread. I truly would not."

Ylia finished her own portion quickly. The taste, as Lisabetha had said, was no longer the wonder it had been at first, though at least it filled a hollow. She and Nisana then made a quick search, though the cat had made a thorough one of her own earlier.

She and Lisabetha stumbled down to the water in total darkness to wash. "I would live on Golsat's trout and nothing else, I swear it," Ylia shivered as she rubbed her face on a far from clean sleeve, "If I could wash my body and all my clothing."

"You!" Lisabetha replied fervently. "I would kill for hot water! And *soap*! Mothers, do you remember soap?"

Ylia laughed. "Well, don't kill me; any I find, I promise to share!" She shook her hands, wiped them on her pants. "It is too cold out here, me for the fire!"

"Wait—not without me—!" Lisabetha caught at her arm, and they ran back to camp.

One adjusts to anything, given need—and so I had, to those with me, so we all had. We functioned together neatly: evening camps had not been shouting matches for long days, and those events that we controlled, at any rate, went smoothly. But more than need joined us after all we had faced together, more than the simple kinds of friendship one has in the ordinary way. Though I seldom say such things, I felt affection for each of my companions—even the Swordmaster. And the Swordmaster in turn treated me, after his own brusque fashion, as a comrade and true friend.

29

Golsat built up the fire and heated water as he finished the last watch, and they were on their way an hour before the sun rose. His trail led in the direction they must go for some while, but finally bent eastward and they abandoned it for open meadow. There were streams amid the tall grasses, mostly tiny rills even Malaeth could cross without aid. They stopped only twice: once to allow Brelian to climb a ledge to look for sign of Levren's fire, and once for a quick noon-meal.

Not an hour later, they came upon a sentry: The oldest boy, Mouse (his real name was Morovon, but no one ever used it), stood at the ready, a long, fresh-peeled staff in his hands. Levren, propped against a tree in the shade not far off, informed the company gravely that he was merely keeping the guard company; none of them would have dared smile in reply.

255

Mouse bowed stiffly before standing aside. Levren sprang to his feet and returned to the camp with them.

He had done his work well: those who had hidden for most of the Planting Month were warmed, rested, fed. The children hung onto him with adoring eyes.

Only the Chosen were silent: Inda had died during the night. She had no desire to live, could not face the thing the Tehlatt had done to her. "The One cares for his own," Ylia heard Sata's subdued response to an even quieter query of Lisabetha's. *Perhaps. If he grants oblivion, then perhaps.*

Golsat and Brelian went in search of fish, taking Lisabetha with them. She hoped to find cattail root, from which she and Lus could grind a meal for a bland flat bread. Marhan stationed himself cross-legged in a patch of sun and retreated into his map. Levren was entertaining the children with some outrageous tale.

Lus brushed hair from her eyes with an impatient hand, set aside her youngest. To Ylia's intense embarrassment, she knelt and could not be persuaded to rise.

"My Lady. My thanks and that of my children, that you have taken such care of us. We would have died if you had not come—you and those who travel with you. I take the blood-debt, mine, my children's—all the children's—to myself."

Ylia opened her mouth, shut it again, chose her next words with great care indeed. "Even as you say it, do I accept," she replied finally. The herder woman, she knew, would have been uncomfortable had she spoken other than so formally. "But how should there be no aid for you? You and these children are the very stuff of Nedao, just as the threads are part of my cloak."

"Nedao is gone," Lus protested, but the words clearly pleased her.

Not only her. There was a silence in the clearing, and Ylia glanced up to see every pair of eyes fixed on them. "Nedao lives. We *are* Nedao, all of us. I am; you, Lus, and these children; these of the Chosen, my arms-mates and companions, the women of my House. Those who escaped to Aresada before us, those who sailed for Yslar. We are Nedao. Where we are, that is Nedao. There was another, once; we all know the histories, when Nedao was an island. When that was taken perforce by the Sea-Raiders, our long parents came to the Plain and again built Nedao. As we shall do, I swear it." She

stopped short, face hot. How had she come by such words?
But Lus' eyes were glowing.

"There *shall* be a rebuilding, Lady." She bowed, returned
to the fire and again took her youngest onto her lap. The child
was so intent on Levren's tale, she scarcely noticed her
mother's return; nor did she pay heed moments later when
Brelian burst into the clearing.

Something strange—Brelian was smiling; no, grinning
hugely, something he had not done in many days and all the
more noticeable against the black glower Golsat wore as he
followed him into the camp. Brelian stopped, glanced about
anxiously, but Lisabetha had not yet returned and he fastened
on the swordswoman instead. "I have bested Golsat! Look!
Five against his two—and larger! And look you at the
color—!" Undoubtedly he would have gone on so as long as
anyone was willing to listen, but Golsat came muttering up
and dragged him off to the fire.

Brelian chuckled to himself as he and the half-caste worked
to wrap and bury their catch in the coals and Ylia turned away
to hide a grin of her own: Brel was well-nigh insufferable, and
Golsat was in the poorest humor she had ever seen.

"I thought you might want to know." She started; Golsat
had come quietly up behind. "There is a pool, yonder," he indicated, "deep enough for swimming. The water is chill, but it
is sunny and likely to stay so for another hour, perhaps two."

"Golsat." She gripped his shoulders. "My undying gratitude. I will have you made peer!"

"Do not you dare—my nose bleeds at such heights!" But he
grinned and Ylia laughed. "Shall I send 'Betha after you?"

"You had better, or she will never forgive you." Malaeth
was not back yet either but, given a choice, Ylia knew she
would greatly prefer Marhan's kettle with water decently
heated. Ylia snatched up her cloak and hurried from the clearing.

Lisabetha arrived, breathless, not long after, and they managed to get each other reasonably clean, though both could
have done with honest soap for their hair, and they dared
wash no clothing; it was late afternoon, and anything wet now
would be still damp when it must go back on. They remained
on the sun-heated rocks until they were warm once again.

Marhan was still poring over his map, drawing lines in the

dirt, mumbling to himself. Ylia dropped down beside him.
"What now?"

"What ever?" he demanded gruffly. "But what think you
—assuming we are here," one blunt finger stabbed at the
parchment, "then I think another five-day. Or so, since we are
more and have children and these Chosen women among us."
He stopped as she shook her head. "Well, we are no nearer
than this, we cannot be!" He pointed again.

"More like—here." She indicated a place two fingers north
of his last. "The Citadel—there. Now, we are already north of
that, so we have crossed both of your points, and we are further east."

"And you know this—how?"

"How do I know anything? But Nisana and I will search
again tonight, and I wager on your tossing sticks, old man,
that I can see the marshes from here, if not the green rock of
Aresada!" He regarded her sourly, finally shrugged.

"And how a man is to argue with *that*! No, keep your hair
on, boy, I meant it straight." He reached out to tug at her one
finished plait. "You have the witching. I never trusted it, but I
know the right of it. When your mother said a thing was, by
the Black Well, it *was*. Here, eh?"

"Less than a five-day, even with these new companions. But
tonight will show more." She met his gaze, her eyes dancing
with mischief. "Of course, you yourself could reach the Caves
ahead of us, if you wished it."

"What, the way you brought Lev here?" He scowled good-
naturedly, knowing full well she had not meant it. "My feet
still work; I'll use 'em while they do."

Evening meal was still going on when she and Nisana left
camp to search, past the pool, now peaceful in the deep-blue
light, on a ways from that. They climbed a low ledge, above
most of the surrounding trees, sat and watched as the last of
the sun moved slowly off distant peaks, and joined then.

No sign of enemy; no other folk, either. That duty taken
care of, they searched north, as far as the combined vision
could reach, arguing fiercely the while. 'Ylia, I swear by your
own Black Well you will not be able to walk back to camp
unaided if you do not use less!' 'Cat, I need what I use, or I
would not use it!' 'As you please, then, wasteful creature. But
do not look to me for help if you—' 'There! Nisana—there!'

There. Once only had she seen Aresada, when she was very

young. The Caves were still beyond their reach, but pale-green rock, and greenish, rock-strewn soil, stunted trees: that was the land not a league from them! They pulled the vision slowly back toward their present location. Marshes. . . .

They blinked at each other. "I was right; we were right! Three days, four at the most!" Ylia was jubilant, nearly shaking with reaction.

'Do not count them,' the cat replied dryly. 'Plans of ours have gone so often awry.'

"No. Let us return to camp, if you're done, at least."

'Done,' the cat said. 'And I am hungry.' She rubbed hard against her companion's cheek, dropped to the ground and bounded back toward camp. Ylia followed, of necessity slower and more cautiously.

She took early watch with Golsat, fell asleep almost immediately after. She slept quietly for some time, or so it seemed. But then her inner being tingled and strange visions moved over her thought: Two swords, one long and heavy, the other narrow and fine-bladed as a dress dagger, clashed ringingly together as lightning crackled overhead. Baelfyr leaped between the points. A dark hall—Lyiadd's? So it seemed, but older, and he who sat upon the dais was not Lyiadd. Darkness thickened the air about him like fog, and she was glad of this, glad she could not see more clearly. Glad the eyes did not turn her way.

Other odd bits of dream followed: Brendan, kissing her mother's hand, Brandt raising him to his feet. A dark, evil shadow sailing across tall forest, sending a tall, skin-clad hunter scrambling back the way he had come. A sword again, and with it a sense of longing. She could feel her hand curling in anticipation of that pale shining hilts against her palm.

Silence. A silence so complete she could not even hear her own breath. Movement—she was moving, leaping forward, dancing back, lightfooted. Fighting. Lyiadd, blood trickling down his chest, staining the dark-red tunic like a ribbon of sweat, his hair hanging red-gold and lank across a thin, golden circlet. A dark-red stone, sullen against his brow. It gave back no light. But she had never seen that narrow band—was this another fight? No, hers against him, for there were the same faces: Marrita's anxious one, the impassive faces of the guard. Her sword, clear and recognizable, weaving in and out around Lyiadd's point.

The inner vision blurred suddenly, as though it could not hold against what had followed and when it cleared she held Marrita, gritting her teeth against a sea of pain. She flung the woman away: blood was smeared across pale, loosened hair, the bodice and sleeve of the blue silk.

"Your death, remember that. Your death—" A whisper caught at her throat, rasped cold across her skin, and a black horror filled her. With a cry, she woke.

She lay flat, eyes wide, drawing air into a shaking body. Silence throughout the camp: the cry had not been aloud, for which she was grateful. But Nisana was already at her side.

'Ylia?'

'I—I dreamed. Sorry.' She caught her breath, steadied it with an effort. 'Sorry to waken you, cat. Just a bad dream.' She closed her eyes; dark fur touched against her shoulder.

'Merely a dream. They cannot harm.' Her thought was soothing. Ylia relaxed suddenly and slept again. This time nothing disturbed her until the early rays of the morning sun slanted down the ravine and into her eyes.

Was this a thing she was to be plagued with hence-forth—or, like Lisabetha's mind-speech, a thing brought about by contact with the Foessa and those within them? I could not be certain, though, unlike Lisabetha—for Ylia's own sake, I hoped the latter.

My opinion on individual persons is not necessarily reliable. Like humans, I take notions and they are not always the right ones. With the girl's cousin, however, this Vess—well, if anything, I was never harsh enough in my judgment of him. That he wanted Brandt's throne I never doubted, though I was the only one who agreed with Ylia on that. Like Lyiadd, he could not entirely hide his thought or his desires from me, and I knew what he thought, how he sought to pressure the nobles ("That a woman should rule! Worse, a girl of few years and little experience!"), how he worked to sway the North ("Your King breaks faith with ye, that he brought a witch to wife, to bear him children of that heritage to rule ye!"). Amusing to me, that last, since clearly Vess had no true beliefs of any kind, though he certainly made an outward professing of this Chosen religion. Well, it is not the first time a human has clutched some belief or other to its breast to win over the adherents of the belief to its bidding, and will doubtless not be the last.

30

Ylia sat up slowly and yawned. A poor night's sleep; she was grateful they intended to stay another day. Nisana sprawled near the fire, sleeping still—or again. The clearing was otherwise deserted, save for Golsat, who tended a small, roughly woven rack of fish over a smoky fire. Ylia could hear a low, melodious chant down the ravine, and in the opposite direction, toward the pool, children's laughter. Golsat handed her food and drink.

"Where is everyone?" The tea was cool, the meat cold, Lisabetha's flat bread tough and tasteless without salt.

Golsat shrugged. "The Chosen are burying the woman who died. As I recall, they put much work into such a thing and will be at it until after dark. Lus and the children are with 'Betha and Malaeth, searching out groundberries and plants. Marhan and Levren left before first light, hoping to bring in a deer. Brelian," he scowled at his rack, "is back at the creek." She bent to the last of a decidedly uninteresting breakfast to hide a smile.

"So we stay here another day."

"Good for us; we need the food, and I could use the rest myself." Golsat eyed her soberly. "What do you think we will find at Aresada?"

"I try not to think on it much. But I suppose the time has come I must. I do not know what we will find. I know there are folk there, a large number of them."

"Do you?" A brief smile, quickly gone. "There is much you 'know' these days, isn't there?"

"Some. But you know much I cannot understand also. I would have starved long since, left to my own devices . . . if I had not gotten hopelessly lost right at the start. We are confounding, each in our own ways, all of us. Don't you think?"

"Sooth. You in a way I never met before, though. But, you do know more of the Caves than I."

"A little. There are folk there, but we all knew that. There are no few. I know of some—well, I know." She smiled at him. "But who is there, which of the folk of Nedao, I will not know that before you do."

"Well—" He smiled, clearly unconvinced. "Marhan is still irritated with you, you know."

"I daresay!" She laughed quietly. "But you know how he is! It goes beyond his dislike of warrior women, I begin to think—as though I were his own baby, his fragile Princess."

"Oh." Golsat laughed in reply. "And you have only begun to see this, have you?"

"Well, he disguises it well enough, doesn't he?"

"So," Golsat replied pointedly, "do you. But he is a good man, the Swordmaster. Narrow in his views, perhaps a trifle. And a little over-swift in arriving at decisions." He touched his eye, which was still a magnificent swirl of color. "He has a strong arm for one so old! But, no insult, mind, I was surprised. Somehow, even though I had been two years in the City, I never really expected—"

"No insult. We have all learned considerable of each other this journey. Look at Malaeth! I have known her all my life, and had anyone ever told me how great her determination, I would have laughed! I always loved her, of course," she added as she swallowed more cold tea, "but I thought of her as—well, a soft old woman, even when I was a child. Fluttery, not too intelligent."

"Unexpected, indeed." Golsat nodded. "But, as you say, each of us has been a surprise to the others." He stared off toward the trees. "Lev—" he hesitated, smiled faintly. "To have become friends, even a little, with him." He met her eyes. "And in such a fashion, who would ever have thought it?"

Ylia laughed, shook her head. "Not I! But—your question of Aresada: There are probably a few from the Citadel there already. A number of farmers and herders from east of the Torth. Perhaps a minor lord or so. Perhaps even a few Teshmorans who escaped as Gors did. Several hundreds, perhaps several thousands. Not many."

Golsat's normally somber face fell even more. Careful hands turned the rack, settled it back down onto the forked sticks that held it above the smoke. "It is a hard thing to face," he said finally. "That there is no going back. That the Plain is closed to us forever. Of all of us here, I should find it easy, but it comes no more easily than it did when we fled Anasela. Nor do the losses."

"No. But we will build again." Golsat met her eyes. "What I said to Lus yesterday, I meant that. There are valleys within the Foessa where a holding could settle, a number of folk could begin again. We will find such a place. We have done it before, our kind.''

"So we have.'' Golsat turned back to the fire to pull his rack from the smoke and dump its contents into dry leaves. "There. That will help. Of course, Brelian will have more—and better—and of better color—'' He grinned then, and Ylia clapped her hands together in sudden delight. "And do you dare say one word to him!'' he added fiercely, but his eyes danced with mischief.

"Malaeth said it best,'' Ylia laughed. "All the wiles of a Narran soothsayer!'' Golsat pulled a face at that, but began to laugh himself.

"You know, I never *could* teach that trick to anyone else, to catch fish with the hands. Brelian has taken to it astonishingly well, but I think at least half the joy of the trick comes of knowing he has bested me and I smart for it.'' He shrugged cheerfully. "So why should I disappoint him?''

"Why indeed?'' And if it brought him happiness—a sharp, dark pain smote at her inner being; she pressed it savagely away, took one last swallow of Malaeth's tea—it was stone-cold—and put the kettle aside to help Golsat rake the hot little fish from the leaves.

He broke one open, worried it apart and held out a sliver of dried white meat. Ylia bit into it, made a face, but chewed diligently and swallowed. "Well, for anyone who wishes a change from jerky.''

Golsat munched slowly. "Why? What is wrong with it?''

"Nothing, if you like fish smoked. I never have.''

"Hmmmph.'' Golsat eyed her sidelong, licked his fingers. "*You* eat plants.''

"I forget, you barbarians eat your meat half-raw and unaccompanied, don't you?''

"Now that,'' Golsat began indignantly, "is not so! I eat bread and rice both, I even eat one or two of the tubers.''

"And smoked fish. Ugh. I think,'' she added as she rose to her feet, "that I had better go make myself useful, since everyone else is busy.''

"You of all folk?'' Golsat looked up. "Do not overtax yourself, Ylia, not before we reach Aresada.'' And, as she gazed at him in mild astonishment, "I do not have my mother's Sight, but I feel you will need all the strength you have there. That is all.''

"Then I will indeed take care," she replied. "But see that you do so as well." She caught up the kettle, emptied the last dregs of tea into the trees and set out to spy the lands, and to gather berries, if there were any.

For what remained of the morning she climbed and walked, searching out a high vantage point. After a long, hard climb up a broad slope and out a long point, she had her view, though she prudently stayed well back from the edge and carefully avoided looking straight down.

Below, spread out all around for leagues, forest ran to the feet of the mountains and far up the slopes. Here the Foessa separated, an outer range bending well to the east, leaving a deeply forested valley some ten leagues by twenty between the spurs. Now and again a clearing, a circle of meadow or a patch of the lighter green that was willow, aspen and running water.

North; she stared intently. Almost at the edge of sight, the forested land ended abruptly, and beyond that, between forest and the blue haze that was distant mountain, a flash of bright green. The Marshes.

Mothers, to be so near! She stared a while longer, finally turned aside, set her mouth grimly and forced herself back down the ledge to lower, safer ground. On the way back to camp she came through a broad, sunny dell and filled the kettle—and herself—with sweet red cupberries.

Brelian was tending the fire, turning another small rack of fish. Golsat was nowhere in sight. Lus and the children had returned with Lisabetha and Malaeth, and the women sat in the shade—Lus and Malaeth picking through their finds while Lisabetha wove a bag of green reeds for the herder woman to carry. The children could be heard in the distance, laughing and giggling as they played an elaborate game of touch.

Early in the afternoon Lev and Marhan staggered in with a deer, and the afternoon was given over to the messy, disagreeable task of cutting and readying the meat. They saved out enough for evening meal and for the next morning, cut the rest into strips. It was a time-consuming task, one Ylia held herself to with reluctance, and only Lisabetha's diligent example kept her at it long after she would cheerfully have quit.

"It is not that I do not mind. I *hate* this," Lisabetha whispered in reply when she said as much. "I am so tired of fish I would do anything to avoid eating it tonight. And I cannot bear it smoked!'' Ylia laughed. Golsat scowled good-naturedly at them both.

They left the hide to the men and slipped away to the pool for a good wash and then a nap. It was late afternoon when Ylia woke; Lisabetha was already gone.

She wandered back to the fire to find Golsat and Nisana alone—he tending the fires and a myriad of smoking racks, she, for a wonder, perched comfortably on his knee. As Ylia approached, they both looked up and Nisana, with a happy little sigh, stretched out at full length. Golsat rubbed the hollows behind her ears.

"Those of the Citadel have not yet eaten?" She could hear them still, faintly now, down the ravine.

Golsat shook his head. "They will be hours yet. I have seen this before, in Teshmor. None of them eat before sunrise tomorrow anyway, as respect for their dead." He spoke without inflection, but the eyes that met hers were concerned. "You do realize how fortunate you are that these we found are so openminded? Few are!"

Open-minded? She thought of Sata, of her female companions who spoke even less with her than Sata did, of the warding signs they one-and-all used against Nisana when the cat was about. But then there was Grewl. *Perhaps.* "All I know of them is that my grandsire, Bergony, gave them the Citadel that was once the King's summer home, and its lands, in exchange for their scrivening and tutoring. Most of them are Osneran, a few Narran. Many, of late, of Nedao. I knew of their chief—the Father, as they call him—Gedderan, by reputation; I never met him. He was said to be narrow, but not as narrow of thought as some."

"Well, I pass no judgment on what they preach." Golsat reached to turn one of his racks, carefully, and with one eye to the sleeping cat on his leg. "Nor on the religion of any. Because there is a thread that runs through all of them, even that of the Tehlatt, which may be smooth. Nor do I care what any man believes, where his inner being goes when he dies, or whyfor, does he not demand I believe the same." He started as the brush behind him crackled loudly, but it was only Marhan and Levren. After a moment, he went on. "Many of these Chosen are not open-minded at all. I have spoken to Narran traders who tell me there is open persecution in Osnera against those with different beliefs—or none at all. They say many of the Nedaoan Chosen are not unlike their Osneran compatriots: fanatics. Willing to convert men by sword, did no other means serve. Or by fire.''

She had watched him in growing astonishment as he spoke, but as he paused for breath, laughed. ''Dead men are won to no cause! What stupidity is this?''

''Men of that kind believe the living more easily swayed with such threat against them,'' Levren put in quietly. ''But you yourself know how they prate against anything AEldra, Ylia.''

''That is true,'' Golsat said. ''One of them that I heard in the market place in Teshmor preached it that your mother was a child of the Evil One himself, sent to drag all Nedao into the Netherworld behind her.'' He scowled as Ylia laughed again. This was beyond belief! ''It is no laughing matter,'' he added sternly. ''If any of those yet lived, they would point to the Tehlatta as the means by which this thing was done!''

''It is dangerous to have them around us,'' Levren said mildly. ''Folk of that kind. I wonder,'' he added thoughtfully, ''what happened to that priest when Lord Corlin's guard got wind of him.''

''Nothing, likely. That is ever the way,'' Marhan grumbled. ''I,'' he added, lowering himself stiffly to the ground, ''counseled Brandt more than once to send 'em away before they made trouble! And those in Teshmor, there were one or two —but he saw no harm in 'em, no reason they should not speak out. So long as no one took them seriously.''

''But folk do; they did,'' Golsat cut in. ''Look at our Lisabetha! She has the Sight—so did my mother, many of the Northern women do. But the Chosen will have it this is evil, a sending to tempt the inner being to evil! Just look what they did to our 'Betha!'' He spat into the fire.

''Well, I have never paid much attention to them,'' Ylia admitted finally. ''I knew how they felt about Mother—anything AEldra. I was not aware, really, how strongly feeling ran until Lisabetha told me. But this Grewl—''

''He,'' Levren cut in, ''is unlike any Chosen I have ever met.''

''But, with me as an example, they must see there is no evil in being AEldra!''

''You credit them with thought,'' Marhan said sourly. ''They do not think. They see a thing and it is either good or

bad, according to what their teachings say. You," he added
accusingly, "are as much an innocent as your father was."

"But they have done so much of what Bergony brought
them to Nedao for—copying the old tales, reviving the histories, teaching lost skills. Marhan, this is important work they
accomplish!"

"Oh, *well*." Marhan fell to moodily poking the embers with
his knife. "I am unlettered myself and see no point to any of
it. That's what minstrels and talesmen are for. But if you want
my opinion—" At that moment, Lisabetha, Lus and the children crashed through the brush laughing and out of breath,
mercifully silencing him.

During her watch at middle night, the Chosen returned to
the camp, silently sought sleeping places near the coals. They
would none of them, save the old man, look at her. *Perhaps*.
Marhan's words, Levren's. Golsat's. She turned them over in
her mind until it was time to wake Brelian. Nisana materialized from her place with Golsat and nudged her. 'Search. Not
here, away from camp.'

'All right.' She was tired, but not overly so. They moved
into the trees, sought out the pool.

'There is a thing,' Nisana began, oddly hesitant, 'I am
afraid you had better know now. Though by your Black Well,
I would rather not speak it.'

'It must be bad, then.' Ylia dropped to the smooth rock,
pulled her battered cloak around her knees.

'I have searched Aresada.'

'You have?' What was she leading up to? 'How?'

'Never mind. Ylia—Vess rules.'

"Vess," she whispered. *I knew he lived, I knew it!* Anger set
the blood coursing through her face. "He dares—"

'Of course he dares. He always has dared. But at Aresada, they
now believe all in the South are dead, for no word has come.
Even so, he would have chanced it. You know that.'

"He—" Ylia's voice cracked.

'We must plan. He will not readily step down.'

"Understated, cat. He will not step down at all. Damn him,
thrice damn him!"

'I agree. He is ambitious; you know that, Ylia. And proud.
And of House of Ettel and, odd parentage notwithstanding, a

noble of Nedao. With all that entails.'

"Noble." Ylia turned and spat. "I will *kill* him for this!"

'Of course you will. Because you will have to challenge him to regain what is yours.'

"I will—oh, no." She buried her face in her hands. "Then *everything* is lost, cat! He will never accept challenge from me!"

'He will not dare refuse. This is your people's custom, remember that! Remember too, the folk of Nedao. Vess will not dare ignore them. Do you think they prefer him to you?'

"I—" She shook her head. "No. But—"

'Then unless you cannot defeat him—you know your law.'

"Challenge by sword and to the death," she murmured. "Mothers, I welcome it! I could have defeated him the night before Koderra fell, before this journey started and my skills were honed by dire need. And knowing now what I know of him, what things he has done, I will kill him with pleasure!"

'Then,' Nisana urged, 'you will remain Nedao's Queen. After all we have faced, you and I, all of us, how could we not win out?'

"How indeed?" Ylia murmured. "You give me hope, cat. Unlike you."

'No. Truth.'

'Whatever it is, I will hold to it." She stood, gathered Nisana into her arms, moved quietly back to camp. Brelian was a darker shadow against the trees, moving slowly around the perimeter of the camp; he was the last thing she saw before sleep claimed her.

The girl had said it, a time since, to her Brendan—something about Nala's son. In light of later events, I should have known the thing was about him, exhaled on his breath, in his movements, his smile, all of him. But the thing itself was so farfetched, so unlikely, that even if I had known then, I would have thought only my own fancy and a thing completely removed from possibility.

*The Nedaoans say there is no need to sep-
arate truth and legend; given time, they will
separate themselves. As with all sayings, it
is not entirely true—but there is a grain of
truth to it.*

31

It was long after sunrise before they broke camp the next
morning, and Marhan held no hope for any distance at all by
day's end: sheer numbers slowed them, as did the Citadel folk
still weak from lack of food. And it looked to rain before
nightfall: the air was damp and noticeably cool.

They spent the night deep in the trees, sheltered from a light
misting rain and infrequent, but chilling, gusts of wind.

The cloud cover broke early the next morning and moved
north ahead of them to hang as a black, billowing mass,
hiding the distant peaks. So much they could see from infrequent clearings and meadows: the forest was as thick as it had
looked from Ylia's ledge. Now and again a chance ray of sun
found its way through the trees to warm cheeks or fingers.
More often, wind tossled hair, tugged at cloaks. More clouds
came from south and east, then, bringing a light rain with
them. The children alone seemed not to notice or care: they
were playing hiding games in the trees between the company
and the foreguard.

Levren spent most of the day with them, for he missed his
own large family sorely and he genuinely enjoyed the company
of children. They, in turn, accepted the Bowmaster as one of
them, hung on him and took great pride in any attention he
gave them.

Brelian and Lisabetha walked hand in hand. Some of his

270

terrible grief had left him since his dream, though his face was still somber with it. But Lisabetha had plaited flowers in her hair, and a sprig of columbine rode in Brelian's cloak. Not far ahead of them, Lus and the Chosen women were carrying on earnest discussion; Marhan and Grewl were chewing over some matter of their own. Golsat had gone ahead at first light to set a way and to prepare camp.

Peaceful. It was that. *A pity it will not last.* Ylia scowled at her hands, pressed her right sleeve to her elbow. A long, rough, white line there, faint but clear against her dark forearm. She would have that to the end of her days. At the moment, she did not expect them to be overlong. She glanced up, pulled the sleeve quickly into place before Malaeth could catch her and berate her once again. Though the scar on her face, near invisible as it was, caused the old nurse more grief.

'What will not last? And why?' She started as Nisana pushed her head free of the carry pouch. 'You look like an owl,' the cat went on accusingly. 'So solemn, and on such a day! I had bettter cheer you.' Sudden concern edged her thought.

'No.' Ylia knew what Nisana had just remembered. 'How would I dare grieve for Brendan, having seen what I have seen?' But she blinked rapidly as she turned to gaze out eastward. She missed him, that truly. And would for long. But: 'Vess weighs my spirits, cat; remove him if you can!'

'If I could,' Nisana began vigorously, 'I would bridge him to Osnera before we got nearer Aresada than we now stand, and leave him to wonder how he got there!'

'*Half*way to Osnera,' Ylia amended flatly. 'There is an ocean between us and them, remember?' Nisana snorted amusement.

'You already know you can best him. So?'

'I can. But—' her gaze went eastward again. She went on, slowly, setting out a thought long unspoken—slowly, because she was still puzzling it out. 'There is something about him—Vess.'

'I know. So you told Brendan; I heard you. Something—' Nisana prompted as she fell silent.

'Something. I don't know what. He is not AEldra. We would know if his father had been AEldra. He is not of the Power at all, and yet—' She paused again, embarrassed. 'Oh, well. Perhaps the tales are true: Nala lay with a servant of the

Lords of the Black Well, and so got Vess.'

'No,' Nisana replied firmly, dispelling her odd thoughts, making them sound even more foolish. 'At least, *I* have sensed no such thing about him. I think I would, though I never attempted to read him.' She considered a moment. 'However. I no longer truly dare ignore *your* hunches, do I?'

'Well—'

'No. I will keep the thought in mind for when we reach Aresada, Ylia. In the meantime, you have your father's skill with blades. And do not discount your arms-mates, your dagger-sworn, and the folk at Aresada, girl. Nedao loves you. Do not dare scorn your worth in the eyes of your own people!'

There was nothing she could say to that. The cat slipped back into her pouch again.

They had not gone far after noon-break when the clouds drew in closely and rain began to fall in sheets. But Golsat came back down the trail not long after to tell of a deep, dry cave he had found nearby. They crowded into the back of that, shared out a hot tea and watched heavy rain turn to enormous hailstones, then back to rain. For a wonder there was no lightning nearby, and the storm was as brief as it was fierce. The sun came out not long after, and within the hour they came to the end of the forest.

To the north, the ground sloped down, and down again. Stands of aspen and willow bunched here and there on the short, yellow-green turf. Huge, overgrown and shaggy berry brambles in full bloom beyond these, further down. A brook cut deeply into the turf not far away, wound through meadowflowers and downhill into the tussocky flats. A faint mist rose here and there, largely obscuring the Marshes and completely hiding any view of the mountains beyond.

"Wetlands," Golsat said tersely. "We had better camp here tonight."

"But it is early," Levren protested. "We could make—well, not a league, but—"

"You of the Plain," Golsat broke in good-naturedly, and rolled his eyes imploringly skyward. "As though you had never seen a marsh! As though you had never lived near water! Were you never within spitting distance of the marshes south of Koderra, Bowmaster? Mosquitos, man! And gnats and bugs and more mosquitos, great black clouds of them! And they are bad now, but after sunset—you wait!''

"*I* go no farther tonight.'' Malaeth let herself down to sit with back braced against a massive birch. She folded her arms. Ylia dropped down beside her.

"You speak for me, Malaeth. If these men wish to go on, we will see them at Aresada.'' Lisabetha cast a doubtful glance at Brelian, but moved silently from his side to join the other women.

Levren chuckled. "Gnats and mosquitos, by the Mothers! As if that were the worst enemy we have faced! But I see we have open rebellion already, and I suppose it would be ignoble to be eaten alive by mosquitos after all we have survived so far. We stay here.''

Marhan scowled, shrugged. "They do not bother me. But as you choose.''

Golsat closed the distance between them. "That is the very least of it, Swordmaster. Look you—'' he pointed out across the lowlands. "Early afternoon, and already the mist is thick. Folk lose their way in such fogs and are never heard from again. Treacherous footing, foul water. At least, one should be able to see such things to avoid them, and with luck we shall. In the morning.''

"Well then.'' Marhan let his cloak fall and stretched hard. "This will do as well as anywhere, I suppose.''

"It should,'' Golsat agreed. He cast a practiced eye at the clouds. "It will not rain again tonight. And I know the lands beyond the Marshes very well. We have most of a day's journey to cross them, less than that distance the day after. There is water, yonder,'' he added thoughtfully. "I think I will go and see what it holds.'' He took Marhan's kettle and set out.

Lisabetha looked up wearily. "Whatever it is, leave it there!'' she called after him, but if he heard, he made no sign. Brelian chuckled. His expression turned to one of mock dismay and fear as she leaped to her feet: He fleeing, she chasing and both giggling like children, they dodged across the meadow and finally vanished from sight. Malaeth gazed after them, a complacent smile on her old face.

Grewl had asked to be of use and sat tending the fire. It was still sunny, but the wind was northerly and chill; Malaeth pulled her small, woven carry-bag free and began sorting through her herbs and grasses. Golsat returned with water for her, but no fish.

Ylia leaned back against the tree, settled her shoulders with a happy little sigh and watched the fire. She had nearly dozed off when she became aware of someone standing nearby. She blinked. Lus' two eldest, Flen and his brother Mouse, shifted uneasily, uncertain whether or not to speak.

"Is there something?" she smiled at them. Mouse nodded solemnly, went to one knee and bowed his dark, tossled head.

"My Lady." He spoke with a child's careful formality. "My mother has told us not to bother you—but—" He tilted his head to one side, gazed at her candidly and with a kind of excited awe. "They say you have magic. That you know things by magic, things we do not."

"Well, perhaps a thing or so," Ylia admitted. She bit back a smile. "Is there any special thing?"

The boy glanced at his older brother, who nodded. "There is a lady in the woods," he said finally. "We saw her, Flen and Norria and Lis and Nold and I. I think—" he added hesitantly, "that she is magic, like the tales from our village. She is not like any of us."

Mothers. She carefully concealed the sudden unease the boy's words gave her. "Can you show me?" They nodded, slipped back into the trees. She pulled her cloak tighter, followed. Flen met his Lady's smile with a shy one of his own. "What was she like?"

"Well—we were playing hide, and she was—just there. *I* think," he added, "she came from the water, because she looked wet to me. And also, she was small. Smaller than Lis, even."

"But a lady," Mouse put in, "not a little child like Lis. And when she saw us staring at her, she was just gone. Like magic." He eyed Ylia sidelong, to see how she took the tale. "Lis saw her then, in another place, and was afraid, but Lis is still a baby, really. This lady would not hurt anyone, I could see that!"

Flen, not far ahead, had stopped and was looking all around. Finally he called out; his voice echoed through the silent trees: "Lis! Li-is! Norria! Nold!" No answer. He shrugged. "They think we are still playing, I guess. Hey!" he shouted. "We have the Lady Ylia with us; come now!"

Silence. A rustling in the brush then, and three children came out of cover. Ylia knelt to be on a level with them: they were one-and-all younger and smaller than the two boys.

Lis touched her face shyly. "Mouse said you would come."

"You saw a lady, did you?" Ylia asked. The child nodded gravely. "What kind of a lady?"

"Little." She indicated with her hands. Smaller than Lis, tiny indeed.

"Which of you saw her?" Ylia asked. They looked at each other.

"We all did," Nold—one of the orphaned—replied. "She was little and dark. She moved very swiftly."

"Is she still here?" Shrugs. More looks. "Well, where did you see her?"

Lis turned and pointed. "There! At the water!"

'Why?' Nisana was suddenly with them; a gentle after-sensation from her bridging touched Ylia, faded. The children gazed at the cat astonished. 'Who is by the water?'

'A lady, they tell me' Ylia replied. Nisana radiated sudden worry. 'No cause for alarm that I can tell. But I had better send the children back to Lus.' Aloud, she added, "you all know about Nisana, don't you? That she has magic, also?" Nods. "She tells me," she went on, "that somebody's mother is looking for him, Mouse." Mouse groaned. "And those with him. Nisana came to let me know. Something about food, and a wash first." The children all groaned in unison. Flen gazed up at her expectantly; she laughed.

"No! Do not look at me like that! I may be Lady of Nedao, but I would never nay-say a mother! Go on, back to the fire, all of you. Nisana and I will try to find your lady, and we will tell you what we find, I promise."

"Promise?" Mouse said hopefully.

Ylia nodded, held out her hands to him. "Promise. By grass and wind, sky above," she added, completing the ancient children's oath.

"By grass and wind, sky above," Mouse replied, clearly amazed that a grown woman should know this. Reluctantly, then, they ran back to the camp.

'Lus really was wondering where they had gone, you know. Now, what is all this?' Nisana demanded.

Ylia shrugged. 'I have no idea. They saw a strange lady, they say, who appeared and vanished at will. Who was wet, tinier than Lis. I do not think they made it up. But—'

'It does not sound evil; children sense that readily. I doubt Marrita could make herself attractive to children. Or smaller, come to that. No, they would fear *her*, however she clothed herself.'

'Presuming she could be here at all—'

'Unlike you,' Nisana remarked sourly, 'to underestimate an enemy. Use care! However, whatever this lady is, I would like to know, the moreso because we sleep here tonight.' She trotted toward the stream. Ylia let Brendan's dagger slip down into her hand.

A shallow, narrow animal track led through the brush to the water, and they followed it, then turned to walk the bank upstream. Several lengths on, they came to a deep pond formed by a fallen tree and the debris piled up behind it. They stood there, irresolute. Nisana caught at her companion's thought. 'Look. Look there!' She bounded across the pond.

On the far bank, less than a length away, were shallow prints in the wet ground. Ylia skirted the water, crouched beside them. Narrow and small, toes overlong for the length of the foot. And there were faint marks where the toes were spread on one or two of the prints: curved, connecting lines. Webs.

She sat back on her heels to keep watch as Nisana sniffed at them. The maker could be anywhere. The woods were silent with the fading of day, and gloomy; a bird flitted from one tall tree to another, the trees themselves rapidly becoming black shadows against the dark blue of the sky.

She touched the cat; Nisana started. 'We should go.'

'I know what this is.' Nisana was speaking more to herself than her companion. 'It must be; it is, by all that's holy.' Her whole furred body was practically alight. 'I return tonight, Ylia; we do. You and I. After the moon has risen. Because this is—because it is—'

'Is what?'

'Invitation,' she replied simply.

Ylia frowned. 'You are not making sense, cat. How are prints invitation?'

'If they were left by one who has, in truth, no form of its own. One who—''

'Great Mothers.' Ylia shivered suddenly. 'Dreyzs.'

'Dreyzs.' Nisana agreed. 'And do not tell me *they* are myth!'

'No, never. Not after all we have seen on this journey. But—'

'Remember the tales. They have no form, the Dreyzs. But there are forms they take to themselves, whether favorite or most comfortable, no human knows. The tales are not specific.'

'But—'

'And if a Dreyzs materialized, if it let itself be seen, if it left prints, then it did so for purpose. Invitation.'

'You have allies in these mountains. Allies who will be told of your coming. *He* said as much.' Bendesevorian's words.

'There—you see? This was foreordained, I know it. But I return tonight in any event.' She took in the growing darkness in sudden surprise. 'It is late; Marhan will be annoyed. And I am hungry.'

Ylia laughed. 'Annoyed, she says. Who—Marhan, of all men?'

Mouse hurled himself at her as they came from the trees. "Did you find her?" he whispered fiercely. Ylia shook her head; he looked so crestfallen that she knelt to speak against his ear.

"We found prints, and we know what she was you saw. Can you guess? No? A water-sprite."

Mouse's eyes went round. "Swear it?" he demanded in a thrilled whisper. Ylia nodded gravely. "It is our secret?" he added, no less fiercely. She nodded again. Mouse grinned widely and dashed back to his brother's side.

They are not like us, the Folk. Not like the AEldra, certainly unlike the Nedao—not even like the Nasath. They have their own matters important to them, their own needs and wants, and seldom do they bother with any not their own kind. Though they did so once, when they swore to the aid of the Guardians against the Lammior. And, once, many hundreds of years later, when they swore to the assistance of the young Queen of Nedao.

32

It was late, more than halfway to morning, when she woke Golsat after her watch. She spoke to him briefly, to let him know where they would go. Then she and Nisana—and Lisabetha, on whose presence Nisana had insisted—slipped away from the fire and into the woods, back toward the creek. Starlight caught an occasional ripple. A breeze whispered through the very tops of the trees, though all was still on the ground.

They pushed upstream. Halted. Silence. Nisana took a few paces to the right, back to the left, again stopped. Ylia remained where she was, as uncertain as Lisabetha how to aid the cat; uncertain, indeed, what she sought.

Light, a faint light, suddenly radiated from her. 'By the Nasath, whose servants we are, we would speak with ye who are their children.' The cat uttered the high AEldran words with an ease Ylia envied, almost singing them in her thought as she cast them to float on the breeze. Silence. 'No harm do we bring, we three.'

Ylia came to stand beside her, moved by a sudden impulse.

"By the grace of Bendesevorian of the Nasath we come," she said aloud, her own AEldran halting, "who are those fore-told." Another silence. Then: coming from everywhere and nowhere at once, a breath, a song: 'Come ye, an ye would speak.' Ylia roused Lisabetha with a light touch.

They followed the water a while, moved away from it as it bent eastward. For what seemed a long while, they walked through deep forest. A meadow then: Moon and stars shone onto grasses so short, so groomed as to seem a lawn. The heady scent of honeysuckle and clover filled the air. There was a hum of bees.

Ylia and Lisabetha halted within the trees: They did not belong here, and both knew it. None of humankind did. Nisana hesitated, but only a moment. The moon cast a warmth over her dark fur as she padded onto the clipped grass. The women glanced at each other uncertainly but followed.

The cat moved into the center of the meadow, stopped, leaped to Ylia's shoulder as the swordswoman came to her side. Lisabetha clung to the edge of Ylia's cloak. The air itself seemed to tingle. "Do not fear, 'Betha, I know this feeling. I have felt it before." And she had; the meadow radiated that same awareness she had known when she spoke with the Guardians. Lisabetha nodded, caught her hand.

A breath. No more than that, and they stood alone, and then not so. Moon glittered on dew, seemed to create forms of its own. They were all three beyond surprise when these forms gathered substance: the Dryads and Naiads of Nedaoan legend. Beautiful, tiny, humanlike forms wove in a dance around them, silent at first. None of them was certain when they first became aware of the music: a light, gentle, tinkling sound—reed pipes, perhaps, and bells. Perhaps, again, none of these; none of them could have said then, nor could they ever later.

They sank to their knees, the two humans, transfixed in the moonlight as a dance of moon and starlight, a joy of move-ment of which they knew they could only see a little, wove around them. Lisabetha rose then, Nisana leaped into her arms, and they vanished among the dancers.

At that same moment, one of the tiny, elfin beings detached itself from the rest.

Ylia bowed; the courtesy was returned. Dryad! She could see it now, at least with the straight sight. But inner vision revealed true form: a bar of light, perhaps four hands high, a pulsating, flickering, eye-searing blue-white. Viewed as one purely Nedaoan might: a narrow, dark brown face, surrounded by long mosslike hair of a darker brown. Eyes the green of new leaves.

"Ye would speak with us." Her voice was resonant, deep. Slender, brittle fingers touched human ones; no illusion, or if illusion, one beyond her ability to break, even if she had wished. "Ye are of the Blessed, those who had the Gifts from the Guardians. And ye are those forespoken to us."

"We are. I am half AEldran, Nisana is truly AEldran. The girl, Lisabetha, is purely of Nedao but she bears her own gifts."

"They are welcome among us, as are you. I am Eya, speaker for those present tonight. It was asked of us that we give aid to you, if there was need. Your need is great, and I fear our ability is lesser. But such as we can give, it is yours."

"And what aid you may need of us, ever, is yours," Ylia replied formally. "I, who am Lady to Nedao as well as AEldran, say it. But for us, for me and those with me, there is little need, for we near our goal."

"The Caves, where already are many of your kind." Eya stated. "Ye have been exiled by war, as we were, on a time." The veriest edge of a numbing sorrow cut the human's inner being: Eya's sorrow. In over a thousand years, they had not forgotten.

"I—knqw of ye, a little," Ylia said, hesitantly. "I have walked in places once yours. They yet breathe of you. And—I know why you no longer live there, of the enemy who was yours." Soft, gentle piping reached her ears in the ensuing silence. "But as to the needs of my people, the Caves are no dwelling place for such as we. We need a place where food can be grown, beasts herded."

"In that, perhaps, we can aid. A place might be found, one safe from the evils dwelling in the Foessa."

"I know of them." She did; knowledge, even here, made her suddenly sober. "Do they dwell so far north as this?"

"Not of recent." Eya's hair swayed gently around her face as she shook her head. "They have been in-gathered to the south for long. But they move ever."

"I know it. And they may no longer be held to an in-gathering."

"No. We were told this also." Another silence. "Ye are the one who battled with that which has made itself the Lammior's heir."

"I slew him. Or so," she qualified unhappily, "I think. But there is danger yet, you must keep guard." Such as these—how could they protect against an evil as great as the Lammior's or even Lyiadd's? And yet, they had withstood the Lammior himself. *Appearances*, she reminded herself sternly. *They deceive. Trust half of what you touch. Less of anything else.*

"We guard. Always. Our enemy was slain tens of times ago, but his armies remained. Even the Guardians could not remove them all. We protect against them. We no longer seek them out. But we know them." She reached; Ylia glanced down in surprise as long, twiglike fingers lay across the hilts of her sword. "Ye carry the weapons of hand. As did she."

Her skin contracted. "She?"

"The shipmen came to our aid at the last, when we would all have been unmade. The daughter of their Lord was Shelagn. She also carried the weapons of hand. Do ye know nothing of her?"

"A—a little—"

"Ye are like her. Much. The Guardians could tell you more of her tale; I know only what I saw of her." She tossed back her head then, and uttered a low, melodious call. A drinking horn was in her hands. "Drink." Ylia drank, gave it back. The Dryad drank in turn. "Then. So. After the fashion of your kind, we are allies."

"The Nasath grant there is no need for such an alliance. Save for friendship."

"May they so grant." Eya was on her feet so swiftly, so gracefully, the human could not follow the motion. "But the moon is fair and there is beauty here. We speak of things sorrowful, and that is not meet." She twirled lightly on one tiny foot, an encompassment of pure joy, and disappeared. A sense/scent/awareness of light passed across Ylia's eyes, was gone.

She was dazzled, unable to move, and it seemed she could suddenly see far more clearly than she had: Naiads and Dryads, Nedaoan legend come to life, weaving a dance together under the moon like a stream bubbling through stately trees. Among and between these, small, upright creatures bounced,

hooved and hairy below, human above, and it was they who
piped. The very grass under her hands seemed to move with
the delicate, heady sound.

Movement beyond the dancers: a larger, dark shape. Awk-
ward: a bear? Three of them. For a moment she was frightened. But they moved to join the dancers, and a squirrel
darted unafraid between their feet. A clutch of raccoons tumbled across the grass, followed by a merrily piping faun.

There was a drawing in that music—suddenly even she felt
it, who had never danced of her own will. It brought her to her
feet, awkwardly. Lisabetha stood not far away, in a puddle of
moonlight, hands extended toward a small, pearl-colored
creature that came barely to her waist. Horselike: a little, in
general shape. Delicate, thin legs, a tail that would have
touched the ground were it not carried so high. A wave crest of
a mane. The jewel between its great eyes radiated a pure, pale-
green light. Lisabetha bent slowly to kiss its nose; it pressed
close to her, was gone.

Gone! But a pressure against Ylia's side told her this was
not so, even as the pang of loss struck hard. She knelt again,
touched the downy cheek. Grave eyes met hers: the beauteous
creature touched her cheek lightly with a soft nose. A fragrance of clover and cool spring winds washed over her. She
cupped the silver-white chin, as Lisabetha had, kissed the grey
forehead just below the jewel. Sank back to the ground as the
Yderra vanished.

A sudden heaviness filled her lap. A raccoon lay between
her knees, all four feet up, its fat little belly exposed to the
night sky, joy and delight radiating wildly in all directions. She
laughed, tickled the soft underfur. It wriggled, stretched,
slowly, slid to the ground, still on its back. Ylia laughed again,
rubbed the hard little head as the small animal righted itself.
Two more bounded across the grass and she and they were
suddenly surrounded by dancers.

She closed her eyes perforce; they were dazzled and could
not handle what they saw. *Blessed ye who have danced the ancient dance with us.* Did she hear that or imagine it? The wild
creatures rubbed against her arm, skittered away.

"Blessed are ye, chosen by Those Who Guard to receive the
Gifts. Do ye need, send. We will answer." Eya, beyond doubt.

"Do ye need, send. We will aid," Ylia whispered in reply.
The music slowly faded. They were alone in the meadow: Ylia,

Lisabetha, Nisana. The westering moon cast long shadows behind them. Nisana jumped into Ylia's arms; Lisabetha held them both close.

Yderra—it is, our legends say, a four-footed wonder: the jewel-beast. The stone between its wide eyes is pale green, clear, and of an impossible depth, that a man gazing into it might be lost, did he not use care. A source of indescribable beauty—fear also, for the Yderra can use the stone to focus its Power and send death amongst its enemy. Goatlike, horselike, and yet like neither, and it is wise as the Nasath are wise. Creatures of myth? Nay —they fought beside our ancestors against the Lammior. And I have, myself, felt the touch of one. And though I live a longer span of years than any of the AEldra before me, I will never forget that night.

They say a man's worth seldom lies in his face, but instead in those skills brought out in time of need. They might have spoken those words for Golsat, for who would have thought when Brendan first swore reluctantly with him, when the Bowmaster broke into a cold sweat at mere sight of him, how very much the company would come to rely upon him—and, in the days thereafter, how much Nedao herself would come to owe him?

33

A chill wind blew across the Marshes, cancelling any warming effect of the clear sky and bright sun. Golsat had them all up at first light so they might cross the low ground before sundown, and camp far beyond.

"Mosquitos and gnats and midges?" Marhan inquired dryly. Golsat shook his head.

"Those as well. They are only inconvenience, however, Swordmaster. I have crossed wetlands before, though, and treacherous footing, sudden soakings, mists, and," he lowered his voice cautiously, "unpleasant creatures which only come out after dark. We could, probably will, face them all. But the women would not appreciate the mosquitos you so lightly ignore. And treacherous footing will likely prove the least of our worries." Marhan nodded, though he was clearly unconvinced.

The ground fell rapidly just beyond the forest, and for the first time in several days they could see many leagues. But the field of vision narrowed quickly as they moved down the slope.

They stood, finally, before the brook they had camped by the night before. Bright green grasses flowed over low, rounded hills. The ground squelched underfoot. Golsat jumped into the water. It flowed slowly, barely rippled as it rolled past his knees.

"It is not so cold," he remarked as he looked up. "Such of you as are able, jump over. Otherwise wade."

Levren tossed bow, arrow pouch, cloak and weapons-belt over, leaped down to join Golsat. "We can hand the children across, you and I, and such of the women as wish it." Mouse and Nold looked rebellious but offered Lev no argument. Malaeth and Pyel were also lifted across. Golsat waded to the opposite shore as Ylia jumped across, the last one.

"Well. Not bad. I warn you, though," Golsat added darkly, "this is probably all you dare look for all day! And this may be the best of it!" With that gloomy warning, he strode forward; the company followed.

Ylia and Nisana took in turns to search. But there was no trace of anything unusual: birds, animals, some of the stranger creatures that inhabit wetlands. No sign of those they had met under moonlight.

"I would almost think I had dreamed it." Lisabetha spoke from beside them, so softly even Brelian did not hear her. Ylia touched her arm.

"No. No dream." But the joy had not remained with her as it had with Lisabetha and Nisana; by daylight, Vess had returned and filled her thoughts with worry of what lay ahead.

Crossings. They lost count. Reedy water, bordered by thick mud. Lisabetha would have fallen except for Brelian's firm grip on her arm. Now and again they skirted high grass where Golsat said there was shifting mud under the water. But there were no real mishaps the entire morning, for a wonder, and they took a short, late noon-meal on the bank of another deep-cut brook. The ground, at least, was dry. Golsat would not allow them to drink from the stream, however, and those who had bottles shared. The sun was warm and they rested a short while before moving out again.

But the third hour from midday, fogs whispered across the ground, rose in purposeful tendrils from the water. The air was chill; the sun slipped briefly in and out of mists and finally retreated to shed a thin, shadowless light on suddenly greyed surroundings.

Golsat stopped abruptly. The company gathered anxiously around him. "This is what I feared most," he said, but his manner was still calm. "Though it is merely fog, in the Marshes that is enough." He caught Ylia's eye; she nodded. "Fog merely." Only one who knew him well could have told how much he relaxed at that. "But we must keep close, for here it is no joke. Ylia?"

"We will lead," she replied. "But we cannot see much further in this stuff than you can, and I do not know our direction. You had better stay with us, Golsat."

"I have a good sense of the direction," Golsat replied, and only she heard the muttered "I hope!" which followed. She clapped a hand across his back, not at all concerned that he might really lose that phenomenal ability he had to set a trail and hold to it. They set out at once.

For long, the fogs grew no thicker, though they rose above any body of water of any size at all and hung in thick curtains over the streams. As the sun moved west, however, the mist grew heavier, and at length they blundered through an ever-darkening, all-encompassing grey.

'Nisana?'

'Nothing. Do not worry it.'

'Nothing—you are certain?'

'Nothing that does not belong here,' Nisana amended dryly, 'save us.' Ylia smiled, ruffled her fur.

Amazingly enough, they came to the end of the Marshes before total dark set in. But the inexorable Golsat would not allow them to rest so near the foul-smelling Marshes and he pressed on, determined to bring them to a place of better shelter that he remembered. The Citadel folk were ready to drop; the men carried the youngest children and Lisabetha and Lus leaned on each other for support. Ylia wrapped an arm around Malaeth's shoulders. The rest staggered on as best they could; Golsat went ahead to set up his chosen campsite and had a pair of fires waiting for them, with plenty of room between for the less warmly clad to huddle. Also, he had set packets of jerked meat and dried fish to heat in the coals, and had made a tea as good as any of Malaeth's.

The children were nodding where they sat, the Chosen women dozed. Grewl lay on his back, cloak pulled tightly around his shoulders; even Marhan and Levren sat with closed eyes. Golsat alone looked as though he had pushed no harder this day than any other. For a long time, the only sounds were the crackling of the fires, wind hissing over rock, Grewl's occasional gentle snore. At length Marhan stirred.

"We reach Aresada tomorrow. I have seen this place before, years past. We sit within two leagues of the Caves, and all of it easy walking. There is a trail not far from here." He looked around the fire. Mouse and Nold blinked, nudged Flen awake. Sata leaned forward, smothered a yawn.

"Who we will find there—" Ylia stopped as expectant faces turned toward her. "We know some have gone there. Many must have headed straight to the Caves as sanctuary. But who, and how many, that we do not know."

"We will reach Aresada at noon-hour," Marhan put in. "High hopes are quickly dashed. But I need not tell any of you that."

"No." Brelian looked up. "To me, it is enough that we who are here still live." Ylia closed her eyes briefly. Levren laid a comforting hand on her shoulder. Brelian, his face pale and hollow in the firelight, leaned to whisper against Lisabetha's ear; she nodded. He pushed to his feet.

"Companions all." He spoke quietly, but with purpose. Grewl blinked, sat up. The undercurrent of low conversation among the Chosen women died as all eyes went to Brel. "I would say a thing tonight, while we are together still. Before we reach Aresada." He stared out into the darkness, brought his gaze—and his thought—back to the moment. "Only this last year I was taken into King Brandt's service. I am not a trained fighting man, such as these—" A wave of his hand encompassed Marhan, Levren, Golsat.

"I have both gained and lost on this journey. My companions from Koderra know what we faced, all of us. But even at the worst of it all, I had an example. One who lost as much as any of us; one no more skilled than I in true battle. She has borne herself ever with pride of House, with courage. With strength in the face of horrors, with assurance in time of need. Though she will not have it, I owe her blood-price, that she

saved my life in the face of an unclean death. Nedao has honor
with such a woman, and to me it is fit we who have journeyed
with her acknowledge her now. Hail Ylia, Lady of Nedao!''

And a ragged, heartfelt cry answered him: "Hail Ylia, Lady
of Nedao!'' Even Grewl joined it.

She was blinded by tears, spoke past a tight throat. "Thank
you—thank you all,'' she whispered. No more words would
come. Levren nudged Golsat.

"Look—for once she is as tongue-tied as you!'' Golsat
snorted loudly, but the resulting laughter broke the tension.
Marhan added more wood to the fires as conversation sprang
up, loud and excited. Suddenly it was there where they could
almost touch it: the end of the road. Less than a day.

But a short while later, Ylia left the fire alone. *Vess.* Damn
him. There was nothing she could do, nothing she could plan
until she actually faced him. And that she anticipated with
grim pleasure. But she could not let the matter lie and inaction
was chewing at her as it always did.

And there was another thing, a thing unexpected. She had
known for years she would rule after Brandt; her parents had
trained her, this was the task for which she had been prepared,
if none of them had foreseen the circumstances of it.

But now that she must fight for her right—*if I misjudge
Vess, somehow, if he is a capable leader, if I challenge him
now, it might destroy the little peace those at Aresada have
been able to procure. What if—*?

"Ylia?'' A tiny whisper broke into black thoughts. She
turned. Lisabetha stood there. "If I disturbed you—'' the girl
began hesitantly. Ylia shook her head, held out a hand.

"No. At least, yes, but I am glad. You push unprofitable
thoughts from my mind, that is all. Another moment and I
might have been weeping with self-pity.''

Lisabetha shook her head. "You mock me.'' But there was
an answering smile in her eyes. "You who have so much courage and strength, the training, the AEldra power—how could
you ever feel sorry for yourself?''

"Because I am as unsure, as uncertain, in my own way as
you are in yours. They say everyone is. Perhaps that is so. I
have merely found the place in my inner being that calls down
doubt of—well, all that is me.''

"Perhaps.'' Lisabetha shook her head. "I certainly have
such a place.'' She paused. "Brelian has asked my hand,'' she

went on finally. "And I do not know how to answer him."

"And you would ask me?" Ylia smiled. "I am flattered. But that, at least, is easy: say him aye, with the blessings of us all."

"I—I cannot. What I told you of Vess—"

She caught at the girl's shoulders. "Lisabetha, by the Mothers, you do not *still* hold that against yourself? Do you think Brelian would?"

"No—neither—Vess was like a snake, holding me prey—not even that," she said flatly. "No. In honesty, I was a fool child, easy game for such a man. Brelian does not hold it against me, for I told him when it became clear he would ask my hand, eventually. It is not that." Silence. "I—dreamed," she blurted finally. "He reached Teshmor somehow, not many hours before it fell, re-pledged himself to Father's aid. I have known it for some days now. I could not tell you, could not tell anyone. I *knew* it." She turned away to stare across the broad, rock-strewn valley. A bleak, watery moonlight touched the landscape, made it alien. "He lay among the bodies outside the City, near the walls. When there was a chance, late at night, he crawled away. He is at Aresada."

"I know. Nisana told me."

Lisabetha turned back, surprised.

'So I did.' Nisana had come silently up behind them. 'One would think you prepared for a funeral,' she added accusingly.

'This is Lisabetha, cat. You know her, she *dreams*.'

'I know you have the gift, child,' Nisana's thought was unusually gentle, and slow—what little Lisabetha had of the mind-speech was fading rapidly, had regained some of its strength from contact with Eya's people but was again on the wane. It would likely not reach Aresada with her. 'But since you know what chances, you can aid us in planning for tomorrow. The three of us—'

"No." Lisabetha shook her head miserably. "I cannot—I cannot go to Aresada. I cannot face him—he—" Ylia caught at her arms, pulled her around.

"And where will that leave your heartsworn?" she demanded harshly. "Will you cost him all, who still grieves for—for Brendan? Where will that leave *me*, who needs all those about me to aid?" Lisabetha's eyes dropped. "Believe me, girl," Ylia went on, "where we are, Vess will not be for

long! Or did you think I would willingly endure his presence?
He has taken the ruling because he did not know I was alive.
By right, he must step down tomorrow and give it to me."

"But he never will!" Lisabetha burst out. "And knowing
Vess as I do—"

"As we both do," Ylia assured her dryly. "But you also
know the laws. I challenge him, he must fight for what he
chooses to call his. And," she added flatly, "I can beat him."
Of that she still had no doubts. "You need only stay out of his
sight, 'Betha. Until he is beyond seeing."

"Until he is dead," she whispered. "But he will not fight
you," she added unhappily. "He fears you; you are witch to
him. He claims to believe AEldra magic evil, but he truly fears
it. He will never fight you."

'Will and must,' Nisana assured her. 'The folk are for Ylia.
Do you doubt that? Well then! And Vess would not dare deny
challenge! His own men would throw him from Aresada!
Also, Vess is proud of his weapons-skill. He will never believe
anyone could best him, not even Ylia.'

"Particularly not Ylia," Ylia put in sourly, "if the men he
has sent to kill me in the past are any indication."

Lisabetha still looked unhappy. "If there is a hole in your
logic, Vess will find it." But she no longer seemed as raggedly
frightened as she had. "I—had better return to Brelian, I told
him I would not be over-long." She fetched up a half-smile.

Ylia smiled back. "Tell him what I said. Give him my blessing as well." The smile slipped, was gone as Lisabetha turned
away. She and Nisana watched as the girl ran back to the fire.
"There. You see, cat? I am not the only one who—"

'Now, I swear,' Nisana warned, 'if I hear one more word of
doubt from you, I will send you sleep right here, where you
stand! I weary of this!'

Ylia laughed. "I—all right. I concede. No more of Vess tonight!"

"As if you could solve the matter here, before you ever see
him,' she began indignantly. Ylia caught her up, hugged her
tight.

"Now *you* will start and we will have no peace at all! It is
late. I should sleep before my share of the watches. And my
hands are cold."

The fires had burned low. All but Marhan and Levren slept.
Nisana sought out a place close to Malaeth and stretched out.

Ylia stood close to the larger firepit, warming fingers and toes. Her father's Swordmaster and Bowmaster conversed quietly behind her, talking of old friends in the Tower Guard, others in Teshmor—the early years of Brandt's reign when both were younger and the world a simpler place. It was soothing; she stood, listened. At length, Levren rolled in his cloak and left the first watch to Marhan.

The old man was cleaning his nails with his dagger when she moved to his side.

"Well. We did it, didn't we? Whatever chances after. Just as we vowed it."

"So we did. And with but two losses, all told." The firelight seamed his face. "D'ye know, boy, there was no way to tell you how proud I was of you so often on this journey. Taking the training I gave you, using it as well as any other I ever taught. But I was, you know."

She shrugged, smiled. "I—I know that, old man. It is how we are, you and I. Your praise would have embarrassed both of us; mine would do as much. It is—well, it is just the way we are."

"So it is, boy," he replied gruffly, but he held out his arms, and she leaned against his chest. His mail was cold against her cheek. After a long, comfortable while, she sat up again.

"Be yet Swordmaster to the House of Ettel," she said.

Marhan scowled at her. "Did ye think I would quit now, after so long at it?" he demanded. She kissed his bearded cheek, went to find a place to sleep.

Perhaps, if I live long enough, I will learn to think beyond a narrow path that is AEldra: particularly if I continue to live with the Nedao, who resolve their disagreements with weapons of steel and not the Power. I had planned, myself, how the situation might be salvaged, and in the end, nothing I thought of was the least use.

34

It was just before midday when they came to the deep gorge through which the River Aresada flows and crossed the rough-hewn bridge that arches over it. They had walked in silence for most of the morning; even the children were subdued.

Thus the first words they heard in hours were those of the sentry atop the cliffs as they reached the other end of the bridge: "Halt! Name yourselves and where ye would go!"

Ylia leaned back, shielded her eyes so she could see him against the glare. Northern by his speech, that was easy. But he wore the dark-blue and white of the Duke of Anasela's livery. Her heart rose. *Erken, alive and here*? That would be a great ally indeed! "We are survivors of the wreck of Koderra, who have journeyed long days through the Foessa to come here. My companions are of the Plain and of the Tower, as you see! With me are Marhan and Levren, of the King's own household. Brelian and Golsat of the King's Tower Guard. Many of the Chosen have come with us. Lisabetha, daughter to Lord Corlin is also of our company, as is Malaeth, chief serving dame to the Queen!"

"And you—name yourself!" The guard shouted back.

"Ylia I, daughter to Brandt!"

292

"The Lady Princess! The Lady Ylia comes to Aresada!"
Even at that distance the guard's joy and surprise were clear.
He turned and cried in an echoing voice: "The Lady Ylia! She
lives and is come to Aresada!" He spoke more, but could no
longer be heard above the sudden outcry, and the cliffs were
lined with people; more sped down the narrow road which led
uphill from the River to the Caves.

They were surrounded; more folk came, and still more,
laughing and crying, shouting Ylia's name and Brandt's, crying Marhan's and then Lev's as they were recognized—
Lisabetha's, that of Grewl.

The clamor died away, finally, and they began the steep ascent, slowly, with questions thrown at them from all sides.
When they reached the flat upper ledges, Ylia pushed free and
leaped to the guard's station, so that she stood well above the
crowd, and held up her hands for silence.

"People of Nedao!" she cried out. Another prolonged wait
while the cheering died away. "The thanks and the love of all
of us for your welcome! Would I had better news for you!
Koderra fell to the Tehlatt, and with the City we lost a greater
part of the men of the South, including our King." Silence.
She swallowed, hard. "The Lady Scythia is no more, also, she
died avenging her Lord." A low moan swept the crowd. "But
many of the City, many of the folk of the South escaped by
sea to Yls; they have found safety there." She paused for
breath. "So it is, my people. But we shall build again, as we
did five hundreds of years ago. And Nedao will again be great
among the lands!" A joyous outcry echoed across the rocks as
she leaped down.

A chant began somewhere deep in the crowd as she moved
forward, the sheer ledges before the Caves echoed with it: her
name, her father's. Nedao. Over and again, building in volume, in intensity.

The guard at the entrance to the main cavern wore Vess'
colors. He stepped across the entry, blocking what he could of
it with his spear. Whether he would actually have denied her
entry, she never knew; he never had the opportunity. Folk
swirled about them, jostling. Her companions were lost in the
press. The guard was swept aside.

It was cool, suddenly; pleasantly cool, half-dark. Torches
flickered against the walls. Bags and parcels, dim shapes, lay

scattered about or pressed into man-cut niches. On, on through a narrow passage, squeezed in as they pressed forward. And then they were out, spilling into an immense chamber: the Grand Temple, large enough to hold over a thousand people. Large enough, nearly, to hold Brandt's great receiving hall. A ceiling, hung with stone icicles, vaulted high and out of sight. Pillars of stone rose from the smooth floor.

She was no longer hemmed in; the folk had stopped, moved aside once within, and she walked forward alone. Footfalls echoed strangely; her shadow, wavering with the air that took the torchlight, ran before her. But there was no hesitation in her step, for she sensed him long before she saw him: Vess. He sat amid stone splendor, a hanging at his back—the egret, snow white, on a background azul within a border: indentee, or. The band, gules, about the near leg tokened bastardy. *He ever wore that with pride.* Two guards flanked him.

And then Levren was at her side, Nisana leaped to her shoulder. Brelian moved swiftly to her other side. Footsteps behind: Marhan, Golsat brought up the rear. A great, sudden calm washed through her: Matters had been taken from her hands and moved of their own.

She walked forward until a drawn blade barred her path. Vess glared at her sullenly. A long scar, nearly the match of her own save not so cleanly healed, ran the length of his face; his broidered tabard was stained and in need of mending. His face was thin, and but for the feverish eyes, deadly tired.

"Cousin." A muscle in his cheek jumped as she spoke. "A pleasure to see you again, and well." A lie, however pleasantly spoken, and they were not the only ones who knew it. An elaborate distaste pulled at his mobile, overly wide lips.

"Hah. And you. Dear cousin." He raised his voice. "Though Koderra fell and most died, yet *you* are here—and these with you." His eyes touched on her companions, one by one. Lighted momentarily as they found Lisabetha, well to the rear and behind Marhan. "Well must you have fought, all of you, to win free at the last."

It hints at cowardice, yet it dares not speak it aloud. For fear of me, or of Marhan? "You fought well yourself, Vess, clearly, to have escaped Father's walls only to reach Teshmor, and have *it* torn from beneath you."

He cleared his throat, distaste once again twisting his

mouth. "And you have brought more mouths to feed. What, another twenty? More?"

"Many of whom can find food for others as well," Ylia retorted. Vess laughed spitefully.

"It will not do, Aresada can support no more folk, we are dangerously low on rations. Try Nar, all of you!" He sat back with finality. An unhappy murmur reached Ylia's ears. No, the people were not pleased.

"And who are you," she demanded, "to say who will stay, and who not?"

He smiled. "You ask that, Ylia of the Outer Circle?"

"I ask it." *Play out his game, then press your own.*

"I rule here. As the surviving male of the House of Ettel, I rule."

"No. I yet live, and Nedao is no barbarous land, that only men rule," Ylia cut in flatly. "While I live, who am First of my father's House, and his named and sworn heir—"

"But *I* rule!" Vess overrode her, his voice high and furious. "As an established fact. And so I have for the past month. Wrest that from me if you dare. *Cousin!*" His light-brown eyes left hers as Marhan strode forward, a towering rage darkening his face.

"Are you fool enough to think Nedao will stand by while you send Brandt's daughter hence?" Contempt spilled from his lips, his words echoed across the cavern. Something in the pale man before them came apart. He laughed shrilly.

"Nedao!" he shouted. "Nedao is no more! That—" a hand stabbed eastward, "that *was* Nedao! If this witch is a true daughter of my uncle and therefore Nedao's Queen, let her return to the Plain, there to rule!" Silence, a terrible silence. Vess snapped to his feet. When he spoke, his voice was under a dreadful, taut control. "There is no room here, nothing to eat, Swordmaster. Shall all of us starve together?" Cold, dark eyes bored into furious pale ones; Vess was no match for Marhan, and his were first to drop. Ylia laid a hand on the old man's forearm then, shook her head. "My battle," she mouthed at him. He shook his own head dubiously, but stepped back. A single pace, no more.

"You rule here as intermediary, Vess." For a wonder, her voice remained level. "We do not leave, any of us. You cannot force us. And with us are women and children, folk who would never survive the long journey to Nar. The people here already would not permit, however you say. And, there are Chosen among us," she added deliberately as he still made no comment. She raised her voice. "You are said to believe in Chosen ways, Vess. Do you condemn those among us to certain death?"

He scowled at his hands. "Chosen. Such of you," he called out, "as are Chosen may remain. Do you wish it. The rest—no. I rule here, and watch you, Ylia," he added softly, "what you say to me. A certain respect is due a lawful ruler."

She let her head fall back and laughed loudly, effectively silencing him. "Vess, you were ever amusing and most often when least intended! Respect, for such as *you*? No. Since you do not step down, as you are honor-bound to do," she was still smiling, but her eyes had gone cold, "why, then, I must give you challenge."

It was his turn to laugh. "Challenge? *You*? Against *me*?"

"I give you challenge, as one member of the House of Ettel to another, setting upon the outcome the rule of Nedao. Or, as *you* seem to prefer, the ruling of these folk." Her voice echoed across the stone chamber. A ripple of loud, excited speech, suddenly hushed. "By sword and dagger I challenge you, Vess, that only one live and the outcome be without doubt!"

He stared at her astonished, pulled himself together with a visible effort. "No. I will not fight against you. You are a daughter of the White Witch of Yls, a sorceress. I fight none of your kind." He raised his own voice. "I am not bound to fight a witch! She could charm my own sword into my heart, if she chose! Ye know her kind, all of ye. She is witch; evil! Will ye have one of that cursed race to rule ye?" Silence. People looked at one another, no one spoke.

Nisana? She was gone, but even as Ylia missed her, she returned. Lisabetha; she had gone to Lisabetha with her thought, and Lisabetha, in turn, pale to the lips, had brought Grewl. "Father Grewl, many of those here who are Northern know your name and know you to be wise in our histories and ways! Your aid to us!"

The old man pondered a moment, then paced on slow feet to Ylia's side. "This woman is child to King Brandt, and she is his named heir. Also, I owe her my life, though she will not have it so. She is not an evil woman, whatever her skills and talents. And, how should any man choose better the King's successor than the King himself?''

Vess gazed at him with ill-concealed fury, and more than a
little surprise. "Have ye lost your senses, old man!" he hissed.
"She is a wielder of the witching your kind prate against!
Would you give these folk up to evil? You have gone soft with
age, and she has besotted ye! No," he fumed, "I rule here.
There is nothing else to say.'' He spun away, trembling with
anger, but when he turned back moments later, his face was
once again under control. "I decline this challenge," he said
formally, his voice pitched to fill the chamber. "I am not held
to fight one I dare not trust.'' And he turned his back with
finality.

'Nisana, now what? It is as Lisabetha said, and as I feared,
and now what do we do?'

'There is a way,' Nisana replied. 'And we will find it. The
folk love you, hold to that. And trust!' Lisabetha laid a hand
on Grewl's sleeve. At the moment she was fully Corlin's
daughter. "Father, is there no recourse?"

Grewl thought again, a long, tense silence. "He says sooth.
No one can be held to battle where there may be treachery of
any kind, or where the parties are poorly matched."

"But, then—"

"A moment." Grewl held up a hand for silence. "When the
Lady Leffna came to the Plain, she and the folk of the Island
Nedao, they came early against the Tehlatta and their enemy,
the Llhaza." Ylia turned to stare at him. What had this to do
with Vess? "A duel was set between the chief of the Llhaza
and the chief of Nedao, setting against the outcome the own-
ership of that part of the Plain that was Koderra and south to
the sea. But that chief would not fight a woman, lest he bring
shame to his clan by the very act. The Queen named her
brother champion, as proxy to battle in her stead."

Marhan caught at her arms, spun her around to face the
anxious, waiting folk before she realized the import of the old
man's words, and he cried out, "What says Nedao? Shall a
champion be found?" A great roar of answer came back:
"AYE!!" And Brelian knelt at her feet, blade borne up in his
hands. "Name me, my Lady!"

She reached to take the sword, kissed the hilts and gave it
back to him. "I do so name you, Brelian, son of Broln, hence-
forth champion to me and my House!" Her voice gathered
strength as she spoke, cut through the babble and subdued it.

She turned back to Vess, who looked as dazed as she felt by the swift events. "Accept my thanks, for having aided my people in their need. But your role here has ended, and as one of the Third Circle you are less fitted to lead those gathered here. Since you do not willingly relinquish what you have usurped, for that cause do I give you challenge." She paused. "Since you fear to do battle with me, you shall fight my champion." She closed the distance between them, dropped her voice so that none but Vess could hear her next words. "Yours to choose, cousin. Will the folk of Nedao tolerate a proven coward as King? However great his guard?"

Vess glared at her, but he knew the truth of it: Refuse to fight her, and he might deal for some time with a disgruntled people. But refuse to fight Brelian, and his own men would drive him from Aresada or slay him. She could almost see the thoughts slipping through his mind as he reached the one choice left him.

"I do accept challenge," he said finally. His voice was harsh; he cleared his throat. "And I shall fight this man of yours, letting the throne of Nedao-that-was rest upon the outcome. By all the forms I shall abide, asking that your man abide by them also."

"I shall," Brelian said quietly. Vess glared at him, but he was rallying rapidly. With reason: he had been accounted one of Nedao's greatest swordsmen. Brelian, by contrast, was painfully young—too young, Vess' appraising eye judged, to be much threat.

"I further ask," Vess continued, "that the Chosen watch over the battle, that the rules be preserved and that there be no interference of *any* kind. That the outcome be without doubt." 'He means us!' Nisana's thought was dryly amused.

Brelian inclined his head. "That is just and fair. I agree." He turned away; Marhan and Golsat bore him off, Levren close behind. But when Ylia would have followed, Vess caught at her shoulder.

"I see you have brought back my sweet Lisabetha," he smiled. It was not a pleasant smile. "I did not really think she would aid me as I wanted. But then, it was worth the chance. It would have been nice, if she had."

"For you, perhaps."

"Perhaps." The smile widened. "She may stay after I kill the boy and exile you."

"Likely she would rather starve with the rest of us," Ylia replied flatly.

"Oh, I doubt that. She was ever pliant, my pretty Lisabetha. A sweet child, though not overly bright. But then, that was never required of women." His gaze lingered on her. "It is a pity. You have beauty, and such a form as to set a man singing. Sweet Lady. A pity you were never interested in what I could have offered you. But, perhaps we can settle this matter more amiably. Come, what say you?"

Ylia looked at him with open loathing. "I would kill you now, this instant."

He laughed quietly. "You think so, don't you? Except that even if you would kill, even if your skill permitted, you dare not kill *me*, lest stupid temper ruin your standing with these folk. Is it so important to you? Brandt's crown?"

"As important as it is to you, for better reasons."

"Is it? I doubt that. But, come. We could share it, you and I." He laughed lazily. A long, smooth hand reached for her fingers.

"If you touch me, I will not be responsible for what I do. Know that!"

He shook his head. "You have that much in common with other women, at least. You all speak so fiercely, and do not mean half the things you say."

"Oh?" And as he took another step; she struck him, hard, with the flat of her hand. The smile was wiped from his eyes in an instant. He dabbed at a cut lip with the back of his hand. Over it, his eyes were tight and ugly.

"You will regret that."

"I warned you."

"You need not count on starving anywhere," Vess whispered. "You know the fate of traitors. Those who seek to overthrow an established rule. I will take great pleasure in your death, cousin."

She smiled, knowing it would anger him most. "Count yourself fortunate I do not call that fate down upon you, Vess. I leave you to my champion's sword." She turned and strode after Brelian and Marhan. Her palm tingled; a bad taste filled her mouth.

*And so I fulfilled my own vow to Scythia,
that I would save her beloved daughter's life
and return her safely to her folk. That she
knew I had done so, that the girl's father
knew as well, I never doubted.*

35

Torches had been brought in; the walls of the chamber were
now visible through a slight smoke haze. But there was a good
draft somewhere high above; the air was stuffy but breath-
able.

Ylia turned back, but Vess had vanished along with his dagger-sworn. She gazed around the chamber, searching for familiar faces—there. Brelian stood in the midst of a crowd, not
far away. Golsat was helping him from his mail, Marhan and
Levren were speaking earnestly, though it could not have been
possible for him to take in their advice since all three spoke at
once.

Lisabetha—there. Malaeth and Nisana were with her, three
lengths from Brelian and his well-wishers. The girl's eyes were
enormous and dark against a pale face; Malaeth whispered
against her ear and she nodded, but the strained look did not
leave her. She would not even glance in Brel's direction.

Ylia pressed through the crowd to his side. The folk parted
as she moved forward, hands touched her arm, her shoulder,
the edge of her tattered cloak. She reached the inner circle at
last, slipped under Levren's arm.

Marhan glanced up, scowled, went back to his nearsighted
appraisal of Brelian's sword. Golsat was rubbing the dagger
against his polishing stone.

"Brelian—" Ylia began. He gripped her arm.

"They have told me already what they know of his style of

fighting, and I myself have seen him." There was a grim intensity to his words, but his spirits were high and this clearly was no simple matter of revenge for Lisabetha. "I need from you," he added with a smile, "only your wishes for luck."

She leaned forward, kissed his cheek. "Yours, Brel. That was bravely done, champion. The Mothers guide your blades!" The light in his dark face told her she had said the right thing. She pressed back through the crowd to Malaeth.

The old nurse's lips were thinned with disapproval. "Now what happens?" she whispered loudly. "That Vess—your father should have shipped him off years ago, I say! Or thrown him in a sack and then into the River!"

"I agree," Ylia replied grimly. She looked at the palm of her hand—it was still mottled red from the force of the blow —rubbed it against her breeches. *Ugh.* Vess hove briefly into view; Ylia moved swiftly, thrust Lisabetha behind her. "But then, who can say what would have happened if Father had exiled him when he had the chance? Unprofitable to read the past, you know that." Malaeth scowled at her, mumbled under her breath, finally subsided.

Save to one who knew her well, Lisabetha appeared cool, even calm. But her fingers were shredding the edge of her cloak. And when Ylia touched her arm, she jumped.

"Lisabetha, trust me. This will fall out well."

"I should not have told him—I should not have had the old Father speak for us—"

"No. He fights for you also, 'Betha. But who else should have championed my cause? Only Brendan. And he is dead." Her eyes met Ylia's then, concern and worry pulling her from more immediate fears. "No, it is all right. *I* am all right, Lisabetha. But there was no one else, only Brel. And did you see," she added, "how swiftly he came to my aid, and how the people loved him for it?"

"But—Vess. I have seen him fight," Lisabetha whispered.

"So have I. And with a more critical eye. I could defeat him, I know that much, and Brelian can also. Easily. Brel is stronger than I am. His blade has a longer reach and is more suited to a fight such as this. It will fall out well. And for your own aid." She smiled at the girl. "I had not the wit to think of the old man, my thanks for that."

"Lady Ylia." A heavy hand dropped to her shoulder; she turned. A deep, familiar voice, cultured and urbane, like the man behind it. He bowed deeply, sweeping a battered hat with a dreadfully torn and fouled yellow plume from his head.

"Erken!" She caught at his shoulders. "My Lord Duke, I am so glad to see you here!"

Erken, Duke of Anasela, now twice an exile, smiled conservatively, but his eyes were warm. "I only just now returned, from a pointless hunt, to find the Caves stirred up. Pleasant to discover *you* as the focus of the fuss. I thought to offer my services and those of my dagger-sworn, if you wish them."

"If I—Erken—"

"I take it you do. Good. We swore to Vess, but of need only."

She laughed. "You need not assure *me*, Erken. I know where your loyalties lie, my Lord, and I appreciate them. More than I can say."

"Good. I have had my fill of words. And little else, these past days. However." He took in the situation with keen eyes. "Where is your lad? There? Mmmm—of course, I know him. Old Broln's eldest—Bren—Brendan, that was it."

"No." Pain ran light-foot across her inner being. "His younger brother. Brelian."

"Ah, yes. He's a good one. Lots of promise in the boy. I think," Erken added blandly, "that we will station ourselves where we can be of use if there is—difficulty, shall we say?"

"Let us not," Ylia replied, matching his tone, "lest the speaking of it cause it. But yes, do so, my Lord. And we will speak as soon as we can, you and I." Erken bowed formally, turned to kiss Lisabetha's brow. Three long strides and he had moved back into the crowd. His rich blue cloak, as tattered and filthy as his poor hat, swirled behind him.

Movement caught her eye: Grewl stood in the arena, gestured. "Malaeth, keep an eye to this child for us." Ylia waved a hand at Lisabetha, a wink and a warm smile taking any possible sting from the words. "Nisana and I must join Grewl yonder, so poor Vess has his guarantee!" Nisana leaped to her shoulder, slid down into her arms as they crossed the chamber.

Preparations were nearly complete: torches marked out an area thirty paces wide, sixty long. Within that area all obstructions had been removed, to the smallest stones. Shadow still reigned beyond the boundaries; strange shapes bent against the far walls as torches flared. People surrounded the fighting ground, three deep.

In a sudden, deep hush, Brelian stepped into the open. Dark hair gleamed in the reddish light; the sword in his right hand, the dagger in his left, shone ruddy.

From the opposite boundary came Vess, sword and dagger bunched loosely in his left hand. He had stripped to boots, breeches and shirt, but against his light-brown hair and dark skin a thin ring of gold caught the light.

Nisana stiffened as Grewl drew near with two Chosen, both younger than he by some years. 'Have a care!' the cat's startled—and half-fearful—thought reached her. The mind-touch snapped. Ylia, after one look at the two, made no attempt to renew it. There was a coldness about the priests, an uncomfortable sense that they could see through to her inner being with chill blue eyes. She was relieved when they chose to stand none too near.

Grewl stood in the midst of the floor, hands above his head. Even the whispering ceased. "Each agrees to hold to the ancient laws?" Nods from both. Grewl moved first to Vess, then to Brelian, gravely inspected the weapons they held out to him. He turned away, then, and stepped back into the crowd.

Brelian took a step forward, brought his arms slowly up, out to the side. Vess matched the gesture. There: a triple crossing of the blades, high, low, before—mere taps. Two steps back. The hand that held the dagger then moved to the small of the back; neither man would use the short blade again, save to administer a death-blow. Vess leaped forward in a series of cat-footed lunges, and battle was joined.

Back and forth they fought for some time. But they were both strong, both skilled, and neither was able to gain immediate advantage.

A clanging, scraping noise: Vess' sword slid down Brelian's and they closed, arms and faces strained. Brel leaped backward, nearly overbalanced his opponent. A rapid, long-drawn clashing of blades. They moved out of Ylia's line of sight. She could see only long shadows battling against the far wall. As suddenly, they were nearly within reach, circling warily. Vess lunged, stopped short as Brelian moved to parry, spun neatly on his heel, and with one deft movement of the tip of his sword, was again out of reach.

Brelian grimaced and the crowd moaned. "First blood!" Vess shouted. Blood ran down the younger man's dagger arm, the least threads of it. Still— Ylia glanced across the chamber; Lisabetha stood still, Malaeth's arms about her shoulders. Her eyes were tightly shut.

"So? What matters first blood, it is last that counts—or so I hear! *Lord* Vess." Brelian was cooly mocking, and if he hurt, it didn't show. "Come. You have not slain me with your lucky touch. Try again!" Vess only laughed; he felt himself in control and his face showed it as he moved forward, sword weaving a blur around his opponent's. But Brelian was ready for his tricks, and Vess made no further touch.

Back and forth across the lit arena: Vess pressed forward, Brelian gave ground. He moved suddenly, then, and his sword described that dazzling, high-wristed maneuver that had been his brother's trademark: Vess' sword spun from his hand and hit the stone floor with an echoing clang. He paled, but Brelian stood back, gestured broadly for the other to regain his weapon.

Vess backed, one slow step at a time, his eyes burning with hate. He would not have been so kind, had their places been reversed. And it was galling to be so easily disarmed, *and* by a puppy of a swordsman. He caught at the hilts, leaped forward with murderous intent. Brelian sidestepped easily, turned, and the fight resumed.

Worried whispers. The two were circling again. Both were slowing; Brelian's arm still bled, but Vess was breathing heavily and the light-footed dance was gone. Gone, too, the blazing hatred. Something more like fear enveloped him now. He feinted—once; twice. Sought to draw Brelian into an unwary attack. Brelian shook his head, smiled; stalked slowly, easily, to the right.

Vess broke first, after all, moving in an old man's parody of his cat's leap. Brelian dropped, sidestepped, lunged sharply. His sword reached past Vess' guard, drove deeply into his side. Vess staggered, blinked stupidly. His sword dropped to the stone floor, for a second and final time, and he fell.

No one moved; the only sound was the wounded man's heavy, whistling breath. But Brelian still stood with sword at the ready, making no attempt to bring forth his dagger. "My Lady!" he said loudly.

Ylia jumped. "My champion." At a nod from Grewl, the two Chosen backed away, and she ran across the open space. Vess glared at her as she approached. Blood pulsed between his fingers, pooled on the smooth stone.

"Give me your bidding concerning this man who is kin to you," Brelian said finally. "The fight was to the death; still, I will slay him only by your word."

Marhan forestalled her. "No."

She stared at the old Swordmaster, amazed. "You jest, Swordmaster! Let Brelian slay him and have done!"

Marhan shook his head. Levren stood beside him. "You cannot begin your ruling sullied with his blood and that of his following," the Bowmaster urged. "Will you slay them all as well? Exile them! They will not return."

"No?" She sighed. Shrugged. "All right. Both of you. But no good will come of this. Either way. But—all right."

"You cannot say so for certain," Levren argued. "I know no good comes of any death, ever. Too much of Nedao's blood has been spilled. Remember when you said that? Will you add to it?"

"Slay me and have done!" Vess rasped. His eyes locked on Brelian's. "I will not live by her grace!"

But Brelian still did not move. "Ylia?"

"No. I do not wish your life, only," she could not help adding, "your absence. We will send you hence once you are healed. Do not return."

"When I am—" Vess laughed, choked and bit his lip. "When I am healed, by all that is fair and noble! You toy with me, woman!" He held up a red-palmed hand. Blood dripped from his fingers. "There is no real life left in me, slay me out-right!"

"I will heal you." Ylia gazed at him coldly. "And I will send you forth to Nar when it is done." She turned to Grewl. "I need aid to move him. I cannot work the healing among so many and he will need to sleep after." The old man chose from the younger men around him, indicating Vess with a nod. The fallen man closed his eyes and sagged against one of the blue-eyed Chosen who had mounted guard over Ylia and Nisana during the fight. The priest glared up at Nedao's new ruler, at his own new leader, turned back to his injured charge.

Brelian set his blades into Grewl's hands. The old man held them aloft, and the people, most of whom had been unable to follow what was happening, understood the gesture and cheered.

"Hear me, people!" Ylia shouted. "Vess, and any who desire to serve him, shall go from Aresada unharmed, with provisioning to aid them in reaching Nar! Those who swore to him but wish to stay may do so, and with my best wishes! There will be no deaths of one Nedaoan by another here!"

A great wordless cry went up; somewhere, distantly, she heard Marhan bellow out: "Hail Ylia, Lady of Nedao!" A roar of sound answered him: "Queen Ylia!" Willing hands tore at the hangings surrounding Vess' rich seat; willing hands assisted her until she stood before the makeshift throne that had been his. The people knelt as she stood there; joy and love filled her heart until she thought it would burst. And still that cry echoed through the Grand Temple: "Hail Queen Ylia, Lady of Nedao!"

Epilogue

Moonlight glanced from tall windows, shone like a blue-white mirror across the floor. A woman stood hard against them, her robes wrinkled as though she had slept and lived in them for many long nights. Her hair hung unbound in limp hanks down her back. She stared across ragged stone pillars, her gaze holding to the flat, close-turfed arena in their midst. She did not turn as the doors opened.

"What news?" Her voice was slurred with the tiredness that went to her bones.

"None." The elderly serving woman knelt behind her. "He sinks no lower, but he does not respond. There is nothing else we know to do." Silence. "Lady, there is nothing we would not do for him—*and* for you. But we have not the strength."

"I know your loyalty, it is not your fault. Go. Keep watch on him." The servant nearly ran from the chamber.

Marrita stared across the sword-field until the door shut, leaving her again alone in the huge chamber. She whirled about, then. "It is here, *you* are here, I have felt you, even *I*, powerless as I am! You are here, Great One! What thing do you want that my Lord did not have or was too proud to give? Is it in *me*? Can you find it there? I am here, Great One—and lo!—there is no thing, not one, I would not dare to save him! Is it within my inner being? Or is it *all*? Take, then!"

She paused, panting a little in the silence. "There is no bargain in me!—I must have what was yours or Lyiadd will die! You cannot wish that, he would serve you!" Silence again. "Take *me*, and you will never regret what you got of this trade!" She flung her arms wide. A faint sound brought her around to stare, frightened, at the sullen firepit.

The fire had burned low a long time since, was only a few glowing embers. They were suddenly quelled; blackness filled the pit, spilled eagerly over its edges. Above the pit, in the far corners of the chamber, Hell's own night puddled, quivering as it slipped down the walls.

Marrita trembled but held her ground. One hand stole to her breast, the other to her throat. The air was thick, hard to breathe, darkening with every breath. A sudden brilliance: blue-edged, sooty lightning tore across the chamber, shattering the windows. She screamed once, an airless, breathy little cry, and fell as though struck.

The chamber slowly cleared as night breezes drifted through broken windows. Marrita lay flat, eyes open and unseeing. Bits of a darkness beyond night fluttered like ebony moths about the spilled gold of her hair.

Appendix "A"

Historical & Informational Data

Peopled Lands

These encompass the smaller Eastern and Northern continent: its terrain is as varied as the peoples who inhabit it. The name "Peopled Lands" was first applied by Osneran traders in approximately Nedaoan year (new calendar) 100. The Osnerans were astounded (and somewhat amused) by the number and variety of small countries existing in a land area not much larger than their whole country, and that so many greatly different folk should live in relative peace so near each other. Besides Yls and Nedao (Nar would not come into being for 200 more years), there were the thick-walled desert City/States of Kerish and Aladar, two days east of the Torth; to the south were the coastal Rangol, Indebris, the warlike mercenary Eddekras. Besides, of course, the later extinct Llhaza and the Tehlatt, the Folk and the Nasath, though these latter two were unknown to the Osnerans save as Ylsan fables, peoples supposed to dwell in the Foessa.

Y

Of the Northern countries in Nedaoan New Year 517 (all future date references are to the Nedaoan new calendar), Yls was the oldest, over a thousand years old. Legend and Ylsan history say the southwest peninsula and forest lands, with fertile valleys nestled between low mountain ranges, had been given the AEldra, along with their unique Powers, in exchange for aid in war. And certainly it is true that the AEldra alone in the Peopled Lands use magic and strange powers, though over the years these abilities have slowly waned, for the AEldra were never ambitious. They had fallen into a somewhat predictable, if comfortable, existence, one generation flowing into the next without any great change. But their pride was what it had always been, and they still saw themselves as foremost among the Northern lands—the Southern and Eastern they dismissed with genial contempt—not realizing they were no longer the fierce sea-people they had been, more than they were still a land of powerful mages. Among the AEldra, only the Five Houses had any of the deep Power remaining true, even though the humblest Ylsan herder-lad might have use of the Baelfyr or be able to bridge.

Though most AEldra were—and are—human, there were, from the first, beasts among them fully aware. Whether the Powers were given also to certain animals among the AEldra, or whether certain of them later took those forms and kept them is not known. AEldra of cat-kind and a few of dog are known; it is believed, as well, that there are AEldra among the great hunting birds, though this is not known for certain.

The Nasath and the Folk

AEldra tradition and history have it that their magic came from the Nasath, the fabled Guardians of the lands. The Nasath, if they do exist, have not been seen for many hundreds of years, nor have the Folk, those to whom the Nasath supposedly first gave their protection. They are seen, on the rare occasion humankind comes upon them, as the ancient river and mountain deities of children's tales and minstrel's lays, the Naiads and Dryads of Nedaoan and Ylsan legend, though their forms are as varied and fabulous as they themselves choose.

Nar

In the late second century, New Nedaoan, there was civil war in Osnera and one entire folk, dominantly traders, won the right to leave the mother country and sail east. They took to themselves the great islands and shorelands at the mouth of the River Aresada, and so founded Nar. Quick-witted and ambitious, the Narrans soon reopened trade with Osnera, and before long they had control of most of the shipping between the old and new lands.

Their ships were ever the target of the Sea-Raiders, who extracted a tithe of the cargo of any ship they captured. The Narrans, loathe to part with any of their profit, learned swordwork of the Nedaoans and the Eddekras, and became the only merchants of any kind to even attempt to gainsay the fierce Raiders.

It is said a Narran can squeeze gold until it cries out, but they also know the value of a well-placed gift, and were ever swift to be of aid in need.

Sea-Raiders

A full day's journey south of Nedao lay the Great Isles of the Sea-Raiders. These folk were never properly counted among the Peopled Lands, though they preyed almost exclusively on the ships of those folk, attacking any who sailed the coasts but holding greatest preference for the triangular-sailed Narran vessels. The black-hulled, black-sailed Raider ships were faster than any merchant cog and struck terror into the hearts of any who saw them. Though the Raiders killed only when provoked and, for many long years, took only a large "tithe" from the holds of those they captured.

The Raiders are believed to be distant kin of the AEldra: Both folk are pale of hair and skin, taller than others among the Peopled Lands or Oversea. Both were originally Seafolk before the call went forth from the Nasath for aid against the Lammior. It is also believed, by some, that the Raiders were those AEldra who did not answer the summons, for there was great dissention among the Seafolk, whether to aid in a war that could not touch them.

Nedao

Nestled comfortably in the fertile Plain between the Foessa Mountains to the west and the deserts to the east, Nedao had belonged to that dark, farming and herding folk for only 500 years. They had come, the Nedaoans, as exiles of a long war and siege by the Sea-Raiders; their Queen Lossana, and her two young sons, all that was left of the House of Lossor; the King and his council dead by treachery, the Great Isles taken from them with horrifying loss of life. But they were determined and strong-minded, and they wrested the Plain from the savage nomads who dwelt there before them.

Even more conservative and complacent by nature than their AEldra neighbors, they settled into their own ways, slowly forgetting the constant threat to their northern and eastern borders, believing—because it was more comfortable to believe that way—that the Tehlatta had forgiven them the conquest of the Plain, and that they would never unite their many warring tribes sufficiently to constitute a threat.

But early in the 6th century, the great Tehlatt chief Kanatan, with the aid of the shaman Urgetz, bound all the clans together, and in the year 507 they retook Anasela. Ten years later, they launched a lightning raid against the Plain itself. Nedao was taken completely by surprise. Teshmor and Koderra, the two major cities, were razed; well over two-thirds of the population was slain, the rest of the people scattered.

Appendix "B"

Chronology

Year (New Calendar)

1	First refugees from Great Isles reach the mouth of the Torth; two years later the last of them, including the Queen and her sons, arrive.
4	Koderra is founded.
7	Teshmor founded; Llhaza driven from the south; Tehlatta forced from the River and eastward.
27	Killdes of Koderra, Lord Prince and eldest son of Queen Leffna, and a group of his friends are slain by Cavefolk when they attempt to discover what is killing the herds west of the Torth.
28	Merreven, brother of Killdes, tracks down and slays the Mathkkra.
177	House of Lossor fails; House of Benald inherits the ruling. Anasela made a part of Nedao. Tehlatta driven further north and east.
207	AEldra cross the mountains and establish land trade with Nedao through the ancient Yls Pass.
220	First repulsion of the Tehlatt.
290	Nar is founded by Osneran traders.
291	Barbarians from the eastern deserts are defeated in a battle at the mouth of the Torth.
299	Trade is established between Nedao and lands to the east. Beginning of the Long Peace. A border guard is formed to take the place of the King's army; Baronry and other landed Holders keep household armed upon which the King can call at need.

305	House of Ettel gains the ruling.
370	Nedaoan Navy is disbanded.
388	Nar and Nedao sign trading pacts.
400	Oaths of peace are exchanged with the Tehlatta.
445	Births of Nisana and Malaeth in Yls.
460	Birth of Brandt, son of King Bergony.
462	Birth of Scythia, of the Second House of Yls.
467	Bergony deals with the Chosen and grants them the Northern Citadel.
485	Marriage of Brandt & Scythia.
486	Birth of Beredan.
491	Birth of Ylia.
507	Tehlatta invade and retake Anasela.
517	Invasion of Nedao. Deaths of Brandt and Scythia.